Wraiths: The Night Sky

Alan Rock

Copyright © 2024 by Alan Rock

All rights reserved.

No part of this publication may be reproduced, distributed, or transmitted in any form or by any means, including photocopying, recording, or other electronic or mechanical methods, without the prior written permission of the publisher, except as permitted by U.S. copyright law. For permission requests, contact a.rock.writing@gmail.com.

The story, all names, characters, and incidents portrayed in this production are fictitious. No identification with actual persons (living or deceased), places, buildings, and products is intended or should be inferred.

Alan Rock

CONTENTS

1. Survival Instincts — 1
2. Be Prepared — 20
3. To Take Risks — 42
4. Live to Learn — 53
5. A Night to Remember — 69
6. Prevalent Mortality — 85
7. Trepidations — 107
8. Simple Patterns — 134
9. Of Methods and Madness — 148
10. The Art of Perception — 168
11. The Pinnacles of Mutation — 179
12. Inspired Magnanimity — 195
13. Insurmountable — 212
14. Ubiquitous Deceptions — 225
15. Contending Life — 239
16. Acclimatization — 254

17.	Contrive	271
18.	Through Contest	287
19.	Torrential Crescendo	299
20.	Noxious Maelstroms	312
21.	Sacrifice	322
22.	Final Strands of Hope	336

DEDICATION

For all those who shaped me
into the person I am today:
You Rock

"The world breaks everyone and afterward many are strong at the broken places. But those that will not break it kills. It kills the very good and the very gentle and the very brave impartially. If you are none of these you can be sure it will kill you too but there will be no special hurry."

—Hemingway

Chapter 1

SURVIVAL INSTINCTS

Trembling, he became aware of the thousand-foot-tall trees, limitless orange grasses, and cold air surrounding him; he felt out of place. His friends were nowhere to be seen. The only thing he could bring himself to do was sit down and wait by the shore– his legs would not let him do anything else.

Sitting down now, he reflected on the ship's fate. His friends were most undoubtedly dead; they had been in the underwater wreck for a few minutes. Griffith had to at least check. There was no way he would be able to live with himself if he left them down there to die.

Standing up again, the cool breeze chilled his damp face; he smelled the acidic water, like sulfur; he heard the sway of grasses, but something was missing– there was no wildlife; the animals must have been scared off by the crash.

Griffith's heart was beating out of his chest, and he felt cold. He thought of his friends; he missed them. "I need to save them," he whispered to himself.

The water looked bloody, but it surely wasn't blood. Griffith had already swum up once before, his eyes now only slightly irritated by the water. His suit continued cooling him; he knew he had to get in and out quickly.

Griffith looked around for anything useful to help this endeavor. He knew how to make rope– he jogged to the vibrant fields of sufficiently strong grass behind him and got to work. After making a considerable length of single-stranded, uni-knotted rope, Griffith tied one end to a log and the other to himself, wading back into the water. The cold numbed his legs; he acclimated to the freezing water as fast as he could, determined to save whoever was still alive and possibly recover some supplies.

His descent was fast, and visibility decreased quickly. Staring into the red, murky depths, Griffith shuddered at the thoughts of what could be agaze back at him. Irritation built in his eyes. The water frightened him, but he remained confident. His feet bumped the wreck, sending a shiver down his spine. He oriented himself with the flashing emergency lights and opened the hatch. The water in the cabin was colder. Opening his eyes again, he saw moving legs; he then saw bodies– there was no saving them. Resisting the temptation to gasp, he began swimming as hard as he could to the air pocket, his eyes still burning.

"Grab the rope and follow it," he ordered, catching his breath and starting to shiver. The five who were still alive were in awe. Before questioning anything, they wanted freedom, following the rope out and up. Griffith trailed after them, his legs aching. He met the others at the surface; they had already made progress toward the shore. Catching his breath, Griffith treaded water before beginning the swim.

It was as if he had disappeared; Bruce, mid-swim, was sucked straight below the surface. Griffith was perplexed. He was exhausted yet pushed on. He tried to yell but had no energy to expend. The rest were unaware of the situation; Griffith would have to deal with it by himself again. He had no feeling in his limbs, yet they continued moving, propelling him toward where he thought Bruce had gone down. In his deep breath, Griffith inhaled water. He could barely keep his head above the water. Finally, a good breath allowed him to descend, flailing his arms around in hopes of grabbing Bruce. He knew they both would be sinking fast; Griffith hoped he could get them back up.

Miraculously, he felt something: Bruce. He yanked Bruce and swam upwards with him. Swimming with a lifeless body was challenging; he was full of water, yet Griffith was making progress. He took a breath of water as he could see the light through his eyelids. He choked up the acidic water, but he made it to the top. It was already hard to keep himself afloat– Bruce made it impossible. He knew he could be saved, but Bruce was close to death, if not already dead. Griffith was struggling, taking in half breaths of water and having to spit it back out. Victoria had begun to swim back out and then helped them get to shore. The others grabbed Bruce and brought him to a flat spot where the mud was compact– to help with CPR. Lucian began rescue breaths and chest compressions while Tanho took off his undershirt and wrapped strips of it around Bruce's bleeding leg. Valeria kept a lookout and helped Griffith catch his breath.

Bruce threw up water after two rounds of rescue breaths, his leg in immense pain. "What just happened to me?" he exclaimed after he caught his breath.

Griffith was still panting and coughed, "You just went straight down while swimming. I didn't see what grabbed you, though."

"Whatever it was, it got my leg real good. Needles. Needles everywhere," he said as he winced again. The markings on Bruce's leg were toothlike, with a semicircle arc of cuts that had been thrashed, probably by serrated teeth. Whatever it was must have been enormous, though– the arc spanned from thigh to ankle.

Lucian concernedly mentioned, "Bruce, it's a miracle you're alive and that your leg is intact, too. We'll have to be careful on this place– what a warm welcome we've got." A red sun crept from behind purple clouds, illuminating the landscape across the lake with a dark hue. They could see the boundlessness of the trees' shadows, streams, and creeks delivering water to the mystical crystal saplings below silver mountains capped in aquamarine blue with cave entrances scattered about. They were mesmerized. Assessing the situation, Victoria gathered the group's attention. Only a few hours were left in the day, and she wasn't looking forward to seeing what night could be like.

"Shelter, any ideas?"

"Bruce is in no condition to travel far; we should split up and find something close by," Lucian responded. The band of survivors agreed, designating groups of two so one could stay with Bruce. As they prepared to leave, Bruce reminded them to be careful. Griffith and Lucian headed around the lake clockwise, moving upwards to get a better layout of the area. Valeria and Victoria started to one of the nearby trees devoid of dense underbrush, leaving Tanho with Bruce. They sat by the lake and tried to figure out how they could help. Tanho unsheathed his belt knife and gathered materials. Dark crystals lay exposed near the base of a hill. Some pieces had already broken off; he knew they would be helpful. Tanho struck the back of his knife on a piece, which sparked.

"We can make fire!" he celebrated. As Tanho began lighting tinder on fire, Bruce looked at the blood-soaked shirt on his leg.

With the fire slowly growing, Bruce gulped and suggested, "We might have to cauterize this. I can feel the blood still draining." Bruce's pale face corroborated it. With no means of safe sterilization, they had to hope the burns and his body would eliminate the invaders. Tanho laid the end of his knife in the fire. When he felt it had heated enough, Tanho grabbed the handle and moved over to Bruce.

"This is gonna hurt, man. Bite something." Without speaking, Bruce exhaled slowly and put his shirt sleeve into his mouth, layering it to cushion his teeth and dampen screams. Removing the now bright red shirt, Tanho couldn't believe they had waited until now to do something about the injury. It looked as if the bleeding hadn't slowed. At least it had only been a few minutes, yet the sense of emergency was present now more than ever. Tanho pressed the hot metal flat, starting at the thigh. Already feeling dizzy, Bruce just stared straight ahead and grunted. The scent of sizzling skin filled Tanho's nostrils as he continued. At the top of the calf muscle, Tanho flipped the knife over, and the sound of the burning got louder instantly. A minute on each incision seemed to stop the bleeding. Bruce continued to apply pressure while Tanho worked his way down. After it was over, Tanho washed some of his bloodied shirt scraps in the water and laid them over Bruce's leg. Bruce fell asleep deservedly. With Bruce's leg no longer oozing blood, Tanho could help them survive; he notched bits off small, long crystals until they were sharp and attached them to a split at the end of a stick with the grass and waxy sap from a log. Tanho now had a ranged weapon: a spear, about seven feet long and, although crude, sturdy.

 He walked to the water and gazed into it. *Acidic; there's no way we can drink this.* Spear in hand, he wanted to try and catch something. With random seeds in hand, he chummed the water. Its red tint created low visibility, but the sunlight helped with that. Minutes passed with nothing. He draped a strip of the bloody shirt in the water; hopefully, it would be noticed. Again, minutes passed. *I know there's something here. I've just gotta wait.*

Immediately after breaking off from the group, Griffith and Lucian began thinking about how they would survive this place. They had been on the go since they landed, perpetually confused, nervous, and overwhelmed.

Watching the ground before him as he walked, Lucian commented, "This place is so strange, it makes no sense. I can't wrap my brain around it."

"The crash roughed us all up pretty bad. We can make sense of it later; we need to get situated; there are probably some wicked creatures here." Griffith's brain pulsed– a migraine developing. Reaching the other side of the lake after a few minutes, they paused and looked back at Bruce and Tanho.

"Fire, I can't believe it! Tanho is amazing!" Griffith said, astounded and hopeful. Lucian did not have a knife like Tanho, leading him to grab rocks and sticks to throw at or prod anything they might encounter. The long, orange blades of grass looked illusional. Upon closer inspection, Lucian noticed they had intertwined, forming weird patterns. Barb-like thorns coated the grass, which would make any venture unimaginably painful. Before getting to the hill that blocked their vision, there was a small valley with a stream running through that they had to cross. Using their sticks to help support them, they dropped into the valley. The stream wound around the hills, so they could not see the stream too far in either direction. The water was still reddish, creating a dull undertone on the rocks and vegetation. Plant life in the valley flourished. It was everywhere. What could only be described as moss covered the edges of the stream and crept up on stone that dipped in. Just upstream, water split and conjoined around a miniature island housing a magnificent sapling. The trunk was similar to Damascus steel and the leaves were a brilliant, amethyst purple. Upon seeing the tree, Lucian had to investigate. The leaves luminesced in stripes alongside the stem. They mimicked palms, reminding them of home. After shoving a few in their pockets, they finished crossing and began the climb.

Lucian reflected, "I can't wait to figure this planet out." Griffith nodded in agreement, still too tired from swimming to speak. As they crested the hill, their jaws dropped; waterfalls, rivers, and ponds separated different colored grasses and terrain as far as they could see. Meeting the regions and the rivers in the middle was an island dense with trees. Lucian squinted at the island. He noticed something was off about it.

"Griffith, what is that?" he questioned.

"Dude, I think that's a building!" he exclaimed, his eyes bulging. Behind a few smaller trees and light vegetation lay a metallic building. They could not tell if any lights were on from where they were. "Maybe they could help us!"

"Don't get your hopes up, though; there might not be anyone home, and how do you propose we get there? That's gotta be a good few miles away, and look what we've gotta cross," he said, pointing at the junctions of broad rivers and dense forests.

"Well, at least we've got something to tell them when we get back. And for shelter, we could stay on this hill, make a lean-to or something against the branches."

"We're fairly exposed on this hill, but if we can keep a fire going, we should be okay. We'd have to make a wall to stop the wind." Griffith thought for a second, agreed, and led the way back down the valley.

Victoria and Valeria were also fascinated by the vibrant colors and patterns of the grasses. They knew that if they went into the grass, getting back out would be a challenge. Traveling to the tree, they questioned how extreme of a situation they were in.

"Other than whatever attacked Bruce, this place seems pretty peaceful. We haven't seen or heard anything yet," Valeria mentioned.

"Looks can be deceiving; be careful." Moving slowly with darting eyes, they continued to the tree. About half a mile in, they came across a pile of giant rocks. With a single knife between them, Victoria held it backhanded and led as they went to investigate. There were many nooks and crannies, but one caught their eye. Five of six sides were fully sealed off; it would be easy to defend.

"It's perfect," Valeria said. Victoria swiftly agreed. "There's no way the boys are back yet, and the sun still won't set for a while; let's head the rest of the way to the tree and see what's around."

Victoria started walking and said, "Yeah, that sounds like a plan. I'm getting thirsty, though. Let's hope we can find water."

The tree was more absurd up close; its trunk was easily a hundred feet around and iridesced brightly when sunlight shone through the leaves. Standing in awe at the base of this giant, Victoria and Valeria were met with an acrid smell. A gust of wind carried an unholy scent; looking around, they spotted the back of a gray carcass behind a few superficial roots to the right of the tree. Whatever it was, it was massive. They both kept quiet and approached slowly. Being careful not to make any noise, they listened to an animal gnawing on bits of the carcass' flesh. This creature must have been small; they heard it moving around, perhaps to eat from another area. Wanting to learn about the first wildlife they encountered, they nodded toward each other, signaling their mutual desire to investigate further.

Closing in, now only a few yards away, their footsteps were increasingly audible. Although they tried their best to move slowly, the sounds of eating and moving halted; the animal was aware of their presence. Victoria and Valeria paused. With her knife ready, Victoria maneuvered herself in an arc around the root system, getting her a fuller view before initiating. The anticipation gave them chills.

At last, they moved far enough to not be obstructed by the roots. Standing next to the carcass was a small, scaly, orange creature. Its long, barbed tail, collaborating with its four legs, two arms, and spearlike protrusion on its chest, gave it a sinister appearance. Many eyes stared at them before it darted up the tree with flesh still in its mouth. It looked dragon-like, seeming to leap up the bark of the tree, its tail following the motion of its body. They stood, watching it before it disappeared into an open knot in the tree.

Valeria was the first to question, "What the heck was that thing?"

"Whatever it was, it's so cool. What if we're the first people to ever encounter that?" Victoria responded excitedly, intrigued by the mysteries they had yet to solve. The carcass continued permeating the air with a pungent smell: the smell of death. They were both familiar with it, but this was different– it was stronger; the miasma of putridness continued to build the closer they were. It was freshly dead, not giving insight into the strength of the smell. Knowing they had to report their findings to the guys, they walked over to it.

"I wonder if that orange thing killed it," Victoria said as they got close. "I think it was feeding on just its skin," she said, looking at patches of missing skin that exposed a purple undertone. They had to hold their noses as they shuffled around the horse-sized animal remains. The purple-blue blood pooled nearest to the roots; blood and flesh had exploded all over the roots, leaving a large crater on one of the wide legs of this beast. Its tail looked chitinous, clearly powerful. A dense orb of what resembled ruby capped the tail, adding insult to injury by red spikes on each segment– they were made of the same material. The body had many visible veins, which seemed to glow. The rough skin towards its neck looked stretched, the veins rising to the surface.

"It looks like it's expanding. Do dead bodies usually do that?" Valeria asked, concerned.

"I think something injected it with venom. That explains the swelling; it must be really potent to cause its leg to explode. I would not want to get injected by whatever got this thing."

"I'm pretty sure it just recently died, so it must be fast-acting, too," Valeria noted, looking at the carcass' quality. Wanting to return, they took a sample of the coarse skin with some peculiar blood and set off, eager to rid their nostrils of the smell.

Back at the lake, Bruce was feeling the effects of his blood loss; his head was bobbing with tiredness by the time Tanho made his way back, holding a deep-red-and-black monstrosity of a creature on the end of his spear. "Bruce! Look what I've got!" he said, showing off his catch.

"Dude, what even is that? It looks straight out of a horror movie," Bruce said raspingly, his voice going away with his dry throat.

"Isn't he gnarly? I'm gonna name him Geoffrey. I wonder if Geoffrey tastes good?" Tanho asked, looking at one of the protruding mouths covered in red spots.

"Tanho, I need water," Bruce said, the world beginning to spin around him. Increased pressure pulsed behind his right eye while he pressed his thumb onto his temple to try and relieve the pain. Tanho's smile faded as he paused, thinking with a disappointed look; he would have to continue bragging when everyone returned. Getting a sense of urgency, Tanho let go of the spear and dropped it to the ground. The creature's tentacle-looking tail slapped the fire, causing a rush of embers to rise in the now almost twilight.

Tanho was also feeling thirsty. He knew that Bruce was unlikely to die from dehydration so quickly, but he still had to do something. *How do I boil water without a pot?* Tanho looked for rocks that could hold water nearby but had no luck. The crystals would not be big enough, so he ignored them. Tanho developed sweat on his brow, which he wiped away. Stopping, he gathered himself and took a deep breath. He gazed across the landscape near and far and let his mind race. *Anything, anything at all that could boil water.* Tanho almost missed it, but he was hunting once again, his mind open and calm. A log partially veiled by grass awaited him a hundred feet towards the crystals. Wood could hold water if it was dense enough; *it just might work.*

Luckily, his knife was serrated and sharp, allowing him to cut partially through the log. He perched one end on a mound of clay and stomped to break it the rest of the way. The pointed crystals helped break up and remove some of the inner wood. Once completed, he spent no time collecting water and resting it over the fire. Before putting hot rocks in the fire to speed it up, he looked at the creature he caught earlier. "That's peculiar; why isn't its tail burning?" Bruce looked over and shrugged, just anxious to drink. Tanho thought to himself while listening to the fire crackle, *fire-resistant skin? How does an aquatic creature develop such a trait?*

I'll have to ask the rest of the crew about it. He left the tail in the fire as he watched the water heat.

Just as the water began to bubble, Tanho saw the girls walking back, still distant. Seeing them made him sigh in relief. They could have been killed or hurt, but their saunter was natural and undaunted. He saw his parents somewhere back on Earth– at home– unaware of his current situation. He chuckled, listening to the dull sound of the bubbles and the laughter of his oblivious parents. The autumn leaves crunched under their step up the house walkway. Chinese take-out again: fulfilling and safe. The signature white containers were placed on the corners of the mahogany table, clearing most of the space. They sat across from each other, sharing a smile.

Just then, Griffith and Lucian approached from the side. "Tanho?" they asked concernedly. Tanho's brain stem was working perfectly. He leaped to his feet wide-eyed before realizing his mistake. He looked at the ground before painstakingly looking up towards them, "So what did you see?"

A quick recount of the vast landscape was sufficient. The stream and the pink tree mystified Tanho. The planet was sure to be full of surprises. They almost omitted what looked like a building. "We're definitely going there after we get situated. I also forgot to mention, the girls should be getting back soon. They were right over–"

"–Here," Victoria interjected, also sneaking up on him. "We saw a dragon! It was small and orange and spiky."

Lucian was in awe, "A dragon? No way!"

"Yeah, and it was eating a pretty big animal. We took a sample," she said, holding up the flesh on the end of her knife.

Griffith was unsure what to think, "I have so many questions... but we should cover the basics first. Is Bruce alright, Tanho?"

"Yeah, he's good; he's just a tad dehydrated and tired. I've got the water boiling. I just need to neutralize it somehow." Lucian looked around slowly, his hand on his chin and his mouth slightly open, pondering. Nobody knew where to start, so as Lucian searched, Victoria, Valeria, Griffith, Tanho, and a fatigued Bruce contemplated the flesh sample. It had lost most of its color but was still bloated. The outer skin looked coarse and tough– the knife had significant trouble penetrating it. Victoria proposed her venom theory, which made them more nervous about being safe for the night. The sky had reached its most elegant and picturesque. A prism of colors blended in eucalyptus-bark-like layers, forming a gradient between the dominant purples, whites, and greens. The waves of clouds reflected the last rays back towards the group, holding out a hand of warm light as if the sun was trying to hold on, inevitably going to let go.

Thinking about the shelter, Valeria mentioned the rock formation and how easy it would be to find refuge there, although it had the highest concentration of deadly creatures they had seen thus far. "Anything beats this lake, this place sucks," Bruce added, sighing and trying not to complain.

Griffith grabbed a few flat slices of crystal and skipped them over the water while everyone talked. He set some down on the water's edge to let him wind up and get a running start. Just before throwing, Lucian made his way back over, almost screaming for them to pause. The cadence of his walk amplified as he told everyone to look at the crystals Griffith had dropped. "What about them?" Valeria asked, matching everyone else's eyes, who also had no idea what Lucian was directing their attention to. Upon closer inspection, they saw the color change when Lucian picked up one of the larger shards. The obverse side was the natural black and purple, while the underside emitted a dull, blue glow. Lucian knew something peculiar was happening. It had to either be the water or the water's composition that caused the glow.

"I have an idea," Lucian announced.

"What idea? What are you thinking?" Tanho questioned. He was met with no response. Lucian grabbed another crystal and began walking away from the lake.

Victoria began to get anxious, "Hey, Lucian! Where are you going?"

Without turning back, he declared, "You'll see!" The bubbles had continued forming mercilessly and began to flow over the top of the log. Tanho and Griffith cautiously took the water off the fire and set it aside. Nobody knew what to do, so they rationalized getting Bruce ready to travel. They'd have to support him the entire way. It would be a long trip, and there would be almost no way to get there before nightfall. Tanho and Valeria would support Bruce on the way there, and Victoria and Griffith would go ahead and prepare for the night.

Griffith looked over at Lucian again, who was precariously cutting strands of grass. "He won't need us. Victoria, let's head out."

"After you." They started walking away, Victoria brandishing her 11" Damascus steel, trailing-point dagger, and Griffith with his 12" carbon fiber, drop-point knife. Lucian began walking back, many strands of grass in tow. He picked up a flat rock and a smaller, round one before sitting down next to the bucket of water.

He began dipping the end of one of the crystals into the water. It started glowing, only up to the line that the water reached. Lucian set the crystal down and murmured, "Oh, I hope this works." He blinked a few times and took a deep breath. He began crushing some of the grass between the rocks until it was sufficiently disintegrated. He set a fraction of the ground compound on the crystal and slowly dribbled it with water. "It worked!" he said, looking up to Tanho and Valeria. "Someone come over here and help me mix." After Valeria walked over, he instructed her to stir the water. He then set the crystal entirely into the water and watched as it began glowing again. Lucian mixed more and more pulverized grass into the water.

At last, five minutes later, the crystal stopped glowing. Lucian cupped his hands and took a small drink of the water, washing it around his mouth to make sure it would not be an irritant– indicative of being poisonous. Bruce, Valeria, and Tanho were skeptical, intently watching to see if Lucian would be alright. The water tasted peculiar– Lucian was unable to describe it. He did not spend long attempting to articulate the taste, instead proposing they get on the move. "We don't want to get caught out in the dark with only Tanho's knife and spear as weapons." Bruce finally quenched his thirst and immediately felt better. They passed the log around, leaving much of the drink for later. Now ready to go, Tanho held the spear with his catch in one hand, supporting Bruce with the other arm. Valeria supported Bruce's other side, attaching the knife to her suit's belt to keep her other hand able to help stabilize them. Lucian followed along, holding his great accomplishment in his hands and a few crystals in his pockets. He found a rock that acted as a makeshift lid. It was not a perfect fit, but it would help prevent sloshing.

Victoria and Griffith were eager for a safer place to stay, not out in the open. Their fear of the dark was renewed, causing them to pick up the pace. The sky had transitioned into dusk, the sun finally releasing its holding on the clouds above– the new, dark shadow highlighting their width. On the way to the boulders, they whispered about the ship's mission. Victoria shook her head shallowly, "We knew the risks. I just didn't think something like this could happen."

"Victoria, you really didn't think anything bad would happen on an experimental, long-distance space travel mission?" She continued forward, staying focused on her foot placement. "I mean, that's why us, of all people, were sent. We're young, adaptable, and can think outside the box."

"Don't you think it's ironic? Ironic that they send twenty-five of those intelligent people to significantly advance the human race, only for nineteen of them to die within the first few minutes, and the remaining few to have no way to send anything back?"

"Hey, we're alive for a reason–"

"–Yeah, and we're gonna die for a reason: everything here is designed to kill us." They walked in silence for the rest of the trip. They had gathered a few sticks on the path to use as bulwarks. They planned out the defense system by making a few piles of larger and smaller sticks at the opening of the niche. Layers of pointed spears would be made to face outwards and skewer any attacker. Next was the flooring; they needed insulation to keep their body heat from draining. Leaves and non-sharp grasses would work perfectly. Some large leaves congregated arbitrarily in small piles between grass fields, making them the obvious choice. Victoria brought the first arm-full inside and breathed a sigh of relief. Maybe there was hope for them after all.

The room they had would be sufficient for the six of them. Leaving space towards the entrance devoid of leaves would let them keep a fire. The wind would lightly blow through and help burn the fire, providing heat throughout the rock-insulated chamber. Handheld spears with crystal tips would allow for precise lunging attacks to their target's weak points. To survive the night, they would need every advantage they could get.

Griffith and Victoria chatted about family, friends, and their upbringings while setting up the ramparts– talking about anything except impending doom. Both of them were only children, and they laughed about its stereotypes.

"Victoria, now tell me this: what made you decide to start training for space? Was it family? The adventure? Destiny?"

"Oh, what do you know about destiny?"

"I just don't want to give up on life. I want to think we're here for a reason. You didn't answer my question, by the way."

Victoria paused, stood from her hunched-over position, and looked over at Griffith. Meeting his gaze, she calmly stated, "Earth just didn't have anything for me." She starkly turned away and went back to work sharpening sticks and firmly planting them angled in the ground.

"This place is anything but boring; both of our dreams came true," he declared with a sigh, a hint of sarcasm lingering on his tongue. Reflecting on his own motives for space travel, he smiled and continued augmenting the defenses, faintly rejuvenated.

Hearing the susurration of crunching leaves quickly grow louder, both were apprised to Valeria and a hobbling Bruce rushing towards them. Victoria was the first to get outside and try to meet them. Their speed clearly indicated a problem, although the obscurity had masked what it was. Victoria hurried to help assist Bruce while Griffith kept his eyes on the open darkness suddenly closing in around them. If both girls were now here, Tanho and Lucian must be stuck out there in the dark.

"Follow my voice!" he bellowed. Moments passed with no response. "Where are you guys?" he said emphatically, the urgency beginning to come through. As Victoria, Valeria, and Bruce neared the shelter's opening, a thundery roar pierced the air, causing them to halt. Their hearts leaped as their minds became overwhelmed with the sounds of abominable horror. All three of them spun around and squinted into the darkness. Griffith stood a few paces in front of them with his feet shoulder-width apart, left arm by his side, and right hand at his hip, hovering over his knife. The hair stood on their necks, electric signals surging through their spinal cords. Victoria unsheathed her knife as well, the adrenaline rushing through her system, causing a tremor through her hand before reinforcing her grip.

Just then, Lucian appeared out of the sinister, pitch-black fog, running at full throttle. He threw his head over his shoulder, looking behind him. "Tanho! Run!" he shouted. Griffith was the first to approach the danger, but Victoria followed shortly after. They had no idea what they were up against.

Tanho's voice was heard but did not hint how far away he was. "On the way!" he said with a grunt. The reflected moonlight shone on Tanho's figure as he flurriedly approached with the spear in tow. Following close behind him was an oversized, gray, panther-like beast that had set its eyes on its next meal. Within a fraction of a second of seeing the creature, Griffith and Victoria sprung into action, running further away from any signs of safety. Tanho's crystal-tipped spear effectively held back the canine thing, discouraging it from an immediate attack. Arming themselves with smaller rocks, Victoria and Griffith began to throw at the beast, hoping to deter it from continuing the chase and buy time for Tanho to make it to safety. Tanho was now clearly visible; his catch from earlier had been left behind, his eyes were wide open, and his mouth was agape.

The rocks had little effect on this massive animal, and there were no prominent weak spots to aim at. It had many eyes, each refusing to give up the laser focus on Tanho. They continued throwing what they could, realizing their attempt to stall was helpless. If they stayed that far out for any longer, there was a good chance they would be caught with the creature between them and the structure.

"Griffith, we need to go back," she said hurriedly as she began to run back. Griffith turned with her but stopped, instead choosing to run out and make himself the prey.

"Hey! Big guy, come over this way!" he hollered. Victoria was unaware that Griffith stayed outside. She was too flabbergasted to yell at him to get back inside. Valeria, Lucian, and Bruce were panting and disheveled, worried about Tanho but entirely powerless to help. It seemed to turn its head to Griffith, but only briefly. It turned back to Tanho, and in a flash, it had clasped Tanho's torso. Excruciating screams escaped Tanho's mouth. Victoria gasped and audibly shrieked, turning away. Griffith was overcome with shock, frozen in place, watching a tortuous scene in slow motion. He had no thoughts, just staring, his brain trying to process how this could've happened. He did not feel scared or threatened.

Rushes of epinephrine temporarily incapacitated his thinking. It seemed too long before his brain stem began working again. The beginnings of a return trip to the fort followed a quick glance to either side to regain awareness of his situation. Before he placed his second step, the dreadful sound returned to all of their ears from the side of darkness from which Tanho had emerged. It was a closer sound, much closer than it was before.

The creature turned its head towards the sound, its four legs and large tail stopping motion. Tanho's flailing body followed in its mouth. As if by miracle, Griffith looked over to see the monster drop Tanho onto the ground. Without another moment of thought, he pivoted and sprinted to Tanho, putting his knife in its sheath. Victoria sensed the opportunity and again left safely. Slinking away, the monster had left Tanho behind. Griffith grabbed Tanho's body and scooped him up, making a weighted jog look easy. Victoria assisted the second half of the way. At last, they were all safe.

Chapter 2

BE PREPARED

It was nearly impossible to see anything in the shadow of the cave. The dull whimpers of Tanho filled the empty air, a wake of defeat converging on their fatigued minds. They would be unsure what to say if Tanho was not bleeding out next to them. Griffith and Bruce started a fire with the leftover wood while Victoria, Lucian, and Valeria removed Tanho's partially shredded, tracksuit-like top and applied pressure to reduce the bleeding.

They only realized how cold it was while the fire grew. The leafy bedding provided some support for Tanho, but it was clearly not enough. He was clearly in shock, so all they could do to try to ease his pain was elevate his legs. They felt the gusts of smoke in their eyes, nose, and throat; the fire grew fast. They would have to moderate their fuel use to keep the fire going throughout the night. Griffith took off his gray undershirt and began cutting it into strips. Tanho's wounds would have to be sterilized before they could be cauterized, or the deeper punctures would remain infested with bacteria. They could only hope it was not too late already.

"How can we disinfect him?" Valeria asked.

"Do we have something that sucks up water like salt does? We can draw the water out of the cells and kill bacteria in the process," Lucian suggested.

His voice was tremulous with an amplified prospect of death. They were all frightened. Nobody said anything. They had no ideas.

"Okay," Lucian said, "what if we inserted the heated knife into the wound, making it slightly deeper but cauterizing each part?"

Tanho immediately responded, "Do it," with significant pain. Griffith put his knife halfway into the forming coals.

"Wait," Victoria interrupted, "I read somewhere that urine can be used as an antimicrobial. We could flush his wounds with that if we decrease the bleeding."

"It is generally sterile, that should work," Lucian added. They continued to slow the bleeding by applying pressure with folded patches of Griffith's shirt. Lucian, getting warm, took his shirt off as well but kept it whole. As they continued tending to the wounds on both sides of his body, they discussed their chances of surviving. It was only the first night, and much more was to be uncovered. A rumbling growl was heard over the crackling of added fuel on the fire. The light emitted from the fire lit up the bare ground before them. From Griffith and Bruce's position behind the fire, sets of eyes watched in the distance amidst two purple wisps, clearly far away.

"I think they're back for more," Bruce noted. They all grew quiet. One of the larger of them partially appeared from the right, inspecting them. It leaped onto the rocks as if looking for a safe way in. Another joined it above the group. Griffith sighed and held up a pointed stick, the spear would have to do. The eyes behind the fire began to disappear, and they seemed to be gone without another noise.

"Wait, they move in packs?" Victoria asked quietly, not trying to interest them again.

Bruce responded, "Yeah, Tanho gave the lot of em' the fish he caught. It distracted all of them... except the one." Valeria pointed out that the dressings had less blood; they could finally sterilize the perforations. Tanho had definitely lost a lot of blood, but he was still conscious, albeit probably for the worse. What he was about to undergo would be agonizing.

Trying to make it slightly less awkward, Griffith told them to look away. He wiped the remaining blood from around the wounds and gave Tanho a stick to bite on. Following another sigh, he began urinating on the wounds.

"This is the strangest thing I've ever done," he stated. Because of Tanho's lying down position, they couldn't flush all of the wounds on both sides of his body at one time. They used Lucian's shirt to sop up the urine, and Bruce began cauterizing. The force behind Tanho's muffled screams made them all wish it was over; yet another round was still to come. They could only cauterize parts at a time, so Tanho had intermittent periods of reduced pain; it only served to enhance the torture.

Finally done with the first cauterizations, they cautiously flipped a groaning Tanho over so that now he lay prone. The wounds on this side looked worse as the teeth shook around more as he was flailed. These wounds did not bleed as much but caused much more pain. This time, Lucian was the one urinating. It felt humiliating for both of them, although Tanho did not think about it much through the anguish. Bruce wiped away the urine and began cauterizing again.

"Griffith, take over. I can't," he said, inflicting so much pain causing him hurt. Griffith picked up where Bruce left off, hearing the sizzling of skin harmonize with Tanho's painful, expressive moans.

"Tanho, we're done. It's over now," Griffith told him after rushing to finish the burning. Turning over, Tanho's eyes were droopy, and his face was sore from biting down on the stick. Imprints lay deep throughout the bark.

"Get some rest, Tanho," Valeria told him. The ordeal had stressed them all, and they needed a good rest.

Griffith said without further discussion, "I'll take the first watch, get some rest." They complied and laid down, although it was difficult to fall asleep, having experienced what they all just did. It was over half an hour before anyone other than Tanho fell asleep. Valeria resulted to staying up with Griffith after futile attempts to drift off. They looked at their friends, the only survivors of a terrible spaceship crash onto an alien planet that was still trying to exterminate them. Even their sleeping faces refused blissful ignorance.

Valeria moved closer to the fire with a light shiver. She waved her hands back and forth, feeling the heat move from her hands to her face and back. Griffith added another log to the fire, "How long do you think the nights are?" he asked her.

"I feel like it took a while to become dark, but maybe that's just this planet's seasons. I just hope we have enough wood to last the night." They decided to brainstorm what they should accomplish during the next day. They would have to get a lot done to be prepared and safe enough to live here– definitely not secure enough with their current defenses. Lucian was tasked with making more drinkable water and adding some sort of poison deterrent to the sticks. Griffith would make some crude weapons to give them a ranged edge. He thought for a moment about what he wanted to make. *Spears for sure, a bow or two if I can find the materials... and maybe a few rock slings.* He was happy with the idea, verbalizing it to Valeria. She had yet to decide what to do come daybreak but was considering helping to improve the shelter.

"We could make this place more cozy," Griffith told her. "It needs a splash of home," he added, chuckling.

"When I was young, my dad and I would go hiking on all these different trails. He would always do this thing when he saw me getting tired. He would..." she chuckled, "He would tag me and run ahead, and I would laugh and try to catch up to him. Before I left for this mission, he brought me out again, one last time. Then, I was the one tagging him." She continued reflecting on her upbringing. She missed it all dearly. It got Griffith thinking about his defining experiences. Although he realized how each moment's influence brought him to this planet, he refused to let it distract him. He would not cut himself any slack; it was his decision to leave Earth, and he was going to live with the consequences.

"Griffith, what's your favorite memory from Earth?" she asked, finally becoming weary.

"If I had to pick one," he said after thinking, "I would say my seventeenth birthday. I'm nineteen now, but I went out paintballing with all my friends on that birthday and absolutely annihilated them. It wasn't really fair, but I still enjoyed beating them all." By now, a reasonably long amount of time had passed. It was hard to tell, but they knew it was probably time for someone to take over. Griffith had been up the longest, so he tried to sleep while Valeria waited a bit longer. While she waited, she poked the fire with the wooden spear, which seared the end.

She had to decide who to wake up. *Definitely not Tanho. Maybe Bruce? He will probably be resting tomorrow anyway.* She tapped his shoulder to wake him and then swapped places. She told him that she and Griffith had been up, so to pick Lucian or Victoria if he wanted to sleep more later. While she drifted off, Bruce now thought about their predicament and how lucky they were to still be alive. He did tell himself they would all probably die, but he refused to let that thought settle.

A few sets of unsettling dissonances later, the day began to break, and the howls started to lessen; they had all but disappeared by the time Bruce had woken everyone except Tanho up. A few speckled clouds and a deep red lay sprung across the dimly lit sky. Bruce had noted the many shooting stars he could see from the corner of the sky the shelter limited him to. The stars now faded while the crew sat up and stretched. Victoria's hair was the most disheveled, but they all had a messy appearance about them. Seeing the numerous blood stains reminded them of their dire situation and few close calls. The hint of urine was mostly concealed by the strong smell of smoke remaining present. They would have to wash their clothing sometime soon, and Bruce may have to give up his shirt so Tanho would have something to wear. They could not see where the sun had begun to peek over the horizon from inside the shelter. The soft breeze had returned, and the temperature rose as the sun lay beams of solar radiation across the landscape. The trees were now in clear view; they seemed unphased by the deadly night. Staring into the dense canopy of leaves, they wondered what may live there. The coverage spanned well over a hundred meters. Enormous creatures could reside there without the group having a clue.

After regaining decent mental functionality, they took their first steps back outside. They were still uneasy from the previous night, so Griffith went out first and looked around. Seeing nothing, he motioned them to join him. Outside and away from Tanho, they discussed what should be done during the day based on what Griffith and Valeria had envisioned, with hints of Bruce's ideas that he came up with while watching the starlit night skies.

After briefly explaining how to make drinkable water, Lucian set off to see if his bucket was still there. He planned to make more buckets and more drinking water first. Then, he agreed he could develop something to better protect them at night.

Griffith proposed his rock sling idea, which was met with positive encouragement. He wove grasses for cordage and looked for other stringy materials for the slings. He decided to bring some crystals and durable sticks back for spears that Bruce could make if his leg was bad.

Valeria would primarily work on the shelter, making it more livable and bringing firewood back to store in case of much colder nights. She would help Lucian with defenses when he was ready, make spears if there was downtime, and tend to Tanho once he woke up.

Victoria was initially unsure of what to do. She could help anyone with their tasks but knew there was something better she could do. After a moment, Victoria was determined to try to find edible foods. She could hunt the fish monsters and set traps for smaller creatures. Her hunting background would help her significantly, although she would have to learn how these completely different animals behave.

Bruce was resolved to stay near the shelter. He could move on his own, but his leg was still in immense pain. He knew he would have to take rests frequently, so he would make spears and other contraptions to help them all. *Maybe I could make a nice axe? Some arrows? How could I make fletchings?*

It took them a while to find their groove again. They were lucky and knew it might not always be that way. Despite the odds stacked against them, hope could not be lost. Although they were separated to get materials, they would only stay apart briefly. They had seen day-dwellers previously and refused to take much of a chance if it could be avoided. Much had to get accomplished to ensure something like what happened to Tanho would never happen again.

Lucian got right to work making the water, getting help from Bruce to make another bucket. He took a mental note of the amount of crushed grass he had previously used to neutralize the bucket of water, so it was much faster this time around. He quickly had two full buckets of neutralized water, which he stashed in the shelter with makeshift lids to prevent contamination. *Not a lot of water should seep through the wood. There should be enough to last the day.* He let them know they had water before he went off again. He knew there must be ways to concentrate a poison he could use on a weapon. During the water neutralization, he brainstormed some. *A concentrated acid? A concentrated base? How could I concentrate them? Are some plants deathly poisonous like on Earth?* He knew that whatever he concocted would be used on giant animals; the poison would have to be fast-acting and very potent. It would have to enter their system and spread through whatever circulatory system they had. Thinking back, he remembered what Victoria and Valeria had encountered. Some orange dragon was feeding on a dead creature. If he biopsied one of the common land animals, he could get a sense of how they were designed and contrive a poison by experimenting with different natural compounds. *Oh! What if we extracted the toxin from a venom-generating animal. We could apply it to anything we wanted, as long as it didn't need to be stored at a specific temperature. It might work.*

Lucian found Victoria at the tree near the shelter. He told her his plan, and they planned to set more traps. She had been careful not to venture too far away for fear of attack. With Lucian, she was less worried. They stopped by Griffith at the shelter to see if he had found any durable cordage material. On his trek by the crystals, he had noticed some vine-like growths that were relatively strong. He demonstrated by trying to cut into it with his knife, where Lucian reminded him to be careful of the possible oils that could be secreted. Taking the warning, he returned to trying to make a sling pouch.

It was remarkable, however, that the vines barely had a scratch. Deciding not to take any of what Griffith had gathered, they walked back to the zone with crystals to get some for themselves. The walk felt short, and Lucian measured it by counting his pace on the way back.

"Isn't it funny that we chose to shelter far away from the water?" Victoria asked him as they approached the water's edge. She was rethinking their situation again, skeptical of their chances.

"Where else would we shelter?" he responded, trying not to sound cynical. "And besides, creatures tend to frequent water holes anyway. We'd just be more of a target. I'm sure plenty of things have been investigating us without us knowing, and our scent is everywhere." They continued walking, looking out for the vines Griffith mentioned. They were difficult to find, but Victoria spotted them growing on a large rock. Strangely, the vines seemed to encapsulate the rock like a spiderweb was laid over it. The vines sunk into the ground, almost as if it were its own roots.

Lucian was intrigued by it, "What if an underground plant is using these vines above the ground for something? Food or sunlight, maybe?" Victoria mildly shared his interest, but the unearthly traits began to frighten her, although she considered the miles of mycelium in some species. They could see where Griffith had taken some, and they started sawing right next to it. The tall grass near them was unsettling; they kept their ears open the whole time, ready to leave at a moment's notice. The wind startled them several times before they finally got what they deemed sufficient. While Lucian was busy counting his pace and thinking about what he could test for with a specimen, Victoria thought about what types of traps to set and what was feasible. Any snare trap would work for smaller animals and perhaps younger ones as well. But for any large creature, they would either have to make a giant pitfall trap or a more straightforward deadfall trap. Deciding that they were still unsure if the animals were edible, they planned on making a few smaller snares and maybe a tiny deadfall trap. When they needed to kill a much larger animal, they could revisit the large deadfall trap idea.

"It's one point seven miles away, in case anyone was wondering," Lucian told Victoria, Valeria, Bruce, and Tanho when he returned to the shelter. He counted one thousand six hundred forty paces. Thinking about it, he admitted to himself that it was not worth counting so much. Before walking out with Victoria again, Lucian noted the purple-tipped spears, the accumulation of sticks and small logs, and an absence of groans. "How's Tanho doing?" he asked, unsure whether to be concerned.

"He's alright, just resting. He was awake to drink water earlier," Bruce told him.

"Yeah, he definitely needs it," Valeria added. Seeing everyone accomplish meaningful tasks helped to ease her stressed and concerned mind. Watching Victoria and Lucian prepare for their future, she began to feel joy. She was confused as to what it meant, though. *Have I finally accepted our almost certain doom... or do I believe in us?* She wanted to believe in the latter but could not accept it.

Victoria and Lucian each grabbed themselves a spear and left the campsite. To get a good specimen, they would want to avoid crushing it with weight. As they walked higher in elevation, they looked for areas that may be sheltered to avoid the larger predators stealing their catch. They also navigated towards the edge of the brush to look for tracks. They kept a fair distance in case anything lurked, waiting for something– like them– to walk by. The ground they walked on was packed, sounding like they were walking on concrete. The brush had no evidence of being beaten down or trampled over. Gusts of wind interrupted the stagnant, humid air.

"Here!" Victoria exclaimed, not too loudly. Lucian looked over to see Victoria jogging to the base of another one of the giant trees. Warm colors reflected off bamboo-like shoots around some of the exposed roots. It looked like they could be saplings, but there were hundreds, much too many for that to make sense. A stream of ominous, red water slowly swept about some of the roots. The multicolored curtain of stalks stood embedded in the sides of the creek, only partially shielding another body of water behind fields of grasses and between trees of varying stages of growth.

As Lucian caught up with Victoria, he approached a fallen log that rested on the elevated bank on the other side of the water. Sticks and debris had gathered beneath, but there was an opening where sticks had been pushed to either side. This path was partially sheltered by the bamboo and roots, so they decided to try it. Having skewed visibility from the plants made them uneasy. They sped up their snare. Victoria used her knife to carve a hook– an *L*-shaped stick that would hook onto the base – an oppositely sculpted stick set into the ground. They made a notch around the upper end of the hook to tie the rope, too, and made their noose. Whenever an animal put pressure on the noose, the hook would unclasp and release the pressure on the bent plant. These shoots acted as earthen saplings would, being flexible yet durable.

Lucian took their sharpened base stick and firmly implanted it in the ground, having to jump on it repeatedly. He then grabbed high up on the nearest shoot and bent it as far as possible. Victoria tied some of the vine cordage to the end and set the hook in place. Lucian slowly released his hold on the bamboo, and the trap was set.

"We've gotta try it," he said, still engulfed by the idea of learning about new species.

"Let's not waste daytime; we can test one later. And besides, we've got to stay away and not make noise if we want something to come by."

"But... alright, I see," he responded, somewhat annoyed but understanding. They began to walk in search of another snare location; they brought enough vine for three or four more.

"Hey Valeria," Griffith said, getting her attention.

"What's up?" she laughed, finally in terms with their situation.

"You know how we've been here for about a day now? What are we going to do?" he asked, still maintaining a half-smile. He looked down again, returning to his latest project before asking, "How are we going to survive?" still looking away from her. He continued his work on a large, flat axe blade, sitting right in front of the pointed sticks. Valeria, who had just stuck another pointed log into the dense soil, brushed her hands together and then on her pants and sat down next to Griffith.

"Well, let's see," she said, pondering. "We're going to keep trying, and when it gets hard, we're going to try even harder. There's no promise we will hold out here long enough, but just maybe, just maybe, another ship will come through."

After a moment, Griffith returned to his normal, more confident state, saying, "It's just strange not knowing what tomorrow or even the next hour will look like. We seem to stand a pretty good chance, though."

"Just don't get carried away, Griffith, stay in the *now*. We can prepare for the future, but letting ourselves be responsible for more than one time at once is just unneeded stress."

Griffith placed the axe head in the split of a strong stick and pounded it into place. He laced the area around where the axe sat in the wood with a sticky substance he found pooling nearby. Applying the glue to the lashings while setting them gave it increased strength. He sat it upright against the rocky shelter, letting gravity encapsulate the joint with the adhesive.

The axe was now complete. A broad face that grew moving closer to the joint added power to any swing. The back of the axe was pointed, a wicked-sharp tip as if part of a spear; it would most certainly pierce anything living with enough might. He stood over it, admiring his work, calling Valeria and Bruce to take a look. Tanho was also interested, but his worse condition made Griffith pick the axe back up again to show him.

"What're you gonna name it?" Bruce asked. "You've gotta name it."

After thinking for a few moments, Griffith knew: "Jarnbjorn. Like from Norse mythology."

"Made of Thor's blood, right?" Valeria clarified.

"That's the one."

Bruce chuckled and exclaimed, "Jarnbjorn, The Battle Axe! It fits!"

Valeria then remembered and asked, "Hey Tanho, you should name the fish creature and the wolf creatures because you were the one who found them."

"Well, I didn't *find* the wolves; they found *us*."

"Fine. But still, get thinking. You were the one hurt by them; it only makes sense. I'll talk to Victoria about what we get to name the orange dragon," she stated while beginning to turn and walk away, deciding to take a break from the shelter. Tanho started to think about being clutched in the wolf's mouth. He could follow mythology with 'Fenrir' or pick something else funny. *Maybe something funnier would help make this place not as scary.*

"Alright, I'll come up with something," he called to Valeria, who was walking away now. He coughed, sending a jolt of pain through his stomach. He curled up and put his arm over his abdomen, wincing. His arm only added to the pain, touching the fresh wounds; he instantly knew his mistake and lifted his hand back off his body, resulting to lie down again and deal with the pain. "Can any of you play chess?"

Bruce and Griffith were the only ones near enough to hear. "No," they said, looking at each other in partial confusion, half an eyebrow slightly elevated.

Griffith rescinded, "Well, I've played before, I guess. I'm not any good, though."

"Can you play in your head?"

"Can you?" he asked, somewhat in awe to see an injured, tired man trying to do something as mentally taxing as playing chess. He moved closer and looked at Tanho again, this time in closer detail. The beads of sweat still forming about his forehead and a slight quiver in his left eye showed weakness; at least his brain was still functional. "You're something, you know that."

Tanho chuckled, this time much lighter to reduce the pain it may cause. "Yeah, I know. But I can play chess mentally; it's kind of fun. Wanna try? I can teach you."

"Maybe tonight, I'd like to finish making those slings before nightfall." Griffith brought one of the pales of water next to Tanho, the rough bark making the pale much heavier and increasing traction. Before taking a sip and lying back to rest more, Tanho noted the awkward smells surrounding him. Nothing reminded him of Earth. When he closed his eyes, he held them shut longer than he needed to blink. He could focus on the sounds of a light breeze bending around the rocks; the intimate breathing of Griffith; the dull murmur of Bruce making a comment; and a low buzz, a soft rumbling whose origin he could not decipher.

Griffith retook his spot and began weaving some of the vines with layers of grasses to form a pouch. By the time Bruce finished preparing the steel he had previously worked on, Griffith had made significant progress. To provide enough force to do damage, the sling would have to be long and the pouch durable enough to hold a substantial weight. He wanted the concave portion of the pouch to be resistant to any sharp objects that could be thrown so the fibrous grasses would make a poor superficial layer. The vines were not malleable enough to weave in the right proportion, but they would work as long as they were strong enough and had few holes for the object to catch onto. He decided to tie two alternating layers of vine together at the ends by the much more flexible yet strong grasses.

Bruce tied another crystal tip to the spear, adding it to the accumulated pile. He heard Tanho lightly snoring and looked up to see his awkward sleeping position. Bruce laughed, causing Griffith to look over.

"Bruce, take a look at this. I'm going to test it," he said as he picked up a rock and set it in the pouch. He held the sling by its two end strings and let the weight slowly descend to the ground. Holding the sling near the end comfortably, just below chest level, the rock set only a few inches above the ground. He was two inches over six feet tall, allowing him to generate tremendous force.

"Alright, let's see it," he said with a sigh, stretching and cracking his back. He was excited but unsure how his sigh would be taken. Griffith seemed very happy with his craftsmanship, not even bothering to look back at Bruce.

Griffith rotated his shoulders a few times, preparing to swing. He aligned himself with the open space most directly in front of the shelter's opening. He reflected for a second, imagining the wolf-like monster chasing Tanho: the screams hanging in the air; the thrashing of a lifeless body; and the shiny, silver fangs dripping an exotic concoction of alien saliva and fresh, human blood. Shivers. Griffith took himself back, envisioning a windshield full of fractalling water droplets whose falling facilitated immediate freezing, a landscape of snowflakes throughout the entire drive. He did not know his destination.

In an instant, he was spinning the rock. Bruce had not noticed anything strange, still partially flustered. Griffith felt the weight shifting, and he only needed to move his arm slightly vertically in a few rotations to maintain momentum. Griffith lifted the spinning sling above his right shoulder and prepared to release the projectile. He envisioned an outline of a giant wolf with red eyes. His breathing slowed, and he could hear it. His peripherals were invisible. The rock hurdled through the air, remaining perfectly parallel to the ground for what must have been over 75 feet before beginning to drop. It hit the ground and bounced upwards before skidding and tumbling further away.

"That will definitely do some damage," Bruce observed, giving a round of applause. Griffith's smile grew; he knew he needed to make more. With a brisk jog, he returned to the rock with the vines without even considering taking Valeria with him, as would be safest. As he approached, he quickly realized that something was different. The rock was still in place, but the reddish vines had turned purple. Even more peculiar was that where he had taken the vines from earlier was no evidence that anything was missing. He thought he was hallucinating, imagining the perplexity. A quick turn in either direction made him realize he was alone, which creeped him out. Deep breaths, he was okay. That was the only noticeable change around him. It was a strange place, either way; this just added another layer of complexity. He was unsure what to make of the vines and was worried about what the color change could mean. To be safe, he decided to throw something at it.

He grabbed a stick and tossed it, standing a safe distance away. The rock did not react. Nothing happened. Griffith threw another stick, unconvinced by the strangely wrapped rock's abiotic nature. Again, nothing. He decided not to cut any of the purple vines and instead walked around, taking a slightly longer route back to camp. He was alone but determined to make more weapons. He took a leisurely stroll around where this rock was, demonstrating to himself his superiority to this extraterrestrial environment. With no luck finding anything else that could make a durable cordage, he walked back to camp to ask Lucian his opinion about the color-changing, regenerating vines.

Valeria now felt that the planet was a fresh start for them, a fresh start that wanted to kill them. It fascinated her how they could even survive this long in a place so foreign and mysterious. She heard something in the grasses to her right, although she could not be sure what it was. With only a split-second glance, she resolved to head straight back to the camp.

She met Bruce and Tanho back at camp and quickly learned that Griffith was not missing and was out towards the pond. Valeria motioned to the bedding she and Bruce had spread around the inside of the shelter. "Tanho, do we need more?"

"I could use a pillow or something." He minimally laughed, smirking, asking, "Do you think I could get a silk one? A nice weighted blanket, perhaps?"

"Of course, Tanho. I got you," she scoffed, smiling while turning away once more. Tanho loved her smile.

They waited around their campsite, the fire permeating the air. As the waves of heat distorted vision, Bruce stared into the familiar flames. Another reminder of what was to be missed. Tanho knew he would most likely be bedridden for a while, a few weeks at least. The heat aggravated his wounds yet provided him enough comfort for it to be meaningful.

He looked at Bruce in his trance and thought, *we can do this*. Tanho had grown accustomed to the pain in only about a day. He knew that struggling and complaining would only diminish their hope and motivation; not mentioning it eased his aches. He wondered if it was only psychological. He hoped it was not, thinking, *maybe I could move around again sooner*.

Bruce looked at him concernedly as if reading his mind, wondering, "Who knows, maybe Lucian will find something that heals you faster. Or better yet, maybe something in the air does the same thing."

"You know, maybe the air is actually hurting me. What if it's slowing it down?" Tanho responded, knowing that it was the less likely of the two opposites. He looked at the ceiling again, aware of each intricate impurity lining his place of sojourn. He wanted time to go by faster.

Outside, Valeria, Griffith, and Bruce began to notice the difference in light. It was finally getting darker. A few stars had already appeared by the time they looked up; they showed up much sooner than expected. The brilliant reds had already begun to fade into an awkward, angry orange. It would be a couple hours before night– a couple hours before all the creatures would appear again. The thought unsettled them; at least they were more prepared this time. Bruce looked at the spears he made, not in the sense of being proud but rather for a reaffirmation of safety.

Victoria and Lucian returned to the refurbished campsite. They both looked confident, a sign that nothing alarming had occurred. Everyone was eager to hear about how setting the traps went. Victoria, being less analytical of the situation, described the beauty of their first spot. She referenced the varying colors and the interwoven nature of streams and roots sheltering a body of water and what looked to be different color grasses. At points, while they had explored, getting higher up, they could see expanses of fresh yellows blending with small, orange trees. It was surprising to them. It looked very different from the location they had all been exposed to.

Lucian added, "It's significantly different from what Griffith and I saw yesterday. You guys should've seen."

"Nothing on Earth can compare to some of those views," Victoria affirmed. She continued recounting the reflective marshes adjacent to ominous ravines. One of the ravines glowed a venomous green, sparking a dangerous curiosity.

"If anything lives there, it must be pretty deadly. We probably should avoid the caverns," Lucian told them. Victoria told them they set out four snares in total. Some were worse than others, but they seemed to be in active places. It surprised them how little evidence of life they could find during the day.

Lucian decided, "There must be other indicators we're just missing. The only things we've seen during the day are Victoria and Valeria's dragon and the dead thing, the one that disappeared."

Griffith thought while they discussed the signs of life. "We don't even know where they live yet, except for maybe the trees." They realized their shelter may not last them that long after all. They needed a place safer and less exposed to the elements.

"If we could clear out some caves on a rock face, it might be safer than this," Valeria told them. "On Earth, it's really just bats that live in them. If we could find something similar, we might be able to make it work, probably with a door, too."

"Something with a small entrance but enough room for us to do most of our things inside; that sounds like a good idea if we can find it," Lucian told them. They agreed that they should find a more permanent shelter as soon as possible.

Bruce confirmed, "Yeah, I didn't even think about the weather. If something crazy happens, we'll be kind of stuck here. What if it becomes freezing?" They decided to continue planning at night once it got dark. Until then, they stocked up on more firewood.

Griffith had completed his second sling, letting both of them hang from the end of the pointed sticks. He thought he should keep one with him at all times but quickly realized that there was no way he was carrying large enough rocks with him everywhere. They were not all that sporadically placed; they seemed to only be in patches near other rock clusters. If he left both of the slings and a decent pile of rocks at the shelter, anyone who needed it could use it. *I have to teach them how they work.*

The sky continued falling. This time, they had an idea of what was to come. Before it was even remotely nighttime, they stuck to the shelter. They tried to come up with anything else they might need overnight. They still had no food source but could go another night without a sated hunger. It would probably be a viable food if they cooked anything long enough, but they agreed to wait for the dissection to decide, at least for now. They had barely felt hungry until now, and they all felt still in good shape. Discussing, they knew they would have to spend some time trying to find sustainable food.

They shuddered thinking about having to test different foods and the possibilities of eating alien foods and alien nutrients. A single illness or ailment could kill them, for they would have nothing to counteract it. The group reminded themselves to be careful; the pressures of living there were beginning to weigh on them. The six of them had no backbone, no supporting structure to fall back on if something terrible were to happen. They could only move forward.

Stars dived across the sky in waves. More trails of ranging lengths followed in majestic brush strokes. The warm colors were slowly washed away, bringing on the cold of the night. It was either the sky or their eyes' adjustment to the reds that caused the onslaught of night to look blue. They sat around the campfire, only incomplete by lack of s'mores. They were united, held together by a desire to survive, although it could be by cause of necessity. Unable to come up with anything else they could need, everyone able assisted in moving things inside.

Griffith brandished his axe, holding it up to the light of the fire. The sight reminded Valeria, "Tanho, come up with any names?" She had yet to talk to Victoria about naming their creature. Everyone curiously looked over at Tanho, who had just sat up for the first time for something other than water.

He looked down at himself, specifically at his barely-covered wounds. Valeria had washed some of the bandages, but they remained somewhat red. "The wolves, I think it would be weird not to name them something with wolf in it. Yet, I'd say we name them *Fenrhor*, Fenrir– like the wolf, and abhor combined."

"That makes sense, and I like it! Those guys are definitely hopped up on something," Bruce remarked.

"And for those fish, I was thinking something like *Fire-Resistant Squid*. Even though it didn't really look like a squid, I got a similar feeling from it."

"And 'fire-resistant' helps us remember. Good idea," Lucian commended, keeping his head slightly tilted up and to the left as he pondered. Tanho, the only one not looking at himself and thinking about the new names, was quick to notice Lucian's manner. He chose not to ask him about it.

"Valeria and Victoria, it's your turn," Tanho told them, hoping nobody hated his name choices. He knew they could still be changed, and they were not the best possible names, but he could not tell what the others were thinking at that moment. After passing the baton to the girls, he stared into the fire for a few seconds, its bright flames burning briskly while a starlit night showed signs of settling.

"Okay, Victoria, what do you think?"

"I sorta like *Pygmy Dragon*."

"'Pygmy Dragon' is cute and simultaneously scary," Griffith commented, beginning to think of names for their planet.

"I guess I'm cool with that name, Victoria," Valeria told her.

"'Pygmy Dragon' it is then," Griffith adjudicated with confirmation by the others. "While we're on the topic, what do you think of a team vote for the planet's name?"

Victoria immediately countered, "What if we had a friendly competition for naming rights?" They were unsure of what to make of it.

"What would the competition be?" Lucian asked, not one to deny a challenge.

"Food. We can decide on teams; whichever team finds the best food and cooks it the best wins naming rights; a friendly challenge, just for fun." They thought it was ridiculous to have this sort of challenge while they were most likely still about to die. Somehow, they all rationalized it for themselves through a combination of livening spirits and getting food.

"As long as we also keep an eye out for shelters and be careful," Lucian lightly demanded. "No dying, please." They agreed on the terms, now deliberating teams.

Chapter 3

TO TAKE RISKS

Just as they proposed that Tanho would work with Lucian, Bruce with Victoria, and Griffith with Valeria, a loud *thwack* was heard in the distance. Without hesitation, Lucian leaped off the ground, a live wire. The spear jumped into his hands, and he had left the shelter in a flash. By then, everyone had figured out why he had left, but they were still confused as to why he did.

"Wait! It's dangerous!" Valeria called out. No response was heard. It had not turned into the pitch-black madness of the previous night yet, but Lucian's lunacy was everpresent. They could either go with him or stay. There seemed no point in leaving the safety of the shelter so close to darkness; a slaughter would be too likely. The five could only hope that Lucian was still in his right mind. They needed him.

As time passed, the group could not tell if it was the fire or the ground's reflection causing the sanguine atmosphere. They collectively had a bad feeling about Lucian's departure. Their conversation had dropped with worry.

"Do we have to go out and help him?" Victoria asked.

"He will be back soon. Believe in him. You guys didn't set snares too far out, right?" Griffith assured, understanding that they needed to learn as much as possible in little time if they wanted a chance to survive.

"Some were farther than others. We were out for a while."

"But we could hear it," Bruce reminded consolingly.

"It could have just been loud because of the trigger we used. Maybe it's just naturally like that."

Tanho had been quiet, thinking. He knew the fenrhor were smart and had good senses. They negotiated with him for his Fire-Resistant Squid, or at least they had seemed to. That's when it occurred to him. "Wait, guys," he announced, getting their attention. "What if the sound of the snare going off attracts the creatures. They'd all converge on him. There's no way he could think his way out of that."

Griffith responded, "Lucian is smart enough to see that. He must have some reasoning. We've just gotta trust him. He should be back soon anyways." They tried not to worry. Tanho, specifically, tried to keep his mind off the many possibilities. *Lucian will be fine.*

They tried to get back to their conversation. Tanho was almost incapable of movement but did not need to move to cook. He was the obvious choice to go with Lucian, who could make anything out of anything– a Macgyver.

Bruce could still move somewhat, but his range was limited. Bruce and Victoria grew up with lots of access to nature; they understood survival wholly. Victoria had already established a good understanding of what was around them. Her sense of direction was the best of the group. Bruce was good at thinking outside the box and getting things done. They were to be paired to balance spatial knowledge and for their similar upbringing.

Griffith was an Eagle Scout, giving him an advantage in that he learned survival at a younger age and had many diverse skill sets. Valeria was cautious, which would prevent Griffith from doing anything half-witted. The teams seemed to work out and would be fair.

"Any objections?" Victoria asked.

"As long as Lucian gets back here by tomorrow," Tanho said jokingly, lying back down with a long sigh. Griffith looked outside; it was noticeably darker than when Lucian left. Nobody had responded to Victoria, limiting the scope of their discussion. They sat in silence, waiting for Lucian's return.

It was a bad sign when they started hearing noises again. Monsters set free, ready to converge on them at any moment. The mightier screams, roars, and growls were unlike anything they had ever heard. This night was somehow worse than the previous.

"What the heck is that thing?" Bruce asked in response to one of the more ominous, peculiar noises. The darkness had definitely situated. They had no idea what any of the sounds were.

Lucian finally broke through the darkness, but he remained partially shrouded by the low visibility until the light of the fire caught his figure. The outline of the spear showed something on its end. He held it top-down but angled away from him. As he approached and his footsteps became louder, they let out silent sighs of relief. Lucian was back, still alive. They were confused and moderately angry that he left with a seeming disregard for his own and, by association, their lives.

Lucian had to convince them. Arriving at camp, he set the animal near the fire and sat near the water on the opposite side of the room, out of breath and panting. He poured water onto his arms, letting it drop to his hands and the ground. Removing the zip-up and using the outside to scrub his hands, he seemed to be in pain. Everyone watched in more confusion as he spilled more water over his hands.

"Acidic blood," he noted. "I'll be okay."

"You know that was stupid, right– leaving while it's so dark out?" Valeria asked him seriously. Lucian was sorry, but his wind-swept appearance masked it.

"It's fine, I knew I could make it back in time."

"There's just no way you could know that! Please be careful."

"Sorry, but I did know. At the first sign of anything being different than what we know so far, I would've turned right back around."

Bruce argued, "Still, that was idiotic."

"Do you want us all to die or to have a chance at surviving?" Lucian exclaimed, a tiredness and confidence lingering on every syllable. He knew that they already had a limited possibility of survival. They needed to take chances if they wanted to beat the odds; the more knowledge the group accumulated as fast as possible, the better they could adapt and hold out longer.

Chance, they thought. It flustered them.

"Hey, he's back, it's alright. Now we can do that dissection," Griffith said. He paused for a second, glancing away before looking back and stating, "Still, that was kind of stupid."

The dissection would have to wait for tomorrow; it was too dark to analyze anything they found. The smell would also attract creatures.

"Wights," Tanho said. "At night, they're all wights– those ghostly entities."

Bruce shifted as the corners of his mouth began to rise. "Why not all lefts?"

"Shut up, Bruce," a collective mind told him, trying to resist a chuckle. Griffith turned away to look outside as his straight face returned. A groan from the eerie darkness reminded them that their speech could still be heard. During their conversation, they were unaware of any of the strange noises.

They were all together, sitting in a makeshift shelter, protected by sharpened sticks, gazing into an unforgiving blackness and hiding from the beasts of the night. For a moment, it was as if their drowsiness was comforting. Two days had passed, and they were as safe as ever. With Tanho's energy being sapped by the wound-healing process, he shifted his body a final time before closing his eyes to rest. Bruce grabbed another fibrous log and set it gently on the fire, watching the reds and oranges with intermittent purples erupt up and out of their shelter.

As they sat silently, shades of a green glow pierced the black fog. Griffith grabbed the non-burnt end of one of the flaming sticks and held it up in anticipatory defense. Their second ordeal had begun.

They remained silent as the glow dotted around. It rose and fell fluidly. The sound of the fire was louder than what the beast was producing. They could not make out any detail, not even an outline. Tanho felt the same rumbling he had felt before, but this time, it was stronger. He sat up, unphased by the creature somewhere in front of their home.

"Guys, do you hear the rumbling?" he whispered concernedly. They released their focus on the glowing light, putting their hands through the leaves and onto the cold ground beneath. Without a word spoken, knives were wielded, and spears were made handy. They sat rigid, taking deep breaths to increase concentration and lower their heart rate. Time slowed significantly; they could only wait for whatever was to come.

Griffith had the urge to throw a smaller rock at the light. His sling limited his throwing potential, so he'd have to wait until it was a close distance if he wanted to try from inside. He knew it was not a good idea.

Lucian tried to understand what the light could represent. "On angler fish, the lights are supposed to mimic small organisms. Perhaps this is supposed to be a bug or an insect. It's strange we haven't seen any yet," he quietly told the rest of them.

The rumbling grew in strength and ferocity as if a mini-earthquake was hitting. The grasses outside seemed unaffected. The light paused momentarily before continuing its movements. Within seconds and after a peak of amplitude, the rumbling had stopped entirely. Their ears rang before settling again. They were confused.

Griffith asked, "Can I throw a rock at it?" slightly above a murmur.

Lucian immediately responded, "No, that's stupid," but recanted. They could either wait and potentially miss out on understanding the creature, or they could implement risk and almost definitely see it. The worst-case scenario he envisioned was gas emitting into the air, forcing everyone to separate and fend for themselves in the darkness.

They decided that Lucian would determine their course of action; he had the best understanding of the possibilities.

"Let's do it, but we should do something to help us see this thing," he said." All Lucian needed to see was the outline, but movement would also teach them about its characteristics. They would have to draw it closer to the light of the fire or bring the light of the fire to it. Settling on the latter, they chose to throw a burning stick out first. When its flames rekindled, the beast would either get interested in the fire, or they would have to forcefully interest it with rocks.

Bruce questioned the authenticity of the experiment, "What if we're just dooming ourselves?"

Griffith told him, "If it doesn't register this fire as a threat, as it hasn't yet, how would it know where the rocks came from?" They decided it was okay to try but wanted it to stick around. Hitting it may scare it off, so they needed to find out where it stood. The variance in the size of the creatures on the planet gave no insight into how far away the light may actually be.

Lucian thought and asked, "What's there in the daytime?"

Victoria told him, "Not much. It's near the grasses and closer to the tree. I don't think any landmarks will help."

"Okay, Griffith, I guess we just gotta hope. Throw lightly," Lucian told him, partially excited. Griffith grabbed the end of one of the warm logs in the fire, taking a step back before taking a skip and lobbing the log. It was heavy, a couple pounds at least, but Griffith threw it far. They watched as the fire's light faded in flight and burst back as it hit the ground short of the beast, which did not seem to flinch. At that far of a distance, the light was of almost equal size. *The bait must be larger than the log.*

Lucian decided Griffith probably threw the log about sixty feet with negligible rolling. The fire was not bright enough to shine on the beast. *That size fire would light up anything within fifty feet.*

"It must be over a hundred feet out."

Griffith was ready to throw a rock. He knew he could throw it farther than the log. Before he threw it, Lucian proposed an experiment. If they threw the rock at the same speed and angle of a known distance, they could calculate how far out the beast was. The giant tree was behind them, out of view from the entrance of the shelter. The grasses were the next best option. There were grasses to the right, opposite the beast, which were closer.

"How far do you think those grasses are?" Lucian asked, pointing to the right side of the darkness. Lucian decided that he could average everyone's guess and hopefully be accurate.

"Groups are supposed to be more accurate than individual people. What do you guys think?" Averaging the guesses, Lucian calculated ninety-two feet. Sensing his cue, Griffith threw an under full-strength throw just above parallel to the ground. Lucian did his best to count the time. Victoria had also done so. They decided it was just under one second.

Griffith aimed just below the light, preparing another throw. "Ready?" he asked.

"Go for it," Lucian said, all the others watching intently.

He tried to throw identically but with a slightly higher release angle to increase the distance. Lucian knew he would have to increase the calculated time because of it. The rock disappeared into the darkness and met its target. The impact sounded like chainmail, confusing them. Before Lucian had a chance to calculate the distance away, the light of the beast disappeared, and movement was heard. They could not tell which way the beast was moving; it seemed to be rushing. They hoped it was moving towards the fire.

The beast appeared near the small and dying fire. Only its massive legs were seen– it looked like it had many of them. Lucian was in awe of how quiet the creature was; it had to have been over twenty feet tall by the length and width of the legs.

It was moving fast and didn't stop at the fire, now rushing towards them. Their sighs were blocked out by adrenaline spikes.

"Oh no," Valeria said in an exhale, "We're going to die."

Tanho got to his feet and grabbed a spear, preparing for the worst. The absence of light from under the massive canopy shrouded all. The sounds of steps grew louder, the creature no longer caring about the element of surprise.

As the beast approached the edge of the fire's reach, dirt and minerals were flung into the air. Many pieces of mantle debris struck the shelter, raining above them. A few pieces landed in the shelter as the loudest sounds they had ever heard began sequencing. They instinctively dropped the spears to the ground and covered their ears. They felt intense rumbling and vibrations through the ground while the sounds penetrated their hands and hit their eardrums.

The glowing light reappeared, flailing and dancing, seemingly being thrashed around. The cries of agony signaled a fight. More vibrations were felt, and more dirt was flung, this time with less ferocity. A dark blue tail flung through the air in front of them.

"What is that?" Victoria screamed, the beasts' brawl overpowering her voice. The ground continued vibrating and lots of dirt was flung, a constant rain bouncing off their rocky shelter. They backed farther into their shelter, sitting against the back wall. The screams began to die down, allowing them to release their vice over their heads. They looked at each other with worried, wide eyes.

The beast soon crashed to the ground; they could hear slamming as if the beast was thrashing itself. The thin, luminous branch of the creature lay clearly visible in front of their shelter. Curiously, they watched as it swung around in the air. The beast was frantic. They looked towards where the end of the creature disappeared, seeing the tails of a dull, gray-and-blue, long animal.

"Are those worms?" Griffith asked worriedly. The more enormous beast thrashed itself closer into the light, the worms following. Giant, squirming worms attacked the creature's many limbs, using their hold in the ground to keep it in place. Some left the ground entirely, climbing up onto the beast. They watched as one bore its way through the blue skin. Within moments, the beast lay lifeless. The worms all left the ground and quickly consumed the beast, leaving modicum bits of flesh and a strange, husky structure. Within another minute, they had grasped the remains and dug themselves back into the ground. The vibrations returned, causing the group to stand up in fear; they wouldn't dare to move any more than that. The oscillations diminished slowly until they were gone entirely.

They were bemused by the entire incident, once again surprised by the new species and paroxysm. This time, they were less frightened, although they did not know what to make of the situation. The only thing they could do was stay by the fire and hope nothing found them.

A light, brisk breeze blew smoke back into their shelter, temporarily masking the sounds of wildlife through a whistling between grasses and other obstacles invisible to them. The smell carried in was rancid; they knew it was this planet's smell of death. To reduce the deathly scent invader, they grew the fire, tossing many logs on top and around, expanding its width.

Bruce moved the speared creature away from the fire to prevent it from burning, revealing a drying, purple pool of blood soaking into the ground. The fire burned and crackled before adapting to its increase in fuel. As the wind died down and the fire began to relax, so did they.

"I think we should try and sleep. There's no point in staying awake if we can avoid it," Griffith told them.

Lucian added, "As long as nothing crazy happens, go for it. I'm staying up longer, though; I need to think." He wanted to explore the wildlife dynamic in his mind. He also needed to stay up and try to get used to the animals' indicators and sounds.

Tanho decided he would try to sleep, with recovery being his priority. He had already felt significantly healthier, but the faster he could get up and move around normally, the better.

Victoria, Bruce, and Valeria had just begun contemplating when they heard thundering steps.

"Whatever that thing was, it's massive," Lucian commented, aware of its slow, loud walking. *Compared to the angler creature, this thing is making way too much noise.*

Tanho slowly and reluctantly sat up again, saying, "We might just have to sleep in the morning."

They sat waiting and listening for the next set of noises to disrupt the silence. They heard lots of heavy walking at different speeds and degrees of loudness, the flapping of a few winged animals, loud hisses, screeches, and brawls. The vibrations had not returned.

Chapter 4

Live to Learn

It was just before the light from the sun would be noticeable when a multi-headed snake-like animal appeared in front of them. Tanho, Valeria, and Bruce were asleep, leaving Griffith, Victoria, and Lucian frozen and unsure how to respond when the hydra with keeled scales approached. It made no noise, slithering across the rough ground, the middle two of its four heads locked on the shelter. It closed in slowly. It was a dull orange with defined scales and dark borders that blended into a vermillion red.

Instinctively, they continued not to move. Victoria was closest to Bruce, and Lucian was closest to Valeria. They tapped them slowly without much movement. As they woke, they sensed that it was still dark outside. Seeing the flickering light reflect on the frozen bodies staring forward, they looked to see the creature, now also unmoving. Its heads darted about in a hypnotizing manner, inspecting the brightness and flowing about each other. It had three eyes on each head, one in the middle and one slightly raised to either side. Each eye was at least the size of a softball. The snake parked close enough for them to see the shadow cast from its extending eyebrow over the rippling blue and purple crescent-shaped eye. This creature also had a pupil, a dilated, dull, cyan diamond from which the vivid and seemingly luminous colors shone a gold that blended in reflection off the eyes' and surrounding scales' convex structures. The gold highlighted the round, dotted, smaller-scaled composition of the main scales; it had the appearance of rocks.

While the others were sitting in anticipation of the creature's next move, Lucian decided it was improbable that they could hit all twelve eyes before mass casualty. Victoria thought about which head she would have to attack based on her position in the shelter. The group was layered; Tanho and Valeria would have to move forward to get a better attack. That would mean Lucian and her would have to take either side while Griffith and Bruce took on the middle two until Tanho and Valeria got in to help.

The bulwarks would help slow down the snake, but they knew it was insufficient. They were unsure if the sticks would even pierce the snake's armor. They hoped it would give them enough time to incapacitate the beast.

As moments of stasis continued, they wished for something to save them and make the beast leave. They knew that most creatures hid during the day and that it was soon becoming light.

The beast produced a sound that reminded them of pressurized gas valves before turning away. They waited in silence as it left the way it came. It began to disappear into the dark shadow ahead of them. They realized the beast must be at least thirty feet long. Spearlike hair protrusions armored its tail, which held partially off to one side as if to balance itself when its heads' movement unbalanced it.

As it moved further into the darkness, they continued to wait. As soon as it was entirely gone, Victoria warned the group in a whisper, "Don't move or make noise. It might be circling around to wait from the back." She realized they were still uncertain of how the creatures thought. They could be more intelligent than the animals on Earth. *Hopefully, they're not more intelligent than we are.*

They returned to comfortable positions slowly, minimizing any noise they may produce from the leafy bedding. They noticed a reduction in frightening sounds echoing around them, and finally, light began to bend over the horizon. As the stars in the sky began to fade, a particular purple and green streak shot slowly, vertically across the scene above them.

Still quiet, Griffith announced, "It's falling!" while directing their attention with a pointed finger. They watched and tried to determine how far away the meteoroid was. As it lowered closer and closer to the ground, they realized a mound of ground would hide its landing.

Griffith, Victoria, Bruce, and Valeria grabbed spears from the side wall, feeling its warmth from the fire, and left the shelter. Lucian was still worried about the hydra from moments earlier; he resolved to stay in the shelter and provide backup if necessary. *Someone needs to be able to help defend.*

They ran spearpoint first in a shape resembling a line. Griffith pulled ahead, understanding the necessity of a new material and clue to the planet. Seeing Griffith's speed, Valeria turned around to check about the snake. She saw no snake.

Her expression quickly flipped. "Guys, what is that?" she called in exclamation, causing Victoria and Bruce to spin. Griffith continued forward, determined to maintain sight of the fascinating meteorite.

There was no wind manipulating the humid air. There was minimal noise, only the sound of Victoria and Bruce's halting and Griffith's continued run. They froze once more, unsure of what to do.

"Griffith! Turn around!" Victoria commanded. Lucian watched in fear as they looked above him. He grabbed his spear and took a half-step farther from the shelter's entrance, preparing for something to drop. Griffith stopped in his tracks, throwing his head clockwise over his shoulder while he turned around, annoyed by how close he was to the hill and that he would likely miss an idea of where the landing site was.

As he spun, he saw a giant, dull, black-and-red spider. It seemed to have more than ten extremities, and they could not be sure how many of them were arms. They saw large fangs dangling below the creature's main body. It stood just below the top of the rocky structure.

"Lucian, don't go outside," Valeria said without losing eye contact with the beast. Griffith gave up on the meteorite, instead walking back and standing in front of them, facing the spider head-on. It seemed to turn its head, although they were unsure if it could do that. They could not tell where it was looking from that distance, close to the grasses off to the right of the shelter's opening.

Griffith made his way forward, pausing after each step; Valeria, Victoria, and Bruce followed him. In the shelter, Lucian grabbed one of the slings and gestured to Bruce before tying one of its ends to a log and throwing it. The added weight helped carry the sling the extra distance. The spider did not seem to notice, watching solely the small, weirdly colored animals holding sticks.

"Get ready," Griffith said, picking up a nearby rock and placing it into the sling. They backed up and prepared their spears, giving Griffith room to swing. The spider moved forward slightly. They hoped it would not get closer to Lucian and Tanho. Griffith continued winding up his swing. He took a deep breath and released his hold on one of the ends at the perfect point in the rotation, launching the rock at the spider with tremendous force.

During the rock's travel, the spider jolted off to the side. The speed of the rock was too fast for the creature to react. They watched as the rock ripped through two of the creature's legs, spewing a greenish gray blood. One of the legs fell in the opening of the shelter in front of Lucian, landing vertically to stick into the ground. Lucian noted the sharpness of its limbs.

The spider released a menacing hiss of steam, which rose above it before disintegrating. It approached them, getting closer and closer to the cave's opening, holding Lucian and Tanho. A second spider appeared over the top of the cave, setting its eyes on them just as the first had. The injured beast almost instantly stopped bleeding; it seemed unaffected in its motion despite missing limbs. To their right, another spider emerged from the grass. The group faced their foes, knowing they could no longer make a retreat to the shelter.

Bruce and Valeria faced the spider to the right while Griffith and Victoria cracked their necks in anticipation of the two spiders' next move. In watching the single spider on their flank, Valeria squinted, seeing movement behind it. Much farther behind the spider and towards the lake they had crash-landed into was a pygmy dragon. It seemed to be slightly larger than the one they had seen before. While Valeria recognized the familiar sight, the spider she was watching moved in a zigzag, approaching them in a haunting manner. It began making a similar hissing and clicking sound, communicating with its fellow spiders, when a long, ivory-colored rod poked from the grasses on the left. It speared the spider, causing its legs to flail and contract closer to its abdomen. It was then speared again from the same side of the grass before being drawn in; it was dead.

Turning their focus back to the two spiders on their shelter, Victoria handed Griffith another rock. As if already learning, the spiders took cover, separating and moving circularly around either side of them. To keep themselves facing their targets, they oriented themselves back-to-back. Quickly, Griffith realized that they were just being corralled.

"Victoria, we rush on three," he said. Lucian picked up two spears and exited the shelter with a determined look on his face. Glancing back and forth at both enemies, he looked for a time where striking would provide them an advantage.

"One," he called, Lucian now farther outside of the shelter, still a distance away from the action. Bruce had no pain in his leg; it seemed to have healed. Victoria and Griffith felt fatigued, but there was no time for that. Valeria was motivated: We are not going to die yet. They were a sight to behold, inconspicuous creatures about to take on spiders on the smaller side of the animal kingdom, a true test of worth.

"Two." Lucian heard the countdown and knew he needed to help somehow. He could throw one of the spears, but he had no time and did not want to risk hitting someone. He continued pushing forward instead. Victoria reinforced her grip on her spear, keeping in mind the knife she wore on her side. If worse came to worst, they could beeline to Lucian.

"Three," Griffith announced at a tone enough for the spiders not to notice a change as Lucian let out a roar of his own. A momentary pause, while some of the creatures' black eyes turned in response to the sound, made the group's rush more effective. They still needed to close the distance to provide a killing blow, which was made more difficult by their heightened heart rate.

Bruce and Valeria's spider was less affected by Lucian's distraction. It immediately noticed that something was awry. It looked back at them, making a dart to their left at a speed they had not seen in any other creature. It waited for a shift in their center of balance, indicated by their foot's orientation, before pivoting and moving to the right. The distance had mostly closed. The spider pivoted again, leaping low to avoid the defended upper body. It held many of its dark limbs fully extended, moving straight towards Valeria. They hoped their spears were longer than the spider's legs.

Simultaneously, Griffith and Victoria moved oppositely about the spider. Either side it went to, it was likely to be skewered. Sensing the danger and explosivity of the humans, it ducked low, hissing, targeting Griffith's legs. Victoria noticed and turned left, moving closer to Griffith to help him attack. Almost instantly, the spider had closed in, but right before reaching Griffith's legs, it turned to its left, using its pivoting power and hold on the ground to make a swift and calculated move at Victoria.

Lucian continued trying to help, rationalizing that the only thing he could do was advance, perhaps helping on a flank.

Valeria lowered herself to give more strength to a thrust as a close-by Bruce began his thrust early, hoping to at least deflect many of the limbs away and possibly penetrate the already weakened creature. Valeria tucked as much of herself as possible behind her spear, held firmly in the direction of the incoming spider. Bruce caught a glint from the spider's many fangs as it passed before him, clipping the end of the spear. The spider's body was lacerated, continuing and plunging onto the end of Valeria's lance. It was not over yet; the injured beast continually flung its limbs toward Valeria, causing her to free her grasp and release the spider. With utmost precision, the spider used one of its limbs to pierce the wooden shaft before pulling it out of its body. Valeria pushed herself backward, now on the ground. Bruce took a lunge forward with his spear, the spider flinching and dodging hastily out of the way before redirecting towards the defenseless Valeria. Bruce closed the distance between himself and Valeria, attempting to get between her and the spider. The vicious beast bared its fangs and launched again, directing its limbs behind it to conserve momentum.

Lucian had moved significantly closer at his rapid speed, allowing him to throw a more aimed throw. His shoulder held true during the throw, aiming just in front of Valeria's reach. It passed through the jumble of limbs and stuck the ground behind it as Bruce slammed it into the ground using the spear as a hammer. One of its legs implanted its spike into the ground during the pound, causing its momentum to stop, hurting its joints, now suffering from a severe jolt. Valeria scooted backward with her hands, watching Bruce plant the spear's tip into the beast's core. It wriggled before dying.

Griffith was still caught off guard by the quick change in direction but rebounded quickly. Victoria noticed the accelerating spider moving towards her, causing her to jump without firmly planting her feet beforehand, her only dodging opportunity. She did not have enough time to direct a spear jab. Her weight shift caused her to jump forward, luckily so, as the spider used its spikes to plant itself below her previous position and instantly push upwards. It scratched the back of Victoria's jacket and sliced some of her dark hair. Griffith completed his turn and jabbed at the now defenseless spider, which moved its limbs about itself in Griffith's direction in defense. The limbs seemed to consume the blow, being reinforced. The spider seemed unaffected, although slightly pushed backward.

Victoria spun around once she landed, further determined to kill the arachnid. Watching Griffith's jab, she began running at full speed towards the beast, incorporating her own zigzag, ultimately less effective than the beast's. Griffith's spear was pulled out of his hands during the spider's fall; it had latched onto it. Her concentration drowned out the sound of Bruce's kill as Victoria whipped the knife out of her pocket. As the creature landed, swapping the spear to her non-dominant left hand, she threw the knife at the spider, not allowing it any time to react. Sensing the immediate danger, it leaped at its only threat: Victoria. She dropped and slid, the friction burning the edge of her shoes in a scrape. Transferring the spear to just above her core, she held it awkwardly in both hands, bracing it against herself. The momentum of the spider's leap combined with Victoria's slide to put more pressure on the sharp edges of the crystal tip. Many limbs hit the wooden stick holding the crystal, but only after the main portion of the body had been pierced. The spider did not weigh much, yet the force of the impact into her stomach took Victoria's breath and would leave a significant bruise.

Silvery blood burst out of the spider, almost aerosolizing. Much of it began dripping down the spear; the pain of the blood droplets on her face reminded her that she needed to get out of the way. The spear was already dropping to the side, only accelerated with her effort. Bruce and Valeria were on the way as Griffith picked up his almost broken spear and finished the job, similarly embedding the crystal into the spider. When he removed it, he admired its luminescent, ancient glow.

Lucian had watched from being unable to assist, but once the second spider was defeated, he ran back to get a bucket of water. The water had begun to leak through the wooden exterior, but very slowly; there was nothing he could do about it at that point. They left the carcasses outside, helping Victoria to her feet and towards the water. She winced, specks of blood burning her face. Griffith helped her up, and Bruce and Valeria brought her back to the shelter. Griffith looked around again. Upon closer inspection, he saw many different creatures on the side of the tree, descending fast. There were at least a hundred: some darker ones definitely spiders, brighter ones pygmy dragons, ones that looked like rocks, some that looked long and crocodilian, and some that were descending in flight. Before telling the group about it, he noticed the giant shadow farther to the left and hundreds of feet in the air; it was moving.

"Guys! There's hundreds of creatures!" he worriedly advised the group before fleeting to the shelter, determined not to be caught outside alone. Lucian met them at the entrance marked by a thin gap between the sticks.

"Did any get in your eyes?" he asked, pouring water on her hands and over her head. She shook her head, nonverbally saying no and allowing the water to flow around without pooling in one spot on her hair. The pain relief was fast, but she admired how long it must have taken for Lucian to presumably run all the way back in pain before. Lucian made sure to use only a little of the water, especially in light of the new news regarding the monsters.

As Griffith returned and moved inside, he reflected on what he saw: "There was a cloud of some flying thing. There were thousands, and they seemed to be descending along with the rest of the creatures."

"Bugs?" Lucian asked calmly.

"That's what I think. Yeah," he responded.

"Makes sense. I guess that adds up." Lucian thought about all the creatures. How were we going to survive this one? They had been on the planet for two day-cycles. They were tired, weakened, and exhausted, losing hope.

Victoria suggested, "We should hole up today; there's clearly no chance of doing stuff outside." This was unanimously agreed upon; no thought was needed.

"If only two of those spiders put up that much of a fight, we're clearly outmatched here," Valeria added.

Lucian thought momentarily before taking Griffith and going back outside to get one of the spider's bodies, "It's just another thing to dissect, and maybe it has venom. We could also use its fangs for something." They walked outside, Lucian looking back at the swarms of creatures descending the nearby tree. He saw many creatures also descending other trees. Some were very shiny. He also saw the bundles of flying creatures periodically spread about the lands in front of them.

Griffith and Lucian arrived at the less mangled body, and Lucian pierced it up with the spear, poking it first to ensure themselves of its death. Griffith suggested, "If we can use the fangs, we might as well get more. That's double the venom, too." Without looking for a response, he jogged over to Valeria and Bruce's kill. With hairs standing up on the back of his neck, he quickly impaled it and began dragging it back, looking around him to avoid a surprise attacker.

He noticed a living version of the creatures Victoria and Lucian had snared; it stood partially out of the grasses to the right of the shelter. It stared back. It looked like a pig, with shorter legs and a cylindrical body. The animal turned and lightly walked back into the grasses while Griffith moved back as fast as he could.

There was little room in the shelter for the spiders as they took up much of their limited space, causing discomfort by being near them. The group decided to chop off their legs for a core dissection. They could use the reinforced limbs for other purposes. *Maybe for new, stronger spearpoints.* Lucian released the spider just in front of their shelter.

Griffith took the opportunity to use Jarnbjorn, his axe, grabbing it from against the shelter's wall. Angling the sharpened edge into the body while the edge itself sat on the joint served the axe as a wedge, cleanly separating the limb with a small hit on the back of the top part of the handle. Blood did not spray this time, although Griffith felt a warmth permeating the body. He cleaved each limb and gave them in bunches of three to Lucian, who passed them inside. There were twenty-six in total. *Fourteen per animal.* They were left below the bulwarks, where they were easily placed without taking up much space. Eager to get inside, Griffith and Lucian maneuvered the bodies to the entrance, which barely fit the spiders' widths.

Tanho wanted to help with the dissection, but he was bored and felt less valuable because of his inability to help. They knew it was not a good idea to keep the scent of the dead bodies near them, and they knew they would need to get rest soon, causing them to make room for the dissection in the illuminated center of the room, near the fire. Lucian borrowed Victoria and Tanho's knives and moved one of the spiders into a flat, supine position. They decided that the snared creature, partially dried, would have to wait.

"We don't even know if either has venom, but if I had to place bets, it would be on the spiders," Lucian said, getting agreement from everyone waiting and watching the dissection. If they were to get rest, it would not be now. You guys should pay attention to most of this. We could learn something, and I could use more sets of eyes." Griffith set a few more logs on the fire to make more smoke and mask the scent of blood.

Lucian did not know where to start and knew he would have to be very careful. "Anyone with any cuts, back up," he commanded. We do not want any pathogens to enter our bloodstreams." They did not have much room to move back, but they knew it would be better for them. Tanho remained close, interested in doing something, instead borrowing Victoria's jacket, which completely covered his healing wounds.

"Watch out for spurting blood, like from arteries. And also don't get above it; the vapor may contain the same bacteria." He was worried it was a bad idea after all. There was virtually no wind, allowing smoke to pool towards the ceiling, only being pushed outwards by the volume of gas and the fire's vacuum for oxygen. He put a log into the spider's mouth to prevent an involuntary bite.

He wanted to test if he could milk the spider's venom, as one would to make antivenoms on Earth. However, he would need somewhere to store the venom, and they had no idea how that could be done. They would have to wait and see if there was something they could use in the body itself.

Lucian soon decided to trace the fangs first in case of mishap, whereupon they would need to pause the dissection. Bruce grabbed a smaller crystal and handed it to Tanho in case it would help. Lucian had never dissected something as he was now, using only his knowledge and deductive reasoning to make well-founded inferences. He further realized that going straight for the venom would help his fatigue and limit his need for concentration, raising his temperature, which was accelerated by the warm fire near him.

He oriented the spider with its face towards his. Inspecting closer, he found subsets of smaller fangs around the eight largest fangs. "Those would shred any flesh that got close enough." Each fang was a combination gradient spiraling between green and purple. The smallest ones seemed more pigmented than the rest. Lucian used one knife to hold back the flesh he cut, Tanho assisting. The incision about the topmost fang bled significantly, and they had to drain it into the spider's mouth. Once most of it was drained, its white inside was revealed. He cut slowly with the precision of Victoria's trailing point blade, hoping to see veins or the gland that produced the venom. Griffith moved the water nearby just in case. Lucian thought about how snakes and spiders from Earth have ducts that transfer the venom from the gland via compressor muscle. He needed to locate those or things that acted similarly.

He soon got to the base of the tooth, the blood beginning to decrease its outward flow, with less blood left. It was harder to position the knives to hold the incision open and allow him to see. He hypothesized that the veins or circulatory system were small or nonexistent, being permeable to spread through the entire animal without the need for a heart. He knew he wanted to confirm as soon as he could. Finally, he came across a yellow, bony structure under the tooth. All three blades were now in the process of allowing Lucian to follow the structure carefully.

A cartilage-like membrane connected to the bony structure. Lucian suspected he was close to what he needed to find. Following the membrane only another half-inch further, he found a rounded structure.

"Definitely the venom sac," he told them. "This is good news." He thought about removing the sac entirely, but should it burst, they would have a bigger problem on their hands. "In a worst-case scenario, we can take it out and use it for whatever. Otherwise, I'd recommend we keep it in the body and milk the venom if it'll let us. We only have to worry about the muscle degrading or whatever nerves it has disconnecting." They agreed with him.

"There must be either multiple connections to the one venom sac or multiple venom sacs. Either way, we should be able to cut a couple of teeth out. Although, maybe we should think about plugging the hole in case it began leaking through the end of the bony pipe." Lucian thought about how venoms typically agglutinate blood. If so, they could plug the canal with a bit of flesh, giving them a tap into the venom without needing to extract the pouch or risk a bite.

He began cutting around one of the lower fangs, increasingly worried about a bite reflex. Holding the knife by the end of the handle, he cut deeper and deeper, utilizing the knife's point effectively. Once satisfied with the lack of connection to the fang, he began trying to cut the bony structure. Reluctant to touch the tooth itself, he placed the knife as Griffith did Jarnbjorn and forcefully tapped the end, using the torque to snap the connection. The tooth fell onto the knife that Tanho held beneath it, bouncing away from the pool of blood in the spider's mouth and onto the floor. The structure did not leak any venom.

They had begun sweating, influencing their decision to pause any further dissection. They instead directed their attention outside. Still, no wind cooled them down; they knew they would have to let the fire die down. Despite the lack of whistling winds, not many sounds could be heard from their shelter. While discussing the spider's strange, vein-lacking anatomy, they watched creatures walk across the wide path formed by the orange, still-mesmerizing grasses. They also had to get to naming them all.

Nothing seemed too interested in them. They saw a few creatures walk by, but none approached. They waited a few minutes in conversation before resolving to try to get some rest while they could.

"Something isn't adding up about today. We should take the chance to rest while we have it," Griffith suggested. Lucian agreed with a yawn. Tanho volunteered to watch, as he was feeling much better than before and had had much more rest than anyone else. He stood up, and they repositioned themselves so he could be nearest to the entrance with a spear.

Tanho thought for a second about his healing and asked, "Bruce, how was it that you ran out there with everyone looking for the meteorite?"

"I hadn't even thought about it," he said, beginning to smile. "I actually feel much better; I didn't even notice."

Lucian thought momentarily, "There's no way you should be healed that fast. Are you sure you're feeling alright?"

"Yeah, I think so," he responded before showing Lucian his leg wound. It was almost entirely healed, with only scarring left.

Lucian tested by putting pressure on the area. "Any pain?"

"None."

"How strange. That's good for you, though." He was tired and wanted to conserve his mental power for later. He laid down without his shirt on. Victoria was glad she had drenched her hair; it cooled her as she lay down, putting the damp hair in direct contact with her skin.

"Before you guys fall asleep, keep in mind we have to name all of these creatures. Start thinking of ideas," Tanho commanded them passively. Before falling asleep, Griffith noted Tanho's expressionless stare outside.

Chapter 5

A Night to Remember

Valeria woke up first. Seeing the brightness and almost perfect, straight-down shadow of the entrance of the rocky shelter, she tried to fall back asleep. After a few minutes, she believed herself awake, energized, and refreshed. She sat up next to Tanho, who sat on a log as a chair.

"What's been happening outside?" she asked in a whisper, adjusting her eyes to the brighter scene.

Tanho looked over at her and the four sleeping on the leafy floor. He wished they had blankets. "There's been a lot of fascinating things, actually. I saw a bunch of, like, everything. Nothing came close to here, though. I'm not sure what it is; I'm happy for it though."

"I'm glad for that," she said in an expressive inhale, raising her hand to support her head while she sat. "Nothing peculiar? Anything new?" she continued.

"There were a few new things farther out, though. There were a few strange, moving rocks. I think they're the equivalent of terrestrial hermit crabs." He sighed, looking up. There were some things with long claws; those were cool; they were super far away, too. I saw some things that looked weird like those Cuban crocodiles running. They kind of hop, but they're really fast."

"That's pretty cool, I guess. Scary, but cool."

"I also saw some little hyena-looking things, which were kind of cute, actually. Some pig-looking animals were running with each other between some of the grasses."

"Were a lot of the animals running through the grasses?"

"Yeah, that's like the only times I saw anything– when they were chased out or moving between sides. It's rather strange now that I think about it. Just like this bird I saw, it gave me the impression of a blue heron; it looked misplaced. How did you sleep?"

"Pretty well, actually. I was definitely tired." She thought about it, remembering she had dreamt about the gray building Griffith and Lucian had seen. They were on the island and found a beautiful oasis within. Someone had told them, "Welcome back," as if they were back home. She wished for it.

"What do you think we should do now? We're pretty much trapped here," Tanho said, wondering. He knew they could not do anything outside, or the ivory rods would pierce them as they fought bats, crocodiles, spiders, and dragons.

"I don't think there is anything else we can do except rest and heal."

"We could revisit our cooking challenge," Tanho said, focusing on his unsated appetite, which only grew as he thought about it. Maybe modified, though, spider only?"

She laughed but caught herself. She did not want to wake up any of the others. "I think we could do that. We should check with Lucian first, just in case we need something from it. And he should find a way to test if it's edible first."

"I hope we won't need to neutralize it like we do with the water. It's unnecessarily complicated." Tanho and Valeria continued relaxing, feeling only partially safe. Tanho also contemplated resting but settled on just staying up; he could now sit up and move around comfortably. It was a dramatic improvement from the previous day's state. It was not very long before Victoria and Bruce awoke within a minute of each other. They both looked disheveled.

"Did you guys sleep well?" Tanho asked. Victoria's damp hair only made the awkward sleeping position have more of an effect on her hair. Bruce was still groggily waking up, holding onto the thought of falling back asleep.

Victoria felt neither good nor bad about her sleep, and Bruce thought he slept well. Tanho and Valeria recapped the situation and told them they should go back to sleep. Valeria offered to take over the watch so Tanho could rest, too. Bruce decided to lay down again, only a denser pile of leaves supporting his head.

A few minutes later, only Victoria, Valeria, and Tanho were awake. Victoria looked at herself in the reflection of the water that was left. After inspecting her hair situation and trying to fix it, she cupped some water to drink, using the leftover water on her hands to smooth her hair. The water reminded her of her thirst, and Tanho had reminded her of her hunger. *At least we can still survive longer without food.* They knew they would need to start eating food for energy soon; their bodies were using stores. She wondered how much weight she had lost. She felt more lethargic, but not different. She figured she was still okay and did not lose much weight.

All three of them watched outside as creatures fought and ran about the grasses. Every once in a while, individual insects would fly or walk by. At only one point did they see one of the swarms they had heard about.

Victoria similarly felt the need to do something. "Can we use the spider legs for anything?" she asked.

"I think we'd have to lash them onto sticks, and we don't have any vines or cordage here. It'll probably have to wait," Tanho told her.

They could not be exactly sure how much time had passed, but they knew it felt longer than the daytime on Earth. Based on the crimson sun's setting angle, they judged they had a few hours before nightfall. Still, other than the spiders, nothing had shown great interest in them or their fire. It was mysterious.

Griffith, Lucian, and Bruce had now awoken. Valeria and Tanho had taken a short nap until they woke up with the rest of the group. Tanho, Valeria, and Victoria recapped, fascinating Lucian. He was sure that they were to have more trouble.

"Something is up about all those creatures outside. I don't really understand it," Lucian acknowledged. Just then, a scaly, yellow frog creature with a flat shell on its top crawled across the path.

"That's new!" Victoria said.

"That one's pretty cool," Bruce stated, noticing the scaled aberrations of a diffused, fractalled orange spread across the creature's body.

As they watched, they saw a type of bird skydiving at a significant speed. Within a fraction of a second, it had reached the frog, standing in the open. The frog's shelled top was not strong enough to resist the strength of the precision blow. The frog was dead on the spot.

Within moments, a swarm of flies began to descend on the site. The bird had noticed, using its sharp teeth to grab one of the frog's limbs before flying away, slowed by the limb. As the flies approached, the group was in awe. Almost like it was planned, the group noticed movement in the surrounding grasses. The flies began feasting on the dead frog, but not before long, many creatures jabbed through the swarm, eating multiple in each bite.

"There has to be at least ten; that's ridiculous," Lucian said. The flies, unable to move through the grasses, abandoned the rest of their kill. Hundreds had been eaten in only moments. They saw the tops of the grasses move again as if the creatures were dispersing. Lucian was sure some would run into each other and fight, but they heard nothing.

Valeria told them, "This place never ceases to amaze me." She had wondered about how such a place could even exist. It was magnificent in its chaos. The view was intense even in their shelter and with the grasses unwavering. Bordered by stone, a path wove and was lost in fiery plants reaching to the angry sky. Distant treetops of varying shades of green and blue connected the warms by a stark contrast. The framing perfectly captured the sun on the upper left, casting shadows on the central path. It was not only a landscape; it was also a wasteland. As time passed, the picture was increasingly corrupted by yellow piles of bone and the occasional fly scavenger. She imagined what she would paint of her time here if she were ever able to return.

"Lucian, do you play chess?" Tanho asked him, a little tired of waiting around.

"Yes, I do. Why?"

"Do you wanna play?"

"In our heads?"

"Yeah."

"Maybe later; I need to make sure I'm not missing anything," Lucian responded. He hypothesized that there was an underlying cause for the sudden increase in animal activity. "Why do you guys think that the nights are so much more deadly?"

They thought and had no answer; it made no sense. They could not find a good reason to explain why some of the larger animals would not come out during the day to hunt the easy pickings.

"Could it be something to do with the sunlight?" Valeria asked.

"I guess it could be; maybe the ultraviolet rays or whatever the sun here produces," Victoria said as Lucian nodded in agreement. Yet, it still did not explain why the creatures in the daytime seemed unaffected. She continued, "How are we going to get back to Earth? How do we escape?"

Griffith said, "I think our ship is a no. There's no way we can pull the ship out, and it's mangled beyond repair. We might have to figure out how to send a signal off the planet."

Tanho added, "If we could only get down there and scavenge the emergency comms, we could send a signal."

"Well, the device would've gone off when we were about to crash. Does anyone remember hearing the confirmation?" Lucian asked.

They shrugged, Bruce saying, "I don't remember anything from then."

Lucian thought for a minute before telling them, "I guess we should assume it sent the signal then. All we can really do is try to hold out and see if someone comes and helps us. We went through a wormhole, though; I don't know if they'll risk a rescue."

"I don't think it's safe to assume the signal was sent. If it weren't... if the atmosphere blocked it, we'd just be sitting here waiting to die," Victoria argued.

They thought about how they would get to the wreck without risking death from one of the fire-resistant squid. Lucian pondered and decided that if they were to have to dive to get the communication device, they would have to research the squid and anything else inhabiting the ominous, red water. They already knew it was attracted to blood and liked to hunt; it was not looking good for them. He predicted that many of the giant creatures lived underwater, as he thought it improbable that they would coexist with such small prey up in the trees. Their mass and center of gravity would also make climbing hundreds, if not thousands of feet up the vertical bark extremely challenging. Even though he knew it was unlikely, he could not ignore the possibility; he did not yet understand the creatures' psychology and physiology.

They figured they should try to extract some of the venom. They could coat it on anything to hopefully incapacitate anything hit with it. They figured the venom would not be as toxic as some from the night animals, but they would have to start somewhere and use what they could get.

"I think it's actually lucky we were attacked by those spiders. It gave us more of a chance to survive," Lucian said.

"They didn't even attack you," Victoria said jokingly, knowing that Lucian had also put himself in harm's way.

Griffith added, "It's a shame the meteorite was lost. If there's a chance, we might still be able to find it."

"I don't really understand your fascination for that thing. It could help, or it might not. I don't think we should travel that far on such a low chance. What would we do with it anyway?" Lucian commented, trying to come up with a reason for Griffith.

"What if it's something from Earth? What if they sent something through the wormhole to help us if they got the signal? That would explain why it didn't burn up before getting so low." Griffith knew it was not certain. *But we have to take chances, right?*

Lucian thought about it and decided he would continue thinking about it later; there was no way they were making a trip there anytime soon to search for it. If it were just a rocky material, it would be a waste and a risk.

They could not stop themselves from thinking about Earth and the chance of being saved. It was the only thing holding them together.

Tanho told them, "We can't rely on being saved immediately; we should figure out how to get to that silver structure on that lake. That may have some answers."

Valeria said, "We better hope it's not an illusion. Griffith and Lucian, you should take us to the hill if the monsters die down again." They agreed it was the right idea; it gave them time to make sure they were not rushing into anything idiotic and to think about what to do about their communication signals.

Lucian gestured to Tanho to pass the spider's body over; they had moved it away while they rested. Tanho grabbed a spear and began poking where he had previously. As he did, the spider's eyes opened and moved while its remaining teeth bit down. It was alive.

Victoria, Tanho, and Valeria screamed, all six jumping in surprise and trying to understand what they were looking at. Quickly, Griffith picked up his trusty axe and chopped the head from the spider's abdomen. Blood pooled once more, the creature stopping motion. Lucian moved to it and shoved the knife cleanly through the middle of the head, realizing they had not done it before. Inspecting closely, he saw what resembled scar tissue in the area he had sliced before.

He was fascinated by the clotting and healing properties that the creature he thought was just dead had. He reacquired the knives he had used for the dissection earlier. He recarved the spider's mouth to get to the sac again. It was deja vu; he knew he had dissected the spider in the same place before. It was no surprise as he cut through the white flesh, stopping just before the venom sac. He was reassured that he was not crazy.

He thought about human platelets and clotting factors, the whole cycle of messengers and proteins stopping bleeding over extended periods of time. The spider here, with no limbs, had significantly healed from a dissection-related injury in a matter of hours.

Not wanting to stay near the spider much longer, Lucian finished cutting to the venom, orienting the spider so that the exposed part would point directly upwards. He instructed Tanho and Valeria to start grabbing spears and bringing them over. Carefully, Lucian made an incision, holding his breath. He dipped the first of the spears into the venom. He lifted it too quickly, however, causing a drop of the clear, red liquid to drop onto the spider's exterior. It seemed to melt the skin away, burrowing farther into the spider before stopping.

"That does seem pretty potent," Victoria commented.

Lucian continued dipping spears into the venom, its unwelcome demonstration causing him to get nervous. He was shakily trying to aim the spear at the venom when Griffith shifted closer, saying, "Here, I'll take over." Lucian did not want to think about what the venom would do to human skin.

They now had poison-tipped spears– javelins that could inflict real damage as long as they punctured a vital body part. They hoped it would help them through the nights should a creature become curious enough to push past the flimsy wooden poles sticking out of the ground. They knew there was bound to be something that could push past the sticks, unaffected.

If they rested the spider down, the venom would spill out and dissolve more, likely causing a foul smell. They thought they should use what they could or get rid of it entirely.

Tanho noted, "We should keep an eye out to see what eats spiders because they would either be too big or immune to the venom. We wouldn't be able to rely on the spears for those creatures if that were the case." He knew he did not want to have to fight one of the larger creatures of the night; even with their arsenal of poison spears, they stood no match.

With the spears now envenomated, they could no longer be stored as they had been. Griffith decided they should be kept lying against the bulwarks like the spider legs. Bruce carefully lifted the spider's head and brought it to the wooden stakes. Griffith drew out bits of the poison with the spear and drizzled it over some of the outermost points. He knew that in an emergency, they might scrape against one of the innermost posts, and he did not want to be the cause of someone's death.

Valeria looked outside at the wasteland-ish scene once more– where they had disposed of the first spider's body parts, scared to consume them. They had been immediately taken away or eaten by some strange creatures. As time went on, they continued to see new daytime monsters. They waited to name their previous finds out of fear of not having good creature name ideas.

"Next one, I get to name," Bruce stated.

"No chance! Whoever comes up with the best name gets to name it," Victoria responded. Lucian continued thinking, indifferent to the needless argument.

Tanho added defensively, "Then what about what I named already? And what about your names? Should we change those if we come up with something better?"

"No, of course not. You know what? Just ignore what I said. Divide up the ones we don't have a solely significant experience with; deal?" Victoria resolved. They agreed while Lucian chuckled to himself. *They are funny.*

Lucian knew they were going crazy cooped up in the cramped shelter, becoming used to the smell of smoke, a sense of death constantly looming, losing hope, feeling disgusting by lack of a nice shower, and growing nervous with the increasingly more prominent onset of night. He wished them fortitude.

For the third time, they watched as luminous stars slowly began to settle the somehow more ominous night sky. The reds turned to blood as the intermittent clouds descended in waves, producing a fog cast everywhere they could see from inside the shelter. Sparkles of blue could be seen throughout the fog's fall, disappearing after it began to rest, supported by the ground. They thought it was pressure as Valeria's nose began to bleed, and their ears felt clearer, although they could not be sure of its cause. The creatures slowly escaped the grassy pastures, making their way through the trees, occasionally causing a glowing wave of blue through the fog.

The stars in the sky seemed to shine brighter than the previous nights, combining with the occasionally luminescent fog to give them the illusion of more visibility. Purples emerged in the sky; it was a perfect gradient, a galaxy. Valeria knew she would paint six crows. Death is upon us.

Their chests were pounding, and suspense held in the air as they waited to hear the first beast on their awkward night. Griffith stared at his axe, unchanging and uninterested in the sunset. The visible lands reflected an aquamarine blue, and the few distant trunks moved with hundreds and thousands of creatures. They wondered how such a place could seem to thrive with life.

Nothing. Minutes passed without sound. The fog seemed to intensify, its density amplifying the lowered visibility. Still, they were reluctant to make noise. They waited in tense anticipation. Griffith added another log to the fire; this night was slightly colder than the last. Not before long, all six of them were sat together, almost holding hands. Why is nothing happening?

The sun made its way past the horizon, transforming reds, oranges, yellows, and black in an epic battle of color wavelengths. Of course, no wavelength of light would remain; black was destined to come out on top.

They wondered why the specks of blue appeared from thin air while creatures were escaping the darkness' encroachment. Soon, the blues began to die out. It took several minutes, but slowly, the last rushes of glowing blue light were put out. The dark fog decreasing their fire's brightness many times over. They knew it would start soon; their trial was about to commence.

More minutes passed as silence bounced off the fog, insulating what they did not know. The fire's carbon emission fought the fog out of the shelter; they were glad it kept outside. It contrasted their home, making them all feel safer.

Finally, something was seen; a fire of varied shades of purple erupted through the darkness before them. It was limited in its nature, mystifying but menacing. Its light shone on the beast which produced it, illuminating its muscular figure. They could only see its front, the flames not being at the right angle to highlight the creature's face. As if warming itself up for battle, it produced a stronger flame. It was turning around, allowing them to see that the beast had four legs and a large tail. They could not be sure of the beast's proportions, but they estimated it to be sixty feet long by the fire's definition; it seemed to intricately wound when spiraling but was, in its entirety, small compared to the beast.

Once the beast stopped turning, its continual fire reached its head. It illuminated a similarly dark, relatively flat face with two brightened green eyes resembling a black panther. If it had fangs, they could not see them. Its jaw extended farther than its head so that the fire produced from within would not scorch its eyes. They wondered what could cause it to create the fire.

In the creature's spin, a blue haze emerged, reminding them of its proximity. Quietly, Griffith reminded them, "We better not attract that guy."

The fire would be the perfect counter to their sheltered status; they would be most certainly dead.

They soon realized the creature was being attacked. *That's why it was spinning so fast.* Eventually, they saw traces of blue light lobbing through the air– a projectile. It must have used the fire to locate the panther, shooting some sort of acid. The panther periodically grunted with a plume of flame.

Screams began to flood the region around them. Within minutes, hundreds of groans, screams, yelps, growls, and roars had elapsed. Both previous nights stood no match to this night; they were right.

Rumbling began, the vibrations causing their spears to roll and rattle as they hit the floor; everything outside seemed unaffected. The sounds of the night continued, stronger than ever.

New shades of blue began to wash through the fog in front of them, giving insight into the speed at which the animal was traveling. Darts of fast animals springing through the grass, giant winged animals swooping down, and mountainous beasts all pushing air around them.

Between the vibrations of the underground worms, an unfamiliar tremble sent waves through them. They were unable to see what it was, but by its frequency, they could tell it was slow and colossal. They all wondered what it could be this time.

The now infrequent flames of many fire-breathing creatures could only light up so much; the strange creatures of pure danger would remain a mystery for longer. In particular, they were interested in the giant ones, knowing that they would have to consume many other animals to grow so much. They wondered how it was possible and how horrifyingly powerful it must be to survive in such an environment.

A bird landed in front of their shelter, the light beginning to show its feet. As it approached skittishly, they saw it had many eyes through which it was watching all directions with an intensity proving its night vision. It had three large, blue wings embellished in feathery, layered tangles that wove to make intricate spirals in a darker shade. It was gone as quickly as it arrived, presumably to escape something or express its disinterest. Their fire was not interesting to *these* creatures.

The bug-mocking, blue light from the previous night returned in the distance, quickly being extinguished as they saw a flying line of blue rush towards it. Whatever it was, it was definitely eaten.

A rise of hissing sounds signaled new engagement. They were from both sides of their shelter. From the rocky insulation, they could not be sure from how many creatures the hissing could have originated. The group of six space-travelers remained frightened, trying to reduce their shaking.

A strong, low-toned bellow pierced the air, being met with silence.

"They all got quiet. This may be the apex predator," Lucian said in response to the sound. He was intrigued, but hoped it would not go near them. He wished it would stay far away.

Soon, the pause ended; the largest creatures were out to hunt. The more they thought about it and heard the sounds outside, the more futile they thought their wishes to escape were. They had nothing to do now except look at each other and hope they were not killed.

Part of them wanted to see more of what was going on to know what they were up against. Occasionally, a creature would face them, traveling at enough speed to let the glowing fog provide some facial definition. It was all strange to them.

Waves of different sounds signaled coordinated attacks; the creatures were intelligent. They watched as blue mixed with different blood, color variances as animals were mangled. It was sure to be a graveyard.

Larger footsteps and trembles increased in amplitude. Right in front of their shelter, a giant, rounder creature met with a two-legged, easily seventy-foot-tall being using a large limb as a weapon. The creature on their left seemed to waddle on four legs, wholly engulfed in spikes. They weren't sure what other parts or material it was armed with by only the movement of the air. On the right, they saw the club slam into the ground, narrowly missing the other monster. The ground shook considerably.

Within moments, the rounder creature, likely weighing hundreds of tons, was flattened and dragged away by the more enormous creature. It seemed to have no interference. Through the moving swirls of air behind the dragged creature, they saw a few smaller ones. *Scavengers.*

"At least there are some weaker ones, too," Victoria said with a quiver and definite uneasiness.

The vibrations decreased and were lost before coming back minutes later. They were unsure of what to make of it all, so they sat against the back wall with spears in their hands, waiting for something to happen.

The relief itself was almost unbearable. The day began to shut down the nighttime machinations. Sounds began to slow until they were gone a few minutes later.

After about an hour of the onslaught, they had begun to get used to the constant fear. Their quivers had subsided, yet their brains continued in overdrive. They believed the cause to be in the air, reverberating through the most powerful sounds.

There were many new creatures appearing as the night went on, so much so that they could not recount half of them. They only remembered the animals from the day before and towards the beginning of the night, although they knew they would remember if it happened again.

Chapter 6

PREVALENT MORTALITY

They were reluctant to move in the morning, so used to sitting in the back of their shelter. After another hour of sitting in their cave, running out of firewood and hearing no movement outside, they left their temporary home. They were all together, standing as tall as they could; it was a sight to behold. Nothing surrounded them, nothing at all. No beasts, no creatures. There was evidence of the battles sprawled across the ground – bones and blood unfiltered. Closely in front of their shelter was the impact divot from the club-wielding monster; the force required to produce it had to be tremendous.

"That's ridiculous!" Tanho said. "It's several feet down!" Everything around them was surprising, especially the barrenness of carcasses. They had all been dragged away or consumed where they laid. The empty bodies had all been picked clean of their respective meats. *From wasteland to warzone and back again.*

They decided not to waste their daylight. After stretching their sore legs, they split up into two groups. Griffith, Lucian, and Victoria would gather firewood and miscellaneous items to help them. Valeria, Bruce, and

Tanho would search for anything that could help them all survive another onslaught; they hoped to find a safer shelter.

Griffith, Lucian, and Victoria turned around and began towards the tree, this time more worried about falling beasts ready to kill them.

"I can't believe so many things live up there," Victoria awed.

"It's astonishing," Griffith said, looking up. "I guess if I were an animal, I'd want to live up there as well."

"I just wonder why the animals weren't fighting on the side of the tree. Maybe each tree has its own subset of animals," Lucian told them. He knew there was a wide range of species on each tree, but they could only really make out the detail of the nearest one. They had not seen many of the creatures battle each other, only ones with some type of physical characteristic that was noticeably different. He thought back to the diving bird, the frog, the lance, and the spider. *The spider.* He thought he had quivered, but Griffith and Victoria did not indicate any notice.

Many piles of bones surrounded the tree's rooted base, likely from other creatures picking off returning ones. Many sticks and branches also lay at the bottom. They dragged a few larger branches armed with deeply pigmented, contrasting leaves back to the shelter, resolving to steal Griffith's axe temporarily.

"He won't mind, right?" Lucian quietly said to Victoria.

"I mean, that's what the axe is for," Victoria told him. Griffith did not express disapproval once they arrived at camp.

They continued looking around between trips, splitting logs into firewood that would fit on the fire and within the shelter, concurrently wondering if being holed up next to the fire resulted in a distaste for the air outside. They figured they would enjoy the *fresh* air if they believed it to be, in a sense, unadulterated by flame, yet within it, diffused with acidic blood and water vapor.

Valeria, Bruce, and Tanho journeyed back to the water, unsurprised to see the vine-covered rock having disappeared. The water seemed blissful, yet they withheld from washing their hair. They would also need to make more water today, understanding they were running low and might not survive another day-and-a-half-long onslaught.

Passing the lake, which held their only interplanetary means of passage, they arrived at the hill described by Lucian just previously. They found the stream complete with the amethyst tree. It was another majestic sight. Valeria told herself that she would paint it as well.

Inspecting it closer, Bruce found that it was very tough and dense. Although it looked like a tree, they were unsure if it was even a tree. It was shorter than they had imagined, only going up to his shoulders. It was quite small in this world of wraiths.

As they continued climbing, cautiously carrying the spears, they were met with glimpses of the same vast views Griffith had described. They went up farther until they were at the top, *another picture.*

That same caustic green remained illuminated from cavernous ravines. Similarly, the ash-gray, blocky structure partially stood out from between and behind smaller trees on a circular island in the middle of a distant body of water. Somehow, it seemed as if electricity shot through the water, a mystery and certain trepidation about what the larger lake may hold.

Exploring the area with less of a time limit than what had been established after their crash gave them more time to look for new clues and manavelins. After a few hours, they began their return, approaching the shelter from a slightly different angle than when they arrived.

When Valeria's group returned, the others were already waiting at the shelter. Victoria recounted that they had no difficulties getting firewood and saw no creatures. Nothing approached them or made any noises during the day.

"How could that be?" Valeria asked Lucian. She was somewhat perplexed.

They looked at him, waiting for an elegant response. After a moment of thinking, he responded, "I think it has something to do with the planet itself; something to do with the air, maybe? I thought it felt different." They concurred. "I think the planet may decide for the creatures if they would go out or not. I'm less sure it's their own idea influencing our temporary peace."

Bruce and Tanho continued discussing what the three had seen on their exploratory expedition. There was potential for a cave, but they had refrained from investigating further out of fear of what could be inside. When they were better adjusted, if at all possible, they would investigate. It was also in the direction of the island. Unsure of what they could do and if they would still be alive to do it, they only hypothesized. They understood they would have to travel through fields and under dense tree cover to reach the lake. Once there, they would have to use some type of boat or go into the water, knowing that nothing would attack them. They found it hard to believe that nothing would see them as prey, considering their recent experiences.

They used their two buckets to wash before Griffith, Bruce, and Tanho went out to get more water. Just in case, they wielded two spears to be carried back by Tanho while Griffith and Bruce each carried one of the buckets. Victoria and Valeria got the materials for the water neutralization while Lucian inspected the spider.

After setting off, Lucian brought the remaining spider out into the open, into the light. He looked for any sign of deterioration or reaction occurring due to any chemicals in the air. Using Victoria's knife that she lent him, he dissected regions of skin to look for canals that could be used for smell. After a few minutes of not finding anything, Lucian went to taste. Inspecting the mouth, he saw nothing immediately, although he smelled the putridness of decaying alien flesh, hastened by the already multiplied bacteria inhabiting the moist environment. Looking deeper while holding his breath, Lucian remembered how deadly the spider truly was. His fear was amplified by how alone he was at this time, although some of the others were within eyesight, talking almost joyfully.

After a few minutes of inspection, he could not find anything out of the ordinary. He would have to return to the theory another time.

Sets of monstrous, radioactive-green, and deep-cyan clouds peered over hilltops. They seemed to rush forward at an alarming speed, even with their height above the trees. They returned to the shelter with an acerbic taste and smell filling their systems. They had no more time in the day.

Together inside, they looked outwards to hear the whistling winds beginning to crash into their shelter and weave about the many strands of grass. The coldness distorted the air as would heat in a desert. As the fire quickly burned much faster, they hastily moved their firewood pile to form a wall between the shelter's opening and the small fire pit. They hugged the wall closest to the fire, behind the wooden-wall heat reflector, to keep themselves warm. The cold, almost-rain being pushed inside caused their exposed skin to tingle. They hoped it was not deadly. *At least nothing hurts yet.*

Moments later, the visibility resembled the previous fog-ridden night. The winds produced a sound blocking out even their loudest attempts to converse. They began trying to lip-read and write words in sections of packed ground, which did not work as the consonants looked too similar, and the ground was dried from the fire's heat. Once again, they could not think of much they could do to gain progress for the upcoming days.

Only about an hour had passed before the cool colors of the wind began to darken. It was a blur of color, hiding all that they knew of outside. As night inevitably set, they wondered if anything prowled through the murky darkness that enveloped them.

Serpentine winds rose in seriousness; a shift of scene, washing aside the lifeless souls in repose, impure air disused, the incandescent fire the sole source of luminance, a story to be promised.

Watching as the rain reached the ground in front of their shelter, they waited to see what the water would do. As if by miracle, it remained outside. The roundness of their structure's ceiling caught and centralized a curtain in water, the mirror further distancing them from the outside world. Fractals caused by the water's cohesion built arches that moved upwards before crashing down again in the symphony of thunderous rain clouds above.

An ashen land, the blaze of last night abate; afflictions abnegated, the absolute insincerity of outrageous weather holding fast, contrasting to the auxiliary salve, an amenity to anthropoid life itself.

The windchill beat their fire, periodically spraying the waterfall door over them. With the water soaking through their shirts, they began to get colder. Griffith oriented them in a circle, huddling closer to conserve body heat. Amid fluctuating feelings, he was made more aware of their hunger. *We should have found food.*

Forward, flurries fleeted their ferocity; finally, the agony of this final performance that they thought would last forever fluttered into a fault, rainfall fading, uncovering the fruitless wasteland that now seemed fertile.

Soft colors seemed vibrant while the sun grew, a prism spread across the opening of their refuge. Lush grasses and wet ground facilitated a stunning growth of fauna. The area in front of them was rejuvenated in energy and health. Even the impression made the day before left no evidence of existence.

Explained through every experience premature, they knew they could not entrust the exterior elegance with their entire existence; each knew the evils they may face, erupting from Earth, incapable of elusion. *Should we attempt to find something edible?*

They were finally able to talk reasonably but waited, still in awe of the tremendous strength of the weather. They were most definitely hungry, unsure if it was the cold or low blood sugar that resulted in a minor shake and shiver. Realistically, they knew they could survive at least another couple of weeks without food, although Tanho would need some sooner to make up for the energy expended by healing.

"What's that?" Victoria asked, pointing, the first to speak or significantly move in hours. A new creature appeared amidst the grasses, still almost entirely enveloped but causing a disturbance from the natural movements. Lucian took notice that some of the grass stalks were disappearing. Soon, a strange claw broke past the orange shroud, utilizing an aberration from a crab's claw to grasp multiple strands of grass.

"It's cutting the grasses; does that mean this is an herbivore?" Lucian observed. Griffith stood up and stretched, wanting to move closer to get a better look, although he knew it would not help him. He had the urge to throw a rock at it.

A few similar creatures were making a high-pitched hissing noise together, harmonizing. They were unsure why they had not seen them before.

"We've been here for four days, and yet today we're only seeing these creatures? What's going on?" Tanho asked.

"I guess it would make sense that we only occasionally see some creatures. This planet is pretty big, so maybe it's just coincidence that we only see some creatures sometimes. I guess the other night would be focused in this area, like a blood bath or feeding frenzy," Victoria told them. They were entirely unsure of what to believe. They only knew their hunger and desire to be safe.

Bruce took a step outside in the build-up of anticipation and cabin fever. Despite calls of confusion, he remained outside. He looked around to the areas that the shelter wall hid. The rocky monument kept its vibrant hue and did not obscure the strange creatures of this strange day. He saw bugs close to the ground, evading a turtle-shelled frog.

Following his lead, the rest of them walked outside armed with poison-tipped spears, determined to attempt to stay outside. They strongly desired to accomplish anything at all; they wanted to bring themselves at least one step closer to escaping the planet.

Their legs ached as if they were atrophied, the result of an undetermined amount of stormy weather and sitting around in awkward positions, hiding from the cold rain. Some part of them wished for more creatures to name. They had yet to formally name them, although they did not want to get too far behind. Something about the unnerving weather had inhibited their thought to come up with good names.

They all agreed that they would probably never be able to take down the largest creatures; if they wanted to make a longer journey, they would have to wait for another day without creatures. As they moved farther out of their shelter, Lucian and Valeria considered whether they should bring any of the spider legs. They wondered if it would be extraneous in energy to keep some with them. Looking back, Lucian figured that it would be too heavy.

As the creatures slowly became aware of their presence by vision– the group's scent had been masked by smoke– they began to back up, causing less noise as they moved away. Two creatures must have collided while this occurred, as one of the same ivory spikes from the spider incident broke through the top of the grass. It was followed by a shriek and panicked running.

Spinning around, they found many species of bug. Giant beetles of many colors traversed the base of their tree, some burrowing into the ground. Most brandished mandibles with spikes that seemed to reflect off a mirror-polished edge.

Setting off towards the lake, they felt a surge of their own energy. The further they trailblazed in a new path with a broader junction between grassy fields, the less they felt trapped.

It was a hunting party. While keeping their eyes peeled for predators hidden in the brush or in the air, they also looked for anything that seemed edible.

"How do we divide up the food in our team setting?" Tanho asked.

Without hesitation, Lucian said, "We shouldn't split up; we're still not confident in our survival as of now. Let's divide whatever we catch in three and do it that way."

"That's no fun, though," Victoria said with agreement from Valeria. "We've got to be able to cook different things at least. But if splitting up is too unsafe, then it's okay; we can wait."

The remnants of feeling from their elongated stay in their shelter drove competition. Tanho looked around before saying, "It doesn't seem that dangerous; are you sure we shouldn't split up? We'd potentially have more food to pick from that way."

Lucian remained hesitant, warning, "One misstep, and we're all dead."

"There's only a few creatures out here. We could be fine, and we outrun just about everything," Griffith added.

Realizing he was the only person unsure, Lucian decided to trust them. *We're all capable people anyway. We're trained.*

They split up into their previously determined groups with a promise of safety first. Lucian and a recovered Tanho were on one team, Bruce and Victoria were on another, and Griffith and Valeria were on the last. Lucian made sure to remind them that it was a friendly challenge and not to put themselves too far into harm's way. He already feared the possible consequences of groups of just two, but it still seemed alright. Every group had at least one person with hunting experience; they would have a better understanding of the abilities of the creatures.

Griffith and Valeria knew they would find lots of creatures below the trees. They hoped there would be new creatures to identify, learn about, and hunt to set them apart from the other two teams. They looked around and saw that the closest tree was opposite them on the lake. Unsure if they should go back to the shelter's tree or go to this one, they hesitated but, before long, resolved to go to the closest tree and get a better understanding of the region. "We can multitask," he said.

It had been a while since they had each gone out to catch food. Griffith had only been hunting a few times, only with his bow; what they were about to attempt with spears was bound to be a challenge. Valeria had knowledge of hunting and field-dressing food but had never done it outside of one of their field days. Due to their generally superficial understanding of the process of killing these animals, emphasized by the unpredictable nature of their prey, they knew they would have to come up with things on the fly.

As they approached, they noted the peace the different species seemed to have. The creatures almost looked indifferent to each other, but sometimes, both of them assumed the noises they heard were communicatory.

They climbed a smaller hill, finding a mini forest of a few smaller trees yet to outcompete each other. Some of them were of ample size to climb. As they drew closer, they wondered how the trees could be a resource in their hunt. They knew they would want to catch something by surprise or set a trap. They could climb the tree and throw their spears at any beast below them, but many things could go wrong. If the poison was slow-acting, the creature would definitely be able to get away, and they would potentially lose the spear. They also realized they would have to lure something below them so as not to spend their precious daylight in a tree they could be trapped in if something sat below or climbed up to get them. It was not a good idea; they were still early in their hunting, so they figured there would be many more opportunities and spots to set up an ambush.

They continued forward, keeping an eye on reference points to build a mental map of the region and its topography.

"The taste usually depends on the diet, right? At least on Earth?" Valeria asked. Griffith confirmed. "We should probably try to get something that eats more clean; it would taste better and likely be more predictable, eating a small range of things we can use as bait."

"Individualists, I think– yeah, that's a good idea," he responded. They began to watch the bugs and smaller, more predatory-looking animals, hoping that something would reveal itself to them. They decided to remain closer to the trees in case they could use them; they hypothesized they could jump to the other trees if needed. "If we need to, we can run back and grab a sling."

Bruce and Victoria leaped at the opportunity to show the others their hunting mastery; they were determined to catch something the others would not be able to. On her trapping expedition with Lucian, she had mentally noted a few good spots suitable to hide and surprise an animal with a trap or thrown spear.

They would likely have to grab one of the other spears, however. They wanted to ensure the poison would not contaminate anything they were to eat.

As they jogged side-by-side, Victoria asked Bruce, "What do you think the vital points are on these creatures?"

"Something tells me it will vary between them, but the eyes and the head are good places to start. There must be some system of nerves relaying information from the eyes to the processing center, wherever it may be." As he spoke, he realized they still had not learned anything about the creatures they split up and set off to kill and later consume.

Seeing the less horrific species blush with color, they wondered how they would taste. "Usually, the vibrancy means it wouldn't taste good," Victoria said. "Whatever we try to kill probably shouldn't look like it tastes bad."

With normal spears, they finally approached the tree, where no more creatures descended the trunk. All of them reached the ground and dispersed. Although the feeling set in that hundreds, if not thousands, of deadly animals hid around them, they walked near the epicenter of alien invasion to move to where the snares had previously set. The hair on the back of their necks stood straight in the silence and returning lack of creature traces. It was as if everything was around them, yet a look in both directions yielded no landscape aberration.

Between the stalks of multicolored bamboo from their first snare location, they saw a flash of movement. Both could not tell the color of the movement, only its speed. It moved fast and in bursts, remaining still about the fallen branches on the edge of the now-raging creek, which masked any sounds of movement.

An innate curiosity compelled them forward. They felt the slight breeze off the hills, cooled by the moving water; it came from the direction of the movement. *A good sign, we're downwind.* As Bruce had wanted to do for a while, he put up his hand to tactically signal and confirm their desire to kill it.

Through the increasing desire to hunt whatever was in front of them and the swiftness of it all, they could not help but wonder if it was too soon to make a risky engagement. Not even an hour had passed since they broke up into their groups. A quick kill could put them ahead of the others; perhaps there would be time for complimentary items on their menu.

Lucian and Tanho believed themselves to be the best-off group. Lucian knew his intelligence would prove to be a valuable asset to the team, although he was not nearly as competitive as the other teams or even his own teammate. Tanho was naturally good at hunting. As they began to walk out of earshot from the other teams to communicate, Tanho thought about the fish he caught and the methods he used to catch them that he had left out in his description of fishing. "Something about human blood; the fish were strongly attracted to it."

Watching the other teams disperse, they now felt that they could communicate a winning strategy. "What do you think we should do first?" Tanho asked.

"I think we should catch one of your squids and maybe even one of the crocodile-looking things. The fish should be later, though, so it's not sitting around and capable of being stolen by something." They agreed that it was a good idea, although Tanho carried skepticism.

"If it's anything like an Earthly crocodile, it will have tough skin. How do you propose that we pierce it with only spears?"

"Yeah, I see, and these spears have spider poison on them," Lucian realized. He came to the very same conclusion as Bruce and Victoria had. They knew they would either have to go back and get new spears or kill something without the ones they had with them. They hypothesized that they could wash one of the spears off with water and keep the other with the poison in case they needed it for self-defense. Lucian knew that it significantly reduced their resilience and defense, but it could be done to save time. They wanted to reduce the extra time they would have to spend going all the way back to the shelter only to return to the lake afterward.

They walked back to the lake, thinking about all the creatures they had seen and which looked like they would taste the best. The feathery creature popped into their heads, but it seemed too elusive and possibly dangerous. After a moment of thinking, which was concluded by their arrival at the lake, they settled on finding one of the crocodilians unless something more extraordinary found its way into their spear crosshairs.

As they dipped the spear into the water, Lucian realized they could tell if it was truly cleansed of poison by letting it dry off and seeing if it still glowed. Within moments, they were satisfied that they could hunt with it safely. Before leaving, Tanho looked at the water– the remnants of their crewmembers dissolved into the water they had been drinking. It held what he perceived as a deathly hue, a premonition that if he were to leave, the wolves would attack again, except this time, he had no bait to distract them with.

Lucian and Tanho began to make their way to where they had seen the longer reptilian creatures before. They saw Griffith and Valeria walk over towards the specific tree, but the entire area was likely to have the creatures. It was just a matter of finding them and killing them.

As would crocodiles on Earth, they believed these ones to also hang out near water. However, something was creepy about how they, too, scaled the tall trees, not succumbing to lethargy or not having enough grip. Unsure of the exact place or direction to go, Lucian directed them in a direction that would keep them safe while they could look for their first target. They walked out in the open before turning back around.

Tanho caught himself, saying, "Wait! We can catch something in the water to use as bait. Those kinds of creatures would definitely eat fish... if there are any."

They had not gone too far before Tanho's realization, but as Lucian had not thought of this, he said, "Alright, Tanho, do your magic." As Lucian crouched in wait and with an extended offer of help, he wondered if Tanho would bleed himself.

None of the animals they were watching seemed right. They all seemed *basic*. After moments of thought and consideration of the extraneousness associated with tree hunting with spears and no idea how to get bait, they decided to go back and grab a sling. Griffith and Valeria could pick off targets from a distance with his invention. They, too, realized the mistake of hunting with poison spears.

The walk-jog back to the shelter was peaceful and devoid of creatures, possibly because they kept away from the grass. As they arrived, they found both slings still in their designated area. He decided to leave one just in case it was needed, but he placed it slightly out of the way so that if the other teams passed by, they would not see it and think to use it. Valeria and Griffith were going to make the most of their advantage.

A little later, they returned to their hunting location and gathered a pile of rock projectiles that Griffith could use. Within moments, one of the frog-looking creatures emerged from around a mound of dirt on the edge of a field of shorter grasses. Griffith knew he would have to be accurate to kill his armored target. He was unsure where to aim, realizing the difference and strange sense of similarity to the animals of Earth.

His instinct and what he thought was muscle memory, from something he was unsure of, made him begin winding up his sling, and before his mind was made, he released the rock towards the frog's head. Throughout the duration of the rock's flight, he deliberated whether it was the correct choice. His brain did not have enough time to process before the rock met its mark.

Valeria took the moment to offer a high five, to which a slightly wide-eyed Griffith met slowly so as not to draw too much attention to them. Once struck, the frog made no noise, which they did not know what to think of.

"I don't think the rock flew *that* fast," Griffith told her. It clearly did, though; the frog had fallen, slumping forward in a ragdollish state. They were not far from the frog, but as they quickly closed the distance, a similar spear emerged from the grass and stole their kill. Griffith and Valeria shared no desire to take what was theirs, even though it was rightly theirs. They knew no animal kingdom – certainly not the one they were visiting – would work that way.

They would have to find something else to kill, but at least their method worked; they killed another one of the species, proving themselves capable in a still limited capacity. Valeria wondered how the spear creatures seemed to be everywhere, yet nowhere all at once. The ubiquitousness had begun to get under their skin; luckily, they had not been the target of a well-placed jab yet.

They decided to stay near the bases of the trees where their lines of sight were open, and they could go in any direction– and, more importantly, launch rocks anywhere. Once again, a creature began to disperse the grasses at the edge of the field. In a clean line of sight, they waited for the dark creature to move further into the open; Griffith did not want the same thing to occur again. Valeria was unsure how to help, but was the one to initially spot the beast; she believed that to be sufficient teamwork.

It resembled the mantis they had seen earlier. While Griffith was now trying to decide where to aim before actually shooting, Valeria recognized that the two types of mantis were likely not the same species. She knew that some Earthen species– like birds– have gender-related appearance differences. Although it was possible that these mantises had done the same thing, it would be the first time they had seen two obviously different-looking types of the same animal in all four days.

Griffith saw the creature's skinny limbs, which would make critical points difficult to hit. It had four arms– two pairs of two joining to the abdomen in separate locations. Looking for carnage, he decided to aim for the uppermost limb junction. The creature's look strongly resembled insects of Earth; he hoped that this creature had vital organs, unlike the spider.

He began swinging the silvery, disc-resembling rock, keeping his eyes on his target. A glance at his hand ensured he was doing it properly. He was ready. He flung the rock and waited, watching as the mantis began to walk just after he had released it. It was a miss.

The creature heard the *whizz* as the rock flew past. It froze and looked to be scanning the horizon. It noticed them, seeing two strange, bipedal animals far away. By now, the rock had crashed into the brush. The creature turned away from Griffith and Valeria, overlooking them as the origin of the projectile. It looked to its left, spotting something obscured by the trees and hilly horizon. Griffith slowly began winding up the sling again, trying to reduce the noise before picking it up for a single rotation before releasing it again. The mantis heard the rock-carrying sling spin through the air, causing it to turn towards them. Like a deer in headlights, it finally stood still, allowing the rock to hit the impractical bullseye.

Bruce and Victoria crept their way forward, unsure of how they would be able to spear something moving so fast. They quickly immersed themselves in the brightly colored bamboo stalks, the sounds of many small waterfalls suppressing their approach. Bruce's shiver resembled buck fever. He did his best to control it while he moved forward; he was not going to make a mistake when everything was of life and death.

They slowed down to avoid knocking into the bamboo, trying to get a better angle and reposition themselves to an area where they could throw their spears. They observed a feathery mass leaping back and forth, up and down the stream. *Chicken*. It looked exactly the same as the one they had seen outside their shelter before.

They knew they wanted to kill it; it looked delicious. Both of them did not register their licking of their lips. They hoped they would not be detected, waiting for any opportunity to arise. Bruce watched as Victoria darted to the side and launched her spear at an elevated, fast target.

It took him by surprise that the spear hit the bird, resulting in a spurt of cyan blood that brought color to the whitish reflection of the metallic feathers. It made no sound. He was astonished that Victoria predicted the movement; he knew it was calculated.

"That was amazing," he said, helping to collect their kill. They moved it back the way they came and did not stop for fear of being ambushed, the body emitting the smell of blood. They dragged it by the spear, careful not to cut themselves on the potentially dangerous feathers.

"That was definitely insane," she said, still in awe of herself.

He complimented her throw before commenting on the creature's mass. "That could feed all of us, assuming it's edible."

"Wouldn't that be a shame– if it weren't edible."

"I'd eat it either way." He wondered how the other groups were doing, but he was relatively sure they were in the lead. It had not been long since the competition had begun, so they had a lot of time to prepare their dish and think about what to do next.

Tanho and Lucian waited by the water. Tanho was using the tip of the spear to mimic a creature splashing around, waiting for something to get interested and move closer to investigate. Minutes passed and they had seen nothing except their own reflections and periodic crashes of things in the grass.

"Wow, I guess they are really attracted to blood," Tanho said. Having cleaned all of his blood-soaked clothing, he was uncertain of what to do. "Should I?" he asked with a pause, looking around in contemplation.

"No, you shouldn't. But *I* will, though. You're pretty beat up already, and we shouldn't need that much. Besides, I'm kind of interested to see how they'll behave." With a grunt, he sliced his hand with the knife and squeezed some blood into the water before putting pressure on the wound to stop it. He did not cut himself too deeply, so he was not too worried about anything bad happening. However, he did recognize the possibility of alien infection, which reduced his ease.

As the blood diffused into the water, hastened by the splashing and consequently turbulent water flow, they knew they would have either food or bait– they were yet to decide. They appeared slowly but all at once. There was a small group of them of varying sizes. The largest ones took the lead and inched forward, locked in on the splashing, looking for something to attack. Just as the lead one moved within both of their reach, Tanho stopped splashing and thrust just below the squid to counteract the refraction.

He held up the largest of the squid, which he estimated to be around 10 pounds. Lucian was fascinated that Tanho could kill it in a single jab, that these fish were so much smaller than everything else, and that they were attracted to human blood.

At first, they were unsure whether to use it as bait or cook it, but considering that they had a lot more time left, they decided to use it as bait.

"Wait, we can just catch another one," Tanho said. Lucian was astonished that he did not think that up, prompting him to chuckle. Being careful not to put acid into his cut, he drizzled some on his slightly bloodied palm beside the slice. He used his other hand to scrub some of it off, letting it fall with the water to the lake. It was not much blood, yet it seemed to do the trick. Failing to learn from their friend's previous mistake, they slowly encroached on the blood-infused water, an army of tentacles surrounding nothing. With the first squid squirming on the ground behind them, Tanho got their second kill.

They decided to take both with them while they were using one as bait so that it would not be stolen. They were trying to attract the crocodile with the smell anyway. Heading over to the tree that Valeria and Griffith had gone to, they worried about how the other groups were doing, both as competitors and as fellow survivors.

Realizing that they now had another necessity to living, Lucian asked himself again, *what is going on here?* The question was not in a sense of surprise but rather connected to all of them and their position on the planet. They had finally reached another milestone but, in reality, were no closer to getting back home. He did not know if they would ever understand the planet and its inhabitants– they could die in many ways before that were to happen, and if they somehow managed to send a distress signal off the planet, *would Earth even send someone after us?*

Chapter 7

TREPIDATIONS

A wave of imminent danger swept about them, the threat of night infallibly incoming once more. The collective knew it was time to begin cooking their catches, seeing which were poisonous, hopefully without accident, in the process. Incapable of cooking with a shield between them for safety in fear of something attacking them, the teams began cooking outside the shelter nearby.

"Lucian, is there any way we can tell if it's edible?" Victoria asked, not bothering to glance at the pile of creatures she and Bruce had caught.

"I think the best we can do, with what we have with us, is to bring the meat to a high temperature to kill off any bacteria. Beyond that, we have to neutralize it so our organs don't dissolve," he said, emphasizing the second step.

"Dissolve. Wow. Okay," Valeria said as if she had not previously realized that the creatures there could do much more in certainly more agony.

Lucian continued, "Most meat we eat from Earth is already slightly acidic; our bodies can handle that; we just need to make sure it's not *that* polarized on the pH scale. I'm not sure what to do for a basic creature, though. We might have to diffuse boiled lake water into it."

It was undoubtedly more complicated than they had hoped. They were quick to shed their beliefs about keeping the food items to themselves and instead focused on being able to consume them. Others were capable of doing it, but for their sake and survival, they appointed Lucian to inspect all the bloodied creatures and do his best to make them suitable for ingestion.

They knew it would be a long time before they were to make it off the planet, if it even were possible. If they were to give themselves the highest chance of survivability, they would have to be able to sustain themselves off the land. In doing so, risks would have to be taken. Lucian especially wished he would not have to play a game against the odds.

Looking around, they became excited that there had been no repeats of what had been killed for food. They definitely had enough food, inarguably too much for what they could use. Some would be stored, and some would be left as a peace offering to the first passersby. Lucian noted that on this single day, they likely gained more useful knowledge than on any other day of their involuntary excursion.

Having had the food the longest, Bruce and Victoria had prepared their decorated creature by skinning it and cutting it up cautiously. They would cook first, with everyone's assistance. Seeing that their chicken would potentially provide enough food for them all, they had built a fire and gathered firewood large enough to be suitable for cooking the largest of the daytime creatures they had seen.

Their fire burned vigorously until all that remained were smoldering coals, signaling their first dish. They could only hope to cook everything before nightfall; it would all depend on the meat's complexity.

The cooking was intricate. They particularly noted the uniform consistency within all of the creatures, lacking organs beyond a stomach or any indicator of a circulatory or nervous system. The color varied between them, which was also perplexing given their completely different physical characteristics.

Their chicken's cyan-like blood mimicked its meat until blood drained from within the porous core. Once the blood had mostly cleared, all color was lost, leaving the absence of color in its place.

First, they sliced the chicken and removed the bones left from Victoria's preliminary removal. The acidic water was poured and flowed smoothly through the thin slivers of pearlescent, mouth-watering food. The imperial crystal displayed its presence throughout the bucket of water through its reflecting light about the sloshing waves. Shadows from the bright light set upon the filet as the water was brought to a boil.

Lucian ground up more grass, particularly the type they had seen the mantis ingest– it was much more likely to be edible. Slowly and with drops of water, he let the basic essence neutralize the stew. Poking and prodding the meat with a normal spear, they confirmed the crystal's dullness. It second as means to ensure the water had diffused throughout the meat.

"I think this should be sufficient," Lucian told them, stepping back and yielding to the intense heat. He let the food cook thoroughly, signaled by a bronzing and darkened gray coloring. He removed the strips from the water, avoiding the heat capable of significant burning. While they began to fill the water bucket with other strips of food, they could not help but imagine the potentially poisonous nature they were surrounded by.

"At least the grass isn't poisonous," Griffith said. "Then we'd already be dead!" The sarcastic statement inherently failed, producing a grim realization they had already had many times before in the half week they had been stationed there.

"Chaos!" Valeria exclaimed.

"Chaos, what?" Bruce asked, trying to tie it back to something they had seen.

"It's here. Everything here is chaos. The nights, the days, the plants, the animals." She paused, "it's the planet."

"It's a good name," Tanho proclaimed in acceptance.

The slices of chicken were now cooling while the next bucket began heating up. Lucian waited on purpose, not trying to diminish the quality of the food but to perform a preemptive test before taking the leap of faith. By now, they had all felt the excruciating effects of expending energy without any intake; the understanding that they could likely survive a few more weeks did not amend the feeling.

"Blood, that's my plan," Lucian said. "Blood coagulates when the soluble fibrinogens become insoluble in the presence of a protein that activates zymogen."

"What did you just say?" Bruce asked with a hand to his head.

Griffith jumped in to respond, saying, "Blood clots when something makes it rigid. So, if we pour blood on some of the food, we should be able to see if it reacts with our blood, telling us we shouldn't eat it. Clotting is just one of the things that can occur."

"Smart," Valeria emphasized alongside the subtle nod of Bruce and Tanho. "But, and correct me if I'm wrong, there's no way to tell beyond that if it's safe to consume? Like I read about the torafugu pufferfish's toxin-filled organs; would the venom be contained within sacs like on the spider?"

Lucian responded, "I don't think there's any way to tell that for sure; maybe if we had the spider and a lot of time, we could tell. We could choose not to eat anything now, but there isn't any telling if we'll have another opportunity to get food, let alone perform more in-depth tests with a creature that tried to kill us and works together with others. You guys should try to think up any other things we can try, but otherwise, we do have to take a significant risk in anything we eat." He took the silence of contemplation and understanding as a signal to begin his testing. Blood slowly dripped following a wince and wiping-off of a crystal. The reddish blood held a peace imbued in its heat, a natural incandescence of mortality and humility.

He dribbled his blood slowly onto the smallest piece of meat. With them all being uniform in color and texture, he did not feel the need to try over multiple pieces, yet he did anyway. It was to be a proper experiment concerning all of their lives, after all. The blood yielded no visible reaction, a relief. They waited several minutes and, after comparing consistency and sliceability, deemed that nothing noticeable had happened.

"So does that mean we should try now?" Bruce asked.

"Unless anyone has any other things we should try. It wouldn't hurt," Lucian commented.

Tanho spoke up, "There are some other tests we can try, but I don't know how they'd relate to these foods."

"Go for it," Valeria said.

"We can place a piece on our arms for a few minutes, then graduate to our mouths, and then to chewing and waiting to see if something happens. If it feels weird, we know that it's poisonous, but that's only for fruits and plants on Earth."

They noticed the awkward smells as they continued preparing food. Tanho volunteered, but Bruce took the responsibility of testing the food. They would do a few tests while the rest of the food cooked. Although it would be nice to eat warm food, they chose to reduce the risk of death, with lukewarm food as the consequence. They opted to warm up the food if they truly wanted it to be hotter.

After several minutes, Bruce responded with a sigh of relief, "I'm fine. What's the next step again?" The previously acidic and likely dangerous meat lay touching the top of his wrist, exactly where Tanho said to place it. The removal of the cooling piece revealed no change in his skin color. The meat left no residue besides the aqueous solution that was replete and allowed to percolate out. It was still intact and seemed to resemble the firmness of beef.

As they prepared more food and the series of tests for each species continued, Bruce finished the last test they wanted to perform. He placed a piece in his mouth, chewing slowly, before waiting once more to see if anything had happened.

He was astonished that nothing happened, although he seemed to manifest it by convincing his brain that something would happen. He believed the weird sensation to be a psychological trick, a character of hysteria, in combination with the strange texture and taste adhering to an unearthly origin.

"It feels sweet but doesn't, and sour but doesn't. I don't really know what it tastes like, but I think it's a balance, a weird balance."

They were not thrilled at his observation, but Valeria pointed out, "I think that's good, though! It's not a bad sign!"

The brim of night peeking over the horizon, with its grim luminance shining a familiar, gallant spectrum of colors, reminded them of their limited freedom once more; it held and was embodied in their decision to not all try the chicken, which Victoria, having the killing blow, named *Esprit*, "meaning: active mind and spirit."

One member from each group would try; just in case they made a mistake in cooking a creature, at least half of them would still be alive. They did not account for multiple possible poisonings from the many species they had gathered, their conscious ignorance of an agonizing death leading them in their food ordeals.

Instead of dividing them all up evenly, they decided to go on a volunteer basis– whoever wanted it could have it. They had a lot to choose from, and after some consideration, they decided not to make a quota for each creature.

"If you want something, try it," Valeria said. Lucian believed they would all just eat the first thing they cooked, but each group wanted to try their own creature, and once the many minutes of waiting were done, they had determined that just about everything was fair. The squid that Lucian and Tanho had caught was the most unique texture of them all, possibly due to its size. They found that the limb-like protrusions were the most tender but could not justify the classification compared to Earth food. Once they had all tried their own creatures, they tried the other groups deemed edible in correspondence to if the group said it was good. All in all, they did not know what was to be considered good or bad– they had more of a sense of 'repulsive' or 'not repulsive.'

One creature they caught strongly resembled an ant or an antlion with large mandibles and a keratinous exoskeleton. That creature had very bright blood and did not pass the blood test. Following that, they had to get a new bucket of water and make sure none of its blood remained to poison them; they did want to keep some, however, at least for the night, in the carcass. *We can dip our spears into the body to coat them in makeshift poison. It could be powerful, although I doubt it.* Seeing that it was the only one that failed their testing, they were pleased with how much they had learned and had to eat. As if singling it out for its unique inedibleness, Tanho and Lucian collectively named their trapping kill *Noxant*. "It's a combination of noxious and ant!" Tanho proudly joked. "But don't enunciate the a."

They had also prepared a frog, a mantis, a crocodile, a lizard, and a beetle. As they went around and taste-tested, they also released names. The frog became *Turtle-frog*, the mantis became a *Mandibles*, the crocodile a *Deinodile*, the lizard a *Tokay*, and the beetle a *Scarab*. To avoid confusing themselves, they waited to name the other random beasts until they better understood them. They did not yet know what to make of the giant with a club.

The rays of darkness shone upon them as if a dream became a nightmare, and they knew of its corruption from when they first fell asleep. The theta waves of monster noises brusquely rushed forward in the sleep cycle that was their worst fear. All together, retreating in their shelter, hoarding alien filets in their corner on top of a plate of wood, they awaited what new things they might see. The food fulfilled them; they could tell the difference now that they were out of the rain and had a rejuvenating energy source. The sun either set very quickly or was hastened by the hypothesized dangers they thought up.

Similar furies of luminous bulbs flew through the air, a flowing sanction to the unlucky creatures who were not stealthy enough. The frequency worried Lucian about the lobber's spatial awareness; so many acidic bombs silently rained from above on the seemingly unsuspecting creatures. Trying to remain confident, made easier by the horribleness of previous nights, they spoke aloud of what they believed the creatures to be doing. Still, of course, they would not be able to truly understand without a better understanding. *Perhaps we will be able to see one in the morning.*

They heard the beating wings of creatures above them. The temperature had increased significantly but was not influence enough to risk a creature attack in the pitch-black night. The awkward battle of humidity fell below their difference threshold but was clearly much higher. Moments later, when they finally noticed the change in smell, they thought it to be brought on by storms from the previous night.

A part of them desired to know the cause of all the fantastical sounds produced by mythological creatures waiting to be discovered. It pained them to be shrouded by darkness. However, it was a blessing in disguise;

their tucked-awayness shielded them from a brutal reality that the many beasts faced alone.

The night was uneventful beyond some familiar noises they had heard two nights ago, along with others that may have just been washed out. It was not as gratifying to see the sun again, but they were still grateful to be able to see.

"Good morning!" Valeria told them. One by one, they awoke from their usual, sporadic sleeping with some iteration of "mornin'."

"I can't believe I actually got some sleep last night," Victoria said. "Somehow, whatever made noise was particularly less violent."

Griffith commented, "Yeah, it was strange; I don't think anything was interested in us either."

"The smoke really does wonders," Lucian added. "The fire makes a peaceful sound and masks the smell."

Bruce responded, "That's a lot of birds with one stone– heat and cooking and everything. I don't think we would've made it this long without it."

Griffith stood up and cracked his back, looking at the darkness' forgiving retreat, streaks and beams of chromatic crimsons piercing the air. He thought he noticed the trees shiver. "I guess we should wait and see what today has in store for us. I'd love another calm day."

"As long as it doesn't come with so many storms at night," Lucian pointed out. He looked over at Tanho, who had been waking up slowly. "Tanho, how did you sleep?"

He pushed off the ground to sit up, "I think I'm alright. Got a little bit of sleep. I think I slept weirdly, though; any chance we can upgrade the sleeping arrangements?"

Griffith said, "I think I'd like to find a good shelter before we start refining everything, but if we're going to be stuck here a while, I don't see why not."

Victoria told them, "We just need to get some wood and employ Jarnbjorn." She chuckled lightly. As she did, a pygmy dragon scurried between the grass fields before their shelter. "Do you guys think we should try and prepare for our escape today? Should we adventure and start seeing what's towards the lake?"

"I think we should see what creatures are out and about today, but honestly, it wouldn't hurt to wait longer so we understand the lay of the land more," Griffith told them.

Feeling more confident than they had in the days before, they immersed themselves in the land and its novel psychology. Only five days had passed, five iterations of a realm so exotic that death encroached on every silver lining.

As hours passed in wait and proposed expeditions, similar animals revealed themselves in front of their shelter. A medium-sized beast that resembled the dead creature from their first day sauntered past, a pygmy dragon in effortless pursuit; *how am I supposed to remember and paint all of this?*

"Gosh, how are we supposed to name all of these?" Bruce asked.

"With time. With lots of time," Victoria answered.

Tanho spoke in slight resentment, "We need to get back home or at least be somewhere safer. I don't like living my life like this– living on death's doorstep, even if this is what I signed up for."

Lucian supported and assured him, "We will likely be here for a little longer. We can't risk long expeditions or too great a degree of variability until we learn this place like the back of our hands."

Halfway through the day, told by the sun's direct overhead beating, they left their shelter. They saw few creatures in any direction, much less than they expected.

Lucian told them, "This resembles the day we landed here." Now farther from the lake, they were in a much better position to see what could be around them. It was just behind them that they found the first dead animal.

As they moved further in a group, they saw more creatures, similar to what they had seen on their second and fifth day. Animals filled the role of the tokays and the turtle-frogs and the esprit and the beetles. A great antlered deer of a lightning-infused green made its way proudly through the open about the tree. Something with a large tail slid across the dry ground before hiding away in the grass.

Hours and hours passed with only short expeditions near the tree for fallen sticks. They laid what they had gathered in layers above the ground– as bed frame rails– using larger logs to steady everything. After a sufficient raise, many were placed horizontally with little spacing, and a layer of fresh leaf litter lay on top. They could cover most of the floor with a new bed in the shelter's remaining space. Now that they were sufficiently elevated, the heat would not be sapped as quickly out of their bodies despite the leafy insulation they had laid on. They had to leave space not bedded where they had not placed leaves before, so the fire had little risk of catching their shelter on fire. An eviction of such nature would mean certain death most of the day.

This night was like no other, not in its fear-bearing quality but in its deja-vu similarity. A malicious howl filled the air and was joined by its companions, its pack members.

Tanho said, "Wow, they're still alive. That's amazing," with a sarcasm that held in the air. He asked, "Why are they back tonight instead of some other night?"

Lucian responded, "Well, yeah, something is definitely happening. We just don't really know what." Tanho especially had trouble sleeping. Bruce and Griffith stayed awake with him for a few hours until they succumbed to nighttime soporific temptations, the signal for Lucian and Victoria to begin their shift.

Overnight, they had all seen the familiar purple flames amidst the otherwise dark and empty landscape. The aura of power swelled the air. Doled sounds drew close and far in a subtle but consistent reminder of their inability to go outside. Somehow, the vision of escape and survival crept into their light dreams.

"I can't remember how many times I woke up," Griffith said when they had all awoken together.

Tanho had slept the lightest, noted by his frequent shifting. There was no solitude in their shelter. He rolled his eyes in awkward fatigue.

Looking outside and adding fuel to the fire, Lucian awaited the sun's welcome arrival. Somehow, Tanho felt cold, and Valeria shivered. Tanho moved closer to the fire, closing his eyes in tiredness as his will held him up. In truth, many of them shared his feelings. It was not even a week since their crash, and the planet had proven both cruel and merciful in its double-edged sword.

"This place is beautiful," Valeira once again reminded them.

Victoria added, "and wants to kill us." In a blend and fury of hidden thoughts shared among them, she expressed, "But what can we do except try and get things done? If that takes time and understanding, so be it."

Griffith consoled, "We can do this. As cliche as that may sound, we have a chance, no matter how slim that may actually be. We can get past the potentially wasted time, heightened adrenaline, and close calls so that we have any chance of making it out alive and reporting our findings back to our people. Imagine that: being the only people to have experienced alien life firsthand and talking on panels about it."

Bruce told him, "As long as our NDAs don't apply and the government doesn't try to hide it or quarantine us for life for having breathed this air without space suits. We weren't really supposed to even land anywhere at all."

The sun made its way into the sky. They saw similar specks flying through the air in a fluttered descent alongside the varying bright, walking creatures holding onto the tree. Before most creatures completed their touchdown to Chaos, the more attentive Lucian, Griffith, and Victoria went outside. The tree to their back left showed what would be invading.

"The spiders are back!" Victoria announced. They returned inside and overflowed the fire, using some leaves to accelerate the smoke production.

Bruce sat up again, sighing, "I guess we're staying here again today."

It's traumatizing, Lucian thought. *It's only been a week, but it has been full of extreme conditions and a berating fear. This place is crazy.* He told himself in a comforting and alliterative joke: *Chaos is crazy.*

***

Every once in a while, a bird dove down at blistering speeds, propelling itself into a target hidden in the tall, grasseous environment. Between the clicks and hisses of spiders, a silence was all that erupted from outside to inside their shelter.

"We can take the spiders," Tanho said. "We should go out and do something to make us a bit safer."

"Tanho, I think this is the best we're going to do for a while, and besides, this is pretty safe," Griffith responded.

"But what are we going to do here in this place but get a better understanding of what's around us? We aren't doing anything to make us more potent attackers. How do we ever expect to make it to that building if we never make it outside this shelter but one day a week?"

"It's only been seven days, Tanho."

"Don't say my name again like that, and you know time probably moves a lot slower here 'cause I healed in like two of these days. The longer we stay here in full view and exposed to the hundreds of deadly creatures, the more likely we will be killed. A single one of those creatures could take us all out for good. Then what are we going to do, huh?"

Lucian stepped in before Griffith said anything, although Griffith knew it was not his place to continue, "one step at a time. But yes, we should start planning for that journey. Next time there are no creatures, and we're absolutely sure of that, we go through the route carefully and scout out the possible places we could get ambushed or envision any challenges we might face."

"Good idea, Lucian," Victoria said. "So we're placing all of our money on this building, which could be some weird plant? And we're planning to go on the second no-creature day from now?"

Bruce looked at Tanho and then back to Victoria, who was watching the fire, "The potential building is probably our only way out unless our people spend millions to have a slight chance of getting us back. I'd say we go as soon as possible, as Tanho said. Lucian's plan makes the most sense. There's no point going so far away into different-looking places with so many different trees, at least without scouting it out first."

"Good talk," Tanho said before putting a spear next to him and laying down on their newly refurbished bedding that held their warmth much longer. He hoped they would not have to get rid of the bed to keep the fire going longer without warming them as much.

Griffith proposed, "Maybe we can do something in the meantime."

"Do you have anything in mind? That's also directed at Tanho," Victoria asked, also wanting to avoid being stuck in the shelter. She did, however, realize that it was absurd to want to leave so often. *It has only been a week; how is it that Tanho healed so quickly and that we have this pent-up energy and frustration in staying here, safe?*

They did not say anything. Griffith told them all, "People in the wilderness survive months and even at sea. Yeah, it's been one week; we're okay. If we make one mistake by overestimating our ability, we die." He stood up straighter, "So if you all want to survive..." he paused, "... we're going to stay in this shelter as long as we can, no matter what we feel." A light echo held within their small cave, and he said, "We need to give as much time as possible to people trying to save us." Lucian realized how obnoxious they all were in being on the planet and trying to get themselves killed. *It doesn't make sense.*

A spider broke their tenseness, appearing outside and looking at them as if craving vengeance. The slender, pointed legs reminded them of the recluse's deadliness. In silence, they watched to see what it would do. Left and right, it danced, likely trying to perceive their depth amidst the prismatically illuminated backdrop.

"What do we do?" Valeria asked.

"We wait," Griffith said in command. He patiently awaited the spider's move. Although they had just talked about staying in control of themselves and reducing risk, he craved action. His craving slowly diminished as another spider jumped down from above them. They had not heard its likely clacking over the sound of the fire and intense focus on the immediate threat. As they slowly armed themselves, he said, "Everyone look away." The second predator eyed its prey. Spiderly communication reflected off the walls, just as their voices had. A beration of noise with a significant, negative, cognitive label surrounded the brain– an infiltration of profane frequencies through which human psychology no longer knew who would win. As if fueling the fire of prey backed into the corner that was their rocky formation, a third and then fourth spider emerged from either side of their shelter.

"Keep looking away; they might lose interest," he said, unknowing of the doubled population of hunters. It was silent, the crackling flame lost in mind and sight, gone. Eyes were closed, for Valeria, Lucian, and Tanho could not bear to stare at the floor, devoid of anything but inebriated thought.

They heard the rough clash of something against their wooden bulwark, causing them to look up in case one had begun rushing inside. They had only taken on two previously, and it had taken two each to take out the two there. Now, they had six capable fighters and may be able to take on three.

The closest spider that had brushed against the bulwark inspected it closely, the primal drive of food refusing to let it back up. It had not hit any crystals nor impaled itself. Once again sober, Lucian believed it to be testing the metaphorical waters that were the defenses of six gamey meals.

"Okay, what do we do?" Valeria, unentranced, in a hushed seriousness. Already, Griffith and Victoria wielded flaming sticks, holding them in the direction of the spiders. They seemed unphased, with dedication and focus in clear view through the chaotic flames.

Lucian took one of the stockpiled spider legs and thrust it into the open wound of the noxant. The leg was not long enough or heavy enough to function as an effective spear, but Lucian had accounted for it. He took a step back from his position in the middle of the shelter, facing the spiders, mentally estimating the distance between him and the spider in split-second racing. *Torque*, he told himself. He threw the poisoned spider leg as a throwing knife, the leg parallel to the ground when his grasp released. It rotated one and a half spins before threading through their entrance gap and hitting the spider's abdomen, piercing one of the eyes that watched the ground.

Although the leg was short, it was heavy. The force behind it concentrated into the sharp point and easily penetrated the fragile body; they could not be sure how far through it went. The consequent scream released any hold the spiders' trance may have had on them; they were winning. Two-to-one odds were much more favorable.

"We better hope no more come. We can take these," Lucian told them, grabbing another spider leg from the few they had moved before the spider's approach. Two spider legs, their spears, and Griffith's axe were the only weapons they had to defend against whatever sat in wait outside their shelter. They hoped for an intervention, although they were not sure any creatures would dare stand up to the army of spiders they hoped were not surrounding them.

Lucian dipped another spider leg into the dead noxant, watching the poisoned spider run off to their right. The blood glistened on the conical spider foot, signaling Lucian to wait for it to take up more surface area before throwing as to not fling toxic blood all over them. Luckily, the blood was glutinous, sticking onto the spider's leg even through the air. This projectile would not hit its target; learning from its relative's mistake, the spider would not fall for the same trick again.

"Its intelligence is frightening," Victoria commented, watching the spider hide its vulnerable body behind a dense intersection of wooden sticks. The three of them, still in view, showed no signs of disinterest. *What are they planning?* Lucian asked himself.

At once, they had all disappeared, jolting to the sides, out of view. "What are they doing?" Victoria asked alarmingly.

"They're definitely up to something. I don't feel good about this," Griffith said. Not knowing what else to add, Lucian kept his agreement to himself. In anticipation of some paroxysm, they grabbed the spider legs that they previously could not reach out of fear of being stabbed and set them against the back wall, acting as their weapon rack. They consolidated their weapons in haste, using the log stockpile as a secondary barricade or projectile ammunition, their arms being the most crucial armament in their defensive and offensive formations.

The trident of spiders returned, dragging a greenish-yellow sac that had clearly been detached from something larger.

"What are they going to do with that?" Valeria questioned. The wall of wooden spikes did not reach the roof of their shelter; it seemed to be enough space for a spider to fit through. As the spider climbed up the side of the entrance, the flailing limbs clearly visible, they prepared for an advance.

In answer to Valeria's question, the second spider, which wielded the ominous, bright sac, lifted it by piercing a meaty protrusion and began climbing the opposite side.

Tanho yelled, "They're going to throw it in here!"

In a temporary panic, all but Lucian grabbed something, waiting a second before preemptively throwing spears and chunks of wood to block the sac from getting inside. Lucian feared for the sac's contents; it could be filled with venom, acid, a gas, or something else they had previously not been exposed to. In a flurry of thought and head-pounding unsureness, he remembered seeing the glowing blue orb used as bait. *Could that be it? What's so dangerous about that?* In truth, it was all he could think of, but it made little sense to him. He was unable to come up with a solution in this moment of anxiety and ensnared hopelessness.

The spider did not overextend its play, keeping the sac out of sight. Once both spiders were positioned on the top arch of their shelter, they wished for the rainfall curtain that had once fallen there. A quick show of the venomously imbued, arcane ball attempted to petrify and weaken mind and spirit. The final spider on the ground extended its limbs in a menacing fashion, taking up lots of space, optimized among a flat plane parallel to the shelter's entrance to appear larger and induce hesitation. It was a symphony of degradation that even the six trained travelers could not resist; the quick onslaught of mindful torture served to reduce the mindless wanderers to a more primal, young, basic-instinct state.

Lucian's mind fell victim to fight or flight, falling back to the brainstem, the foundation of thought itself, where conscious, intelligent thought is censored entirely. In mere seconds, morale and confidence plummeted hand in hand. A surge of Tanho's fenrhor thrashing emitted from the entrance of the shelter, as far away as it was.

An instinctual, mindful vision signaled the spiders' attacks and consequently evoked emotional responses, a method that could be deemed purposeful but was, in fact, nothing at all. The spiders used what they had learned and had been naturally gifted with: an emotional intelligence capable of manipulation and trickery coupled with a versatile associative-tool-use capability to outplay anything they took for prey.

Flinging wood and launching a few spears into the empty opening or off the roof onto the wooden spikes did nothing. They were quick to halt their impulsive action and employ some backed-against-the-wall strategies of their own. Griffith's signal induced their stoppage, after which Griffith and Lucian aimed at opposite corners of their upper exposure. A well-timed fake would over-advance the spider's plan.

When objects stopped flying out of the shelter, the spiders knew a chance had arisen. Implanting one of its legs into the pouch's extension meant it would have to swing to release. The spider began building momentum with a quick backswing, where the sac was lowered and moved towards the shelter before it would go up and out to swing in far enough to hit its target. It was silent. The slow initial rocking exposed the underside of the pouch, where Griffith, aimed at the left side of the opening, reoriented himself and threw at the right side. The spear missed on the spider's backswing.

They watched as the spider reorganized after being somewhat surprised by the projectile; they had another chance. Lucian was not to be outwitted, collecting himself in strategy as the others regrouped their consciousness. It would be a second before the spider could try its luck again; Lucian had precious seconds to think, the others reframing their existence and watching memories play before them, the shelter's entrance the screen.

"Blitzkrieg!" Lucian shouted with unprecedented intensity. At once, the clash of fight or flight and conscious, intellectual thought interwove neurons and firing synapses in an iota of time. Unified in effort and life-related dedication, new thought awoke; it was a language of strategy and war where Tanho was reminded of his baiting trick. They still had their pile of food, and before they had all risen to their feet, Tanho spun his head over his left shoulder and picked the top filet of esprit.

It was three spiders plus an injured one– lurking about– against six reinvigorated survivors. Lucian and Griffith were first in their order to make it to the wooden entrance. The bastion's gap could only fit one at a time, channeling them and reducing their initial offensive capability.

Griffith went out first in order, launching himself in an upward jab. Bruce quickly made his way in front of Lucian to get outside second. In surprise and caution, the two spiders backed up, crawling upwards in a regathered retreat. The third spider retreated directly before them, separating itself from its collective kind. The injured spider did not hint at its presence; they could not be sure where it hid.

In the moments of escape from their shelter, Lucian thought it ironic that he signaled their attack but did not rush out first. As he, the third person in their line, finally left their almost tomb, the spiders began to counter their counter. The one with the sac bounced about the structure above them while the other moved closer. It seemed unaffected by them all in a rushed attack, pumping energy and enhanced focus. The spider's bravado came with purpose, an attacking opportunity on somewhat blinded foes, and an understanding that it may not survive the attack.

Right after Lucian was Victoria. As she rushed forward, she watched Lucian and Bruce look over her. Her subconscious registered that they were watching the spiders from above as they began their retreat. She did not expect the spider's lunge just as she moved out of the shelter. In a flash, a black spear moved through her vision. The spider was giant; Lucian, Griffith, and Bruce thought, *how did we not notice before?* Somehow, their spears were not oriented in the right direction to intercept the exceptionally fast spider's movement. The jab nicked the right side of her chin and implanted itself beside her clavicle, inches into her shoulder.

The seconds that followed fought between passing by too fast and drawing out too slow; a silent and disgruntled scream harmonized with the symbolic stabbing of the smug spider; the pierced brachial plexus nerve network shot spikes of anguish straight into her spinal cord, a surge stabbing her brain as each nerve strand synchronized the song that was the spider's imposition into one intense, shadowing loss of consciousness. Her immediate fall to the ground significantly increased the distance between her and the attacker so the rest could help fend off their foe.

Griffith was busy eyeing down the forward spider, who seemed to coordinate its attack alongside the one from above. Victoria's scream caused him to turn around, but after realizing that the other four were right there and able to help Victoria, he turned back to ensure the spider would not have an easy target. The spider that had advanced a few steps stopped and reevaluated.

Bruce smacked the spider against the top of the shelter as it dropped. By Victoria's fall to the ground, the spider leg unfastened itself from her shoulder, spurting blood. Some glistening liquid stuck onto the leg, dripping slowly until it was flung onto the wall, after which all the blood on the leg lay against the wall in an inverted pyramid. Each individual droplet had a forward-facing tail that moved away from the leg's impact zone.

It definitely had a concussion, if at all possible; the torqued force of the spear-hammer immensely overcame the gravity behind an angered showcase of power. During the quick ordeal, Bruce left his guard down, relying on Griffith's advance to keep him a safe distance from other attackers.

As quickly as Victoria had gone outside, she was dragged back inside by her feet. Valeria and Tanho went outside to neutralize the threat or get everybody back inside. On the return, Tanho realized that more spiders could come for them at any moment.

Just a few steps outside, while Lucian and Bruce stabbed and killed the spider, Griffith remained, limiting the other spider's movement. They were glad the spider only managed to inflict that much damage, considering it had thirteen other legs. Above them, the middling arachnid swung its mystery pouch back and forth hypnotizingly, a metronome of danger catching their eyes against the livid sky.

On one of the swings, the spider rocked backward, then forwards, releasing the pouch. "Inbound!" Lucian shouted. From twenty feet above them, the pouch held a slow arc, raising only a foot into the air before beginning to drop; with Lucian, Bruce, and Tanho's eyes dilating in emotional response to unavoidable danger, it was impossible to brainstorm anything resembling an adequate solution in time.

Bruce shoved Lucian, who pushed Tanho and Valeria back into the shelter. In the moments of gravitational acceleration warranting just over a second in drop, Bruce launched himself, with Griffith's additional push, through the shelter's entrance behind the other four. Griffith remained outside.

The pouch of liquid folded in on itself, flattening, before a hole was made, and liquid shot up and out a few feet in every direction. Bruce and Griffith uniformly turned a shoulder and put up their arms to shield against the likely dangerous solution, all while spears clinked to the ground. A sizzle percolated their minds as drops of liquid dispersed among the wooden bulwark and the impervious ground in front of them.

Tanho watched from the back as a single drop made its way through the opening in the bulwark, embarking on a journey, the mission intended by its insect commander. The drop had scattered as a larger glob hit the bulwark with speed and split into many small pieces. Slowly and with a moment of pause, the drop engulfed the floor in flame.

The rock-insulated cove now held heat too well; the temperature inside skyrocketed within seconds. Seeing the intensity of the inferno, they knew they would not be able to make a break for it. All they could do was douse their clothing in water and cover their mouths to avoid suffocation, pushing the bedframe and leaf litter as far away as possible.

Griffith remained outside, alone. Over the crackle of their bulwark bursting into a fiery blaze, any sounds Griffith produced from the outside were inaudible. In helpless staring, once again backed into the corner, with Victoria still bleeding profusely from her carotid artery's almost audible pumping, they could not help but watch as the figure resembling Griffith spun about and melted into the liquifying sticks in a raging, fervent flame.

Rising embers melted again before escaping the heat as gas, hiding themselves in the group's imagination as the series of spiders corralled Griffith like a tortured animal. A quick break in the flame revealed the equally angry sky once more but held a darker hue, the shadow of a many-legged, round creature.

They shriveled into the back corner, farthest away from where their fire had sat, waiting patiently and using their thin clothing as heat shields. They could not move their hands farther away, or their faces would feel like they were on fire. The battle of wind patterns periodically prompted winces, exacerbated by the spontaneity of unpredictable fiery outreaches.

They did not know how long it had been but thought it had been a couple minutes. The fire died down, its intensity being its downfall as fuel was used all at once. Their bulwark and pushed-over, temporary shield of logs were all but gone; the only remnants of the battle were the coals and ashes, the latter of which now had free reign to fly and escape the burn.

The portal to the outside world was reopening, strangely complimenting the grasses and sky, which held true despite the slightly opaque smoke. Their door, now larger, allowed them all to take the chance and leap through to find Griffith. They had to wait longer, using whatever was left of their water to make a path against the scorched rock.

Griffith had still not appeared; they hoped he was still alive. They could not be sure if the fire had reached him. *Hopefully nothing splashed on him.*

They all eventually made it outside, the smoke still rising at an angle. Looking around, he was nowhere to be seen. A bit farther and to the right of where he was last, a fair amount of blood droplets led them to the other side of their shelter. The sun's heat accented the light burns on their arms as they approached. On the opposite side of the refuge from the entrance, Griffith sat, one leg extended, against the rocks. His right arm was almost fully extended to where it met a spear that he held upright. His left arm attempted to cover the gash that spanned his whole right arm. There were four spiders in all: two lay in front of him on either side, a few feet away, and the other two were farther out but also dead.

Ensuring nothing else was around, they approached Griffith cautiously but speedily. "Are you okay?" Valeria and Tanho asked simultaneously.

"I got 'em," he responded in a grueling manner.

"Yes, that is indeed what you did," Lucian analyzed, looking at the dead beasts that lay ceremonially about him. "How did you get all of them?"

"Just get me a fire," he told them. "The wounds need to close." By now, blood coated his entire arm and began dripping onto his leg, the floor, and down his side. The top of his left eye was bleeding, beginning to obscure his vision. Instead of bringing him to the fire, they decided to bring the fire to him.

With just about all their wood reserves gone, it took a while to start a fire again. Victoria was still bleeding, but did not look nearly as bad as Griffith did. Valeria stayed and tended to both of their wounds while the others brought wood back and Tanho sparked the tinder bundle of grass.

Griffith knew he was in a dire predicament; he could not be sure of all the places he was bleeding. All he could do was hold out, waiting for another searing pain. Valeria used whatever strips of cloth they had tucked into their waists and around their heads to bandage Griffith's wounds. Upon closer inspection of his state, he had lacerations of various sizes and depths scattering his body. His left ankle was bleeding at the sock line, leading her to imagine him using his foot to prod a spider away; his thigh was also cut, remarkably close to the femoral artery, a hint of some blindsided attack and quick reaction; there was a small stab wound on his left, upper back; *how did that get there?*

His shoulders were slightly raised and he held his eyes closed throughout the wait to the fire. The spider legs would undoubtedly have dirt and bacteria on the ends, having them be what they use to walk on and pierce things; soon after their meet, Lucian split off to get water for the flushing. Some of him still wondered if it was safe, but they had not felt any negative feelings they could attribute to the water. *Admittedly, I don't know if we could correlate anything to anything. Besides, anything we've ingested is bound to have some sort of long term side effect that is unavoidable if– and we do– want to survive.* Bruce opted to tag along.

"Boil that water quickly! Or else we might have to just cauterize now!" Valeria told her as they approached in return. Victoria and Tanho were both around Griffith, who was now hyperventilating.

Victoria distressfully told them with blood still slowly making its way out of her shoulder, "The blood seemed to be stopping, but apparently not enough. He started this right before you got here."

"Tie a tourniquet then! What are we doing?" Lucian shouted. Tanho stood farther away with his spear in hand, looking about the grassy fields and roots towards the tree. Apparently, something was watching them.

Bruce reminded them, "He's lost something around twenty percent of his blood!" Quickly, and as they had practiced before, they tied a tourniquet around his arm and focused on his leg. There was no spurting, so the artery was definitely fine, it was just pumping into the broken blood vessels. Somehow, his selective silence and seated position shielded his confusion and disorientation from Valeria. Lucian thought she may have just been stressed. Either way, Griffith was about to die unless they acted fast. He hoped it wasn't anything that got into his wounds, or else Victoria would be dead too.

They moved the clothing away from his leg, exposing the purple skin. While water boiled, they applied pressure. Lucian clarified, "I think it's just mild internal bleeding." Griffith was the most knowledgeable in first aid; they wished he could treat himself, although they knew they were also substantially qualified.

Lucian was very efficient at neutralizing the water, tossing in a new crystal that had no fire residue, just in case. It reminded him that whatever flammable liquid the spiders had used could be poisonous as a gas; he hoped it was not so.

Through the breathing, pale and clammy skin, and unfocused eyes, Griffith remained generally quiet. "It's hypovolemic shock, right?" Valeria asked.

"Yup, that's it," Victoria clarified. "Another ten percent of blood or so, and he goes unconscious." She still felt a numbing pain in her shoulder, but fought it; she could not afford to let the one who saved them all perish.

Chapter 8
SIMPLE PATTERNS

Tanho did not really know what he was looking at. There was some unfamiliar noise that kept reappearing around him; he hoped it was not of dangerous origin. He tried to stay near but refused to offer his help to the others. They'd be ambushed if they took their eyes away from the wilderness surrounding them. They were all stranded outside and now had no protection; *we should be trying to keep us all alive by refortifying our shelter.* In a sense, however, he felt bad for Griffith's predicament, realizing that he was in a similar state just a few days ago. Something about that kept him anxious, but he did not know exactly where the feeling came from.

After standing around, pacing, and watching the brush lines, he slowly walked back to the group. Seeing Griffith's eyes and the direness of his situation being able to blind them all from their group's safety gave him a similar, foreign feeling. *Is this what it feels like to be Lucian?*

Amidst the painful sounds of dripping water into open wounds– removing bacteria– and the muffled screams and sizzle of cauterization that reduced his focus, Tanho caught a bird out of the corner of his eye. It had dove into the edge of a grass field to the right of the tree, to the left of their rocky outcrop from where they all were. Moments after its disappearance, it had dragged its kill out into the open. "It killed a spider!" he announced, somewhat surprised but looking to distract himself and the others if they needed it.

They finally had a better look at the bird. Although it was a fair distance away, the size defined it in its more considerable intricacies. The pattern resembled that of their esprit, but the feathers on this bird were much more modest and slicked back. Corroborated by what they had seen throughout their time on Chaos, they knew it was built for speed. *Feathers*, he thought, *the feathers we had from the esprit were burned in the fire.* He was reminded of the arrows and fletched spears for some of his favorite bushcraft weapons, and it made him more anxious in its sorrow.

The bird admired its kill before digging in, ripping past the legs and into the strange, white core. "How tall do you think that is?" Tanho asked.

Lucian, Victoria, and Bruce were caught up in sterilization and cauterization, so Valeria answered, "Five or six foot tall, maybe?"

Within moments, as the bird had almost finished consuming the spider's insides, something struck its side from within the gold-scarlet grasses. Blood poured to the floor, but against the background, they could not tell what color it was. Within ten seconds, the beast was knocked out or dead.

"What the heck?" Tanho announced in perplexity, taking a step backward. Griffith winced in sweating discomfort, causing Tanho's stomach to phantomly ache. Lucian looked over to see the commotion, his hands slightly bloody from wiping it away from the burn sites. A smaller snake appeared around the backside of the fallen animal, looking around. It spotted them but did not seem too worried about its safety; instead, it resolved to eat its meal. It had excellent, bright camouflage and was of the same waving, interwoven nature of the grass.

It seemed to recoil its tail up above itself. As it did, Lucian noted the rattlesnake-resembling tail– although it did not have rings but a longer and sharper-looking end. He thought about the giant snake creature from one of their first days: *is it similar? A baby?* The beast brought down its tail in front of it and jabbed at the bird's leg, amputating it.

"A blade," Tanho murmured in confused awe of the animal's allusion and complexity. The snake carved into the leg and devoured it before chopping off other parts in a motion resembling a scorpion striking with its tail. It soon sated itself before disappearing into the mysterious grass.

They half-carried and half-dragged Griffith back to the still-warm cave. The heat provided a sense of solace in his soporific state. "What are we going to do about our defense? We're exposed to everything now," Tanho questioned.

Lucian was beginning to get lightheaded from the repeated exposure to fire, which was amplified by having to listen to Griffith's pains. "We should build it back up, or we could move somewhere; I don't know," he responded.

Victoria said, "I think rebuilding is the obvious choice. No use in keeping ourselves a target for the spiders." She felt the first and second-degree burns on her arms in their full intensity as her shoulder jolted in pain. "Do you guys think this needs to get cauterized?" She did not want to; she feared its pain after hearing Griffith and Tanho and the remnants of Bruce having gone through the ordeal.

Sterilizing the knife again to the best of their ability and cleaning the blood off, her already water-sterilized wound was burned shut. "You guys realize how dangerous cauterization can be, right?" she said after she regained her senses, reopening her eyes as the pain began to subside. She only felt the pain from the burns that lapsed over time with the dribbling of cool water; the deeper, more intricate incision's effect would persist.

She was met with agreement. Yet again, they all knew it was the only way. She looked over at the bruise beginning to form around where Griffith's tourniquet was cinched. She wondered what most of them did: *how did it happen?* They did not want to know superficially; they wanted to see it play out despite the injury. He was probably the only way they could see what had happened on the other side of the fire. Out of respect for the returned warrior, they let him rest.

Daylight waned over the next few hours, and wood was carefully collected. They took turns carrying spears in protection on further expeditions, but they never had to go far to get wood; in their generosity, the trees left many sticks at their bases. They took mental note of the size of some of the logs, easily being a few feet in diameter. The abundance of such logs on the ground seemed like the tree considered them insignificant. The few of the group moving sticks and logs would only have a means of transporting them with an elaborate series of pulleys and cordage.

Cordage, Lucian thought with a tired sigh. He remembered their dissection and thought about it. His weary mind filled with images of diagrams of deadfall traps and pitfall traps to ease the thought of frightening nighttime enemies.

He remembered the moving rock with vines on it. *Where did that go?* It was confusing, all of it. *Interplanetary Travel, who knew it could end up like this?* It was a blur; he did not know what to think, as was customary of Chaos. *Travesty*, he described to himself, referencing Chaos and its continuous shocks, sudden shifts in their minds, the change from optimistic to critical skirmishing in oscillation.

"Want to play chess?" Lucian asked, responding to the week-old invitation from Tanho's dire state.

"Let's do it!" he exclaimed, excited to have a challenge at something he was good at. "Rock paper scissors; winner is white, first game; best of three."

"I'm a little tired, so only one game now, the rest later– but deal."

Tanho was starting as white. They sat down next to the pile of sticks at the shelter's entrance while Victoria and Griffith rested. Valeria and Bruce brought leaves back and sharpened the sticks so Lucian and Tanho could implant them. There were already some impressions in the ground, but they had to extract the unburned bottoms before putting the new sticks in, which proved harder than they thought.

A chessboard of alternating colored squares appeared, the eight by eight grid engrained in habitual memory. As if reminding himself, Lucian recalled the dark bottom-left and top-right squares and followed his rule as if the colors of each square were not already present in his picture: if it's the same– odd to odd or even to even– then it's a dark square. 'A' represents the number one, so 'A1' is dark.

Tanho won rock paper scissors and said, "E4." From different perspectives, the line of pieces behind pawns stood strong and unmoving as the new image in their minds saved to have one protruding pawn.

The simplicity of the first move prompted no thought, for it was familiar. Lucian knew which moves worked and which moves did not without thought. He matched the pawn, going "E5". The two pawns stood face to face, unable to see each other. It was still easy, still the opening– still theory.

"F4," Tanho aggressively prodded.

Lucian did not recapture, even though he could without immediate consequence. He registered the immediate weakening of his center and the need to defend an overextended pawn if he wanted to not lose material and hasten Tanho's piece development. Still, he did not spend time on his move, "Knight C6."

"Knight F3," Tanho said, adding pressure and threatening to build a strong center. As he said this, Bruce and Valeria looked over at them. Besides their fairly blank stares, they still efficiently planted the sticks into the ground, multitasking. Their minds and bodies did many things simultaneously; they kept track of the moves, registered threats, predicted, prepared, and outwardly kept doing the job. The mind flipped back and forth instantaneously to do both in the illusion of a single moment.

The board became more complex, adding threats and tensions. "D6," Lucian said after a moment of thought. He finally pried out the stick-end embedded in the ground, looking around before tossing it to their wood pile.

"Bishop C4," Tanho said, being aggressive and implementing a dangerous threat of invading with his knight and taking one of Lucian's minor pieces. Of course, Lucian saw that, though, and he could just as easily defend with his own light-squared bishop.

Quickly, Lucian realized it was not much of a threat. He used this understanding to implement a mind game, immediately responding with "knight F6" to lure out a lost tempo.

With a few seconds of thought, Tanho replied with "Knight C3." The center of the board increased in complexity, yet was still easy to understand. The few initial moves set the foundation for how the game would turn out, and there were still many places where mistakes could be made. It was less a game of strategy and more a game of understanding. The board more clearly seen would be the winning one.

"Bishop E6," if Tanho did not realize, his bishop would be taken without consequence.

"Bishop captures E6," neutralizing the threat and doubling Lucian's pawns on the E rank.

"Pawn captures," the doubled pawns hurting Lucian's chances of castling. Somehow, their eyes saw the wooden stakes in front of them, where they were to be placed, and the chess board invisible behind it all. The vision persisted. The intimate game knowledge and experience shimmering between them echoed spatial intelligence in their multitasked concentration.

"Castles kingside," moving the king to a safer square out of the middle. Moving two pieces at once would seem challenging to envision and store in the game's memory, yet they both appeared in control of the game.

"E captures F4," the pawn decentralizing and allowing for the bishop's discovered attack. Lucian knew Tanho would have to keep track of the strange pawn movement. *I hope it gives me an advantage.*

For the next few moments, Tanho looked strange with his eyes closed and his orientation to the ground before changing to the sky. Deep in thought, calculating, finally blocking out the outside world enhanced his thoughts and memory. "Pawn D4."

"Good move," Lucian said. Tanho looked at Lucian, noticing no extended blinking before he said, "Pawn E5."

Tanho could either move forward and attack the knight on C6 or capture to try and win back his pawn. "Pawn captures E5."

Lucian moved his head back slightly and squinted his eyes, his face otherwise blank. He paused the implantation of the next stake for a few moments. "Tanho, I think that was a mistake. Pawn takes E5."

With a smirk, Tanho said, "Queen takes queen."

Lucian was slightly confused, "Rook takes queen."

Tanho realized he was slightly losing by now, but the game was far from over. It was still a complicated position; Lucian was bound to miss something and blunder. "Rook D1," lining itself with Lucian's rook that just took the queen.

"Bishop C5," activating the piece and getting his king ready to castle. "And check," Tanho could either block or move the king.

"King H1," putting the king in the corner, light square. Both sides had lost their light-square bishop and queen, leaving Tanho's king in a reasonably safe spot.

"Rook takes rook," Lucian forcing the knight to undevelop into the back rank. Now Tanho's rook was trapped from the middle by two of his own pieces.

"Alright, knight takes," Tanho said, with no other choice because he was in check and not ready to forfeit the game with an unintelligent blocking move. If he moved his knight in front of the king, Lucian's bishop would allow the rook to take with checkmate. *I can't let that happen.*

They were both fully involved in the game now, the chess board the only thing they could see despite having their eyes open most of the time. The information hitting the cones and rods in their eyes and being sent through the optic nerve to the occipital lobe in the brain was being ignored, sent straight past the influence of the hippocampus' memory generation, and diffused into nothing.

"Castles." Although a pawn was hanging, available to be taken, Lucian wanted to continue the attack with his rook. Castling would protect his king, as Tanho's king was, and bring his rook into the game. Tanho did not have to think about which side Lucian castled to; it seemed second nature in his wrapped-around understanding of the game thus far that kingside castling was the only option.

Tanho did not know what to do; he could re-develop his knight or bishop, try to neutralize the attack slowly and counteract on the queenside, or make room for his king. "Pawn A3," he said, overlooking the undefended pawn he could have defended by developing his knight to C3. The pieces began to blur from sight but were still clearly visible in the subconscious. Each piece had many moves to choose from, all of which had to be registered by the brain and analyzed to determine the best possible approach. The feat of memory, correlation, and piece coordination proved less their knowledge and more their love for the game.

Bruce and Valeria occasionally looked over, even calling their names at one point, but the game was too profoundly interwoven in conscious thought. "Rook D8," attacking the knight and re-implementing the checkmate threat in the corner.

Finally, Tanho realized his mistake, collectedly defending his pawn with "Knight C3."

However, Lucian placed his rook on D8 as an in-between-move for a reason, to amplify the threat that "Knight F6 takes E4" makes.

Tanho thought about the position; the knight was free for the taking; nothing defended it. It was not a good idea to take it, however, because of Lucian's rook. Tension in thought and between Tanho's eyes enhanced, amplifying the feeling of understanding a losing position. He saw the pieces more clearly, the strength of his focus shielding him from physical feelings. "Bishop D2," defended by his knight on F3, helped open up his rook.

"Knight takes bishop."

"Rook D1," he said, eyeing the rook through the knight. Tanho would win back his piece in one move, and now he could trade at any moment and get rid of the checkmate threat for good.

"Okay Tanho, I'll win a piece. Knight takes Knight F3." He felt he was winning, not by the position of the pieces, but by an innate inclination of winning and the impossibility of a surprising move on the board.

"Rook takes rook," he said with a smile and a light sigh of relief. The checkmate was no longer a threat; *maybe I could beat him in an endgame.* He still threatened to kick out the bishop, but it would be shallow; the bishop was not trapped.

"Knight C6 takes D8," taking the rook that gave him a check, now comfortably up by two pieces.

"G2 takes Knight F3," the game's complexity encroaching its memory-dependency peak. The pawn moves from minutes ago now were very significant; if one forgot where their pawn was, it could decide the game with a promotion or passed pawn.

To simplify, knowing he was winning, Lucian moved "bishop D4." He wanted to make Tanho think, anticipating a strong attack so that he could whittle down the pawn structure and go for a checkmate.

"King G2," moving forward and allowing the trade which would double his pawns. It was close to over for him.

"Bishop captures knight on C3."

"B captures C3," the game dwindled. Tanho was almost ready to resign; it was about over for him. His lips pushed into each other in a moment of frustration and silence to not signal it to Lucian. He was annoyed with himself for having lost his own proposition.

Lucian knew it was won as long as he remembered the position of his knight and pawns. "Pawn G5."

Without a moment's notice, "I resign," emerged from Tanho's irritated voice. "Good game," initiated by Lucian, began the customary handshake.

"Wow, that was good, Tanho. You had some fight in you for a while there. It was a hard game to keep track of."

The rest of the evening went well, dozens of sticks replaced the burned ones. They hoped the defense was still strong, but it was all different. They thought they could see between the sticks much easier, which reduced their sense of safety. The bed platform was now gone, some assorted leaves insulated the floor, and they hoped the fiery pouch did not leave any poisonous residue they overlooked until it was likely too late. "Well, even if there's still poison in the air, it's too late now to go anywhere else. We would normally smell it, right? I haven't really smelled anything," Victoria declared.

Griffith and Victoria, more tired than the others due to their energy being sapped to heal the wounds, felt a strange feeling before the others. Griffith was basically asleep and did not register it over the crackle of the refurbished fire that now had a stone ring. Victoria held her hand over the wound and occasionally jolted in pain when the muscle shifted in a particular manner. She felt a rumble.

"Guys," she announced. "There's rumbling."

"Didn't this happen last time? What was it, like five days ago?" Lucian asked, still tired but holding himself awake, displaying his eagerness to figure out the planet; Chaos was the most arcane matter of them all, the most pertinent thing in their mission to escape. Tanho confirmed the feeling, being more knowledgeable about the initial shaking and being injured the previous time. Lucian added, "Wait, that makes sense. Last night, we had the fenrhor, which was like the first night we were here. Then, the spiders the next day, which was this morning. Then the rumbling of the worms."

"Wait, that's really strange," Tanho observed.

"So it's like a cycle?" Valeria asked.

"That's what we'd want it to be because then we could predict what will be upcoming and prepare for it. There was the one day without any creatures. I hope that one comes back around so we can go explore," Victoria told them, increasingly hopeful. She realized they felt much better about their situation now despite her and Griffith's injuries and the shelter basically exploding. They recovered quickly and held a chaotic passion.

Lucian looked up with the fire's luminescence contouring his face, "I guess we'll have to see tonight and tomorrow. If I'm remembering correctly, we have a lot of chaos to look forward to." The grimace of renewed threat began to eat at their hopefulness. "But we've already survived this long; what's another few weeks," he said, immediately regretting the effect of lowered morale; he could have worded that better. "We can take it day by day. We've got this," he corrected.

Night emerged with dark eyes that consumed the luminous lands, dwindling down the oranges and replacing them with an ominous, ever-darkening purple hue. Slowly, with a silent yet electric potency, large creatures traversed the trembling ground. *How do the underground creatures know when to come to the surface; why this night specifically?* Lucian wondered. "So if it's anything like last time, we'd notice the blue light, the snake, and large birds at a minimum."

Semi-frequent, fluttering wings signaled the birds' presence, but the feather-suppressed and intermittently silent flaps refused to reveal where the bird was. "Could it even be a bird?" Valeria asked.

"Owls fly pretty silently," Tanho responded. From inside the soot-scorched shelter, they would be lucky to know where any creature was at any moment. "They're really cool; they have leading-edge feathers with trailing-edge borders, and they can fly at like two miles per hour. The feather tips are serrated to dampen the sound and stuff."

"Why would they want to fly that slowly? I don't think they'd catch anything if they flew like that," Valeria said.

The soft winds swept about them, bringing leaves of different trees together in tornado-ing collections, a taste of each world represented and thrown together, beaten against in a symphonic finale, after which the vibrant colors erupted upwards only to fall down and recollect. Where light was bereft, chaos shined.

Creatures swept about the grasses on either side of their shelter's entrance. Disorderly influence raised internal temperatures, permeating their skin through salt and an invisible steam. The protein messengers of epinephrine release strained in continued use, resulting in catharsis for two adrenal glands and a sluggish intellect for several supposed strangers. They were dendrites in their own nerve-relay system, with wraiths whose monstrous sounds composed competitive inhibitors, similar neurotransmitters that reduced the epinephrine energy spike caused by initial, sonorous shocks. The slow swash of enhanced strength and determination brought on forehead furrows, through which the eyes of many minuscule beads of sweat refracted the fire's light into theirs.

The blue light returned; the similar yet arcane mystery of five days ago was unveiled to them but not to the other creatures. Quick snaps of the luminance joined pained screams that drifted, windblown, to rest. The interest of the light attracted more than whomever it had consumed. The slow encroachment was masked by gusts and mastication heard intensely through an inner vibration. The light was gone in a struggle, rising hiss, and tumble through grass.

They looked around at each other with a slightly raised right eyebrow, hinting an interest easily understood. They silently, unitedly, wondered what it was, the pain unrecognizably diminishing with tiredness and fatigue.

Again in awe of their survival come morning, they took a long and deep breath. The sun, in its welcome ferocity, patiently absorbed the darkness and dark sounds. As predicted, the wind had dulled down to nothing, and animals of all types began to descend to the ground. They moved outside and looked around at the many trees as they had done the first time. Thousands of creatures approached their position– on the ground of Chaos. They hoped that this time, and this night, they would survive the onslaught. They had scraps of food remaining, most having been toppled over in escape from the heat. The reserves would hold them over, but waking up to every loud and startling noise appended energy that they needed; Griffith and Victoria especially needed to preserve their vitality, likely having to fight an alien disease, if their bodies could even recognize it.

The ground rumbling had subsided early, just as it had the first time they were met with the worms; it made lying down and falling asleep much easier. Griffith remained lethargic, taking a few slow sips of water, the rest re-arming themselves to feel safer while the first creatures touched down on the planet. The beasts were likely to spread out in hiding before hunting; if pack animals could group together, any individual hunters right below the trees would have no chance of survival.

Chapter 9

OF METHODS AND MADNESS

The day passed rather uneventfully, a surprise to them all. It was as if their door was a one-way portal, allowing only them to enter.

"Maybe it's because we're fairly out in the open," Tanho said.

"Well, the rocks would provide shade, right?" Lucian responded.

"Yeah, but all of the shade would be on the other side," he argued, looking at their back wall. "Although, maybe the creatures just hate being in the open at all. The grass is a good hiding spot when there are so many aerial predators." They could still see many birds and insects flying around through the opening, now slightly larger than before the fire.

Griffith noted no changes to his condition, the healing likely initiating underneath the burned skin. They hoped his healing would undergo quickly so he could travel the next day with them; although Griffith's body would probably still be healing his leg, Tanho's arguably worse injuries healed in just about one extra day.

They had to make it there before they could worry about using their empty day. A darkened night, more intense than the rest, asserted itself hurriedly. An anarchal silence marked the transitions of creatures and light. Although each night held horrors, and they had been exposed almost every night, they still built nervous tremors that came and went over and over again with the anticipation of death.

The sky was marvelous, nourished with stars that held no pattern and colors that cloaked the threat of murder. Despite the stars' shimmer, the exterior of their shelter became void, the fire losing the skirmish.

As silence waned, their brains froze in anticipation. A metronomic clock counted down the stars' inevitable decay. It was hot. *Temperature; catalysts.* The brooding mutation of light craved energy.

Spontaneity, a transcription failed, augmenting their builds through natural selection in horrifying enhancement. Every evolution, indiscriminately long per cycle, would further optimize annihilation in and of itself. Time held an infinitely accelerating degree of terror ordeal-ing in gruesome competition– the other bestial incarnations equipped with similar, unpredictable adaptations.

The fang of obscurity lapsed, baring intense reality in the form of abrupt, brash clamor. Battle cries of vicious fiends lacerated the air in threshed slashes. Sleep would not be an option; it was far too volatile just a few steps in front of them. They knew they would likely see the club-wielding colossus with an immensely malignant power. They were nothing compared to it.

"At least that means it's less likely to target us. We mainly have to worry about crossfire and the smaller creatures," Bruce observed.

A few of them clutched their spears, however insignificant it was. *One more day. One more day until supposed peace,* Victoria and Lucian thought. It was almost the only realistic thing they all could look forward to. Tanho kept himself busy with tingles about his stomach scars. He knew it was a psychological reaction to his atmosphere, but the knowledge did not ease the unwelcome feeling.

The wispy insignificance of their previous lives faded into clandestine darkness. Fires of shallow colors flared in fields of many distances, masked by their lack of depth perception. The picture-motion scene before them flashed intermittently as if composing the stars. A fierce flavor saturated the air, a bloodied riddle to vexing origin. Its scent was mystical in an exhilarating ferocity, heaving a denser air that was only slightly harder to move through. It concentrated the ideal, warm, catalyzing temperature for optimal battle.

Lucian wiped a bead of anticipatory sweat from his brow; *one more night,* haunted by howls and screams, held them from an exploratory mission of what could be a final survival.

A chaotic combat began somewhere in front of them. A toxic, bioluminescent bug quarreled against a smaller but faster predator. Perforating bites oozed a dull green, mixing light and blood. This beast could shoot flames, but in the midst of a close-range skirmish, was wildly inaccurate. Flames shot in spears fast enough to seem like the fire would die, but it did not. In the slow minute of contest, one of the spears flung just above their shelter, a jolt of unneeded remembrance to their present situation.

They chose not to speak, partially to not attract any sensitive-eared creatures but also because they preferred to pretend they did not exist. Only slow shifts escaped their cave throughout the night, kindly unheard by what lay right outside their home the entire time. Their movements had brought them to the back wall, and none remembered making their way there. It was instinct– instinct that brought them together yet set them aside from the native organisms. They had never felt so out of place.

A series of fantastical creatures blipped in and out of their one-way mirror of existence, the painful cloak blending ground to sky in luminescent annihilation, the spark of curiosity slowly burning it away until dawn breaks, too late to expose the wraiths of the night sky.

The surreality fell with the stars– they had meaning again. Griffith held his head up but looked down, "That was brutal. Maybe if I could sleep through that, I'd be more back to normal." He stood up but had to hold the wall for support, the limp in his left leg evident.

They walked out just past daybreak with peace restored to their fruitful land. "Come on, Griffith, give it a try. We've got to try," Lucian told him, standing tall in the bliss of redirected sun and serene breeze.

Tanho jogged out and brought back a good walking stick for Griffith. Nothing would get in the way of their exploration– Chaos was too dangerous to stay on. "If you need to, you could stay back here. Would you be fine by yourself?" Tanho asked.

Valeria added, "Or I could stay, but we could use everyone on the journey."

Griffith responded slowly, "Alright, I'll start, but I'm coming back if I need to. If you guys need to go faster, I'll stay home, too."

"Just see what you can do," Victoria supported.

They began their trek past the lake with spears and axe in hand, the use of Griffith's leg initially aggravating the pain but then soothing it in psychological hope of their escape. Subconsciously, they knew it was unlikely to happen now, today, or even within the week, but they were itching for progression.

They passed the multicolored fields that now had scorch marks and dissolved color, continuing hastily to the overlook they had seen the building from. Its polished silver brought more mystery. They were going to find a way there, hopefully this day.

"I really wonder what that is, and I really hope it isn't nothing," Victoria told them. She thought about Chaos and its intensity, "if people were ever here, this place would be way more mysterious."

The hill felt more treacherous than they remembered, but they made their way down cautiously, still faster than they had in their previous, smaller expedition. "Woah, Griffith, is your leg better?" Lucian asked him with raised eyebrows. Griffith was making steps downward with his bad leg, still using the walking stick but more as a habitual movement and less of an aiding support.

"I guess so, I barely even noticed. I wonder why that is," he said, somewhat happy that he could walk but not yet rejuvenated from recovery. He seemed to exert more effort than the others, but Lucian was unsure if it was just less energy or if Griffith was still injured.

At the bottom of their steep hill was a sloped field that curved intricately around large hills, rocky outcrops, and intermittent trees. The much smaller trees bordered the right side of the field and had a relatively dense underbrush, contrasting with the openness of the short plants in their field. A bronzed green flew beneath them as they moved onward, soon passing a curve where they saw a dense crimson forest. Almost everything in the forest was crimson. They were surprised they had not seen much of any bright red from the top of the hill, but they realized rocky pillars and trees with dense, leafy canopies obscured the forest from them. At least that meant it was likely not that large across.

The air tasted different as they got to the boundary of the red forest; an acrid, red-water-resembling irritation built in their noses. Seeing no way around, hoping no creatures were about, and hearing the slow current of water ahead of them, they trekked through. They took a mental note of the sun's position so they would not get lost in the forest, and occasionally, Bruce marked a tree with an 'X' with his spear. Red thorns outlined the bottom of each tree, some of them up to a few inches long. They looked like seeds, locust tree thorns, or some other strange defense mechanism, completely detached from the tree or any vine. Upon closer inspection, they were coated in some viscous liquid.

The red woodland was relatively barren except for the trees, spikes, and fibrous thickets. Instinctively, they moved around the sometimes large red bundles of plants and closer to the water. Past fallen trees, wastelandish piles of dried blood, and a few cow-like carcasses, they found a deep-purple river. Although it still carried the tinges of bloodshed, the water was ominously magnificent.

"Anyone care for a swim?" Griffith asked, now leading the group on his relatively natural-looking leg.

"Well, considering we can't see into it at all, and we don't know how deep it is or what's in it, yeah, of course!" Victoria said with a beaming yet mock-ish smile. Lucian closed his eyes and pictured what they had all seen at the vantage point. His brain sent back clouded forests but also clearly defined river highway intersections. His picture began to move, the wind waving leaves and treetops while water flowed down the occasional waterfall. By the vague colors and estimation from his memory, downstream would bring them closer to the strange structure.

Corroborated by their time-generated estimation and sun re-orientation, they went downstream, hoping the sound of the forty-foot wide water would not disguise the sound of a stealthily approaching paradoxical creature. Occasionally, the tips of rocks broke the surface, dividing water to either side, accelerating and seemingly concentrating the noble streams. One of such rocks lay farther out of the water than the others, where a small island was inhabited by an elegantly draping crystal tree.

"Another one!" Lucian announced. Its amethyst brilliance amidst the red backdrop emphasized its exquisiteness. They could only admire from a distance, the small island offering no bridge and the water's inhabitants unknown.

"Look over there!" Valeria called out, picking up speed from her already hasty jog. She saw an opening through the trees, a brighter space shining rays past the surrounding canopies. They moved closer but stepped away from the river to inspect the opening.

As they approached, they saw carcasses. "Why are there so many?" Tanho questioned.

Lucian stepped closer with Tanho to the edge of the trees, the sun's beams just inches from their feet. "Don't go in there, just in case."

They all looked at the empty land in front of them, devoid of life, replete with death. "It's a perfect circle, how menacing," Victoria said to their right. The circle of nothing had likely killed all that entered in the night. None of the likely hundred animal carcasses of assorted species was even partially consumed.

Valeria also walked to the edge of the ring, pausing before hypothesizing, "What if one of the big creatures lives around here and takes the carcasses back as trophies."

"That's kind of farfetched, but they could. Or maybe it's just a very poisonous zone, in which case we should back up," Victoria replied.

They returned to the water, wondering about the strange zone. As they approached the forest's edge, signaled by new color and light, they redirected their mental focus. On this side, there was a region near the water where no trees grew, a buffer likely caused by toxins in the water infiltrating the nearby ground. It was one of the intersections they would have to cross to continue their journey.

"This smaller stream is definitely not safe," Lucian said. They looked upstream, to their left, and saw the water fade and bend until it was hidden by red trees and raised elevation. The currents were brought together downstream, mixing purple with purple. Upon their clash, a foam raft of white bubbles held together, shielding the transformation of the water into a light electric blue.

They walked over to the merge, and their nostrils felt rejuvenated. Lucian acknowledged, "Maybe we shouldn't stay near the fumes for too long, just in case it's actually harmful." The sun was still not close to the middle of its arc, so they figured they had more time before storms started developing.

They now needed a way to cross the river and return safely. Tanho suggested, "We can follow the other river upstream. Hopefully, there's a way to cross up there. Or maybe a dead creature will hint at how to get across."

"Yeah, that makes sense," Victoria said. "With the way the walk here went, I don't know that any tree logs will be helping us – with how warped and bendy they were."

As they began up the other river, they reacclimated to the strange smell, realizing it was not bizarre enough for them to consider it likely poisonous, but still worthwhile to not stay inside for very long. Lucian said, "At least there are animal carcasses here. They've got to get here somehow, and I doubt they'd stay if the air was actually poisonous. Yet, we're humans and biologically unrelated, so we'll see."

Bruce added gravely, "There's no hope for us without this building." Although they knew it was not entirely true, they felt a dependence on the building. Victoria thought about it more, realizing that she, too, had a subconscious motivator; she was unsure what they would do if the building turned out to be a hoax. Although the others probably came to the same conclusion, she, and presumably the others, did not mention it to reduce any impact the building's actualization may cause.

This water obviously differed, with slower waves in a seemingly more viscous solution. The water smelled more potent than the other, with hints of sulfur amidst chlorine. On the other side, they could see a large field of low grasses. Many large willow trees with visible bundles of leaves like spoked wheels were spread throughout the massive area.

"How beautiful," Valeria said, examining the yellow-orange leaves and wavy wood. She wanted to build her mental image more, but she kept going with the rest of the group, hoping to inspect them firsthand.

"It really is something," Griffith confirmed, but he was more worried about finding their way back. After a few moments of pause and light jogging, he told them, "Make sure you guys realize we have to follow the path all the way back. I don't think we've been keeping track of our pace." The sun would continue to serve as their time management tool but would not help them optimize getting back with so much lateral movement.

"Look, there's an underwater spring!" Lucian pointed out. They picked up pace ever so slightly, already moving at a decent pace. He estimated they'd been on the flank river for over two miles. As they drew near, they felt a cold rush over them in the air. "Cold groundwater is coming up here, which is why there's so much in this bulging pool."

"And I didn't even notice, but the river isn't as wide anymore," Victoria told them. It accentuated the bulge in the outline and made the already viscous liquid appear flat. Now, standing over the water, feeling the heat being sapped from the cold water and air, she had an idea. "Lucian, come here," she said, beckoning the others to catch up to her. She asked him, "Do you think this could be a supercooled liquid?"

He knew what she was thinking, and after a quick glance further upstream, with no hint of accessible crossing, he responded, "It definitely could be." He decided not to speak up, letting Victoria explain to the others.

"Because it's so cold, it might be below the liquid's freezing temperature. Although it's usually only with purified liquids on Earth, there's a chance it may do the same thing here – we have no idea what this is." She paused, but they had a good idea about her proposal. "All we need is an agitation, and since we can't shake the river, we can try one of these," she said, picking up a stick.

She tomahawked it a few feet out to reduce the backsplash. The stick made a full rotation before impacting on its end.

"What?" Valeria and Bruce said surprisedly, responding to the stick's weird behavior. It bounced a few inches off the purple fluid before landing again, with reduced force, and sank relatively slowly.

"That's strange. I didn't expect that," Lucian told Victoria. "I thought your idea was going to work, or at least I wanted it to."

"Non-newtonian fluid, Lucian?"

"Yup, I wouldn't have thought it was that dense. Maybe the sun has something to do with it, or maybe the water is flowing below to concentrate just this pocket with whatever is in this stuff."

Victoria picked up another stick, throwing it from a lower angle, more horizontal and parallel to the pool in front of her. "Let's hope this works." It skidded a few feet across before hitting a jagged protrusion, catching it, and sinking it into the liquid.

"No way. Are you thinking what I'm thinking?" Tanho asked her. "That's so cool."

"Yeah, let's do it," she said, adding, "But we should test with a little more weight first. Lucian and Tanho found a decently sized rock, rolling it over first to be mindful of anything dwelling below. Seeing nothing where the rock was, they picked up their weight and rocked it back and forth, throwing it out into the liquid. Just as they'd hoped, it very slowly descended.

"That's good," Lucian said.

"Yeah, it should be able to hold us up if we keep moving," Tanho explained.

"Should lightest go first?" Victoria asked them.

Griffith mentioned, "I guess that makes sense; it gives us the best chance of figuring out if it's not going to work if we go based on weight."

"Isn't that you, though, Victoria?" Valeria questioned, somewhat confused.

"Yup, it sure is," she said, smiling. She took a few steps back, stretched her legs as if they weren't already warmed up from jogging, and did a high jumper's run-up. She continued forward, without the jump, keeping quick feet in the line inches downstream from the center of the spring. She calculated that there would be denser with the viscous liquid, assuming a longer dissolution reaction by the liquid's water-like flowing towards the river convergence.

She glided across, stepping down hard in each motion to conserve the fluid's solidity. She jumped forward to make it back up the bank, turning back to them and waiting. "Come on, that was easy!"

Tanho, Valeria, and Lucian crossed, bringing them one step closer to the building. They were now on the edge of their overlook's visibility, entering the page as a minuscule particle hidden to primate eye.

Griffith thought about his leg but chose to ignore it. He had traveled a considerable distance on the leg already. He stretched extra and picked up speed slowly so as to not blow out his leg early. The liquid would need extra weight each quick step to keep him from sinking. As he began to move across the surface, he could feel his leg pulse with each step, but no matter what, he could not stop. Lucian's crossing just before him made him more assured, keeping him relatively calm as he grabbed awaiting arms at the other side, helping him up the small ledge.

His injury reminded Griffith of its presence, as if it was forgotten entirely before. "Let's just get going," he said as Bruce crossed. They danced through fields and forests sectioned off by rivers, easily crossed by the rivers' erosion in downward-sloped travel. Each plot of land brought them closer to the giant lake, presumably at the bottom, as they had seen from up above now a few hours ago.

Judging by the distance they had traveled, they knew they were approaching the final island. Keeping near the water's edge at all times, they were sure to only go downstream in the right direction. As they approached another river junction, hopefully, their last, they watched the purple-green forest grow before them. It was not dense, allowing them to see the many ravines scattered throughout.

"Very ominous," Victoria commented as they reached a narrow part of the deep stream. In the distance, mostly shielded from trees, near their lake, a similar toxic glow highlighted the jagged tree bark. A few types of trees were noticeable, some with higher and some lower canopies, all in similar pinks, purples, and greens. It was a pleasant contrast to some of the boneyards they had encountered.

Using a stick to ensure they could approach the edge, they looked into the first ravine. The bottom was filled with spikes, and one side wound out of sight. A few unidentifiable impaled creatures spattered the sides with reflective blood. The stalagmites were crystalline green, similar to the glow they were now nearing. The gorges were abundant yet left large enough gaps between them to reduce their anxiety about landslides and ground collapses.

At last, as the sound of rushing water amplified, they could see the island through the trees amongst the lucent green heatwaves. This ravine was much larger than the others. It emitted a caustic smell of potent earth.

While the others displayed death, this one gathered opaque fog to make the illusion of a bottomless abyss. They backed up quickly.

Purple water touched purple land; the water was doubtlessly concentrated. Mixtures of many underwater springs of different solutions gave this lake a more-dense-than-water appearance. It held its murky viscosity close to the river estuaries but began to settle farther out in stagnant, level water.

About this vast picture, backdropped by every color biome except blue, lie a silence and emptiness by drowned sound, unchanging trees, and no animals. The yellow trees on the far right side were particularly noticeable, taller than the others by a significant length but nowhere near the largest near their shelter. The colors produced an iridescent effect on the water, likely due to some reflection in new molecular structure, creating a kaleidoscopic blend across the flat surface. Warm-colored petals of empyreal flowers spiced the mix, spinning on their descent under the clearest layer of liquid. Some petals remained on top; the white-hot sublime lilies reflected light and cast shadow to further dimensionalize the mosaic.

"How do we get to the center?" Valeria asked.

"We probably just need a boat," Bruce suggested as he returned to the trees. They followed him.

"I guess a boat would work, but we would need to be able to hold all our weight; maybe we make two or three boats."

"Teams of two again? Rematch?" Victoria asked as Lucian's eyes dilated. They set off and attempted to produce a craft to keep them dry.

Griffith and Valeria opted for a simple raft, using a broad base of less dense material to keep them above the water with a higher center of gravity, less likely to fall over. Griffith assorted layers of larger logs and ensured they could float on the mystery substance. They were held together by dense grasses found in bundles nearby; Valeria closely inspected for fibrous hairs or hidden stingers before collecting their makeshift cordage. Their raft did not have to be held together too tightly; it only needed to keep the logs together. Griffith's leg felt better but was not fully recovered from the crossing. They would need smaller sticks on top to act as the platform, but it was somewhat unnecessary.

Bruce and Victoria opted for a similar strategy but used larger logs from fallen trees that sloped upwards on one side. These logs would help them steer with paddles like a modern boat.

"This log seems heavier than the others," Bruce told her, straining.

"We better not use that then," she responded. The lighter and sturdier, the better. We just need to slowly make our way across. I'll go get some cordage." She, too, gathered grasses, quickly weaving many longer strands so that they could make several loops about each section of the boat.

Lucian and Tanho also went for a raft design but kept it efficient. As soon as they were out of earshot, Lucian suggested, "Because we know the liquid is so dense, why don't we make a layer of big logs and then use two smaller ones perpendicular to keep them all level. We would only need to attach the ends and keep the big logs from floating apart. The logs should be buoyant enough; we should probably save as much time as possible to get back home in case something bad happens."

"Seems like you've thought this through. Sounds good to me!" They inspected several fallen trees and collected wood with fewer protrusions that could reduce drag and still give them points to attach cordage to.

"Well, that wasn't so bad," Bruce said, stretching his fingers after lifting the weight optimally to reduce cuts. They pulled their rafts together in the middle of two estuaries, where the lake would be most stable. Lucian and Tanho completed their raft the fastest, followed by Griffith's team and then Victoria's.

They opted to conclude their mini-competition there, concerning their safety and not falling into the water on their way across. They made crude paddles from misshapen sticks, which Lucian and Tanho gathered as a triumphant *see what we had time to do while waiting for you guys.*

Slowly and cautiously, they boarded their crafts, ready to explore. The sun was soon to be vertically above them. "I guess we only have about an hour here before we should go back," Griffith said, his leg in an awkward state of neither pain nor normalcy. They moved slowly, careful not to let the liquid splash on the way into or out of the water. It was peaceful, the stirring current of paddling making purple particles rise in underwater secondary waves.

"Now it's time to relax; we made it."

"Yeah Valeria, we should all take a break. It would be nice to relax here for a while," Victoria said.

"It's very peaceful," Tanho corroborated.

Lucian subtly reminded them, " Yeah, let's do it. We can hang out for a little and still have some time to explore." He just wanted to make sure they could get back home in time. The return was bound to take less time, the unknown and spontaneous safety considerations already having been considered.

They explored their side of the island, with trees and shrubs more normal-sized, grass greener, and a blackened wall with a silver wire a few inches from the side.

Wide-eyed in surprise, Valeria jumped back with an audible gasp against a tree. Victoria's mind raced of possible detriment. *Maybe we should go back.*

Valeria, still shocked, called out, "Humans are here!" If anyone was inside the structure, they would have known that they were there by now.

There was no point in being silent. They backed up and regrouped. In back-to-back style, they looked in all directions.

"Swimming!" Tanho announced. "Something's in the water!" They looked over, Lucian and Griffith with only a glance, to see bubbles and a small wake moving towards them from where they had launched their rafts.

"Why? What is even going on?" Victoria alarmingly said to the group.

"I think something's happening! Did anyone hit a tripwire?" Lucian asked. A light rumbling developed.

"Did anyone hit anything? Touch anything? I mean, I fell back against a tree."

"I don't know what to think, and what's that smell?" Bruce asked.

"What smell? I don't smell anything," Lucian responded.

Griffith threw up, managing to say, "That's horrible," between breaths. The smell rose and hit them all. It was putrid, some angry blend of chemicals that appeared out of nowhere and was invisible.

"I feel horrible," Victoria said, holding her hand over her eyes and forehead. They all fell against each other, stumbling towards the silvery wall.

Refusing to speak so he could hold his breath longer in case the smell was a poisonous gas, Lucian figured there had to be a secret entrance. The building was definitively not natural on the planet, and there was no obvious door from what they could tell. *How can I find it? What would I do if this were my island?*

They almost forgot about the bubbling, only being reminded by the obnoxiously loud roar behind them. "Something is definitely going on," Griffith said, wheezing. Moments later, the smell subsided. Valeria and Bruce were on the ground, gasping, while the others caught their breaths against each other and another tree.

"Is everyone alright?" Victoria asked, able to breathe relatively normally once more.

Before anyone could respond, Lucian pointed to the water, where the bubbles were, and yelled, "Run!" Seeing the startledness of those around her, Valeria accelerated to a sprint before taking a quick look behind her. Now out of the water and moving in their direction was an awkwardly humanoid octopus, standing on two muscled legs, and its body sporting many defined tentacles. The legs were shorter, letting the larger mass of the head and arms be closer to the ground. It was a dark pink color.

"Get around the building! We need to get inside!" Lucian directed, the most aware of the situation so far. They could not take chances with being attacked, injured, or killed. As they approached the corner, they learned they were faster than this octopus creature. However, as they turned back around to look for doors, their eyes scanned the waterline across the lake.

Tanho took a double-take, refusing to believe his eyes for a few seconds in surprise. There were monsters everywhere, some new and some familiar, some large and some small. They climbed trees and moved around the ravines. "There are so many!" he called, panicked.

"We need to get inside, now!" Griffith shouted.

As they continued around the side of the building, being careful not to set off any tripwires, they saw the creatures begin to swim. They followed the wall to the far corner.

"What if there's no door?" Bruce asked. There was only one wall left. *What if the door is locked?* They ran near the wall and saw no apparent door.

"What now?" Valeria hastily questioned.

"We need to get in," Lucian told them as if they did not already know. He looked up; the over twenty-foot tall walls could lead them to an inner compound if the roof was not enclosed. *We can check the roof, find a secret entrance, or fight our way out directly.* "Anyone smart enough to hide a secret entrance would do it well; we don't have time for that. We should figure a way above and into the walls; some tree should do."

We just need to find a way in, Griffith thought, biting his teeth together as he focused on moving quickly. He was in front of the others and the first to spot a suitable ramp. He led them in an arc to approach the tree from the right. Upon closer inspection, the tree was slanted on another tree. It was flawlessly seamed into the ground, although it looked like it had fallen mostly over. The hungry cries of wraiths waned through the trees and soared across the water.

They climbed up the tree, a few feet of distance between each of them, into the green and purple canopy. Some of the trees produced the purple-fanged flowers from the water.

Further elevated, they saw the barbed wire lining the roof's edge. It got much darker above the building, the dense cover meant to shield the structure's existence.

Thinking quickly, Griffith slammed his axe onto the dense barbs. The wall was thick, definitely meant to keep out some of the more dangerous creatures. The trunk grew shallow just when he needed it not to. The leaves obscured vision as smaller branches increased resistance. Sounds dulled as he stood on the axe face, pressing inches deeper into the wire. Its rounded nature sprung the sides closer to his leg, but Victoria and Tanho were close behind now, jabbing spears into the sides of the wire and pulling them away.

He paused atop the wall, one foot loose and one on Jarnbjorn. The drop was steep. Griffith looked down and subconsciously trembled, hidden from the others. *This is gonna be fun.* They would have to drop the full twenty feet to get to the ground inside; no inner structure offered its assistance in their drop. He grabbed the longest spear that they had brought and held it point down.

He dropped. A few feet at first, becoming faster and faster. The spearhead implanted itself into the soil. He held on tight, bracing his hands. As his grip began to slip, his momentum decreased. The spear pole brought him to a slowed descent so his knees could absorb the rest of the landing. "You're next!" he called to Victoria, tossing the spear up.

Lucian was the last person in line, keeping an eye behind them. By the time Victoria landed at the bottom, the octopus had multiplied. "There's gotta be a hundred of them!" he said.

Their humanoid run-crawl out of the water and towards them was worrisome. The octopus is intelligent, developed alongside the human brain but wired completely differently. The octopi are the humans of the ocean. The distinction and complexity of octopus-human hybrids' existence mean their creators are pure genius, relating billions of years of continuously differentiating ancestry into one being and controlling it. The presence of the building and the humanoid creatures subconsciously affirmed their beliefs: somehow, someone diabolical had created them and likely manipulated their existence.

Just as Lucian caught the spear, looking down at his friends, he trembled with the shake of the tree as one of the creatures began climbing up. It lowered its center of gravity, as they had done, and held limbs extended to the side and back, capable of being brought in, raised, or lowered to maintain balance. He froze, instinctively holding his breath. He had to remind himself to breathe, looking back at the monster approaching him, soon to be within reach. He moved forward slightly, approaching the edge to which he could step on Jarnbjorn's side. With a quick glance back, the background filled with blurry movements, he knew he had no other choice and no time to stand still. He lept, and his heart fell as he did, cautiously dragging his back foot to bring the axe and remove the other creature's possible entry. He almost impaled his head as the spear descended and began slipping through his hands. As he landed, legs weak, they heard similar thumps outside the walls. As he stood straight again, the sounds became more frequent.

"They're banging on the wall, I think," Bruce told them, tapping on the inner wall, almost mimicking the sound.

"It sounds like it," Griffith said, pausing again before saying, "I wonder if they'd kill us or just bring us somewhere. As they are seemingly conscious and intellectual, they'd probably have a cage to throw us all inside."

Chapter 10

The Art of Perception

Standing in the inner compound, they were trapped on all four sides. Looking to the middle, they saw arrays of glass containers, some slightly filled but each a different color. Adjacent to the arrays was the laboratory, a small glassy room with a double door facing them and the strange chemicals. One side had a gray-marble-ish countertop with matching gray cabinets, elegant in design. The structural supports prevented them from seeing the other side of the building, but its small size and remoteness on the island led them to believe that there was an underground portion of the place.

"We need to be careful; someone might be here. Someone probably sent those things for us," Lucian said, returning his gaze to the barbed wire. *They better not be able to get over that, or under it, for that matter.*

They moved through the garden of toxins, complete with rows of flowers, all mixed with different species. They did not dare to touch them. Victoria led through the garden, now staring through the open, welcoming doors in front of her. A white marble staircase was going down, leading to two doors, one straight ahead and one to the right. A picture frame interrupted the smoothness of the left side wall.

"I guess we explore, right? We want to be here as short as possible," Tanho explained. They cautiously checked the drawers and cabinets amidst the dying sounds of drying octopi. Before long, they had checked every cabinet, finding nothing, and the creatures enveloping the walls had subsided their rudeness. The other creatures were drowned out or remained nearby, likely waiting for them to leave. The area was not quiet, yet they could not pick up on any noises, or at least any recognizable ones.

Nodding in affirmation, they moved down the stairs, following in each other's footsteps and the knocking of the spear's end to ensure they did not trigger any traps.

"I hope we find whoever put us here, or whoever wants us dead–" Valeria stated.

"–and I hope we can use something here to bring us home. I'm rather tired of this," Lucian commented. The door was a forest green, made of some reinforced metal. They watched their reflection grow on the door handle.

"I have a bad feeling about this," Griffith expressed with unwavering dismay, "and I don't usually feel like that." The door handle was silver, how Earthy. The ceiling corners were unusually barren; they expected to see a few cameras, but they were likely hidden well. *Who knows, maybe with this advanced technology, these people have many smaller cameras.* The thought produced a shudder, unnoticed.

Still stealthy, they crept through the door, eyeing another door at the end of a long hallway. The interior burned cool, flowing with a light blue hue that blended floor to accent wall. The shadow of rod lights about the rest of the ceiling obscured fine detail. A circular dot-light lay in front of each door on the side, alternating left to right as the hallway progressed. It looked to be about ten doors, each with a glass panel to the left or right, depending on which side of the hall it was on. A furtive walk, hugging the walls to avoid being seen through the windows, brought them to the first door and first view.

Putting his hand into a fist to avoid getting fingerprints on anything, Tanho supported himself against the wall and gently lowered his eye to the bottom corner of the glass left of the door.

"What do you see?" Bruce whispered from behind him. He continued to grow nervous as they held spears and the axe and moved further underground down a long and narrow hallway.

"It's a... it's a lounge," he said with a quizzical tilt of his head.

"What? Really? I thought it would've been more menacing than that."

"Yeah, I thought so too." They moved on.

Lucian suggested, "Maybe our way home will be easier than expected. I wish we got here sooner."

"We did just break into it, though, so it's not like they were waiting with open arms– whoever 'they' are anyway," Victoria responded while crawling beneath another window. Assuming nobody was in the close corner of the room, they could alternate from the hallway's left to right to avoid being seen by anyone.

The next door was to a staircase with a window into a storage room and two elevators. On the right side of the door was a poster with destinations:

Floor 3 - Surface Access & Phototropic Experimentation

Floor 2 - Design, Refinement, & Simulation

Floor 1 - Assimilation Access, Control, & Biological Innovation

After a brief pause of memorization and conscious understanding, Victoria questioned, "Why do they say innovation instead of experimentation?"

"This does seem fairly cutting-edge," Griffith said, inspecting the neatness of the storage room, filled with blurry labels of boxes whose contents would likely remain undetermined.

Tanho gave a hand motion, signaling their travel to the next door. Creeping up slowly once more, he told them it was a lab room with more doors inside that seemed to go far into the underground wall. Seeing how far back it was made him realize that this and the following few gaps between doors were significantly larger. "These rooms must be over a thousand square feet."

"Don't you think we ought to go back and see what's in the lounge area? We might find something else useful, and I don't want to get caught here in the hallway," Bruce suggested.

"Good thinking, I agree," Griffith affirmed; as he began to turn back, Tanho halted them with a closed fist.

"I saw something move," he whispered. At that moment, a goosebump feeling rose from the shoulders, up the neck, and about their foreheads; a silent shiver, an endorphin-filled full-body rush; game time.

With the quietest pivoting squeak on reflective floors, they began a swift yet cautious slink back to the lounge. If anything were to come inside, it was sure to be surprised. As long as, by some miracle, they had not been detected yet.

Lucian softly said, "I hope they think they're safe enough to warrant not having cameras everywhere."

Now, back at the first door, Tanho used closed hands to try to open it. "It's locked; of course it is!" he announced in a slightly more powerful voice, still hushed. Lucian looked up and to the right in thought. Just as he did, Victoria ripped off the laminated nameplate from her shirt, shoved it into the door jam, and pushed.

"It's a classic Earth door, that's for sure," she said as she gestured them inside.

"Wow, you're full of surprises," Griffith told her, smiling, "nice one."

They moved away from the window but remained close to the door. They were mostly sure that nothing human would come from the surface access door, so they moved behind the door, not caring about their visibility from the window. The door was locked again, and now they could interpret the room. A few couches surrounded a man-made, wooden coffee table; a lone fridge stood next to a sink below cabinets; and a wooden door labeled 'Storage 1' held the back wall together. A few paintings of buildings and cityscapes filled empty space about the light-colored, woodish walls.

"I think we need to see what's in the fridge. We could get some food to help us recover from the trip," Bruce recommended. The fridge offered a few unlabeled snack bars and a plate of moldy food with saran wrap over the top. They shared the few bars, holding onto the reflective foil they were wrapped in.

Tanho walked around, pacing the corner. "We should check the storage room for weapons and clear the building."

Lucian added, "If there's someone here, we can take them to control and make them tell us how to get back and why they're on this planet in the first place. Remember, nobody is supposed to be here."

They could reanalyze the situation now, in a more relaxed state. Some of them without shirts, all in rough, muddied condition and partially malnourished, were not prepared to take on an armored foe.

"We have to consider the possibility of creatures being dispatched on us here. We need a general battleplan, something we can fall back on so we have no confusion on our role. Team synergy likely won't be enough in such close quarters or without conversing."

"I agree, Griffith," Lucian said as Victoria and Tanho nodded. They all acknowledged it, but it felt like another level more intense; somehow, it felt more trying than living in a rock through the nonsensical attacks of the nights for two weeks.

They continued calming down in the lounge, spending a few minutes ensuring they were not being trapped before moving across the hall to the storage room area.

"It's bound to be a high-traffic area, a whole department of experimental research on this floor, so maybe we should only send a few of us. Maybe two?" Lucian asked. "Griffith, who do you think should go?"

"Tanho and Victoria, are you up for it," he responded.

"Let's do it," Tanho said, cracking his knuckles and grabbing a second spear, this one the shortest and with the least surface area. They both held their knives in a pocket sheath as backup. He peeked through the window and saw the empty hallway. Unlocking the door, they quickly jogged to the other door and glanced through that window, too. They disappeared through the unlocked door.

"And now we wait," Griffith said. A couple minutes passed with nothing. The air did not change in the room, remaining at a constant temperature. No sounds were heard other than the light hum of the burning electricity in the strange lightbulb system.

"Let's go check out the storage and see what they've got in here," Valeria proposed. A stretch into strut brought her first to the door. This door was unlocked, too. "Woah, check out how many gels there are!"

"Gels?" questioned Lucian.

"Yes! Gels! For nutrition and energy and stuff. Look, here, these ones are for stamina," she said, inspecting the white basket full of packets labeled "Stamina" in the same foiled packet style as the fruity bars.

"There are so many different types – there's 'Strength,' 'Vision,' and 'Recovery' too."

A yellow warning label was printed onto the width of the middle shelf and along the side of each packet, reading: Do not consume more than 2 within 4 hours. Do not consume more than 6 per day.

Valeria read aloud, "lasts for two hours," under the stamina gel's warning label. "These people have been working on a lot of groundbreaking work. On Earth, people would go crazy for something like this."

"As long as it works, yeah. Who knows, this may be a failed prototype," Griffith reminded them.

Lucian glanced at the gel storage, furrowing his brow before smiling, "These people are geniuses; I don't think they would just give up on something like this. They might have used their gene splicing in all of these creatures to identify compounds that react with our nervous system in beneficial ways. For there to be multiple types of stimulating compounds, they definitely developed something cool."

"How do these things even work? I can't imagine eating a gel," Bruce said, his mouth quivering in deep disgust.

"Gels rapidly diffuse the compounds into your bloodstream, quickly circulating to all your cells. Typically, they are high in carbohydrates, just like an energy drink, but immediately target the active muscles. So for the best results, if we have them, we should have them as we use those muscles or eyes if we do that. I don't know how that would work, though."

"Let's stock up; we should take a few with us just in case, I think even a vision one right now might be worth it, but we should probably wait," Valeria explained as she stood with an open posture, still facing the piles of gel consumables. Putting a few into their pockets, separated by type so they could grab the right type without looking, they mentally prepared themselves for some kind of battle. The further they were to travel into the lab, the more likely they were to be seen, captured, and killed in that order.

Tanho and Victoria opened the door slowly, partially scaring Valeria and Bruce, who were more encapsulated in the gels than Lucian and Griffith. They carried a few medical scalpels and shards of glass.

"It was very quiet in there, so we broke a few glass bottles, flasks, or whatever they're called," Tanho told them.

Griffith responded, "Yeah, we found some gel things you eat here, which apparently enhance an ability." He handed them two of each, "Don't have more than two every four hours, and they last for two hours each."

Lucian reminded them, looking at the door, "We should clear this place out quickly now that we've sort of understood what is going on here."

"I concur," Valeria said.

"Concur?" Bruce replied questioningly. "Why use that word?" he asked, verbally enunciating "haha" in a chuckle.

"Whatever. Why not?" she shook her head.

"Okay, let's go!" Griffith said as Tanho opened his mouth to say something similar. They moved toward the window and looked around again, seeing nothing living.

"Tanho, are you sure you saw something earlier?" Lucian asked as they crossed to the staircase. "Should we go see what it is?"

Griffith told him, "We should get to the main control area– where we will be the most powerful compared to them." He continued as they moved through the staircase door, "Here, if we get caught, we will be locked in a room and eliminated."

"It's just so strange that it seems like they don't know we are here yet; I thought we made quite the commotion, and only one thing seems to be on this floor."

"Maybe it's a holiday," Victoria quipped.

They moved downstairs swiftly, figuring Tanho and Griffith take the front, Lucian and Valeria the middle, and Victoria and Bruce at the rear.

They organized for efficiency, as Tanho was cleverly adaptable, and Griffith needed information to use his strategic planning. He was also the one who killed the spiders by himself, proving his ability to fight. What looked like two floors of stairs passed before they were met with the door. The stairwell echoed greatly but ensured that they were still overwhelmingly alone.

The inside of the building was spotless, empty, and dull compared to the outside life. Yet they were sick of the beauty; the safety of being inside a reinforced building brought them inner security, but the protection was only shallow with the possibility of the world's creators living inside.

Another greenish door with the same silver handle lay motionless before them. Carefully, they opened it to the apparent simulation floor. This hallway had no windows up front, only a few towards the end. That was likely to be where the design areas were. The first door on the right, made of a more padded material, was labeled 'Sim 1.' They could hear many sounds emitting through the door despite its soundproof appearance.

"Why is this hallway empty too?" Tanho asked. They walked down the hallway in silence, this time with less zeal. They reached the end of the three simulation rooms and peered through the first window. This room had blueprints and scrolls on which diagrams were drawn, most on a table towards the middle. They could not see exactly what was on the papers from the window, but they could see that this room had many layers of added security. A barred airlock, chains, and many layers of smooth-edged, reinforced glass prevented just about any possible entry.

"You'd wonder why the entrance was not nearly as boarded up compared to this. I guess that means either we're still walking into a trap, or this room is really groundbreaking that even other workers aren't allowed inside," Griffith figured. They spread out more in this hallway, taking up more space to close the distance if anything or anyone came out of a door.

Griffith made his way up to the door, inspecting the panel on the side, "and it's a handprint scanner or something. I can't be sure."

Just past the barred room was a closet with nothing useful inside except they could probably find something to do with random short cables. *Better cordage, or just to electrify or spark something,* Lucian thought.

More empty rooms followed, along with another lounge, which they decided not to enter.

"Something's still upstairs, right? I guess we better take the final floor- hopefully, there are some weapons there," Griffith led.

They quietly moved to the staircase again. The elevators displayed the same floor as when they had walked in, the first floor.

"I hope it's not just a meeting. Or actually, that might be good for us- we could take control without anyone noticing."

They opened the stairway door slowly, listening for anything, before creeping down another four flights of stairs. Now furthest into the base, they could not help but wonder what lay below the bottom level. The stairs continued, but the transition into a cheaper, more typical service lighting dissuaded their plan to continue their descent.

The final level- likely the most influential, important, and protected. The ominous 'Control' label etched itself in their minds; this area would be where they would take their stand. Immediately after they peeked through the small window, they were agape with the sheer size of the area. The middle of the large room had a fountain of purple liquid decorated with indistinguishable, elegant stone designs. Walking paths around the familiar purple, crystalline trees wound to many large rooms, offices, and three large boxed and windowed zones in the back. Two were smaller than the other. They could not be sure how far back any of them went. After looking around and seeing nothing moving, they opened the door.

As it creaked open, the ground shook. An amplified metal tapping vibrated the whole compound every few seconds. Interestingly, nothing seemed to fall from the ceiling. The building had state-of-the-art earthquake resistance. It would make sense; the rumbling of the worms and the massful creatures trampling the surface were sure to disrupt any experimentation. The labs were something special if they were somehow stabilized within the bunker. Measuring fine quantities or performing an intricate brain dissection would easily be disrupted by constant earthquakes.

"Where would the main control area be?" Bruce considered.

"They couldn't place it way off to the side unless it's even more fortified than this; a bunker inside a bunker, if you will," Lucian explained.

"They probably have it sealed in some protection, but it's so crucial they wouldn't hide it away. Left or right?" Tanho asked them, hoping it was indeed the first room on one of the sides.

"Well, if nobody's even here, let's just split up and catch up if need be," declared Victoria.

They moved through the door, leaving one of the spears as a doorstop in case it would lock upon their entry. The rumbling was cause for concern, but they would have no real benefit in returning up– they were effectively trapped either way. Griffith, Valeria, and Bruce, on the right side of their two-two-two formation, went right, leaving the others to go left.

"At any sign of trouble, meet back here," Griffith assured, wiping his forehead and taking a deep breath. He eyed the bulge of the gel packets in his pocket; *I hope I don't need to find out if they really work.*

Chapter 11

THE PINNACLES OF MUTATION

Tanho, Lucian, and Victoria rushed out of the stairway. They knew they were quite central in the room, the stony pathway being symmetrical. A quick arc left turned them away from the others. Looking up, boxes of storefront-like boardrooms, labs, and homes stacked to the ceiling, a few in each column. A few black staircases and hallways webbed the wall together, a strong fire escape of interconnected mystery. They could see that some catwalks met in the middle of the room, attached to the ceiling. Estimating, the few flights of stairs added up to 200 feet to the ceiling.

The first door, with panes of the same reinforced glass as the scroll room on the sides, was clearly the control room. As they got to the door armed with a similar biometric recognition lock, a hulking crash drew their attention. It was behind them and close.

"What the–" Tanho began to say as he locked eyes with the culprit. A pure-white wolf the size of a lion, a pure-white panther, and a massive pure-white spider entered the room. The wolf had a royal purple and a deep red eye.

"Run!" they heard from the other side. Any other warning they could have given was drowned out by the demented howling roar of the largest beast as it began strolling toward the fountain. It sized up the room– its new play area.

Now, giving up on the possibility of breaking into the control room with some machiavellian resourcefulness, they had a new but recurring objective: to survive. They got to the nearest set of stairs and climbed halfway up, the metallic clanking of each step failing to conceal their location. Each room on this level had many windows, definitely not defendable, but it made it easy to see what was inside.

Lucian strolled by each room, searching for anything powerful enough to incapacitate the creatures. Victoria followed, doing the same, but glanced at the other side, seeing the other group climbing up and away from the prowling panther. The wolf still made menacing growls about the middle, the spider nowhere to be seen. She found it curious how the thing could disappear, but she could not focus on that problem for long– they needed to find a way to group up with the team and kill these beasts.

Lucian held a jog, glancing through any window. Thus far, he had seen only desks, conference tables, pens, books, and the occasional computer or terminal. He guessed that most doors were locked, which was an added consideration. Lucian still had a spear, and both Tanho and Victoria had knives. He hoped that the spear used to prop the door open was either still in place or in an accessible area; either Bruce or Valeria would need it, and he was not sure who held their remaining one now.

The wolf, gallantly prancing around the middle fountain, used low growls to coordinate with its subordinates. Its mere presence was threatening; it held its head high and observed both groups. They communicated, the wolf the leader, armed with an enticing violence. It looked open, undefended, unguarded, except everyone knew it could not be true. Partially rough and tattered fur masked any scars left behind from previous fighting. They wondered what hidden abilities they were now facing.

The spider pierced echoing clicks through the cavernous space, disguising its whereabouts by reproducing the noise before the previous one faded. The noise seemed to rattle their heads, the blood in their necks turning icy. As their skin prickled, the spider made its appearance, leaping up from the cave wall on their left and landing straight in front of them. They were almost at the next staircase, but the spider blocked their path.

"Left or backward?" Victoria asked, primarily to Lucian. He did not respond, nor did Tanho, the all-too-familiar shiver of mortality causing hairs to stand straight. Victoria led them backward, passing the useless rooms of randomly assorted supplies and fragile desks.

Encapsulated, indefatigable, and ravening, the spider took to the hunt. Instinctively weaving left and right, dramatically shifting its entire weight onto a couple of its many polished white legs in effortless boast, it closed in fast. It desired the chase; it desired pursuit; it was an apex predator.

As it closed in, likely about to feign an attack by an outstretched, bladed arm, Victoria, Lucian, and Tanho darted right. A large room gave them space to move around, but the spider would be able to dodge and move about more effectively. *Do we tire it out? Will it even get tired?* A small room would appropriate stabbing; it would effectively back them into a corner. No room was safe, yet they had no choice.

It was a larger room, mostly empty– not ideal for combat against a superior wraith. Still, checking that their space was limited and not wanting to risk a reckless attack, they opened the unlocked door.

The spider curiously stood outside, almost frozen if it were not for the repositioning of its lower limbs in preparation for a jump or dodge. A loud click: broken glass. The entire wall shattered with a targeted tapping vibration coupled with a click likely produced at the end of the single leg point touching the center of the glass. Swiftly, it had full access to its targets and made a barrier of glass shards to prevent their escape. It watched, entranced, as three four-limbed enemies grouped together far too close around a metallic desk, having moved rolling chairs in a line in front of them. They were crafty; they were different. The all-white walls and miscellaneous furniture would camouflage it, offering no benefit to the warm-blooded movement in front. The spider had no need to seek an opening.

"Run!" Griffith shouted as the creatures crashed into their cave. From the swift exploration of chartless territory to utilizing its every aspect impromptu, they took to the stairs. The strangely albino panther slinked towards them with a sparkled gleam from the ceiling's lights. They were slower than the hunter and likely inferior in standard combat; it could leap up stairs faster than they could climb, even able to sprint more than double their top speeds.

Naturally, the panther is aggressive, using its speed, agility, and tree-climbing capability to outmaneuver prey, splitting off weaker links and consuming them safely above. They are impressive climbers, capable of jumping over fifteen feet vertically, leaping up trees with all one hundred fifty pounds of muscle.

"We need to surprise it; there's no evading this guy," Griffith called as they rose another flight of stairs, their pursuer closing the distance. They conserved energy, stopping upward travel in hopes of surprising it on a flatter plane. Looking over the left-side edge, they saw the wolf, amplifying the growled sound with an occipital association, inspiring added fear– they would not get used to being prey.

As the panther leaped up the stairs, it was obvious that it had not been in this room before. It looked around constantly and was not fully used to standing on the dark metal. As its ambivalent eyes sympathized to violence and might through one scarlet and one sinister, dilating pupils ascertained a crimson fervor.

Triviality. How important is our survival? Have we truly learned anything by being here? Of course we have; this is groundbreaking. Extraterrestrial life and perfect gene splicing. Earth would be annihilated. Griffith took his axe, flipping its molded handle to the pointed end. Assuming that the creature was no ordinary panther, hopefully, a lot of force behind a small point would pierce the skin. *We need to warn our home if it has not already been affected.*

"Look at its tail!" Bruce alarmingly shouted, finally avoiding eye contact in an upward motion to look for useful structures. A quick glance while backpedaling yielded a spiked tail weaponized with wide spikes. It looked like a club and did not hinder the panther's movement; it was flexible, allowing a potent tail wag to whip significantly more power.

"What do we do?" Valeria asked, hurried as the panther confidently stood, likely waiting for them to make a sudden move.

Quietly, Griffith said, "Let's get up or down one more floor, bringing it with us. I go on one side; you two go on the other." They nodded– it was a relatively basic strategy. "Hit it with your spear, Valeria. When you do, I'll try to catch him mid-turn and spike its head." It seemed awfully reckless and required precision. Griffith considered letting Bruce make the hit, but experience was crucial. They turned abruptly and ran to the next staircase. The panther began its next chase, building the desire to kill.

"Hold," Tanho held out his hand in front of the poised spear; they needed to conserve weaponry. "I think it's time for a gel."

"We couldn't possibly hold up fighting for two hours; we should have both," Victoria recommended, no longer making sudden movements while the long-legged spider stood blocking their escape. Unable to truly consider the downsides of saving space for a recovery gel, they began carefully unwrapping strength and stamina.

"Wait, split the stamina one so we can have a recovery if we are badly injured," Lucian realized, already having swallowed his strength gel. The spider remained in watch but began moving side to side. He unwrapped the stamina gel and took a third before passing it on.

"How does this work?" Tanho asked, not feeling much different, the layers of instilled fear persevering through any neurological form of confidence-building distraction.

The white ceiling lights flashed as the similarly colored creature lept to the ceiling. Several powerful and destructive legs snapped a tendon-muscle system at that moment, exploding with intense force in a momentous impulse.

Tanho launched the spear at the blocked-light shadow, a similar levered javelin toss pushing forward force from shoulder and bicep to bicep and forearm and finally to wrist and fingertips in rotation; each mechanism of additive directional potency grew enhanced and exceedingly amplified by desperate, fast-acting neurological chemicals surging nerve cell to nerve cell, competitively inhibiting the brain's natural transmission to the thalamus, overriding limiting brain signals, and further exciting the muscular system through rapid drain of energy, refilled by pure synthetic.

Rough, metallic clangs, the inferior wooden spear hoping to pierce before breaking the fragile tip against a dense target that pushed itself from the ceiling to their position. As Victoria began aiming her spear while kicking off to avoid impalement, Tanho's weapon redirected the front-facing leg spears, giving way to partially embed in the large spider's core.

The spider's surprised pain made it partially flail its legs, a small break before it was to reconcentrate focus on them again. They knew the spider, as any large, carnivorous creature, would be able to ignore injury in search of food. The slight shift of spider thought allowed the surgically precise roll to cover. Victoria evaded easiest, as the spider opted for the group of two targets, one of whom threw the spear, instead of the single, less threatening one. Lucian and Tanho strategically dropped from crouch to the ground in an explosive roll.

They could not speak– it would take breath and time, arguably priceless while actively prey. Victoria used the space to throw her spear well-aimed, with a wind-up incorporating a step forward, landing to the side of the suspecting target. It lept quicker than they could have, and with more ferocity than before, to the back of the room, its more comfortable landing zone.

Seizing the space allowed, they sprinted to the glass shards, offering the possibility of an ankle cut instead of a certain death. Lucian held on to his spear until the last possible moment; seeing the spears already used being broken in half and the other close-range weapons offering no use, he twice feigned a throw to create hesitation before tricking the spider by actually throwing it. The spear narrowly missed the main body, as the spider had a swift reaction time. The strength of the throw enabled the spear to scrape barely into the spider's side, oozing light-purple blood. The spider did not let the other wounds bleed, opting to keep the end of the spear embedded inside. The acidic poison on the tips did not inhibit the creature– it did not seem to notice.

As the wooden spear clattered about some desks, they jumped over the glass and turned left, dedicated to find some type of other weapon.

Leaping up three stairs at a time while the incessant clicks echoed throughout the room, they gestured to the strength gel, tearing it open and swallowing one each before reaching the next platform half-flight. Griffith knew their situation was dire. He ripped open another strength and ate it, the slightly sour apple aftertaste more amplified in his mouth the second time around.

Now, at the top of the stairs, they heard the tapping of claws on metal. As it climbed the stairs, its white shadow was visible between railing bars, and the sound became increasingly more defined, as if its claws were protracting the closer it was to them. *How did we get so much room between us? Maybe it was accelerating slowly or trying to instill hope,* Griffith thought.

With the rushing charge of strength-inducing endorphins, he felt the rising tingle and mental clarity of one fighting without the effects of the clicking and growling. Bruce and then Valeria had passed him on the stairs, going right while Griffith went left. He peered from the side of the staircase railing, watching the panther bound up to the final platform, catching his eye before Griffith backed up, starting an audible, flat-footed run. He spun around rapidly, holding the top of the handle with one hand and the spike with the other, flat against him to prevent sudden attacks.

As it broached their level, it turned to Bruce, moving towards a target now separated and mostly undefended. From its experience hunting creatures capable of holding tools as weapons, it learned how attacks could be forged by anything; it was used to the fighting and psychological patterns of human prey. However, they were different.

The clubbed tail was slapped by a spear; it was far more reliable to safely swing from a distance instead of jab from closer ranges. The sudden, albeit weak, attack barely drew the panther's dead-straight vision, offering no space for face-on attack.

He had to think quickly, backpedaling in wait for a strike or opportunity. As the panther gaited left and right, low to the ground for ease of leap, it curiously kept pace with Griffith instead of charging in. It could have sensed that they were somewhat skilled.

Another spear swing was met by a reinforced tail. A double-quick tail slap with unnaturally fast reaction time broke the spear, leaving the glowing crystal end to fall back towards them, splinters and rather pulverized wooden shards in previous glory's wake.

Griffith felt as though he might have to take on the panther by himself; if he made any sudden move, he was sure to be chased down, beaten, and killed.

"A little help?" he asked, almost beggingly. He did not want to give away his strength just yet.

Bruce picked up the spearpoint, Valeria holding the knife, and alarmingly yelled, "Incoming!" As both auditory and tactile distractions, the thrown sharp objects forced the panther to open its eyes, perk up its ears, and look back.

The sudden movement – a lunge – in front of it refocused it on its target. The strange feelings of pain and releasing endorphins would have to be ignored, at least until after the hunt.

It was flung into the opposite railing, eyes closed, tumbling. It waited before attempting to get up, ensuring its head was okay.

Whereas one would typically run away from the fight after landing such a blow against a deadly and powerful creature, the situation was different. They were not normal foes. Nothing could prepare them for ruthlessness like these humans had.

They closed in, Griffith seizing the stun to deliver another edged blow to the head. The first pointed hit was aimed at the side of the head, near the ear, where the cranial plate would likely give way for the spike and where he could get the most leverage. This blow was aimed at the neck, with intense speed that forced the firm grip on the axe to slightly slip in just the swing.

This attack bounced back and did not pierce even the white fur. The panther began to move again with a whirring tail that forced them all to back up. It raised its head slowly and looked again into Griffith's eyes before evolving into a teeth-bared smile.

This time, it would offer no such opportunity for attack. It prepared itself for a hasty chase.

The spider gave them a few seconds of head start, hiding behind the wall before again beginning a pursuit. Strangely, the growling had stopped– they could not be sure when– and the giant wolf was now nowhere to be seen.

Finally, they looked up instead of to the side, spotting a lab in its achromatic glory, the lights partially dimmed. *Chemicals.* It would surely be a reactive compound if anything were to kill the beast. Lucian was sure to be in his element if enough chemicals were available. From what they had seen with the water purification, Victoria and Tanho knew they had to get him there. With just the point of a finger, Victoria signaled a location for their split: Lucian was to make a break for the chemicals, while Victoria and Tanho took the spider in a different direction. The new team of two was the distraction.

The spider could easily outpace them, and they no longer had any ranged weapons; projectiles were their only option to hold the spider at bay, hoping it lost track of Lucian.

He did his best to shrink, hunching his posture and moving ever so silently at reduced speed. Slowly climbing the stairs, he wondered where the wolf had gone. It was no longer his problem, though– he needed to concoct the perfect poison.

Through the laboratory's windows, Lucian saw cabinets and shelves of chemicals. *Perfect.* The sliding doors inside were locked by a hand scanner. Lucian studied it, needing a way to get inside. The scanner had a place to put your hand, lining it up by keeping the wrist and thumb in the same place each time.

He looked to the windows. He had no pointed weapons to concentrate a force upon, and no piping or metal showed itself. He contemplated kicking the window down but disregarded the sound it would produce.

Yells reminded him of time– he did not have much. He could see no other identifiable lab, and they would likely also be equipped with the same locking mechanisms. He needed to find a way inside this one.

Can I short-circuit it? No, it must be watertight. He tried prying it open with his newfound strength. With no give, he still decided not to use the two-thirds remaining gel he could ingest on strength, at least not yet.

The clacks of claws on metal reflected around the large expanse as he took a step back and looked at the scanner and the door. The lights about the scanner were intriguing, lighting up where the hand was to be placed. Just then, his brain worked deeper through his heuristic of biometric scanners and returned the word *reflection. What does that mean, Lucian?* he said to himself. He said the word in his head repeatedly, looking around.

He tore some gels from his front pockets, unwrapping a few and dropping them off to the side where the creatures would be unable to find them. *What if I gave enough gels to the monsters? The side effects would surely kick in– whatever they may be.* He still stuck to his plan, but he now had an idea of what to do in the worst-case scenario. He cleanly opened four gel packages and cleaned the inside with his hand and pants cloth, orienting them into a square before pressing the intersecting lines together to reduce the ledge's definition.

He slowly placed the reflective sheet over the glass-topped scanner and put light pressure into the mold, holding his hand in the correct orientation. The palm print previously used on the scanner had yet to be wiped clean, leaving an oily residue on the surface. An opaque backlighting of the previous print brought definition, tricking the scanner into providing Lucian lab access. As the door began to open, he wondered why the bunker was not in lockdown and how the wraith at the top level played into the whole situation; the cleanliness, powered lighting, and inopportunely-timed powerful creatures from the stairs were not adding up.

It still has eyes, Griffith thought. The eyes could not be as reinforced as the rest of the panther. If he could damage the eyes, it would have to rely solely on sound. Regeneration was an issue; if it was only injured, it would likely be able to heal. He would have to lodge something inside the eye socket or remove the eye and surrounding tissue entirely to have a chance.

The menacing grin and pompous bounce to standing position caused them to step back despite their intent to kill. It was time to run once more.

It was now more irritated than before, having been tumbled and shallowly attacked. They had a single knife between them, and it would be hard to break the crystal point of Jarnbjorn off, enabling them to remove the panther's depth perception, requiring both eyes. The glimmering claws would give no access for a stab; if they went in close, they would surely be dead, and there were still two other monstrous creatures sharing the room with them; the knife would have to be thrown.

"Bruce, you're up," Valeria said after Griffith put two fingers over his own eyes and gestured to the panther, along with a hand mimicry of throwing a knife. He needed it to pause to put strength and accuracy behind a throw. He needed a surprise and a clear line of access to the eye. If it were looking at him or slightly to the side, he would have the most space to throw. Yet, they were still elevated and on a metal path, so a surprise would not be so easy.

The panther built up to a sprint, closing the distance incredibly fast. There was no chance they could make it to the next staircase or even bend, where they could pivot faster than the panther. Bruce, being slower, was in the back of their running line. Sensing the rapid closing-in, he spun and dropped to his back just as the panther made a leg-sweeping leap.

Redirection. The intense momentum and power in speed from the irritated beast let a mistimed jump open up for a powerful judo-esque kicking throw. With the metal floor as a strong hold, Bruce used his powerful legs to kick just behind the panther's claws, following down the arm and into the side, the middle of the beast, where the center of gravity would allow his kick to transfer the most force. The launch was explosive, motivated by trying to dodge the razor-sharp claws and the forceful tail.

Both Valeria and Griffith had stopped to face it, adopting a "no one left behind" policy. They were to try and face it, at least until their attacks were entirely futile in saving Bruce. It was unnecessary, though; the launch provided just enough force to move the panther in a trajectory that would bring it over the railing and to the bottom floor. It reoriented itself quickly, having swung its massful tail in Bruce's direction– a miss– to slightly null some of the force in counterbalance, from which it could then face the railing and outstretch its arms, clawing at the uppermost railing bar as its body slowly crossed that threshold.

First, one claw managed to go over the railing, and then a second one followed soon after. As the paws braced to hold the weight of the entire panther, and as Griffith moved closer to try and smack the paws with his axe, the sharpness of the claws sliced through metal, leaving the panther to silently fall to the ground, where its landing was unheard. Simultaneously, a heavy metal pipe hit the walkway and began oblongly rolling towards them.

A second weapon– a second way to remove the panther's sight. Luckily, the panther did not fall perpendicularly to the railing, making the hollow pole have a point and consistently sharp edge. It was an excellent stabbing device, especially if they could use the sharp edge to disconnect all tissue from around the eye. If they could push horizontally after embedding the metal, they could effectively scoop out the target. They hoped the eyes and surrounding tissue were weaker than the neck with its fur coating.

There was no time to waste. The wolf was on the prowl and the panther was warm with pique. *Could the wolf be invisible? Where did it go?* They had no time to speculate further. Now was time to set up another plan of attack; it was unlikely the same strategy would work again.

They moved down the path, looking into strangely oriented rooms that were not methodically designed at all. Metallic clacks and faster clicking frequency raised blood pressure; they kept moving and sweating, strength coursing their veins.

Leverage. Their armaments would be more deadly if they could further amplify the force behind the small impact point. Between deep, calming breaths, they looked to the back wall of each room.

"There might be a service exit. Look for secret doors, too," Griffith led. He supposed that they could find another means of escape from the room. They would only have to get Lucian, Victoria, and Tanho to enact their escape. There was likely more to learn from the building, but they had already discovered its malicious intent. It was more worth it to escape while they were still able to use their new knowledge to make a new plan.

They slowed their jog, now farther away from where the panther was audibly rising stairs, both parties conserving energy for battle.

"Someone definitely released these things on us. They must be hiding something," Valeria deduced with a visible facial dread of raised eyebrows and confused lips.

Bruce looked into Griffith's eyes. " There's no escape for us, even at the surface." He pursed his lips and gritted, "We fight." Valeria and Griffith soon matched, "We fight."

The panther would be less deadly in an enclosed space. Its dense tail, assuming it could not break through thick walls, would be unable to swing, and it would have to move forward and backward. If they found a well-equipped room, they could lure it in and put the panther in a spot open for attacks; they could surround it with more floor space. *How do we keep it from charging directly at us?* The sight of the claws now brought more fear; even a metal desk would not be enough to stop the blades if pointed straight.

They continued moving until the panther had reached their level, inhaling in a pause before sauntering ominously in their direction.

"It's accelerating! We need to go!" Valeria said, watching the walk turn to jog while its head stayed low.

They pushed into a room with lots of shelving and labeled boxes. They read a few labels as they moved to the back of the gray-tiled room, *nothing we can use.*

Simple metal shelves would provide a temporary barrier and allow them to slash or stab through. Boxes and paperweights could be thrown. Wires; cables they could use to reduce its mobility. *That's it. That's the way.*

Refusing to look towards the door, they bundled optimally-sized wires to throw through the shelves. They knocked a few boxes strategically off the shelves, kicking them out of the way.

Scratching at the door– it was here. Griffith stood in the center aisle, hands out to his side, directly facing the creature; it was a taunt. It opened its mouth in a humbling growl, exposing a diaphanous blue-violet saliva that dripped to the ground. The afflicted metal began to corrode, the coating of color vanishing.

Griffith looked to his left and right, seeing Valeria and then Bruce behind the shelves, and cracked his knuckles against the axe handle, bidding, "Alright, bring it on. Let's see what you've got."

Chapter 12

Inspired Magnanimity

Lucian immediately got to work making chemicals, using beakers instead of the proper mixing flasks and only estimating the amount of each solution he began to mix. Each chemical on the shelf was a high concentration, although different. Lucian quickly realized these chemicals to be of much higher molarity than normal, ordered chemicals. *This is the good stuff.*

His first idea was to make something very sticky– something that could be thrown at the eyes or mouth and would reduce its power. He quickly found cyanoacetate through the alphabetical sorting system. While placing the chemical in a beaker, he scanned for an empty vial. He then found formaldehyde, nitrate, and baking soda and quickly poured some of each into the vial, careful to put the stopper on immediately to reduce vapors influencing the contents.

He grabbed the polyethylene container of highly concentrated hydrofluoric acid, an already labeled vial of hydrogen cyanide, and another beaker which he filled halfway with sodium hydroxide. He made sure to take the ones with the highest concentrations.

On the way out, he placed the sodium hydroxide strong base right outside the door at the scanner and a chair propping the door open. No alarm sounded as he began to follow the sounds of apparent sword fighting.

As he approached the staircase down to their level, he looked back to the lab, knowing that he had to go back there soon. The chemical possibilities were endless, and he could create very potent and designed poisons to fight the various surface creatures.

Still, the wolf was missing as he saw the spider dancing and slashing at Tanho and Victoria simultaneously. Both of them had impromptu shields– Tanho using a metal pole and Victoria using a conical metal lamp top. Each of the spider's explosive motions left dents in the metal where the sharp tip had partially embedded and still not broken off. Lucian observed them enter another room and move around, evading a charging attack and deflecting any attacks. They continued stalling.

Lucian slid the hydrofluoric acid to the side while in motion, the friction bringing it to a stop against the railing to the right side wall. He opened the vial of formaldehyde solution that he had prepared and dumped it into the cyanoacetate. He shook the beaker slowly and then quicker, now accelerating his walking into a jog while keeping his legs tense to optimize how quiet his steps were.

Victoria and Tanho slid around a brick half wall, turning back to see the liquid splash all over the spider, dripping onto the floor, rapidly becoming more viscous in contact with the air.

"Ready your weapons! Sixty seconds!" Lucian called from around the corner. He would have to back up, unable to damage the core of the beast quickly. He went back to his other container and opened the door to a room, looking left for any sign of the wolf. Across the arena, he saw a wall of glass shatter, his brain filling in the audio waves with the sound the spider had previously made. He looked back, peering his head around the corner to watch the spider stumble and swing many of its legs, ridding a miniscule amount of the quickly setting liquid. The few heavy drops flung onto the flooring and inside walls, mixing with the initial dripping to repair some of the holes caused by the spider's stomping and pivoting.

It thrashed more and more as it began to stiffen, crashing into desks, tables, and lamps, auditory stimuli coupling with the spider's mental beginnings of panic from forced visual and physical stagnation. The wait for a paralysis crescendo lingered, continually slowing movement despite the spider's resilience and determination. It fought to keep the glue from curing, shaking and still managing to walk towards Tanho and Victoria, now keying in to its affliction.

They backed up, still cautiously, but relieved of some pressure. Tanho stood up straight instead of his slightly lowered and more agile posture, watching the spider struggle as its strangely prismatic eyes were half swallowed by the cloudy fluid.

Together, he and Victoria walked backward to the other side of the room, picking up speed as the spider continued moving towards them, rather quickly.

In an explosive slash, the spider lunged and fully extended a limb in a swipe at Tanho's waist, taking advantage of the poor foot placement and backwards orientation. By moving around the room backwards and keeping one eye on the spider at all times, his mind was not comfortable with the remainder of space behind him; it was hard to move backwards.

The spearpoint shimmered as it began its arc, accelerating closer to his stomach. Victoria dropped the shield and firmly grasped his back collar and pulled, bringing them backwards and to the floor.

As the spider had used a burst of energy, it took a moment to recover. This moment completely set the superglue, freezing all of the spider's lower limbs and half of its body. It flailed its upper limbs before stopping, conserving energy to try again soon.

Victoria stood up and threw her makeshift shield. *It didn't react; it really is stuck.* She moved closer, still weary of the spider's power. It was standing upright, keeping its core above the floor.

"Make a cut! I've got acid!" Lucian instructed.

Victoria moved away from the mouth but stayed near its eyes, weaving between frozen spider legs while out of its vision and using two hands to make a long slash. She used her weight and leverage in falling to the floor to slice deeper and keep slicing momentum. Lucian got closer and very cautiously scooped and splashed some hydrofluoric acid over the cut, ensuring it would seep inside.

As foreseen, the acid did not have much of a reaction on the outer layer. But inside, they could hear the bubbling corrosion of soft tissue as well as the creaking of straining legs. Standing out of the way, they moved around to where they could see more eyes. They moved up, rolling back in the head while its core shifted and struggled against its own immobilized legs. More bluish liquid pooled out before the many iridescent eyes stagnated in lifeless agony. They could not speak as they stood, unmoving, watching the body finally come to a stop, some type of neurological spasm manipulating the torso for seconds after the eyes died.

Tanho picked up a white pen holder and flung it at the stiff spider. It bounced off with a clack, the spider inanimate. He still did not trust that it had been killed.

Victoria stabbed it again, "anything would react to that. I think it's dead." They took the conical shade and placed an edge onto the joint between the core and leg. Griffith used the side of the axe to send an impulse directly into the joint on the angle of the thin metal object. It was like a horizontal swing of the axe, but much more accurate. A few taps of escalating strength were enough to separate the leg.

"Okay yeah, it's definitely dead," Tanho admitted, picking up the fifth leg they had dismembered.

***

The panther trekked forward, sniffing the air and inhaling its own poisonous fumes. As it moved forward, a drop of the saliva hit its leg, rolling off and leaving no observable change.

"Come at me, big guy," Griffith beckoned, putting his back to the panther and moving away, *it's the chase.* He tried to look frightened and less stoic, opening his eyes more and inhaling audibly to mimic a stress response.

It began to follow him, going through the doors and then to the main entrance rug meant to reduce dust. A drop melted through the rug and into the less defended tile. It stared into the back of Griffith's head; it wanted to chase, but something felt off. It turned to the left, leapt up the side wall, pivoted away from the back corner, and kicked off the wall, eyes now locked deep into Bruce's soul.

"Watch out!" Valeria screamed while the panther jumped up.

Bruce stood, frozen, eyes matched intently. He smiled, unsure why. He could not be sure if it was the feeling of death, or just that of chronic lost hope. As time slowed and the panther drew close, his brainstem pulsed fight, flight, or freeze while his amygdala screamed. He held it back, and in a moment, his pupils dilated and his muscles flushed with epinephrine adrenaline.

His legs backpedaled as he used his right hand to fling a cable roll. Bruce's left hand grabbed onto a full shelving unit and began to pull. He did not realize the swiftness of his secondary reaction time until they all watched the unit crash into its white-furred side. The cable hit the back wall, its landing unhearable over the sounds of dissolving metal and crashing.

The tail snapped back, smashing the metal supports, wooden ledges, and boxes full of miscellaneous items. It clawed and leapt once more. This time, Bruce was more prepared, running out of the way, pulling on bars to increase his momentum. He moved back through to Valeria's side, where Griffith now stood tall in wait behind an invisible corner.

It slid against the tile, retracting claws to not cut through the floor. It was a weakness; the panther had to control when its claws were extended. Even if it were able to do so rapidly, they could still take advantage of it. They could cut the tendons, inhibiting brain signals to produce movement– it would take a long time to get used to, and would be harmful in fight.

From still behind the shelf, Valeria yelled "It might have regular panther anatomy!" She noted how their experience on the planet changed their mindset. They knew it resembled a panther, *but maybe it actually is a panther.*

Griffith looked at the panther, first from nerves centering the brain, then as very lean muscles, and then back to the fur. Its leg movements felt more predictable, seeing, imagining what was going on inside. Its skin was durable, even the fur not giving way for the crystal-sharp blade.

It charged him as Bruce passed to Valeria, her ready to hand him more cable. Griffith, instead of moving backwards, pushed forward, instantly transferring weight from one leg and side to the other, mixing up which side the swing could come from. He opted for the spiked end again. It felt heavy in his hands.

It went for his neck, jumping with arms outstretched in a deadly hug and its tail slightly upward. Griffith held the handle with two hands, smashing the axe into the side of the panther's head once more while also deflecting the arm of the right side claw. The force transferred through the spike tip slammed the panther midjump into the shelving. It got up instantly, and moved to open space.

It knocked over the remaining shelves, reducing the area for all of them to walk on. Within seconds, it laid low and locked eyes with each of them at the same time. It tilted its head slightly while the three of them spread out. The plan was simple: find a weakness and exploit it.

Valeria took a long and flexible cable and tied a simple lasso. She opened it up and left it flat below her, making sure the panther could not see what had happened. As it danced over with Griffith, she fed the wiring through shelving supports and held it firmly in one hand. After she pulled it taut, she would have to wrap it around something to not have to hold the entire force with just her hands. She held it halfway through a mostly collapsed unit, so she could pull it back far enough to wrap around.

Bruce took note of her plan, and Griffith had nowhere else to go.

"Get over here!" Bruce shouted and turned the corner to Valeria's new position. He had coiled the rope a few times, holding a weighted cable end.

Griffith jumped over a few boxes and went to them, the panther not wanting all of them to get out of the door. Griffith saw Bruce through the open spaces, and took the outer arc in rounding the corner. Leaving room for Bruce to throw his rope in a similar arc at the panther's mid-air level so that it would hit the panther from the side instead of straight on. With the panther now in bounding stride to make it to the corner swiftly, the cable fed between the forward and backward legs, feeding length until swinging around the panther's front-right leg as new axis of rotation, slowly closing the cable-end in, fully wrapping itself around the panther's front legs. With the equal force of gravity, the cable did not yet slide off, offering a preemptive pull to cinch the front legs even more.

As the ground made contact, Valeria pulled too, wrapping her coiled end around a support pole. It struggled greatly, but its limbs were constricted by elbow-like hinge joints that gave it mostly forward and backward mobility, particularly useless when both front legs were tied together, so straining backwards was not feasible.

Griffith closed in again as the closest shelf, the one that Bruce was using as a brace, fell further down. Bruce struggled and fell backwards, using his feet as added traction. The unequal force and the panther's shifting spun it slowly, giving Griffith access to the side of the body, which he quickly capitalized and overhead chopped with the blade. He had practice splitting wood, as he had done growing up through scouting and just for any fire, aiding his strength gel in maximizing damage. Griffith did not aim for the middle, where he was likely to come across bones, a very intricate network that would require too much precision to slice between. Griffith aimed for the side closest to him, placing only half of the blade over the panther to reduce friction over time, allowing for a more damaging cut.

The crystal struggled at first, applying an intense initial resistance before pushing through and between the small hairs. The panther growled as its stomach developed a significant gash. A tensioned ping snapped across Valeria's cable and Bruce's cable began to unwind.

Griffith took their strained sounds as a signal to continue attacking. He swung multiple times, his axe raising and dropping with more blue blood each time. It was working; no doubt, if he hit the panther in its center, the axe would not have cut through.

Griffith used the momentum of the previous swing to hasten his next, now targeting the animal's tied wrist from a diagonal angle to hit perpendicular and transfer the most force over the still-sharp edge. It began to cut.

The panther stood again, blood dripping from its stomach, the minor wrist injury unaffecting. Griffith was pushed back by the risk of impenetrable claws.

"We have to let it bleed more. It'll weaken," Bruce said. Valeria still held on to her cable as both Griffith and Bruce moved closer to her. Holding onto the cable, they could keep the panther farther away and let it bleed out slowly. It was not an easily healable cut, and it could not apply pressure to the wound to aid the healing process. Its back legs were being pulled through a gap opposite where the panther wanted to go– to get to them. It pulled and as soon as its front legs were free, it scratched against the cable, breaking it instantly.

"It has bled a lot; just avoid its attacks," Griffith assured them.

They could've made a break for the door earlier, but now it was not an option. The panther's white coat began absorbing the superheated blood, producing a steam similar to that of its mouth. It growled at them, a furious look on its face, and began its retreat to the door– they let it go.

They stayed in the room for a solid minute, resting against the wall, stretching and flexing hands and arms, and observing the room's carnage. The blood had cooled, producing less steam. It coated a large portion of the far side of the room, scratch-marks and impressions by the struggling creature causing imperfections in the liquid's surface.

Upon leaving the room, walking with consciously open eyes to search for remaining enemies, they saw its body. It lie to their right just twenty feet from the door. In any other situation, they would've tried to get the teeth or claws, but they could not be sure if it were even possible, if not deadly for them. Across the room, they saw Victoria, Lucian, and Tanho. They were all still alive.

They met on the second level, being cautious of the wolf still lurking somewhere. Tanho gave Bruce and Valeria their own white spear, the legs straightening with a process resembling rigor mortis.

"Do you guys know where the wolf went?" Lucian asked.

"Nope, we lost it pretty soon after we began fighting," Griffith responded.

Tanho added, "We think it left, but I have no idea why." They were still roughed up by the intense battles.

"How was the spider? It looked very scary," asked Valeria.

Victoria answered, "oh, wasn't so bad. Just a long reach, fast speeds, and unpredictable behaviors. And I can't forget to mention how strong it was. Lucian made a glue for it and we got to its abdomen after that. Died pretty quickly when we poured acid in it."

"So how was that panther? Didn't look too difficult," Tanho smirked with smug tone.

Bruce defended them, saying, "But you didn't see what else it could do. It had highly corrosive saliva and was resistant to head injuries." He left out the failed eyesight removal, keeping their integrity of success.

Now back as a group, Griffith changed tone, "So you got into a lab? Lucian, what other things can we get from there; what's useful?" "Well, we've got the basic acids and bases and things like that, but we can definitely make explosives and toxins. I think it will just end up being situational, and besides, we have to remember the reactions for them to work out. For instance, there's this really simple reaction with potassium permanganate and glycerin that lights basically anything on fire– I want to try it."

"Alright, we should get a few things from there and then find a way out of this place." They knew it would not be optimal to carry beakers and containers everywhere, seeing Lucian with his hands full.

"Maybe we just take one thing that different people can wield while we still have the spider legs. We can put a nice poison on the tips, that might be useful," Lucian suggested. "The fire thing is useful, it even works with wet materials. I think we should use that."

"Good with me, but that acid is really nice. We just need to worry about exposure, but it's like that with everything," Victoria praised as they approached the lab.

Lucian confirmed for all of them, saying, "they can all be placed in pockets. We don't need to take the big things; carry light, you know." They grabbed the chemicals through the propped-open door and made their way to the large rooms at the back of the room.

"So this is the assimilation access point, it looks like," Victoria presented. They went up to the door, unable to fully see through to what was going on. Curtains blocked most of their vision. It was far too late to go back to their base and there was no reason to. This base had more than they ever could gather, and was safer assuming no more creatures would come in and that they were not being watched.

"Which door do we go through?" Bruce asked. They went to the left-most door, the closest to where they were, and the largest of the three rooms. There was a large warehouse-sized door next to the double doors. All was quiet as they grew more curious, touching the door handle.

"Locked, nice," Griffith said sarcastically. It was an easy pick though– Lucian showed them a hidden panel and pulled out his rectangle of foil. *Magic.* They subconsciously registered that this room had higher security than the rest of the rooms. It was something they could not ignore. Watching the lock buzz green refuted their thoughts of taking the control room– there was still time and they seemed to be alone again.

Lots of lab-equipment, chemicals, vials, and mechanical devices. Claw-like machines and tangles of wire hung over the gigantic vat of blue solution centering the room. Their nostrils and eyes burned of formaldehyde and a scent of sulfur seemed to float in that few feet off the floor.

They propped the door open, "we need some ventilation in here," Bruce said. As he turned back from placing a chair in the door, he saw an unlabelled panel. "Woah, take a look at this!"

Inside were typical gas shut-off valves, gas monitors, electrical switches, and the breaker. One of the switches was labeled Computer Systems. They had not registered the computers and chairs that had been turned off to the left side of the room, focusing more on the large room, trying to figure out exactly what it was and what it was for.

"Let's switch it on and see what these computers have for us," Victoria suggested. After they turned on the power and the computer systems switch, she went to the main system and found the power buttons in the form of a single switch in the middle of the array under a transparent cap.

There were multiple layers of computer screens, having diagrams, development status, and chemical levels with variable settings from top to bottom, respectively.

Lucian pointed and gathered, "look at that one! Something is being grown in the liquid!" It was small and still very much developing in the image.

"What is it?" Valeria asked.

"Four limbs? That's basically all we know. Well, that and it's in this gigantic area. They're obviously growing something, maybe it's the creatures we encountered up top. That would confirm what we've been thinking." Griffith observed.

"We need to get out of this place, off this planet," Victoria felt, the cumulative feelings from the previous two weeks adding through a scared reminder of hopelessness all at once. She looked down to the end of the room, which had a type of railway that continued and bent to where they could make it to the surface, however far away.

Lucian spoke up, "Maybe from here we can send a signal to our people. I didn't see any satellites up top, but they could be integrated into trees or something. Worst case, I think I could salvage to make a signal and send it into space, past the atmosphere as Victoria hypothesized a while back."

They moved back to the large room and scanned again for the wolf, completely unsure when it left. There was only one way out, unless it had found a secret way or was just inside one of the side rooms– the stairs. If they were caught off guard in the stairwell, they would not be able to defend themselves; if the wolf was able to get past their spears, they would be very likely to have casualties.

Next was to the lab, where Lucian could prepare his firebomb in the form of a two step process. Just a few vials and other containers of potassium permanganate and glycerin to be thrown against a target. They were not sure what would be effective against the giant creatures they had seen at night– they could not get close and did not know what would affect what. The corrosive acid was supplied, and another version of superglue was all placed in two unbranded backpacks they collected from the back storage room. Nothing within the backpacks gave them any clue to their previous owners.

On their way out, Victoria thought, "Wait! Before we go, we should make a knockout gas. Something rapidly diffusing and potent to give us some time to run, another last ditch escape attempt."

"Oh wait I've got the perfect idea," Lucian said. "Just you wait and see." He hid his quick concoction and they left the lab.

Clicking. *Not again.* "What! It's back?" Lucian questioned with an open mouth. It peered out of the same room it had just died in, flaking off superglue.

"How is it doing that? It couldn't move earlier," Griffith asked as if they would have an answer.

The panther, no longer bleeding from its stomach but still bearing the unhealed injury, appeared from the storage room opposite them. It walked slowly towards them, leisurely instilling torturous bouts of 'oh no, not again.' They managed not to get seriously injured in the first round, but they still did not want to have to do it again.

Valeria was reminded of how close their fight actually was, mightily dependent on their unlikely lassoing of its legs. At least now they had an injury to work with, somewhere they could focus, especially with poisons.

"I didn't think we would have to use these already, but here we are," Griffith said. He and Victoria carried a backpack each, and were somewhat aware of what to do with all of their glass containers and snuggly packed vials.

"We've got this, just another round with these idiots," Tanho said between his own doubts in deep breaths. Tanho's group would fight the spider again, both sides of the fight having experience now.

The panther was now standing on their left, the spider patiently waiting on the right. As to not get pushed into a corner and to fight with more equal footing, each group pushed to their opponent. As Tanho and Victoria stood front, wielding spears, and as Griffith and Bruce began poking and prodding the panther backwards, the wolf reappeared through the stairway door.

Victoria stared into empty eyes as the zombied spider combined successive lunges with feigns and multi-directional hits. Its own legs were durable in deflecting and keeping distance from the beast, allowing them to push it backward almost to the corner of the room. She kept her hair out of her eyes through strategically-angled head movements that aligned with her shoulders in momentum conservation. The spear acted as a bladed staff, strength parrying and deflecting every attack in fluid motion; one attack from the upper right led a counter-clockwise swing, both hands collaborating to hook each of its remaining attacking-legs, negating each blow and creating space for Tanho to draw closer in a yin-yang clockwise and forward arc, pushing the spider into discomfort.

Its eyes held the same multicolored hue that now confused its dark undertone. Part of its body had lost its support, five legs missing and a very serious injury of corroded innards. *It doesn't seem to have control of its body– what could be causing that?* Lucian asked himself. To not get in the way of their fighting, his vision relaxed, cognizant, placing movement in his left-side peripheral vision.

"The wolf is back!" he yelled. It could not be coincidence, the wolf had to have something to do with it all. The spider's injury grew darker until it was solid black, the incisive weak spot fulfilling its healing potential. *How fast can it heal? Faster than we did? We need to take advantage while we can.*

Griffith jabbed and thrust the spear to the panther's face, aiming for eyes. Against three pointed spears, the injured creature was forced to back up– it was at least still smart enough to recognize that. Valeria grabbed a vial of acid and tossed it upwards. With a gap between Griffith and the panther, the vial began its fall down to the panther. Bruce stepped forward and used an overhead swing to slam the glass vial against its back and neck, breaking it and releasing its contents in a small horizontal wave. While much of the acidic solution slid off the hydrophobic fur, the continued exposure began to break through. The panther did not react, it did not seem to feel the burn of its melting skin.

She grabbed the fire-making vials and waited for an opening. Aiming for the face twice would be difficult, but the panther began to grow predictable, fighting-patterns continuing using its tail and front claws as primary weapons. It could not force itself forward, its claws not cutting through the spider legs.

Bruce advanced to match Griffith's efforts of corralling the panther against the wall. They had to keep the points facing the panther due to front-facing attacks. It swung its tail, changing its center of gravity lower and backward. They backed up a step, avoiding the swing to hold on tight to the spears. Bruce anticipated the shift and took another step to the right to begin a stab to the back.

As it quickly slingshot back to guard the attack, its face was unguarded, prompting a throw that, between two angles of attack, the panther could not protect, at least the one paw required to maintain steadiness. It was a good shot, the panther could not avoid being affected, and began taking extra effort to block its face.

They stood at their toes, light footed in explosive jumping and side steps. A vial of purple potassium permanganate flew by and was deflected by a backhand. She grabbed another, signaling Griffith and Bruce to initiate another attack. Bruce prodded the tail, neither weapon giving in, but pausing the panther for a well placed jab to pierce the skin towards its hip. No whimper or growl emerged, the panther opting to begin a counter-clockwise spin in attack. Griffith was forced to let go of the spear and move further right and back towards Bruce. Valeria moved left and threw the vial.

With the spear poking out of its side, it did an explosive push-up, sacrificing internal damage for the vial to miss its face. It knew the vial was bad news. Glass shattered and quickly settled as Griffith got his weapon back. They only had two more, but could sacrifice more time to get more after the fight. She took out both remaining two, handing one to Griffith and making a fake swap to Bruce.

Within seconds, the new plan was initiated. They did not want it to learn more. Griffith javellined the pointed leg at the beast's right side, then threw the vial weakly upwards, giving the panther plenty of time to see and react.

Bruce swapped the spear to his weaker left hand and pulled nothing from his pocket, disguising his closed fist as holding the next vial.

It had to move right, instinctively watching the poison fall to its left, cross-eyed by Bruce's suspicious movement. Valeria moved from Griffith's shadow and side-armed the vial with a raised elbow of leverage. Bruce lunged to the right, further jabbing the weapon directly to the beast's chest, aiming behind the shoulder blade, hoping the curved ribs would guide the point deep into vital organs. He fell forward putting all of his weight behind the thrust, two hands holding on to the middle and back.

The reaction occurred almost instantly, beginning to ignite with bubbling and the emission of steam and smoke. As the sharp tip penetrated further and further, the panther moved, switching sides with them. This time it let out a growl, low and weak. Its face began melting, fur burning and charring, settling on the floor or fusing to burning skin. The fire intensified as its claws scraped through, failing to remove the concoction. It clung to the floor, a sort of fire-reducing roll that did not cease allowing oxygen to energize the flame.

Chapter 13

INSURMOUNTABLE

Once the others were a fair distance away, the wolf finally made its purpose known. Amidst their fighting, the panther had led them farther away, separating both teams. The lion-like wolf made its way to Lucian, Tanho, and Victoria, now surrounding them in coordination with the spider.

"A new enemy… and two at once at that," Victoria said in a deep breath. She prepared her muscles to push past tiredness. *Another gel would be great, but there's no time for that now.*

Lucian fumbled with the bag, pulling out a small flask before the wolf's bark caused the slightest shiver and hesitation, forcing Tanho to stand in front of Lucian in defense, Victoria on the side with the spider.

"Let's get this spider out of here; this thing is something else entirely," Tanho said, staring into its different, dark but living eyes. The space was closing in fast. "Lucian, throw something!"

Lucian threw the flask of acid at the spider, hitting its mark as the missing limbs acted in phantom. The blighted spider still felt its previous limbs and acted on their presence, resulting in the burning sensation that failed to reduce a new round of clicks. The wound, too, went dark, black in the fusion of cells that rapidly grew but were undoubtedly corrupt.

Its eyes began to melt, dissolving, deconstructing, and forming a uniform, highly viscous liquid. The acid shriveled the keratinous layer of skin, de-moisturizing and blocking blood flow before it could even spill from the eye sockets. It still made clicks, but they seemed to crack. The smell of chemical burn returned, and the melting flesh and disassembled fluid-filled eyes released an invisible gas, rapidly diffusing. It kept moving.

It leaped and danced, pushing off the wall and now rolling. The wolf armored itself, its fur becoming more dense and rocky. It seemed much bigger up close, almost standing taller than them. It snapped its mouth, a drip of silver saliva beginning to drop from the right corner. It held itself low and stomped a step forward, preparing to push through Tanho's spear and latch onto human flesh.

The spider made a sudden, amplified click that drowned out noise as a temporary flashbang. It set forth three of its remaining eight legs in a quick flurry of attack, forcing Victoria to parry one and duck low. Lucian remained at medium height, the remaining jab not reaching far enough as the spider tried to push closer. The wolf, too, pushed forward; they were being squeezed together.

He took another beaker and smashed it into the floor beside them. The green and noxious gas created a smokescreen, prompting the wolf's involuntary reflex to avoid it. The spider followed suit, giving them a few more seconds of avoidance as they held their breaths and used one hand to block their noses.

The safest bet of escape was the spider, all three of them independently acknowledging the wolf's difference in power. They rushed it, Lucian swinging the backpack over one shoulder as they moved to attack the spider as a trident. The spider seemed as uncoordinated as the wolf must have been, a defensive backing up and aimless flailing in their direction, the loss of its eyes now affecting something.

Tactical; decisive. A quick swing and stab broke the skin and pushed deep, doing notable innard damage. When the leg released, the spider did not bleed, wounds shimmering gray and black. It backed up further, out of reach, leaving the dust to settle in gaseous distribution while the three cut down a stairway to breathe.

"Lucian, look!" Tanho alarmed in a point.

He looked down– red blood. As his brain connected nerve signals to stimuli and counseled pain-relieving adrenaline, a pain was felt in the form of a diagonal gash from the left-side clavicle to the right pectoral. He fell back, looking up and now palming the injury on his left side over his heart. Magnified heartbeating, distorted in circulating white blood cells and platelets.

Recovery, Victoria thought. She grabbed one from her bottom left pocket, estimating safely between a half and two-thirds. *Let's see if this works.* The pool of blood proliferated down Lucian's chest and began dripping further down to the ground.

Tanho analyzed the situation around them. "The wolf, it's the wolf. It's gotta be."

Victoria dragged Lucian to the corner and handed him his knife, returning with Tanho to the fight.

Once the gas was no longer visible, they peeked up from the staircase and observed the wolf partially stumble over itself. Bruce, Valeria, and Griffith had put a few more holes into the panther, waiting for the gas to diffuse.

"It's the wolf, we need to kill it!" Tanho shouted to the others. Victoria took out bottles from the bag and lobbed them at the wolf. Some hit, and some missed, the wolf coming to more consciousness, enough to begin to dodge and fight against the inhibiting chemical invading its system and circulating.

They closed in, prompting the panther and spider to fully dedicate themselves to the wolf's aid. More vials and flasks, a dangerous battleground of corrosion and poison gases. The wolf was much more affected than the dead creatures were, opting to move to the group of three and away from the chemicals. Only, they had chemicals too, and it knew that, they merely had not been throwing them until now.

More chemicals prompted a jump, admitting Valeria to throw the spear in foresight of the landing and knee-bending suspension of a graceful yet frightened bounding. It stuck in, somewhere on its face. Immediately, both Victoria and Tanho threw theirs too, sticking into its shoulder and neck. The panther and spider caught up, flinging themselves recklessly in venomous attack. The panther salivated and dripped much faster, and the spider opened its mouth and revealed a spiked tentacle-like tongue, all black in a dysmorphic, decaying figure.

An unpredictable opponent is one to be feared. Unless, of course, that opponent had no eyes and was clearly being controlled and brainwashed by another. Then, a skilled assailant burning for vengeance and mortality could counteract this direct, unplanned approach with one of finesse and cognitive proficiency. In being adaptable and versatile, quickly thinking and using one's own mastery to de-escalate and conclude may often be the most efficient solution.

They did not merely fling themselves onto the group of five skilled individuals collaborating in common enemy. They put forth a violent attack that could not be prepared for, using their genetically modified abilities to the fullest extent. Faster and faster potently poisonous jabs supported a backwards jump from the wall to swing at knee level. Although they were spread out, they could not spread out far enough against the railing to all avoid each attack properly. While Bruce tried to block an attack he usually would have dodged, and Victoria deflected more jabs to prevent casualty, it was impossible to make more room.

The animals adapted, switching the patterns mid-barrage to exploit the weaknesses of Victoria's weaker, unparryable side and Bruce's forearm soreness. At once, both Victoria and Bruce sacrificed injury and bloodshed to open the attack for Tanho and Griffith, Valeria holding on to both backpacks for their maneuverability.

Weakened tissue succumbed to extreme directed force, the spear perpendicularly stabbing the spider's face and skewering down the middle, impalement. Griffith's axe flung sideways and chopped horizontally into the panther's face, slicing cartilaginous nose bridging to exploit the weak nasal bones of its skull. It buried deep, and all ceased, the flailing of the spider too slowing down to make way for another spear stab and knife prod. Dark, barbed extensions slowly began climbing the spider's leg-spear from the injury site.

"What's that?" Valeria yelled, watching as the tendrils grew from where they had injured the spider previously. The tentacles began making their way out of the panther's eyes and back. They backed up instinctively, and Griffith sliced the blackened tentacle moving his direction. Instantly, they moved toward him from left and right. He dropped to the ground as fast as possible, but they checked there, too, beginning to constrict as they wrapped and released his grip on the axe. Five thick strands poked him with thorns tighter and tighter as he tightened his core and stretched his chest forward.

Tanho grabbed the axe and slashed but could not cut all the way through. The injuries repaired themselves regeneratively. Victoria, Valeria, and Bruce turned their attention to the wolf. It had to be that, *that thing*.

They ran towards it, Valeria still carrying both backpacks of various chemicals, mostly empty as they had thrown so much already. A full-on attack was pointless, but their previous attempts resembled pointless, too. Chemicals were an advantage, Valeria arming them all, holding one bag over the shoulder and one in her left hand to reach in with her right.

Chemicals splashed pointlessly onto the floor and dripped to the ground level. They had three spears and one knife. A silence of focus resonated in their eardrums between low growls and incessant axe slashes. The wolf made sure they were only on one side of it, the walkway not allowing more than that single direction of attack.

They stabbed at it cautiously, swinging claws and low advances offered no opening. Valeria threw a vial up to land behind the wolf. It hesitated in backing up and made a surprise leap forward, met with spear points that did not break through its hard fur and skin.

It began a backpedal and opened its mouth to bare teeth, revealing new and smaller tendrils than the other creatures. They were obviously pointed and coated with a clouded liquid, either poison or saliva. It seemed to be waiting for something. *Spores? What if spores were in the air, infecting us?*

"Hey! I've got something for you!" The wolf spun suddenly and bared its open mouth to the surprise, hunching and arching its back with its head low to look bigger and more threatening. Before it could react, Lucian had stuffed the knifepoint into the wolf's mouth, a kebab of gels layering the blade. It scratched back aggressively, marking up both of Lucian's legs above the shin as he heel-kicked it in the chin to elicit the opening of the gel packets and release of blood in its mouth.

Infectious silence of disregarded senses, a focus unbending. The malignant wolf fought its tongue in blood sputter and claw-withdrawn slash. Blood swelled Lucian's wounds, but his sense of pain was, too, relieved; he flinched and stumbled back but halted and clutched the railing in wait of what the beast would do next. Lights seemed to buzz a white noise drowning out even the wolf's movement and clattering. Warm blood circulated at every heartbeat, ringing in vibrations, tattering the ear's hammer, anvil, and stirrup.

The content of saliva increasing secretion to flush its mouth facilitated the swallow; the blood, gels, and saliva blocked its airflow. As moments of struggle with the knife ensued, it swallowed, flexing the muscles of its throat and tongue to push out the blade. They could not be sure how much gel it had swallowed, yet it renewed a half-senseless hope.

They watched and waited as six doses of stamina gel and one dose of strength began rapidly dissolving and being absorbed into its bloodstream. They had about forty-five seconds– the time for human blood to circulate from the heart all around the body. *Effects should be almost immediate. Hopefully, this creature either has a heart or a centralized organ network,* Victoria thought. She watched as Lucian fell over, *blood loss.*

Bruce waited a few seconds before moving forward with the spear. He quickly backed off, though, seeing the bundles of fur increase its hardness before growing into jagged spikes tipped with purple. It held its spine upward before contorting it down, spikes growing on spikes, resembling the thorns, as it closed its eyes with its mouth held open, dripping familiar blackening blood. He wanted to attack, but there would be no point. It let out a loud bark and whimper before it fell on its side, laying restless instantly. More vine-like tentacles made their way out of the wolf's mouth but slowed to a stop within moments, the afflictions of drug overdose affecting that too.

A single royal blue flower with hundreds of feathery strands in a fire-like orientation began developing on the tip of the tallest one, only two feet above the body. It was large, a foot across from petal to opposite petal. As it bloomed, Bruce whacked it off with the side of the spear, moving towards Lucian. Valeria dumped vial upon vial onto the flower as Victoria watched to ensure no more generated.

The spider and panther had definitely been controlled; they had not observed any other behaviors from the creatures they had killed or seen killed. The ominous blackening was also a surprise, yet by the creatures' shared reactions and the wolf's ability to read them, it was an obvious deduction. Valeria pictured, *definitely something resembling a parasite, but much more plant-like. Something that sent signals to the wolf and gave it a sense of control over the others once they had died. It always seemed to be observing– and its return was prompted by the deaths.*

Victoria turned back to Tanho and Griffith while Bruce went first to Lucian. Tanho had collapsed while slashing away, but Griffith's red face did not hint at any purple. They had killed the parasite fungus in enough time. She observed the strange body of the panther, more unnatural than before, as she ran back over in a light pant. It looked smaller and somewhat different in look and even texture. Already, it had lost some of the brightness and shine from the fur, partially due to the chemical decomposition, but it was different than before. She picked up the minimally dulled axe and safely broke the rest of the vine away from his shoulder, hoping that her slashes were powerful enough to not cause too much vibrating and exacerbate the thorn wounds or administer any extra poison through their tips.

Griffith wheezed and coughed as he fell to the floor onto his hands, dripping blood from his arms while some soaked into clothing or collected at the lowest point of his stomach. He ached all over his core from the hundred dots where he had been spiked. Victoria assisted in opening a recovery gel for him, propping him against the wall away from the carcasses.

Tanho groaned and got to his knees, still mostly closing his eyes in exhaustion while smiling intensely, chuckling from the intense soreness, "I kept chopping until all of the panther's usable energy ran up, but by then I was too tired to finish the job." He coughed deeply from his lungs between words, the intense workout instilling a feeling of phlegm. Each of his slashes had required the parasite to use some energy to regenerate and continue constricting. By the rate of its growth, it would use energy quickly and only come from a select energy storage, the processes of utilizing even carbohydrate and fat energies very complicated already.

Victoria inspected closer after Griffith and Tanho were more stable- the life had been drained, looking frail in the face. Some discoloration in the vines, now likely dead or disconnected from the others, was noticeable towards the ends and in stripes beginning to slowly make their way back to the base carcass.

Bruce and Valeria ensured Lucian was healing, helping him put pressure on the wound as he came back to.

"I'm good, I'm good. Kill that thing; it might not be dead," he groaned and began closing his eyes and tilting his head up to attempt to reduce the pain.

They used a spear and jammed it down the length of its body through the mouth, ensuring it would pierce the throat and any organs present. As the body lay on its side, they went from the stomach side and pushed the spearpoint through the roof of the animal's mouth, using a tap and series of pushes once the point had lined up to the center. Its esophagus was cut, its lungs and brain pierced, and the whole body was overdosed. Hopefully, it would not come back; hopefully, the flower signaled the end of the battle, the war concluding victory, taking into account the calamitous injuries sustained.

They needed food. Raiding break rooms was probably the only sensible way to get it; they could make their way back to the surface and hunt and cook, but that was better saved for when the night was less approaching, and armies of creatures did not sit above, likely in wait. Victoria, Valeria, and Bruce slowly assisted Tanho, Lucian, and Griffith to a safe room on that level. Victoria stayed with them while Valeria and Bruce went to one of the break rooms.

"I think there was one or two on the bottom level at the stone," Valeria said. *Plus, I can admire the fountain just a bit more. Oh, and the trees.*

"Get back here quick; we need to go over what we know as soon as possible," Victoria reminded them as she walked around the bland office room to find any cloth they could employ. *This place just keeps reaffirming its craziness.*

It was their time to recover while mostly out of view and in the general protection of the building. It was not the safest idea, as anyone with any control over the facility could lock them all inside and potentially release more dangerous creatures. However, going back out and fighting any of the creatures as nighttime approached was much more of a risk. Tanho sat against the wall as Griffith and Lucian laid down, head to the side, flat on the carpet. Griffith laid his shoulders flat, even pushing them into the carpet as a brace to psychologically reduce feeling.

The scarring on Griffith's legs was more evident now, the sweat and blood tracking it differently, now drying in a contour to the scar tissue. Lucian's legs were also red, still releasing blood in indiscernible pumps. Pressure from weak hands barely slowed it, synthetic compounds propulsioning white blood cells to flush the wound, overseeing the healing of platelets, neutrophils, macrophages, and fibroblasts.

Platelet-generated fibrin clots build about the wound, prompting neutrophil proteases to break up potentially perilous microbes embedded during the injury. This allows macrophages to consume dead cells and bacteria, allowing the fibroblasts to build the new cellular matrix and collagen support structures. Within ten minutes, the innermost layer of skin had fused shut, accelerating the dermis and epidermis' full repair.

"I would love to see what this stuff is made of," Lucian said, inspecting the gel packet once more for any hint of its fascinating composition.

Griffith felt the slow departure of ache, now bending his legs so that while he lay back, his knees pointed up. "Yeah, and there's no allergy warnings either– must be fairly advanced."

Valeria and Bruce returned with a backpack full of snack bars, protein bars, and unlabeled bottles of what could only be presumed to be water.

Bruce told them, "We poured some of this water on one of the crystal trees down there, and they didn't glow. We tested with a drop from one of the vials to ensure they were activated, too. So I think we're probably good; they don't smell bad, and everything we've had here has been good so far."

Griffith and Lucian were the most parched, the energy and healing processes utilizing water faster and merging with the effects of intense battle sweating. They slowly sipped water until they would feel stomach pain from drinking any more; they had to keep themselves in relative fighting shape.

Lucian prompted, more rested but tired in his eyes and slouched posture, "Okay, quick recap: We found a building with chemicals both outside and inside. It's a large bunker with office rooms, decorative design, and trials through simulations, labs, and larger labs. Something was on the top floor, so we don't know how the three guys got in, and even if that top floor enemy is still here, or an enemy for that matter. *They* seem to be designing creatures and assimilating them into the world above." Griffith gestured and Lucian gestured back, signaling his turn.

"Precisely, Lucian. They are modifying animals or generating animals somehow and releasing them against each other at the surface. The nighttime spectacles are likely their doing. It doesn't seem sustainable if so many animals die each night. Still, if the animals could be created from nothing, and there are multiple of these bases around this planet, we have much more to worry about than just what is going on here... much more to worry about than just our lives."

Victoria remarked, "I've noticed they seem to all have unique abilities, or adaptations, within their similar, if not same body systems. The corrosive saliva, the crystalizing fur, the clicking sounds, fire breathing. The only exceptions are defensive, but even then, dense shields are easily adaptable; defense would rise as offense rose too."

"So what's the next step? How do we use this to our advantage?" Lucian asked the group half-rhetorically. "Now we know– without a doubt– that we're being played here."

Valeria looked to the floor and noted, "We could destroy this place; surely, it would be a major setback for anyone using it."

Bruce added, "As long as we get what we need to survive first. Temperature-controlled rooms and lab equipment would be hard to come by anywhere else... that we know of, at least."

Finally, Tanho spoke again, saying, "What if, hear me out..." he began whispering, "We ruin this lab's objective, complete with destroying the lab to elicit a response. And when whoever comes to end our wrath..." He left it open-ended, the blank being obvious.

Griffith posed, "How would we do that?" Then he whispered, asking, "And do we think we're being watched or listened to?"

"Definitely," Lucian said.

"I've got an idea for that," Tanho responded emphatically with a thumbs up. It made no sense to give them all this access relatively unrestricted.

The white creatures must have been released for that intention: killing. He spoke lower than before, prompting them to move forward, "We should make our own creature, one of complete mass destruction. We kill the lab and the planet they've spent so long working on.

Griffith asked, directed to Lucian, "Can we make a place where we all can speak privately? Can you make a scanner or something similar to that effect?"

"I can surely try; you guys will have to help me find the right things, though."

"We should split up again– some of us getting materials for the scanner and the rest getting into the control rooms. Lucian, do you still have the foil?" Victoria suggested and asked with the beginnings of dilated pupils.

Lucian handed her the foil, miraculously still in one piece despite the scratches of red, healing skin peering through his tattered and bloodied clothing.

"Just holler if you need anything. We'll keep the door open as long as it works that way," Victoria said, Bruce and Valeria following her to the door.

"Good luck."

"Yeah, good luck," Valeria and then Bruce said.

Chapter 14

UBIQUITOUS DECEPTIONS

I keep fighting the urge to sign, but yeah any high-def cameras would see it. He quieted again, "Okay, let's see. We have to assume, if there are any bugs, that they emit radio frequency signals like the ones on Earth. We also have to hope there isn't much interference with any of the computers or systems this place is equipped with," Lucian explained.

"... and we have to worry about how long we're here. For all we know, a group of armed soldiers is on their way here right now– by plane, maybe. I doubt they'd want to fight through all of that outside," Griffith said.

"What do we need?" Tanho asked at a normal level. We have to make sure we're not too conspicuous– gotta hold the plan as long as possible.

"Copper wire, brass tubing, some toothpicks, cotton, and the knife you pulled from the wolf. The rest I'll look around for. Just go see what you can find; we can probably separate; just stay armed at all times and don't use connector doors." He first went to the lab and made a quick-setting, weaker glue. The next items would be harder to come across: electronics.

Connectors, conductors, and an RF voltmeter. I can probably disassemble a radio, radar, or microwave, especially if we have multiple– one to deconstruct. He stared ominously at the standard United States power outlet before getting up and limping in aches to the door. He did not want to exacerbate the wound.

He went just one room to his right and began searching boxes, particularly the ones sporting electronics-related labels. Minutes later, he emerged holding a box of electronic parts and radios. Radios– we can communicate over long distances and listen in if someone else is nearby and using these frequencies. I wonder what the range of these things is? He met back up with Griffith and Tanho and began constructing.

Griffith started explaining his findings as Lucian fought looking up in thought while using the knifepoint to align every metal connector in preparation for the radio's frequency detector, "I couldn't find any toothpicks, but I got these thin metal sticks and a few screws. I also found some brass plumbing equipment– a few valves, maybe. I'm not sure what they're called."

"And I found some copper wiring, still rolled up. I guess we didn't find any actual cotton balls, but I found this fabric that is similar– probably could be made softer. I'll get to work on that."

"Should we go help them, see what's up?" Griffith asked.

"I could get help from one of you in case I need more than two hands for something. Up to you."

"Alright, I've got it; I'll stay, I need more rest anyway," Tanho said.

Griffith got up, carrying a few radios set to the same frequency, "radio if you need anything!"

They made their way to the double control room, chained up and empty. All three of them stayed close this time, spears prepared. The door was no longer propped open, but they resolved not to go open it again. In the back of their skulls and brains, concussive metal crashing and clicking and corroding swarmed their senses, subconsciously and paroxysmally admonishing the unpredictable world they still inhabited, fauna and flora feverishly venturesome.

There was no need to worry about the sound they were producing, at least not yet. Victoria held the spear leg up to the glass and looked at Valeria and Bruce, "ready?" she asked.

"Go for it!" Valeria replied with Bruce's nod of consent.

She javelin-ed the spear at the reinforced glass, neither side wanting to give. Immense pressure and weight behind the spearpoint forced its way to a dent. Still, the intense viscosity of the extraordinary liquid in panes comprised of potassium nitrate instead of sodium on the surface strengthened it. It applied a significant normal force back onto the spear throughout the conical region from the partially buried spearpoint to the outside. The spear slowed incredibly fast, preventing even the spear from holding itself in the wall, clattering to the ground.

"Guess we've just gotta break the chains," Valeria said as she stepped forward and looked through the backpack. "Nothing's left that would really do anything."

"Can't you just pick it, Victoria? I mean, after the chains, the biometric thing is easy enough. Hopefully, the reflection trick works on this, too." Bruce looked at it; I could probably bump this lock open with something. "... and try bumping it."

"What?" Valeria questioned.

"You'll see," Victoria said. "Yeah, I guess it might work." She finagled the lock with small metal bits, intricately twisting and tapping. She moved on to a larger piece of metal shaped like a key and bumped the end in, hoping to jostle the pins and allow the fake key through to the next. She continued trying but could not get past the first pin. "This thing is deceptive. Should we smash it open?"

"Yeah, I guess. Bruce, do you want to give it a go?"

"Sure, maybe I'll try to spear the lock. Could I borrow your spider legs for a moment?" He backed up a couple feet and began throwing. His first throw missed the 3-inch lock by less than an inch. It deflected off the waist-height chain and dropped.

"Warm-up, it's okay," Valeria said in response to his miss, a sarcastic edge in humor releasing off the final syllable.

Bruce threw the second one at ninety percent strength, remarkably hitting the lock in the upper right, next to the joint where the lock's end joined the base. It refused to budge. They knew it was heavy, but the material must have been dense and firmly joined together. He threw eight more times of varying strength, aiming to induce a crack and then expand it– he failed in both objectives.

"Chemical embrittlement," Valeria said.

"I guess it's come to it. Let's go to the lab."

"I'll stay behind, Victoria. I want to try some more. Maybe I'll come up with something," Bruce said.

"Just be careful. Stay aware of the door, and everything, for that matter. Expect something to come out of one of the many rooms, and expect them to be silent," Valeria warned.

"We'll be right back." Victoria and Valeria went upstairs to the lab. Diffusible hydrogen had to enter the steel, its small atomic radius allowing it to travel into the structure and make it more affected by stress. The affected, embrittled metal is even weaker at high temperatures– when the hydrogen pairs separate into atoms. The consequently expanded metal would similarly increase hydrogen absorption, collaborating to amplify embrittlement and stress susceptibility.

"Okay, we need a simple exothermic reaction to produce heat and speed up the process, preferably something with hydrogen gas as a byproduct, so we can contain the hydrogen gas molecules in the metal."

"Sounds good, Victoria. I'll find some way to generate a lot of heat." She looked around and found liquid methane with a prominent Highly Flammable danger tag. Perfect! Soon after Victoria found a metal bin and a basic flint sparker, they returned to the room, seeing Griffith and Bruce lifting up the large metal chain still intact.

"Lucian found radios!" Griffith said.

"Woah, that's amazing! Have you checked any of the other frequencies yet?" Valeria queried in excitement.

"Nope, not yet, we're all still recovering up there. Lucian is pretty bloody; I ought to tell him to wash up." He looked at his arms and chest, dots of blood and lines of bruising causing any movement to ache. It was not a sharp pain, more a sore tension stemming from muscle.

"Yeah, we ought to rest soon, maybe get some sleep," Bruce stated. They all looked rough and rugged from the battle-sweating and injuries. They had all taken some recovery gel, a remarkably quick-healing synthetic coursing veins and wounds that would enable them to keep pace with the perilous world around them.

Valeria coated the chains and lock with liquid methane, placing the metal above it to contain the heat. She put it at an angle against the door to allow for some airflow, allowing the oxygen-dense air to keep the fire breathing and introduce hydrogen to the mix. She let the first bit of methane burn until it was extinguished, and then she burned more below to let the flame reach up. The metal soon became visibly hot, a glow emitting heat waves. Capitalizing on the heat-releasing metal, hydrogen split into two atoms and began diffusing, making its way into the structure of the metal.

Victoria took some water and began heating it, producing water vapor and coating the inside of the metal with higher humidity. By working in more humid, wet conditions, moisture could diffuse and cause corroborating corrosions and weaknesses. Bubbles of oxygen and acid contaminants could intensify their efforts. They burned some extra paper and cardboard below the metal in hopes of increasing temperature and diffusion.

Lucian stared at his crude radio frequency detector, I really hope we get what we need out of this thing. He put it on a box next to him and slowly raised himself up, holding his arms forward and slouching his shoulders to reduce pain. "Let's see if it works!"

Tanho held up a radio and pressed the side button, resulting in a beep, "Hello, testing. Are you guys doing alright down there?"

"Let's go! It works!" was heard over the line before Tanho released the button.

"Yeah, we're good down here. I'm just trying to embrittle the lock; it's tough," Victoria told them.

"What, do you mean it's working?" Bruce asked.

Lucian responded, Tanho still holding the radio, "Well, I sent a signal through some copper wire, magnetic fields, blah blah blah. Now we can test for electric conductivity… and with a little luck, we can electrify a needle and make a cool compass."

"Wow, so no more need to follow the sun? We could travel at night; that's awesome," Griffith responded. They had all begun their deception, consciously altering their knowledge of what was happening, not just lying about their project but making themselves believe it was real. While deep in their brains remained the understanding of radio frequency, acting as if it was a compass would save them from meticulous scanning by someone behind a camera. *For all we know, we're just in a big simulation room right now.*

Lucian walked around the room with the device, doing a pacing maneuver, pretending to be deep in thought, and occasionally blurting out random thoughts or facts about animals they had encountered. "Ah yes, the bird dove and ate part of the frog." One corner in their room acted as an alcove; Lucian checked it thoroughly for bugs and then the entryway walls for anything. *This room is clear from anything emitting radio frequency, and now we have a small spot away from the windows.*

"I guess it must be approaching night now; I seem to be getting more tired," Bruce said as he overhead slammed the crystalline axe onto the region of the lock and chain with a high surface area for more hydrogen diffusion. It broke and fell to the floor, leaving sharpness in the metal on both sides of the break. *We're in.*

Victoria pulled out the foil packet appliance and immediately propped open the door. The room seemed from an older time period than the rest of the building. It had a bland concrete interior design, supporting desks, and a middle roundtable likely for strategic planning. From the fountain's orientation, they were on the right side. On the right side of the room, the wall was armed with computers and desks from many years previous – large PCs, none of them even flatscreens.

"They must be equipped with some special program, only operable on these old things," Valeria said.

"Let's see if we can turn any of these things on," Griffith commented as he looked on the left side of the room for any switches or a similar red button. Why were these turned off in the first place?

They found an array of switches behind an easily accessible panel. Valeria switched them one by one, finding that one set activated lights, another did computers, and the last turned on the main display with multiple larger screens and a few buttons, now backlit.

The smell of a stunned petrichor descended the ventilation as they were drawn to the single, centermost screen. A virulent tempest accelerated its blossoming, exponentially amassing in regions downwind from bodies of water. As night began to close in, smaller storms sent out feelers in preparation for the main event. They sought to merge, conjoining in marriage to frame a destructive yet curative magnanimity.

Through the beginning of this feeler storm, Valeria stared at the image on the screen, silent. As thunder crashed above, crescendo fleeting crescendo, a tear rolled down her cheek in a desperately eroding stream, releasing the flash-flood of lightning buzzing ear to ear. A ringing was heard, falsely fading, for the crescendo had not yet descended from that dark cloud; the climactic ending, clashing arc-pulses vaporizing electrons, was far too berating to anticipate. Strong crackles soon faltered, tears drying up, listless fire in petrified woods, for the cloud had moved on, and so did she.

"Let's get Tanho down here quickly," she whispered with her head looking to the floor. Victoria called it in. They did not speak until Tanho arrived.

"Lucian's just exploring with the compass thing. We found this space–"

Griffith pointed, "Look, Tanho, look at the screen." Within the dark gray screen border was a black one, contrasting the illuminated picture of Lucian.

"What?" he exclaimed.

"Guys, what does this mean?" Bruce asked.

"We can't assume the worst just yet. They might've just put his picture here to confuse us," Griffith explained with hands confused about whether to be by his side or at his waist height.

Victoria stated, "But we still can't ignore it. Don't be alone with him; someone watch him all the time. We can't let him get a knife to our throats, just in case."

Griffith looked at Tanho, "You're just here to consult about the behavior of some of the creatures we've encountered. Don't give any hint of suspicion; he can't know this has happened yet."

Valeria continued looking at the picture as they tried to turn on the rest of the computers by the buttons on the side. It was an image from the interior of their ship in which, through the windshield, they could see Chaos; Lucian was standing at the back of the ship, facing everyone else, who were all unconscious. Light streaking in the window told them they had just breached Chaos' atmosphere. Lucian seemed to be holding something silvery, indiscernible. Could it be a knife? No way, right? Why is he the only one awake… and standing?

The middle screen was locked on that picture and would not change. They unplugged it while searching for hints for the login and password for the computer system. Every computer was locked out.

"Alright, I guess I'll just test this," Valeria said. She grabbed the radio from her waist and pressed the button, "Lucian, come in."

"Yeah, hey, what's up? Everything alright?"

"Yeah, we found these computers locked by username and password. One computer is displaying white, unlike the others. Do you think there's a bypass for the login?"

"Hmm, I'd have to take a look, I think–"

"Nah, it's probably not worth it, Lucian. It's alright. What do you think about a login and password? Anything we should try?"

Victoria added, "If you had created this elaborate base as a super mad scientist, what would your login be?"

"Easy: something I had invented myself. Something I had developed and would only make sense to me. It would be a seemingly random pattern; the username and password would distantly correspond."

"Yeah, but what would you pick?" Victoria questioned?

"Maybe simply Panther for the username. For the password, I'd probably do a genetic sequence of sorts. Maybe for these people, the genome tag for increasing genetic variety between offspring. So it would be in the sex cell, the X and Y chromosomes. This is quite the longshot, but maybe the first 16 bases."

Valeria inquired, "What are those?" Valeria set up the radio and got ready to type the password in.

"C T C T A A C G C G C A A G C G."

"Wrong password, but I guess that means the username is correct. Security question: What is the correct animal?"

Griffith spoke, "I doubt it would be an animal. What else is related to animals or fauna? Lucian?"

"I don't think we should risk getting locked out. We should get to sleep soon, and think about it: we could find more hints in the offices, maybe, or the other control room."

They did not respond over the radio. "Why would he want us to stop? Are we getting close?" Bruce wondered.

"Better be safe than sorry; we might as well go back up," Valeria stated in reminder. Thunder ominously ranged in, occasionally beginning to vibrate the building. Still, nothing fell from the walls or ceiling.

"Let's get back to the room. Let's not let anything else happen tonight," Tanho ached. They returned to the room, and Lucian informed them that the entire space seemed clear of bugs. From the outside, he could not be so sure, but they had a blindspot, and as long as they faced away from the window, their lips could not be read.

"Anything cool down there?" Lucian asked.

Griffith responded, "Not too much; I didn't expect to be fully locked out. If we could get the passcodes and other logins– assuming there are multiple– we could really uncover the truth."

"But oh well, should we get to sleep early tonight? The storm seems real bad tonight," Victoria asked. "Who's first watch?"

"Sure," Griffith volunteered.

"Same, I'll join," Tanho said. He remained in a slight shock that could have been noticed, but they had been through quite the series of events that day. For as intelligent and observant as Lucian is, I wouldn't put it past him to already suspect something.

If the thunder and rainfall could be ignored, all that would remain would be a visual flickering. Life was quiet, waiting, regenerating, mutating. In only that day's cycle, the lake-side meeting of so many creatures would have resulted in mass death. Many grander brutes and fauna had not shown up to the event, waiting for their next turn in their cycle to unleash their power. The variance of the smaller creatures– the minor, trifling beasts– ensued only the strongest survived; natural selection extreme. A whole species may have been wiped out in the single day, but scale and range made it more unlikely. If the individual found a single partner, thousands could be unleashed in just a few hours– daylight, growing by consuming the exotic, esoteric fruits of the mystical trees they returned to every night. Instinctual urges brought the already-matured adults back up, back home to the world of continuation and species betterment.

The humans, too, were evolving. Sleep was much easier now, despite Lucian's suspicious behavior in the picture. Nothing seems wrong yet; if not for the picture, I really wouldn't have suspected anything. But I suppose he could be good at deception– some people are like that. Griffith was slightly daunted by the image. He and Tanho considered it better to stay conscious longer than to try and sleep adjacent to the subject in question immediately after stumbling on such a surprising insight.

Introspection, key to REM sleep. Delta waves slowly rock regions of the brain, revealing your innermost desires and, in doing so, subconsciously storing and processing your thoughts. Rapid eye movements, darting back and forth in visualizing the future, can let one shape reality. Lucid dreaming, elaboration on thoughts, wants, and needs further promotes the registration and encoding of memories, instilling foundational scenario emissaries to preemptively account for possible outcomes. As the three of them slept, newfound knowledge transmitted about and about, recirculating underlying feelings through images of being hunted by horrible creatures, taking an exam, and running from cold killers. Lucian, too, felt the anguish of their entrapment; Lucian dreamt of a way out.

"What do we do in the morning?" Tanho whispered.

Griffith leaned forward from his relaxed position against the wall, infuriatingly still aching. He kept a low voice for the others, "We should probably get some food; it doesn't make sense to rely on all the reserves we have left. This seems to be our new base, but I don't like it necessarily. Maybe we explore."

"With all the creatures still out?" Tanho said almost too loudly, hushing himself.

"Well, the longer we stay here, the more trapped we may become. In the event that soldiers really are on their way here, we need to get out very soon, or we'll be dead. We haven't even seen the surface since the octopus people. Speaking of, I still wonder what their deal is."

"Octopuses have quite the nervous system... if we are to fight them, everyone should know. I don't know how octopus-human hybrids would work, but if we have to worry about their intelligence and camouflage capabilities, they would be quite formidable... and yeah, we should get out of here first thing."

"Can you still fight? Do you think Lucian can? I think I'm good." Griffith was not sure if he would be able to sleep; his eyelid muscles remained energized. *I should really try to sleep, though. Healing, albeit fast, is still important for my reaction and strength.*

"I should be good. Probably, at least. I'll just stay back a little more and take some recovery gel here in a minute. Lucian got it the worst. Maybe we should wake him up soon to have some more gel."

"Nah, we're good for now. If he was in more pain, he would be awake right now. His surface injuries seem alright; we should just wait and take gels before we head out. We don't want to run out, though; we should be careful; we're not invincible."

"Trust me, I know." He looked at his fully healed injuries and lightly flexed his biceps and forearms. He looked to the side, *Victoria and Valeria, maybe? No, Victoria is in more need of healing.* He gestured to Valeria and Bruce, and Griffith nodded.

"I guess they should probably be asleep right now," Victoria said. They moved farther from the sleeping crew, just as Griffith and Tanho had. No talking about Lucian.

"How was fighting the spider, really?"

"Scary, that's all I can really say about it. I've never really had to fight something so... advanced."

"I couldn't agree more, truly. The panther was quite dangerous, and if it really was just learning from us the whole time, I couldn't tell!"

"I did not at all expect them to come back. We have much to learn from this place; I hope we make it through and out." She frowned.

"It was shocking, yeah, but that's the nature of this place. I feel I've sorta got used to the whole 'I'm about to die all the time' thing."

"Not to be too cynical, but I hope at least one of us makes it home; that'll be enough."

"We can get all of us home; none of us have died yet... well, except for the people that died in the crash. All of us are okay." She chuckled lightly, attempting to soften the mood. They paused for a long while. A clock seemed to tick audible seconds by despite their failed attempts to find it. I'm probably just imagining it.

"What do you think the significance of the purple water down there is, Valeria?"

"I mean, on Earth, people do water fountains. Maybe it's either drinkable or has some special ability. Knowing what we now know about these people, I wouldn't put it past them to have some sort of magical chemical only found on this planet that sustains life itself or something."

"That's absurd, but also probable." They stared together at the glass wall and listened for any sounds beyond the sleeping breaths of a possible imposter. Through the rest of the night, the outer existence only sent forth water sprays through sound waves passing through and simultaneously reflecting off the glass wall.

Chapter 15

CONTENDING LIFE

"Good morning," Lucian joyfully said to Tanho, the last one to wake up. There were no visual cues to the day and night; they heavily relied on their circadian rhythm to awaken. They were in sync, too, waking up at very similar times.

"Alright, everyone. I'd say we go outside today and soon, so if you were injured, have a recovery gel or part of one, and let's get a protein bar before we go out," Griffith proposed orotundly before he stood up and stretched.

"Should we take a bottle of the purple water and restock chemicals?" Victoria asked as they left their carpeted office.

"Quickly; sure, let's go. Tanho, wanna join? We'll catch back up in five." Griffith, Tanho, and Victoria went to the lab and loosely filled one backpack. *We don't even need to be outside too long anyway, just long enough to get some more crucial information.*

Armed with a bundle of spears and refilled pockets of gels, they set forth slowly up the stairs. They peered into each hallway but saw nothing–no signs of whatever had been there previously. They slowly rounded every corner, ready to throw at any monster that lay in their path. They continued to the surface, making it fully out into the chemical garden.

"Alright, how do we get back over this wall? I saw no hidden passageways," Valeria asked them.

"Easy," Lucian joked, looking at the bundle of spider legs. He grabbed one, and they watched him closely with an inner shudder. He threw one at waist height to the metal, where it made an indentation but did not stick in. "Oh, wait; give me a minute." He grabbed a strength gel and ate it, "It'll help us fight the creatures, too." They, too, had strength, not to be outmatched.

Just in case, it's better we're prepared. After a minute, Victoria grabbed one and threw it another step higher. "Remember, step closest to the wall for minimal torque," she reminded obviously. She went first, being lighter as the preliminary test. A simple staircase, close enough to take the bottom spear out and bring it with them. The spear bundle was heavy but easily made into a rather deadly backpack with cable, of which they had two large rolls in another bag.

At the top, they laid an empty bag across the wire that they would leave for that purpose. They now had four smaller, compact backpacks they would keep light and close to their backs for optimal fighting and storage. As they took turns going up, Lucian was in the middle. Griffith decided to go last to help take the spears out of the wall, which proved harder than anticipated. He had to pull in jerks to impulse the joint back out through the metal hole.

During their descent down the same tree they used to get up, they recalled the horrifying colors of the hybrids. *Where are they now? Underwater?* Griffith thought. The rafts they took to get there were still on the shore, only moved slightly. "Let's get off this island as soon as we can."

They slowly paddled in the same groups as before and docked back where they had started. There was nothing in the immediate vicinity, but the air reverberated anything but silence. Winds accelerated the buzzing sounds of giant bugs. The air was refreshing; they could not even notice their breathing, as slow and easy as it was in the oxygen-rich environment.

It distracted them, only for a moment, to the wake they left in the water. As the bubbles reached a few feet from the shore, they finally saw.

"Behind us! One of those octopi!" Valeria announced while taking a half step back. Bruce dropped the pile of spears to not hit anyone with the pointed ends, and he held his own up.

It inched forward slowly, like a crocodile sneaking up on its unsuspecting prey. It did not jump out of the water however, instead slowly peaking and matching their eyes, but not pausing when locking them. It continued slowly and did not drip a single drop of water down. It flashed a yellow and then orange, the muscle-enclosed pockets of pigment expanding and contracting rapidly to reflect out just those colors. It defaulted back to a strange purple and sometimes reddish-pink, mimicking the water.

Its protean upper body made it a strange foe. They observed it carefully, cautiously awaiting its next move while trying to learn as much as possible. Lucian considered, *Octopus' neurons are mostly in the limbs, little in the brain itself; if its humanoid, muscular legs are like ours, it would be able to feel pain there– it would care about those limbs more than the independent arms.* "Guys, when we attack it, target the human parts– it should feel pain there," he alerted.

They now had ranged weapons and planned to use them when needed, keeping them farther away and safer from the mysterious attacking behaviors of every enemy they encountered. It did not seem to be communicating with its brethren, but that could not be known for certain. Now that they were no longer on the island, they could quickly run away if needed. After a minute of no sudden movements and curious looks, it backed into the water and disappeared.

"Alright," Griffith expressed. They turned around and continued their explorative journey for food. It was not long before they observed the first creatures. An esprit disappeared into a thick brush section as a large deinodile snatched a turtle frog from the water's edge. *Some creatures can survive in this water– good to know.*

Before they knew it, several deinodiles surrounded them, teeth bared and armored with rough hide. Their next fight was about to commence.

They saw food. *I wonder if it's thermal vision. We're not their usual prey, so why are they doing this?* They snapped forward in a coordinated and swift advance made to bring the group closer together and towards the other predators. They were fast, running and standing over two feet off the ground. Luckily, they were in a flat, barren field, where they could not be easily surprised. The spears were partially deflected against the rough skin, but a jab angled against the hide pierced partially through. Tanho's spear was mostly stuck into the side, causing him to have to drop it. He could not pick up another spear yet, having to pass through Victoria, Bruce, and Griffith to get one. They were all rather busy very quickly.

Griffith and Victoria went in one direction and created an opening, forcing two to back off. They moved through their created opening and could now work additional angles of attack. Bruce handed Tanho another spear as Lucian baited a deinodile forward. He led its head upwards before falling down and piercing its softer, weaker neck with the length of the spearhead. He turned to find another emerging from the water, passing his kill and stopping suddenly. This crocodilian was multitudes bigger than the previous ones, *must weigh over a ton.* Yet, it was able to stand up. It was not very long to help it turn faster, clearly the same species as what they had just killed. *Maybe we just killed its offspring.*

As Valeria and Victoria attacked one from either side, landing a deadly blow, Tanho finally got a spear and, with Griffith's assistance, killed the few-hundred-pound deinodile to retrieve the spider leg. The final smaller creature fought Bruce, who, once sensing this was the last remaining, quickly disposed of it via a quick step back, prompting an advance and an overhead slam of the spear through its head between the eyes. It was dead instantly. He propped his foot on the head of the beast, now lying a foot off the floor, and removed the spear, turning to Lucian and Victoria.

"That's a big guy," Victoria said.

Lucian responded quickly, "Probably their mother."

"Well, if something just murdered all of my kids, I'd probably be pretty mad," Bruce explained.

"Should we go, or do we fight?" Griffith asked. He eyed it down with a squint, one hand at his hip. He took the axe from his back and swapped the spear to his left hand. As it bent its knee and began moving forward, he flung the axe towards its long head looking down– so its eyes could see its targets.

"Watch for the tailwhip," Lucian reminded as he, Victoria, and Tanho went to the right to surround it. The axe hit just above the nostrils, hitting on the axehead but not cutting through enough to stick or do damage. The beast was decorated with many scars, primarily located on its head. It began a fully supported run towards Griffith and a turn towards Lucian.

Bruce and Valeria got the pile of spears and launched at the beast's head– the side would not do enough damage against the protecting skin. This giant deinodile's hide was much thicker and denser than the smaller ones. Both of their full-force throws did not stick or cause a flinch.

"We should get out of here!" Victoria shouted. "Let's get a different kind of food!" They began moving upstream in the direction they had come from. The giant followed Lucian and Victoria in the slowed turn, allowing Griffith to retrieve the thrown weaponry. As they continued near the water with no way to easily cross, the giant Cuban crocodilian took the straightaway as a reason to pick up speed. It accelerated quickly, bounding, becoming fully airborne behind the impressively strong leg's explosiveness. Within moments, it had crossed three-fourths of the distance. They darted left, perpendicularly away from the water.

If only we had anything to take its focus off of us, Bruce thought.

Valeria took a vial of vibrant poison, acidifying the tip of a spear. She passed it to Victoria, saying, "Get through the skin!" The spear continued its turn in a quickly decelerating pivot. At peak height, arching its back as it walked, it was close to ten feet off the ground.

Why is there such a big tree-dweller down here? It makes no sense, Lucian thought. He knew they needed to induce a weakness in its movement. He used his spear and targeted the ankle, wherein an Earth ankle there would be tendons and muscles required to support movement. He flung it from a quartering-away angle, using its forward momentum to get around it and avoid the tail as it swung the other way, keeping focus on the group in front. The creature's structure held a muscular tension inside the skin, preventing it from being weakened by the single injury. The spear filled the small hole, leaving a bridge of flesh over and under, which could still carry signals. *We might need to sever the entire backside– it would fall over.* "Target this ankle from the back! Get rid of its support!" he announced. The animal's front left ankle was the only one transporting a spear.

They rotated around, taking advantage of their quick pivoting ability and the deinodile's slow turn speed and large turning radius. Soon, Griffith and Tanho threw theirs as close to the same spot as possible, re-arming themselves with the pile Bruce carried. Before more could be lodged to the creature's support beam, it executed a tailwhip, forcing a drop to the floor that was quickly taken advantage of by placing all six of them in one direction. As they stood, it faced them and began moving forward, cutting right to force four of them towards the water. It arced left and pinched

Tanho, Victoria, Bruce, and Griffith, leaving Lucian and Valeria trying to cause some distraction. Bruce dropped his underarm spear bundle to the ground, allowing him to move more efficiently; he still held one, which he launched at the turning deinodile's eyes.

It hit the upper right eye, causing it to turn away before shifting its shoulder backward to claw the spear out. It had absurd flexibility, retreating to the water, pushing through the plants on the edge, and taking three spider legs with it– eleven remained.

"Alright, we have food," Tanho joked.

"Yeah, let's get out of here and maybe stay off the rafts for a little while," Victoria agreed. They turned and began walking back to the deinodiles they had defeated. Seeing the assortment of vibrant beetles and lizards escaping with large chunks of their kills, they all stopped.

"Hey! Get off the food!" Valeria yelled to scare the creatures; they did not budge until they escaped with their food. There was no reason to continue forward, as nothing but small and tainted scraps remained from everything they had killed.

"They were pungent, but I didn't think they were *that* pungent," Lucian said. They were reminded of his antics, prompting a slightly awkward silence masked by heavy breathing, quickly absorbing oxygen. The oxygen in the air was dangerous, but it prospered, growing life. It barely, if at all, was usable by their Earthan lungs. As Lucian observed his breathing, he pondered, *our lungs can only absorb four to six percent of oxygen on Earth. Assuming we get around six percent here, that's still not too helpful– great, more disadvantage for the humans.*

I don't really want to eat a beetle, Bruce thought. He went forward to the deinodile that he had killed, eyeing a lizard gnawing off the front-right limb with a combination of shaking its head, rolling, and clasping down harder. He kept moving swiftly from behind it, knowing it was almost entirely focused on getting that scrap of food. It must have perceived his footsteps as another lizard, or even a beetle that would not fight it, as Bruce stabbed it through the center of the back and held it on the end, upwards so it would not fall off. It did not die, though, and the wound was still closed, not letting more than a few drops of dull blood spill. It squirmed and squeaked with its mouth open, claws extended, and tail whipping around. It was bright yellow, with some variance from the other lizards by pattern and shade. Holding their next meals in the air was difficult.

As he turned around, he said, "This must be twenty-five pounds!" Its tail was long and whipped through the air. Bruce had to hold the end of the long spear to avoid the tail, and barely. He swung the spear down and back towards Griffith, who missed once before stabbing it in the neck and holding it to the floor so Bruce could stab it there, too, separating enough nerves to calm down the creature. After separating the head, it lay still.

Griffith put the lizard's head on his spear and inspected the mouth, which was still open. He did not dare place his hand in there or look too closely in case it still had muscle reflexes like Earth creatures. The lizard had many fangs and layers of crisscrossing saw canines that could easily cut through flesh. *The gator's tough hide must have prevented it from running off so quickly. We can use that to our advantage.*

"Should we return with just this? I mean, it's definitely enough for us." Victoria asked.

"Might as well, but where do we return to? I think we should camp out outside the base as long as possible and observe if anything goes in and out. That base is our best shelter; we shouldn't waste it as long as it's accessible," Griffith explained.

Tanho added, "As long as we can get rid of that one creature I saw. I know it was real."

"Alright, agreed. We should hang out outside and clear the building before we rest. Let's just cook the food outside and keep it in a bag," Valeria concluded. They went farther away from the water, staying far away from everything they could. *No use fighting when we don't need to.*

They made the fire and crouched around their cooking food. It would surely attract other creatures, but they would get to that if it came to it. Every fight could be their last; there would be no shame in turning away from a battle. Coals began to form as the oxygen heightened the fire lit by knife and crystal. Warm bundles of carbon continuously glowed warm, the slight gusts of wind agitating it for a second before returning to its glow.

Cutting and skinning to the best of their ability, Tanho noted the strange stomach cavity. He was familiar with it, being so similar to the other creatures they had killed, with the exception of the white creatures in the lab. He did not drain the blood for the lizard as they had for their previous kills, this time leaving the stomach acid and strange cell lining there. Almost everything on Chaos had no vital organs; *maybe this stomach thing could be a target.*

Lucian took a look at it, "Whenever they eat something, they must digest and absorb it quickly via this pocket. We should test and see if this is an effective poison." After using all the liquid on three spears, they flushed the stomach with water, watching some soak into the flesh, and continued cutting. The innard meat was very striated and went back and forth from tough to soft with no visual hint of its change.

They began cooking over the blistering fire, letting the rising heat raise the temperature high enough to destroy any bacteria. Fast-moving particles invaded and bounced off the fleshy structure, breaking down fibers and connective tissues. In just a couple restful minutes, the food was ready. The filet-like cuts of lizard were ready to be eaten.

"The smoke must somewhat mask the smell of food," Griffith remarked. Creatures left them alone while they cooked and ate. They quickly covered the fire and removed as much trace of their presence as possible across the dense ground. The coals swiftly burned, and the leftover flame was smothered with grass, leaving a random, inconspicuous pile. They retreated behind a hill and finally began their stakeout.

They watched all directions cautiously, ensuring nothing snuck up on them. If given enough time, the creatures could be silent, and the aerial animals would have the element of surprise.

After a few hours of monitoring Lucian and waiting, they had still not seen any issues. Eliminating the threat would be the obvious choice if Lucian were some double agent, but they needed surefire reasoning. *How do we actually test his loyalty? If he's been in a deep-cover of sorts for this long, he would have no trouble waiting until the right time. How do we make the false, right time?* Victoria thought.

Bruce wondered, *did that picture actually show up? We need to know why.* Scanning around once more, he said, "The spear things are back." Across a river, they observed a small group of beetles being speared from out of the air, pulled into their grassy demise. A few amphibious frogs leaped near the water, were grasped by tentacles, and brought in without making a sound.

"Alright," Griffith responded, slightly worried.

"Yeah, maybe we should just go back to the shelter while the octopi-people are eating. I don't think anyone is coming after us. Let's clear the place and just rest; we have food," Tanho said. He did want to test out the newer poison spear, but there would be time for that as long as it did not evaporate off the tip. *It would be great to have the synthesized, flammable poison from the spiders, but I guess we'll have to wait... should only be a couple days.*

They swiftly moved to the rafts, silently entered the water, and slowly made their way across, free from the annoyances of beetles or octopi. They made sure not to trip any wires and made their way back into the compound via the same strategy as before, smoother with practice.

"We clear each room one at a time. Nothing gets past. Nothing hostile stays alive," Griffith led. They left the backpacks at the end of the hallway and went diagonally from room to room. The first few went by quickly; they did not have to fully go into the room to see the whole space. They checked the closet of the break room and, after finding it devoid of life, took a few more gel packets, this time from the bottom of the pile in case it was somehow tampered with.

Unbeknownst to Lucian, someone was always watching him. They continued room by room, reaching the door previously harboring *something*. Victoria looked through the window first, holding a closed fist to indicate staying still. She watched the room intently with a squint of focus.

"Nothing," she whispered. Victoria and Tanho entered the room to be sure and found nothing. It was a standard office room.

Griffith told them, "It must be here still. Let's keep going." They checked every room and went downstairs, seeing the immediate simulation areas and locked rooms at the end of the hallway. All the doors were still locked and chained, but they went to look through the windows before going to a simulation. It was quiet.

Opening the door revealed a seamlessly tiled white room, only noticeable as some came up from the floor in a few circles on the floor. Some pillars reached eight feet high, while some were only a few inches off the ground. *Empty.* They went to the second one and found it also empty.

They went downstairs to their same room before Lucian said, "So where did it go?"

"Hidden escape... lighting trick?" Valeria proposed.

"If there were a hidden door, we would probably never find it. I'm unsure what it could be, but it doesn't seem here anymore."

"Alright, Lucian, what's the play?" Bruce asked.

"We just stay alive and fortify the place. Some booby traps wouldn't hurt." They flinched internally; utilizing traps meant arming the suspected murderer with means to do something. Lucian had no game yet– there would always be the possibility he would take one of them hostage, but there would be no benefit to killing them *yet*.

We have to be much more careful when or if we escape; that's when he would strike, Griffith considered.

Victoria, Tanho, Valeria, and Bruce looked to each other and then to Griffith. When Griffith gave a thumbs up to the group including Lucian, so did Victoria. It was settled.

Simple tripwires and door handles set off loud crashes of falling metal, looped cables set up weighted traps to suspend trespassers in the air, and a weighted board with crystalline spikes stayed above the door as a last resort.

"Tomorrow should be the same day as our first," Lucian said.

"Wolves tomorrow night; yeah, let's stay here for a while and work on sending that signal," Tanho said. They agreed to the plan. *Now, we need to figure out if Lucian would sabotage the signal or do something else malicious. Maybe we should confront him now– the alternative would be too risky.* "Lucian, could you run over and grab another thing for bedding? Might be nice to have more support."

"Sure thing," he said as he got up and left the room.

"Alright, I was thinking we should confront him and see how he reacts. I should be able to read his subconscious limbic system behaviors in response to a couple questions. Griffith could direct a few questions, and the rest of us can watch and see what he does."

"I guess that makes sense. To be fair, I'm kind of tired of watching everything and being scared of him as well," Valeria affirmed.

Victoria commented briskly, "He better not be able to deceive us then."

"Deception is obvious; focus on the eyes and lack of certain behaviors," replied Griffith. "I'll ask a few normal questions first; don't spook him."

Moments later, Lucian returned with two jackets that he set on the floor next to them. Victoria and Bruce lay looking at the ceiling while Tanho began explaining more octopus anatomy.

"Hey Lucian, what kind of tech did you use for that detector?"

Lucian calmly smiled and explained, "It's radio frequency stuff from that radio. It's not too bad, but if I hadn't built one before, I probably wouldn't have been able to." He kept his arms to his lap and sat crisscrossed facing Griffith; nothing about his body language signaled distressed limbic-system responses.

"Oh, that's pretty cool. We ought to go around and search a bunch of common areas. The people that may be watching us are pretty smart; I don't think they would give themselves up easily."

"Yeah, that makes sense; I can show you how to use it. It's easy but doesn't have much range; I don't really know how to extend it." He looked down and then forward, raising his shoulders as he glanced to where he set the receiver in the corner, disconnected from its mobile power source. His pupils remained only dilated by the darkness of the room, not noticeably adjusting from the questions thus far.

"That should work. Hey, what's your story, Lucian?"

Victoria sat up as Lucian responded, "It's basically just been school and the program. Lots of studying and researching my own interests. Once high school was done, I was put into contact with them, and after a bunch of testing and preparation, here we are." His breathing was calm and regulated. His arms and legs remained mostly still, and he began bouncing his right leg. His feet were directed to Griffith. Lucian rested his back against the edge of the pillar separating their alcove.

"What about outside of school and studies?"

His feet shifted slightly, leading his legs and hips to angle more to the left. His arms crossed nonchalantly as he said, "I did an occasional bit of fishing– oh, and I played a bit of piano. I oriented myself alongside studying and learning a lot– maximizing what my brain can store and handle." He thought about the lingering light headache he familiarized himself with after long days and nights of almost continuous research and notetaking-encoding. "That's where I learned a lot of this stuff; it's how I'm well enough able to survive, too, as I studied and looked into it. The resources from the program were very comprehensive." He returned to a more relaxed state of hands by his waist. "What about you?"

"Well, yeah, school and scouting– got lots of outdoor experience there. I've been hunting a fair bit– it helps with understanding the creatures and why they do what they do. Then the program reached out, and now here we are." He paused, "Hey Lucian, I've got something to ask you."

"Go for it," he responded, particularly confused.

Griffith waited, allowing dull suspense to build before looking up, matching Lucian's eyes, and asking, "On the ship, how were you the only one awake... and with a knife?"

Confusion– some combination of synaptic artillery, first directing frequency translations through the thalamus and temporal lobe before running several times through the prefrontal cortex. The hippocampus enlisted support, searching through memories in a neuronal kaleidoscope; labyrinthine chemical trails instilled emotion through amygdalin mystique; cognitive ties of simple retention, encoding, and recalling of one mostly fatal ship crash. Adrenal surges coalesce at the frontal lobe, switching posture– stress in its most primal form, pushing limbic influence into a shift of footing.

Lucian looked to the side, closing his eyes beyond the typical furrow in contemplation. *Did that really happen? There's no way.* He moved his hips to the center, less relaxed. His arms awkwardly crossed, deep in thought.

"That didn't happen." He felt the eyes watching him intently.

After a minute, Griffith responded, "But of course it did."

"We know what happened," Victoria added.

"Let me just explain what I know. We went through the wormhole. I woke up as we went into the water. Griffith led us out a few minutes later, and here we are. I was strapped into the seat the whole time– at least until we got to the water." Lucian remained nervous, lightly sweating but trying to hold himself in a confident manner.

"He's telling the truth," Tanho said.

Victoria gestured outwards, "Agreed, he doesn't know about it."

"About what?" he asked.

Griffith paused and looked around as if they had not already swept the room for bugs before saying, "In the control room down there– it was a picture of you, standing, holding a blade while everyone was passed out on the ship."

"Okay, yeah, something is up for sure. We really need to find a way out of here. The traps we made are definitely not enough; they're crude at best and don't account for numbers or high defense."

Valeria added, "We have no heavy machinery or artillery. Someone or something is playing games now."

Chapter 16

Acclimatization

Sleep was impossible, the night filled with restlessness. At some point during the night, though, they all managed to close their eyes and lose track of time; it was a strange, listless night in *their* insufficiently fortified structure.

Tanho stood impatiently in the corner of the room, mere inches away from his spear, leaning point-down against the wall. Griffith fidgeted his thumbs before touching each forefinger to its respective forefinger counterpart. He contemplated aimlessly through roundabout arguments and justifications– dull thought had no benefit.

"Alright, what's out today again?" Victoria asked.

"That pygmy dragon is out today," Lucian said.

Tanho continued, "And tonight's the wolves and giant purple panther we saw."

"Is now a good time for naming?" Valeria proposed.

Griffith answered lightly in a higher, understanding tone, "Maybe that's better saved for the return trip at this point; I'd like to work on getting home."

"Understandable," Lucian agreed with a nod.

Valeria re-offered, "We can't be sure, but today is also the big pig guys; I guess that means today marks the three-week anniversary."

"Three weeks in this wretched place–" Griffith proclaimed.

Valeria cut him off, correcting, " –wretched *and beautiful* place." They mostly nodded, it's true.

Lucian led, "So there are two routes we can take here; we can either put efforts into researching the creatures in the hope of staying alive as long as possible, or we can try to send signals into space and hope someone can bring us back home."

Griffith responded, "I doubt they would just send another ship without some sort of sign of life. I don't think we have any way of really calculating our position in space with regard to the wormhole we came through– but it may be beneficial to get a signal to space, and hopefully, eventually, it would travel through the wormhole, undistorted, so they send someone."

Victoria was provoked, "Would they just leave us here to die? There's no way to account for possible time distortion or even if the emergency transmissions made it through the wormhole. Chances seem slim yet again."

Every plan previously proposed seemed irrelevant. Constant change, continuous on Chaos, underscored every proposal line. The signal was obvious; it was likely their only way to communicate outside the planet without developing a complex series of levers and pulleys to excavate and repair whatever damage was done to the ship and then hope it works. Some of their crewmates were trained in ship repairs, but the goal of the mission much preferred specialization.

What was less obvious but easily justifiable was their long-term survival. Clearly, a home in the bunker was not right, but it could be used temporarily as long as they had guards and swept every room for hidden gas dispensers and bugs, as well as cameras, scanners, and detectors of any sort. If it were remotely possible to sweep the entire building and disconnect all power sources, including hidden ones, it may have worked. Something outside and all their own would be most beneficial; *we can try and find the cave-like structures we considered before this.*

The rest of the day was simple for Lucian: make the transmitter and find out how to send the signal out of Chaos' atmosphere. They needed to explore more and get a good sense of the landscape. Griffith, Tanho, and Victoria went upstairs to test the simulation rooms while Bruce and Valeria returned to the main control room to see if they could get security cameras up and running.

As they went upstairs, they remained cautious, confused, and hoping that the planet's founders had not made their way back into the base. Each tile remained equally pristine, blank in indescribable light. Each step was light, producing small taps as their target door got closer. The handle was cold, and the room was stale; pushing through, levers and switches made up the entire back wall, supported by a few monitors where average height would make buttons obsolete.

"Alright, simulation 2 is closest," Tanho said as he flipped the red and gray handle over.

"Computers would be cool too, I suppose," Victoria mused. She turned on the main room's power that they had passed on their way in. With the screens now lit up, they saw their second simulation room come to life. From two opposite upper corners, cameras showed life in some vast expanse. The corners of the room were invisible, a seamless transition from ground to sky.

Tanho and Victoria left and went to the room, entering from the left side of the screen and walking around on the rough, open terrain.

"Woah, this feels so real!" Victoria exclaimed. Each step on dirt and then the grass was different, as if they were stepping on the actual thing. The door closed and completed the illusion. Looking around, the sky was a bright yellow-red, and a few scattered creatures moved in the distance in most directions. Within moments, the smells rushed in and settled; *it's probably coming from the ceiling.*

"The air is so refreshing," Tanho told Griffith. He looked up to the corners of the room, "And I can't see the cameras; that's kind of scary... but cool."

Griffith alerted over the intercom speaker, emitting a surround sound from above them, " Moving you guys to the cliffside." Disorientingly, the floor carried them across the ground, accelerating through trees before moving diagonally upwards.

They both closed their eyes as Griffith moved them up and down, learning the controls. Gravity didn't seem to affect them in this transition state, but they did not dare try to jump with their eyes open.

"We're here!" he called. They opened their eyes to an aerial view of a cliffside close to their original camp.

"Take a look at that," Victoria said as she pointed to the right. They moved closer, slowly this time to not nauseate. A circular cliffside cave, somewhat accessible by walking from around a bend to the right, held what looked like a suitable, safer home.

"See if you can go inside," Tanho requested. Moving closer and closer, the inside began to light up as if in response to their flying box's presence. As they moved inside and each nook lit up, a strange weight was lifted off their chest– nothing was living inside.

"Tanho, Victoria, what is that?" Griffith exclaimed.

They looked closer, inspecting, before Victoria said, "It seems to be some kind of animal remains. Maybe whatever was here last wasn't hungry for the rest."

"That sounds plausible. I guess the nighttime creatures may use this for safety; I don't think it'll be a suitable house. Besides, it smells horrible down here."

He navigated them up to their ship's pond. "I wonder if we can see through the water."

"Don't!" Victoria quickly responded.

"Yeah, we might get soaked."

"Good call. Alright, let me make it nighttime, and maybe we can see some creatures."

"Any way you could increase our brightness, though? Maybe give us some tools or weapons, just in case? Tanho asked.

"Oh yeah, let's see what kind of swag we can get you." Just a minute later, he had sent two gray coats. Another minute later, a sword-shield and an atlatl with a back-quiver of arrows appeared between them.

"That's so cool," Victoria commented.

"Hopefully, we can take them out of the room," Griffith's voice announced. As the day quickly turned to night, the sun leaped over their heads and produced the purple sensation they had experienced through many nights before.

Bruce and Valeria still held spears and maintained a balanced center of mass at all times. Upon entering the room, they located the computer area dedicated to monitoring activities about the facility. Turning the power back on, they were no longer met with the earth-shattering image– instead, the screens turned on normally. *Did we imagine it all? No way.* All the screens in their section lit up simultaneously, displaying a few outer cameras but nothing inside.

"Do we have any other views?" Valeria asked.

"There's no way to know for sure, I imagine they have ultimate control over what we see. But there's nothing else I can press here," he said, standing over a panel as Valeria stood farther back, taking it all in.

"That was kind of anticlimactic, wouldn't you say."

"Well, yeah, that's how it goes with the short straw. The simulation stuff sounded intriguing."

"Wait. Take a look at that," she said, gesturing to the upper left camera view. It displayed an angle of the metal structure above. Based on the perspective, it had to be in a tree.

"What about it?" Bruce asked, tilting his head.

"It moved."

His eyes opened wide as he stood up and stared intently. "What? I don't see it."

"Bottom left; watch." Staring, a gray limb appeared and disappeared. He went back and tried to select that camera to move it– it was not set to patrol. To their dismay, it was not capable of moving around.

A few minutes of watching the outside cameras yielded no results. They called over the walkie-talkies, "Guys, come in."

"Yeah, what's up?" said a masculine voice they attributed to Griffith's.

"Go," Lucian attended.

"We've got some movement on the surface, but it disappeared. It's likely in a blind spot."

Valeria continued, "We think it may be inside."

After a pause, Griffith asked, "Description?"

"A gray arm, probably two or three feet long. Be careful. Last seen five minutes ago up top." They moved back to the main courtyard and navigated back upstairs to Lucian, who was still working his way about the signal.

"It's probably nothing, you know?" he said nonchalantly as he spliced bare copper wiring.

He chuckled, "Yeah, I don't really have any idea what I'm doing... but at least I know some Morse code."

"We definitely saw something. Well, Valeria surely did; I probably did."

"Probably just an octopus moving around up there... maybe it died and is going to be eaten; they lose color and parts of their flesh as they die. I don't think it's anything to worry about." He continued pressing a metal wire into the crevices of the crude device in his lap as Bruce and Valeria left to make a chemical run.

As soon as they left, he placed a spear to his right and one of the chemical flasks to his left, one from the pile Bruce left as he cleared the backpack. *They had better not take all of what we have there; it could be useful.*

Wielding their new weapons, they awaited an enemy. Tanho looked into the darkness with a smile, *I wonder where they are.* Rushes and crashes entered in a muffled symphony, Griffith raising the volume from the other room.

"See anything?" he asked.

Victoria responded, "Not really, it's pretty empty."

"Over here, all I've got are numbers; the animals are numbered."

"Start with something in the middle, then. Let's inspect it," Tanho requested.

"Number fifty, inbound." In front of them, something aquatic spawned.

"Fire-resistant squid, cool." Tanho walked forward, and Victoria followed. *Can I touch it?* He took the end of the atlatl and slowly pushed it, causing it to begin flopping around.

"That's so cool. Does it feel real?" Before waiting for a response, she took a decisive step forward and decapitated it. "Yeah, real."

"Let's try something a little higher: 60?" Tanho asked. Moments later, a bug appeared and began flying away. It was large enough for the lightbox to shed light onto the insect's reflective legs. Tanho took his atlatl, nocked an arrow, and threw, propelling the extension of his arm to fling the arrow.

"Nice shot," Victoria said sarcastically.

"Warm up. Warm up," he repeated, nocking another arrow before letting it down and saying, "Whatever." They watched it get farther away, descending before a purple flame erupted upwards and scorched it.

"How about lucky number 7."

"No, 17,"

"Which one is it, guys? Both?"

"Fine, both, but give a break in between."

"I'm good with that; it's much safer anyhow."

"17 is on the way– closer to 50."

"Wow, okay–"

Tanho looked up, interrupting with widening eyes and disbelief etching across his face. He drew a quick breath and sparsely released some to say, "h–o–l–y... s–h–i–t." Crushing the fire-resistant squid beneath its foot stood a mountainous giant. Barehanded, the large man looked to his new surroundings. His brain was fully developed, yet his lifelong experiences were pre-implanted; he was now conscient. Instinct taught him to attain a weapon, especially when caught out in the open.

Their first instinct was to run. Victoria was the first to make it to the room's border, Tanho taking a different route– it materialized right between them. They both clashed roughly simultaneously but at different angles to the room's squareness.

The giant left the bounds quickly, searching for a stick. While Griffith called, "Go in the same direction," it found one.

"Shut this thing off!" Victoria yelled as she dropped the sword, its weight slowing her down. They slowed and Tanho nocked an arrow into the hook of the atlatl, turning around. A wolf produced a lowly growl from behind, and now the giant took to the light; it ran straight towards them.

"I can't! I don't know how!" Griffith shouted through the intercom. They darted to their right, setting up the wolves and the club-wielding giant to brawl.

Can they even see us? she wondered. A wolf leaped upwards to the giant and was backhanded with his non-dominant. It landed beside them and locked eyes. "Yeah, it can see us."

"Griffith!" Tanho threw down the quiver and speared the blunt atlatl at the wolf as it approached with its ever-gleaming claws. Two other wolves began attacking, causing the one next to them to leave, but their battle naturally led to the lightbox. They moved away, but the creatures followed in battle, preferring the light. *What kind of simulation is this?*

After the giant's club clipped the back of a wolf, they retreated. He looked down upon the two humans, now frozen some fifty feet away. Their appearance warranted a glance at his own limbs.

"The caveman berserker dude is gonna attack," Tanho stated. He watched as its large, slitted eyes went from up to their left to down and to them. The wooden log-club went into a more active, variable position, close to shoulder level, using gravity as an additional force accelerator.

In front of them appeared a massive jumble of long worms resembling maggots. Tanho took a step back from surprise but froze, refusing to even speak. He locked eyes with her; she covered her mouth as the giant was, too, surprised and stopped. It looked at them and at the illuminated zone; they were highlighted. Victoria took the shield from her back and looked at Tanho, trying to telepathically communicate, *a distraction— anything?*

As the worms descended in rumbling, Tanho slowly took off his jacket before emphatically waving his hand, also trying to nonverbally capture the giant's attention. When he saw a dilated pupil, he threw the jacket up, slightly bending the knee to reduce his upward momentum, keeping his legs glued to the ground. *Griffith, what's going on?*

With a swift motion, she gripped the shield's edge tighter, winding the shoulder back as if preparing to pitch. As she twisted her body, her arm snapped forward across her body, releasing the thin shield with a wrist flick. The frisbee took form, soaring through the air with a spin to keep its path true, arcing down as its weight overpowered flat uplift before finally striking the groin.

A single step back redirected the lingering worms, which immediately went to the movement— hunger can act as a strong motivator. As arms went down, the center of mass shifted down, increasing force and pressure applied to the ground, somehow seemingly sensed by the underground dwellers.

They launched into the bottom of his foot, inflicting a pained groan that sounded human but was devoid of inflection or resemblance to words or language. Victoria looked up, *Griffith, come on. Where are you?*

As the giant fell to his knees, the wolves returned with company and began tearing into the giant from the Achilles. Tanho and Victoria took the opportunity to sneak away, bringing the light with them. The light then cut off, a familiar miasma of blood and darkness as they took to the ground, sensing each other and waiting.

Finally, Griffith opened the door, and the sound was reduced to nothing. As the two of them left the room, he asked, "You guys good?"

"Yeah, yeah."

Victoria just kept walking, reaching for the walkie-talkies as Griffith told them, "Bruce and Valeria got cameras; they're all exterior, and something was up there and then disappeared. They suspect it might have made its way inside. Could be that thing you saw, Tanho."

Upon clearing the hallways and rooms above them slowly, they had made it to the surface without any sign of the gray-limbed creature. They had grown much more efficient in clearing the building through repetition, building spatial knowledge and re-lived feelings of uncertainty and anticipation each angle-swing.

"The signal is ready," he said as he flipped on the surface power. Together, they stared at the empty sky, the sun finally rising, where storms would gather in half a day. The window was relatively short for the signal to escape without wasting lots of precious, scarce materials– if the hypothesis was correct, little to no sound waves would reflect back to them.

"Alright, here goes," Lucian said, looking from their rudimentary satellite dish to the button on his handheld device. Out loud, he annotated, "dot, dot, dot– S... dash, dash, dash– O... dot, dot, dot– S." The satellite-dish light was lusterless as they waited; no signal bounced back, as it had the day before– the day of the spiders. He repeated the signaling six times more; "life path number seven."

"I almost forgot about those– our signaling key. Emergency signals only; this definitely counts," Valeria reminded them.

"Why life path numbers again? Why is that the key?" Victoria questioned.

Griffith explained, "Single digits represent the life path numbers just because they reflect levels of experience, outlook, and certainty... it already existed, so that's what we were taught. Ten through nineteen were for very specific messages."

"Ah, yes, our favorite signal: twelve repetitions– do not come, we are dead." Lucian locked eyes with them and nodded, slightly biting the inside of his cheek. They nodded and moved on.

They enjoyed the sunlight, even if the dense, overlapping canopies absorbed most of it. Several days of recluse-like activity affects the brain. They had been on the ship for a while; it affected them greatly. Having so many of them together made the time pass much faster, though, allowing for communications and games and laughter; it was similar to that now, with only the brisk hunting party of three to get another week's worth of food. They were stocked up and had no need to risk more exposure. The thoughts of moving to the cave slowly disintegrated, the brain still lingering on to central synaptic connections but with lack of use, dismembering the more far-out, less useful links for more important ones, such as their need for recreation.

With improved knowledge of the simulation chambers, two people could control from the outside, allowing four people to be inside at once. This left no security or real failsafes, though, so usually only one group was rotated in and out, allowing for uniformity between each simulation and allowing for competition.

"Is it time for exercise?" Victoria asked, several minutes after looking up between the leaves, listening to the familiar breeze and the silence of their particularly peaceful day. If they only needed to go out twice a week– once for food and once for the signal– the workout regiment would have to be held. For safety, Lucian set up the light in view of one of the cameras they could manually turn at the surface; they would not need to visit the surface and risk capture every day. Every time the surface was reached, they reflected on the mysterious being on their first day there and the gray limb they saw on their first day on the cameras. It was always, *someone might be watching,* but they had become used to that feeling. *Hey, survival is survival. We're not trying to get ourselves killed.*

They meandered back down, grabbing a few gels for their simulation. By working the muscle until almost failure before ingesting a stamina and recovery gel, they could surpass their limits and tap into a therapeutic headspace.

"Can't wait to be completely exhausted by the end of this," Tanho lied.

"Well, this time... we're going to stop before the gels lose their effects. Thanks for testing that, by the way; we all really appreciate it," Bruce chuckled, laughing by the end.

"I'm sitting today out," Tanho declared as he opened the door, still limping in a slight writhe from full-body soreness. He sat down in one of the many chairs. Now versed in sim-room operation, all could feasibly take turns; instead of their typical groups of two, Lucian joined Bruce and Griffith for the exercise regiment. Griffith and Bruce could focus on more strength and sprints than the others, targeting their workout to speed and strength as preference.

He stepped inside with them, signaling Tanho, Victoria, and Valeria to start everything up. The ground transformed as it had many times before, with the sky blending colors, clear and bright. They looked down as their eyes adjusted to the unnoticeably artificial sunlight. They stretched on the flat, dirt-ridden ground, knowing the dirt on their clothing would disappear as soon as they exited the simulation.

"The glitch in the system a couple days ago sure was something," Griffith told Lucian as he touched his fingertips to his toes.

"Yeah, maybe it just hadn't been up in a while– had to warm up some more before letting you stop it. Definitely not safe." They did light jogs before moving into the strength part, utilizing heavy shields and some logs they materialized before the main events– creature combat. With the safety of tested controls and working shut-off buttons, they recognized that the lower the creature number, the larger the beast. Scratches emerged after fights with some of the smaller creatures, yielding more care and better armor. While in the slim, lightweight armor, real training with some of the more dangerous creatures was possible. *We've got to learn all we can about them before we have to fight them for real.*

"After the storms tonight, we'll see the big crocs again. There'll also be those frogs and esprit and spear dudes. Let's just fight a few of those, one on one," Bruce said.

Griffith questioned, "So you wanna fight a chicken, too? I think I'll pass on that one."

"Well, wouldn't it be smart if we wanna get food?"

"Maybe, maybe."

They had mapped a bunch of the middle-tier creatures in a process of traveling quickly away as soon as they materialized. The esprit would be fast, yet killing it as soon as it arrived would not be fair. They gave it some time and then made themselves known. The long-legged creature would easily win in a footrace– the main option was range, most useful in the form of a primitive bow or the atlatl. Griffith and Lucian's preferred primitive ranged weapon was the bow, while Bruce favored the atlatl. Bruce was swifter in his release and struck the esprit from roughly twenty-five yards.

After some target practice on moving esprit, they switched to the more dangerous creatures. Single spiders were the choice target; they worked too well together. It was far too risky to put multiple spiders in coordination even if Griffith had won that battle before– but there was more on the line then... it was more real.

Griffith aimed his bow at the spider, who easily deflected the arrow in flight. "Damn, that was a good shot too."

He dropped the bow and grabbed his spear and shield. The shield in his left hand held loose for purposeful sliding down his arm. The convex curve of the front side allowed a punch to deflect a few spider limbs, providing a valuable opportunity to surprise it. The spider learned very quickly, though, especially in the case of the bow; Lucian drew the bow back and induced a reaction.

Bruce had yet to show his hand, and he kept it that way; he kept that element of mystery and began moving around the spider, providing the flank that the spider was smart enough to keep extra attention to. Even a single extra limb pointed in Bruce's direction could be the difference between a clean kill and a more difficult, risky one. The lance, this time with a single metal tip to prevent catching on one of the limbs, would be the weapon to deliver the final blow– it was the spiders' weakness as long as it was a little bit longer than the longest limbs.

Griffith moved in with three arrows of support from behind him before a quick atlatl sling, opening space for a targeted shield bash to the left side and a spear from the right.

"Simple!" he exclaimed, brushing a light sweat from his brow. *Every time, I'm way too nervous.*

Lucian swapped to the lance, and Griffith grabbed his bow from behind him.

"Ready."

"Ready."

"Ready."

The spider appeared, looked around, and put up more limbs in defense. It was already surrounded– suspicious. It looked at each of them individually, spending a good few seconds analyzing.

This time, Bruce tossed an arrow up over the spider with the atlatl pre-nocked. His back facing the beast, he spun, twisting his right arm counter-clockwise to angle the arm extension perfectly. He flicked his wrist down as the force transferred into the atlatl, and the arrow began its descent in the arc, releasing the arrow, too spinning counter-clockwise with minimalist, dark fletchings. Griffith began pulling back his bowstring, letting out a quick shot without ample time to stabilize– although, the quick-shot was rehearsed with a good feel for his personal weaponry, modified the exact same way each time.

Lucian ran forward with the shield ready and lunged the spear with enough force to deflect two limbs and embed, finished off with the atlatl from the other side.

"Bruce, you're up," Lucian said as he stretched and relinquished the shield first and then the bloodied spear.

"Look good in that suit," Bruce complimented, referring to the light armor.

"Hey guys, could I get a sling, please? Do we have that?" Griffith asked.

"I'll take a look," played ambiently in Tanho's tired voice. In moments, the sky dropped the string and a pouch with premade tubes for the string to pass through.

"How did you guys do that?" Lucian questioned, standing a step backward.

"We're just good like that," Victoria announced.

"I'm going to figure that out later. Anyways, I'm ready."

"Shoot."

"Yup, go for it," Bruce ended. Griffith began winding up the sling with a sharp-looking crystal from the ground. He slowly sped up, getting a feel for the weight. Lucian grabbed two arrows and held both in his shooting hand, nocking one and shooting right, then quickly redrawing, nocking, and shooting to the predicted movement left. The spider was taken aback by this and likely the situation it was placed into as well; it saw the swinging object and strange creature but had no time to learn about it. It began to roll away, utilizing the tips of its feet to propel each time one was passed over, allowing it to traverse uphill. It outran the spear but not the force placed onto the rapidly spinning crystal. It held sturdy in the air and went clean through the spider, even slicing a leg off after escaping the main body.

"Great hit," Bruce laughed.

"Alright, I'm good for today, I'll head out and work on our surveillance, and I'll prepare tomorrow's hunting gear," Lucian said, prompting the simulator to shut down and show white before the door automatically opened. "See you guys later. Have a good workout."

Chapter 17

CONTRIVE

"What's today's target? Do we want some momma deinodile?" Tanho asked.

"I doubt you're going today. You don't get to decide," Victoria declared. She glared at Tanho jokingly.

Griffith proposed, "Let's go for some chicken and lizard. I think the frog will be too fatty anyway. Oh, here's Lucian."

As he walked in carrying sharpened metal poles wrapped in tape, he ecstatically announced, "Tanho has been helping me with these weapons here. Take a look; we've got a perfectly balanced ranged weapon which, upon impact, delivers this spider venom… and, remember that dragon you guys got? Well, I extracted the venom from its tailspike, and it'll release both simultaneously. I didn't test it because I wasn't sure how I'd clean anything up, but I have a feeling the result will be something to behold." They smiled, imbued with hope in response.

Griffith and Victoria received one, proving their aim through training and in the field. Lucian held on to the last one, the only one employing the tailspike as a delivery method– the tip of the spear with a semi-sheath and two carefully excavated tubes straight into the venoms.

"So we shouldn't use these as walking sticks?" Victoria queried.

"The bottom end is fine, just not the tip."

They went to the camera room first, noting the dull light before switching to some of the other cameras. Tanho stayed behind

"Wait, look at that." Valeria pointed to one of the repositioned cameras.

"Is that a frog?" asked Victoria.

"No way, that can't be a frog." They moved closer to the screen, looking farther up as they approached the elevated image, now full-screened. Instead of a flat helmet of dense shell, it now had a spike.

"Woah," Lucian said plainly. They sat and waited longer to see what would happen. It soon jumped into the grass and disappeared. Before they left, however, another creature appeared– a large beetle greater than even the frog made its way from the smaller trees and into the field, likely in passing.

"That's bigger than normal, right?" Griffith asked.

Confirming, Bruce exclaimed, "Yup!" They watched longer as a group of small creatures emerged from the grass. There were six of them, no more than two feet long and half a foot wide. Within seconds, the long spear protrusions generated from nothing and stabbed into the back of the beetle.

Valeria gasped. The beetle flinched and stretched its back outwards and up, visible from however far away they were in the quality of the decent camera. The six small creatures began going closer to the beetle, penetrating farther from multiple angles.

After some looked away, Lucian brought them back, saying, "Look, it's still going in."

Looking again, the spears drew in farther. It seemed it was disappearing.

"Wow, the beetle is ingesting the spears somehow," Victoria observed. After a minute of this, one of the small creatures was eaten, prompting the others to detach their spears and retreat to the grasses, likely bleeding from their foreheads.

"Okay, I thought I noticed the creatures being weird two days ago with everything out, but I didn't know they could do that.," Bruce told them.

"Yeah, when we all watched the creatures fight with the night-vis, I thought the wolves might've been a little slimmer and quicker," Victoria added.

"That night, I saw a bundle of lights instead of one... but thought it could've been camera resolution messing with me, and it was super late," Valeria said.

Lucian collected, "Alright, something is different, but we knew that would happen. You guys have seen the panel– you know how it says 'Updated Sample Needed' as the description beneath every creature ID? I think they change more than we previously imagined. Let's go get this week's food."

Griffith called over the walkies, "Tanho, the creatures are slightly different. Can you come cover cams?"

He sighed before returning, "on the way."

Walking outside, they knew it would have to be a quick mission, yet again. It was not very safe on the surface; they would be much better off staying underground as much as possible. The abandoned bunker had plenty of space, even if they were being watched.

"Tanho, how you doing?" Lucian called.

"Good, animals have cleared, it seems. For now, at least."

They climbed the new ladder up the wall and used a rope to rappel down. The one coat they used on the barbed wire remained there; they hoped nothing could climb the rope and figure it out.

The rafts they had tethered to trees further up on the island were still in good shape. They crossed smoothly through a dense region where the wind had congregated the flowers until they reached the opposite shore.

White-spider-limb spears, an atlatl, and a sling in hand– the metal poles used as defensive weapons, they looked for their first prey. Not before long, an esprit appeared through the tree line. Bruce stepped forward with the atlatl, much quieter than the sling from a long distance. He watched it peacefully, knowing the heavy arrow would have to decapitate the thinner esprit's neck to achieve a kill. They crept forward until he and Lucian had a clear shot on a still target.

"3, 2, 1," Bruce counted off before launching, hoping Lucian would shoot at the right time to impact at the same time.

"Good job, guys," Griffith said, running over and looking around for predators before attaching the sling to one of the motionless legs. They helped drag it out, cut off part of the neck, and stop its bleeding. Using a dense cloth to hold pressure on the body, they could bleed the creature back at their base without risking blood dripping into the water and something attacking them. The layer of clear to purple liquid seemed to provide some type of insulation from whatever may lurk below.

As they started back to the rafts, a band of spear-bearing small creatures approached out of the grass uncharacteristically.

"Yeah, let's go," Victoria told them.

Twilight skies infested their dreams, nightmares of sorts shared, no summit in sight.

An intoxicating sunset invaded the night sky, a myriad of purple and pink lining every wave of cloud; through the sun's waning moments, reflective clouds instilled the final warmth of the day, relieving the day and welcoming the graveyard shift: pure darkness in its grim onslaught.

A multi-fractal-ed shroud blanketed the sky; the moon was blurred yet beautiful, peering through in a tesselated circle, the bladed waves cut darker lines through the sky. Blue is just a description; from the other side of that wall of that sully overcast, where the brisk mist sent wind every which way, we gazed to see the fabled spectacle glum, blue in immortal under-glow. They longed for its clarity– an unobscured view, for they were sad, and the moon was too.

Crimson skies mirror violent eyes through a moon's blood-soaked tears; power entwined, might unraveling, hell incarnate rains from above. Enchanted mystery, through and through, lies beyond that blanket of ill-fated clouds. It is not yet over; we remain standing strong; the stars tremble before us, for fleeting sighs, we belong.

The emerald hills launched waves of forest to tangerine sunset. Speckled trees easterly illuminated, lining valley-horizon in peak after peak. In the distance watched a lonely ocean, surrounding and ever-encroaching further into the damned island, fruitful and vast yet slowly sinking; that life may seem condemned, but the plants and animals, flora and fauna, they do not care. *In the end, life finds a way; we will find a way off this fucking planet.*

Bloodied hands fall on brazen sands; a roll reveals the bleeding red sun, blinding with blood. The enraged galaxy circles above, offering its wisdom in twinkling stars. There's got to be a message. Music plays a familiar thunderous symphony– sad, dark, lonely, scary. Something is outside the cherry velvet curtain, satin providing hospice to the creatures outside; *no, I'm hiding from them.*

The moon peered over the horizon, becoming morose and gloomier as it rose. It carried a darkness, that young moon; it burnt out all the lights as its midnight rays conquered every corner of the cityscape. Obscurities manifest monsters, behemoths of mass destruction with the mind's generous, unlimited potential. Amorphous demons with spikes and horns condescend the ultra-black moon, masked and shrouded to carry out an unsolicited mission: death, decease, and demise– a mortality aforethought but futile. *Good night,* a hopeless disregard.

They spent hours watching the single camera, seeing many stealthy creatures line the grasses and occasionally chase a giant, gray pig.

"Those guys must be the primary food source," Tanho commented, feeling better.

"We haven't seen them chase anything or kill anything, only be killed," Valeria added.

They remained bored and holed up in their bunker, left only to play games, design weapons, and build up their living quarters. They had been through every storage room, compiling piles of wires and tapes and fleeces. In their room, seat cushions wrapped in soft clothing made pillows, layers of jackets made mattresses, and soft fabrics were reserved for blankets.

Lucian commented, "It's reminding me of that circle we found."

"Hey, would you guys want to catch up on naming things today? We can turn it into a game." Griffith suggested.

"–and let's take a look at the green caves through the simulation," Bruce decided.

"Well, maybe not. It seemed to emit things, and we know we can smell through the simulation. Might not be safe," said Lucian.

"Let's play a naming game. We've experienced the same animals now," Victoria beamed.

"Spear throwing? Knife throwing? Poker?" Griffith listed, excited to do something else for fun instead of learning about the planet.

"Poker is too risky," Valeria frowned, "I'm naming something at least; I'll earn it, though.

They thought for a minute before Tanho proposed, "Paperclip sculpture building contest– no supports, paper airplane competition for distance and hang time– must resemble a plane and can use as much paper as you want, and creature design contest– best suited for this planet?"

"How will ranking work?" Victoria asked.

"One through six, then split evenly, and people can choose which they name. We can basically take as long as we want for naming, though. Maybe we have a naming ceremony when we get fresh air in four days."

"And the time for the competition?"

"Let's go with six hours– make it interesting. Better yet, till sundown. We don't really have anything better to do."

Lucian commented, "Well, I could work on the labs and research that creature incubating in our vat, maybe even prepare to make some stuff of our own."

"Oh, come on; you can have some fun this one day," Griffith pried.

"Plenty of time for that stuff; take a break," Valeria too convinced.

"Sunset it is." They went back down, careful to avoid the traps still there. Lucian gathered some paper clips, pencils, and supporting malleable paper and tape. He brought everything to a lab bench on the other side of the building and sat down. The large clear glass didn't bother him; the others would have to come all the way inside to see his workspace hidden by the sinks.

Lucian began connecting triangles of paperclips to make a dodecahedron of triangular and pentagonal faces. 120 paper clips utilized just under half an hour, the first structure was complete. He began making hexagons now, connecting one after another with a slight bend to try and keep each connection at the exact same angle.

An hour and a half gone, 112 hexagons covered most of the lab bench. He began connecting edge to edge until he built an unsupported bottom half of the sphere. Placing his first paperclip contraption inside, he used six additional paper clips on the outer side and three towards the smaller side to make room for a single paperclip chain to connect it in the middle. He repeated this for the five sides he could before building up the rest of the sphere and connecting the final strand. Now, he had a ball in a ball of paperclips held in place with what seemed like tensegrity.

He gathered three standard 8.5 by 11 sheets of paper, using one as the body and two as either set of wings for the F-16 he made. With the weight distribution slightly towards the back, Lucian made a light glue concoction to hold the wings and body together before misting an acid mixture to the back of the airplane and quickly drying it to make the wings slightly less heavy and lock their position. Holding the paper in the correct orientation with gloves, he sprayed the more pure solidifying mixture to areas that would unbend or break easier, giving them more strength while maintaining their weight and aerodynamics. He placed another paper cap on the nose to protect it during his trials; after checking to see if anyone was watching from outside, he gave it a few test throws.

It was time to design a creature; he immediately went to amorphism, a quality that, with the life structure of Chaos, would be nearly invincible. One of the leading, obvious drawbacks would be being engulfed, as a quick reaction time would cause any venomed stab or sting to hit nothing but air, the body capable of separation. If such a beast were caught off guard and engulfed, it would need a rigid exoskeleton to prevent being crushed or immediately digested; next, it would need a method of escape, which could also tie into its lethality and deadliness. *What fits?* With the picture of axe heads in his mind, he drew three black spear-axe heads that would act as ultra-dense blocks still capable of morphed structure. His vision left bladed hooks that could be aimed in different ways or aligned to maximize leverage and slicing ability; placing them aligned could make it easier to slice, but in multiple directions or into a single point would enable carnage or piercing power. *If my creature had reinforcements mirroring the amelanistic spider's legs, it could be indestructible.* He drew several sketches portraying the dynamic motion of the bulwark and the three connotative heads moving about and orienting in one direction to cut holes through solid metal walls to fit through.

With my design, aerial combat would be challenging, particularly against anything that could move too fast to see in certain light levels– improving eyesight and hearing is obvious, but a ranged weapon could be helpful. With the regenerative properties of many of Chaos' creatures, it would be viable to shoot out part of its body as projectiles, which would also help it cut through a creature's stomach.

On the right side of the paper, he began detailing distributed nervous function in bullet points. *Do not partake in needless fighting,* he thought, envisioning his creature fighting for sustenance and defense. If the new being could strike some type of fear and hesitation, it could pick its fights and reduce danger to itself while still being notably unkillable.

"Alright, who's up first?" Griffith asked, looking at the row of paper clip sculptures under blankets and paper airplanes alongside rolled-up blueprints.

Versed in some psychology, Tanho said, "Let's just go random– spin a pen." It would be a slight advantage to go first, as people would establish their voting standards and would be more likely to vote well.

"And then for ranking, 1-6 depending on place, best is 6, and ties go to the highest of the two? Three categories: difficulty, ingenuity, and likeability– how much you like it." Griffith asked. They nodded; it gave them all more opportunities to win that way.

Tanho was selected for the paper clip sculpture first, saying, "Well, here we go. I've got this pretty cool thing right here." He moved the cover sheets and held up a full-size acoustic guitar that supported itself with an endoskeleton looking like ribs and a spinal cord; the internal and external skeletons elegantly blended in an all-silver guitar that wished to be played.

They saved conversation for later and wrote down their rating out of ten in half-point increments. They could change the rating later, but kept the anonymity.

Valeria went next, saying, "I took the idea of chain linking and rounded it to make this spiraling sphere with a base of the same pattern to hold it in place." The pieces blended together to form a galaxy of orbits, with single-paper-clip circles representing either vortexes or planets.

Griffith constructed a miniature German shepherd. It was intricate but definitely did not take the entire time; the pointed ears and strong shoulders were very to scale, portraying a fierce companion that would have to be kept as a memento to Earth.

Lucian showed his intricate inception and how the complex shapes created illusions as he rolled it across the floor. The labyrinthine shapes blended and morphed as the phenomenon rolled to a stop.

Bruce took his sculpture and put it on, sleeve by sleeve, revealing the suit jacket with a line for outer pockets. He used three paper clips as a button clasp, binding and completing the elegance. He kept it on as they moved to Victoria.

Victoria built a peacock feather, implementing layering to make some areas thicker and denser to convey softness on the edges instead of a stronger middle. It was skillfully positioned to wave with precisely angled spokes that acted as the barbs. Rings of different densities formed the eye, centrally placed and powerful.

"The paper airplanes should probably be distance, accuracy, and looks– does that work?" Valeria confirmed. They again nodded and brought their planes and some paper to the right side of the large area, constantly surveying for potential dangers and security breaches. They oriented on a line that spanned the room's length and would serve as their accuracy meter. They would track each throw for distance with the papers, keeping it as a placeholder to visually compare before closer inspections for closeness. They lined all the planes up randomly and voted.

"Three throws, yeah?" Lucian urged. They accepted, and he went first, the competition being based on skill and craftsmanship rather than influence by others. The competition was over quickly, and Lucian and Victoria smiled through their apparent victory. Valeria frowned and went back to the room first.

"And now, for the final showcase... let's see, spin the pen," Victoria developed through a dramatic tonal shift. As luck would have it, she went first, unveiling by scroll the intricacy that was her monster; its body was surrounded by curved blades that moved in coordination with each other. The wind wove together familiar blades that sliced up and engulfed anything daring enough to run into it. The body itself would seem entirely made up of the blades themselves, but cuttlefish-like cells would blend the whole mass into its background; it could learn and relearn which colors are optimal in fighting each individual creature, depending on how long it had been since a color-spectrum perception mutation.

Valeria displayed and detailed her creation, a small creature with densely powerful limbs, some with needlelike tips to inject anything it touched with a potent venom and gas concoction; with that kind of failsafe, an affected creature would either die from the venom or the rapid expansion and diffusion of the gas. She conveyed it like a jumping spider, similar to the larger ones on Chaos in intelligence and design but to where each limb could inject. To further the destructive capability, she explained the reaction time similar to how small things on Earth can move and react so fast; with legs so powerful and accurate, it would be difficult to kill.

Bruce, too, designed a speed-specializing creature, but this one has resistant hairs secreting a slime that protects from any sort of digesting or potent pH enzyme. It invades the body with protracting spear points that clasp open the wound. The obvious countermeasure is keeping distance, but even that is difficult when the enemy you are fighting can disappear in a moment– distracting and misleading to hide in plain sight, mirroring the ground beneath or behind it.

The pen chose Griffith, unveiling his creature that detects body composition and scent to completely morph into its target. Through a single touch, it could change its whole body rapidly and store it for later use; it could observe, learn, and mimic the behaviors, too– the ultimate observer. Preferring assimilation until getting close enough to instantly change into its true or favored form allows surprise, even sporting the ability to rapidly concoct a potent narcotic from its own blood and diffuse it to the air, potent in spaces of low ventilation but can be directed to a specific target.

Then Lucian conveyed the destructive power of his hydra, an omnipotent cataclysm with a ranged weapon utilizing potential to generate immense power in an instant and the patience through high-functioning and distributed neural systems; *crazy but difficult.*

Tanho showed how his design secretes a gel and can shoot webs that absorb all the nutrients from living cells through an electrochemical gradient and negative pressure combination. By returning the gel to its own body, it could utilize the chemical nutrients for personal benefit, even storing and separating for high-dose poison cocktails and projectiles to compliment its primed spikes hidden beneath the gel mucous layer.

Tanho said, "Okay, now that we voted, I just want to say we probably can't actually make these here. We need much more time to figure out how the creatures here work, let alone make new things entirely."

"We have all the time in the world; it's okay," Lucian said. "Let's see who won." He was eager to conclude the ceremony with naming distribution, continue reverse-engineering creatures, and try to figure out the experiment's downfall while he still had the motivation.

Victoria and Griffith both tallied scores before Griffith revealed, "From first to last: Victoria, Lucian, Tanho, Valeria, Bruce, Griffith. Alright, alright."

Not to immediately rub it in, Victoria stood up more and said, "Okay, there are one hundred creatures exactly according to the range of the simulation, but we've only encountered about thirty, and named like eight. Maybe we go through and write down what all of the numbered ones are in the simulation and distribute the ninety-two. I'm cool giving the extra two to Griffith and Bruce."

Lucian confirmed, "Let's go for it. Oh, and which creature do we think will work to our goals?"

Valeria responded, "Maybe Victoria's. I think it would be reasonably easier to overexpress some genes, creating sharp protrusions and blades like the snakes'. The color-changing would just have to be figured out, and we would have to make sure nobody catches on before we're done– that might take a while.

Griffith concluded, "Well congrats, Victoria, and let's get back to work then."

"Good to know you're still doing well," Tanho told Lucian.

"Yeah, still figuring things out, but I think I just had a breakthrough in understanding how their body structure is so versatile; I'll clue everyone in at the same time soon."

They went upstairs, calling, "Valeria, Victoria, let's head up!"

To the opposite side, "Griffith, Bruce, going up now!"

They all reconvened at the bottom level at one of their two upper-level access points, armed with spears and a few makeshift concussion grenades. Walking up the stairs casually with no hints of danger from the security feed, they reached fresh air once more. With the Morse code signal hopefully set far into space, they waited for a return signal and continued to imagine some signal returning "received."

"Before you guys go out, I learned a bit more about the creatures."

Griffith responded, "Do tell, Lucian."

"So my theory behind the creatures not falling over until the leg is fully cut off is either full-body hydraulics or something to do with quantum fields. Because the creatures heal so fast and have so much liquid inside of them, not too much is lost to injuries, allowing internal hydraulics to support lots of weight. I still haven't found any evidence of pressure manipulation, so we'll have to see and maybe analyze a live specimen, as dangerous as that may be."

Valeria commented, "Not looking forward to that."

"As for the quantum field hypothesis, something at a quantum level could be scaffolding on a molecular level, holding with immense strength. Getting a little farther out of earthly boundaries, something with quantum entanglement could allow cell-to-cell communication from longer distances; maybe that is how some of the creature's reaction times are so fast with a dispersed neural network."

Tanho added, "I read about some of that stuff a while ago; if these creatures are utilizing quantum properties, we might have to worry about probabilities and attacks that we can't perceive with our human eyes."

"I'll keep looking into it and see what I can find out," Lucian concluded.

"See everyone later. Be safe," Valeria mentioned caringly.

"Yeah, see you guys later."

Victoria, Griffith, and Bruce set off over the dented wall, sharing a single raft over the blissful layers of liquid below. Some paddle strokes created whirlpools, upsetting the purple below into a twirling spike, an upside-down tornado that touched air before collapsing or moving away and losing its tail.

While some of them were out and about, Lucian, Valeria, and Tanho continued in the laboratory, using their developing specimen to learn more through a readily available source of tissue and circulatory fluid. Progress was slow, but that's what they expected; there was no way to account for time-dilation, the speed of signal travel, or possible interference causing distortions. It was left to hope and continued effort. *Minutes, hours, days, weeks, years, decades– we may drift farther from humanity... forever.*

Chapter 18

THROUGH CONTEST

"Are we ready to head up to the surface again?" Victoria asked after finishing breakfast with Lucian and Griffith.

Griffith responded, "Yes, definitely. I'm so glad we still get fresh air–definitely better than being stuck in here."

The radio buzzed, "Come in. Over."

"Yeah, Tanho, what's up? Over," Victoria answered.

"When you guys come up, could you bring some caffeine or energy, please? My circadian rhythm alarm clock hasn't told me it's time to wake up yet, and I need a boost."

Dilated pupils and neuron firing; she looked down at the table to avoid displaying any expressions. Griffith also paused for a second, looking around the room partially in search of that caffeine. Lucian closed his eyes and cracked his neck very audibly to both sides.

"We'll bring some up soon, over," he said.

"Alright, thanks; I'm really falling asleep up here, haha."

They got up, and Griffith grabbed a miscellaneous gel packet. "I'll head up now. Grab Bruce and Valeria, and meet me there." They nodded and walked out swiftly.

"Valeria, Bruce, let's head up to the surface now, Griffith's already on the way."

Lucian added to Victoria, "Yeah, it's time to catch some rays– get that vitamin D."

Bruce and Valeria stood up at the same time and began walking. Bruce grabbed six spears, and Valeria carried the axe. The many flights of stairs led to an unknown destination, a relapse of remembering to facet a burning fire. As they reached the first actual floor several flights up, Bruce left two spears propped against the wall, *just in case.*

Tanho and Griffith met them in an office room previously swept for bugs and listening/looking devices. Tanho exclaimed at a moderate volume so as not to pass into the hallway, "There are creatures out today, and a lot of them, in every direction. Even the water seems stirred."

Griffith continued, "We don't know if there's a deeper meaning behind them yet, but we shouldn't go out today. Tanho, you mentioned the creatures seemed different again?"

"Yeah, they seem to have evolved again more than last time. There seem to be new and larger things too– whether it be a new species entirely or they are only released today of all days, there's no way to tell just yet."

Victoria paced back and forth before looking up and stating, "I want to think it's just some blood moon, but it still doesn't feel right. We should see if anything in the simulation room has changed. Tanho, you should head back to the cameras. I'll join. We need to make sure that nothing surprises us."

Upon reentering the security room, the change in the volume of creatures was evident. There were several times more creatures than they had ever seen, most large and in groups despite their typically solo hunting strategies. Large groups of flyers and small animals were also present but avoided the larger creatures. Not much fighting was occurring; *it's something about the grouping, surely.*

Minute by minute, many creatures left the waterside, most heading west. A few groups of each size remained to explore and move about, seemingly not in search of food. Tanho and Victoria watched intently to try to figure out what was happening.

"I wonder where they're going," Victoria commented. She looked around the screens and reflected on how much they had done here in so little time.

"Wait, take a look at this," Tanho said as he pointed at a screen of numbers. "The temperature in the tunnel rose by two degrees; that's weird, right?"

Victoria did not respond, focused on switching a few of the largest screen regions to view cameras in the tunnel. Once up there, she watched the camera showing the deepest into the tunnel. A spider squadron slowly crawled into the frame. Their eyes opened wide as Victoria sprinted to their office room.

"Change frequencies and be clear!" she yelled over the radio, enacting another protocol– like their signal phrases– for not alerting possible enemies. She changed to their first predetermined frequency Lucian created outside the radio's standard range and waited until she heard all four other names followed by "clear."

She announced, "Spiders approaching from the tunnel. Lots of creatures on the surface. I think they're coming in from assimilation. Over."

Griffith asked, "What's the best course of action? Over."

Lucian replied, "I'll send our panther vat down there at speed to break when hitting something. Then we get to the next safest spot and work from there. Over."

"Go now if you're doing it. There isn't much time. Over," Victoria directed as fast as she could talk.

Bruce said, "Valeria and I are grabbing whatever weaponry we can. We'll meet by the stairs. Over"

"I'm grabbing some chemicals, and then I'll be there. Over," Griffith furthered.

"Tanho and I will keep watch and prepare for whatever comes next. Good luck. Over." She returned to the security room and perceived the squadron of spiders present a regiment of fenrhor, fire-breathing panthers, and pygmy dragons and centipedes with dagger-like claws. Beetles with highly flammable pouches continued forward, teeth-bared for battle.

On the surface, the purple and clear liquid stirred and engulfed smaller creatures wandering too close. Mosquitos and falcons patrolled the skies through rapid shadows spotlighting the ground. Tanho and Victoria could not help but watch as the waves of creatures not going through the tunnel returned to the surface, escorting a band of giants.

"This is shaping to be quite the battle; I hope Lucian and Griffith can somehow block the tunnel or something," Tanho said, his eyes still glued to the screens.

Victoria's eyes darted quickly to the spears, envisioning herself picking one up and fighting. "We've still got some time to think of something. We'll make it through, just as we have every other time."

They watched as the vat with a still-growing panther rolled down the tracks and crashed into a layer of wolves too thick to avoid it. The slightly more viscous liquid covered some of the creatures and created a layer over the ground. It stuck to some fur and feet but otherwise caused little interference.

On the surface, large deinodiles and giants began redirecting the liquid, digging and pooling large quantities of the mysterious water away from the giant pond. Tanho thought, *I don't think they'll be fast enough to care right now. The tunnel is more important.* Many small creatures continually appeared on the cameras.

Lucian grabbed as many cables as he could before meeting Griffith at the lab, grabbing as much sodium hydroxide, nitric acid, sulphuric acid, and hydrochloric acid as possible. Back at the staircase, they began pouring it in different regions of the bottom level. The hardened material softened through stabs with the spider-leg spears.

"They're here!" Valeria shouted, watching as the spiders broke through the large glass wall and began scaling up to the rooms on each side, making room for the wolves to run around the fountain in the middle. The stone floor clattered with the impact of sharp glass, claws, and spikes. It rose further as more and more sound came from the tunnel– a series of grunts and clacking echoing the room. Seeing the group, the wolves beelined to the door. Bruce slammed the heavy door shut and held onto the handle, bracing for the initial impact.

Instead of a slam, scratching ensued. The sharp claws slowly penetrated the reinforced metal door. Peering through the door, Bruce saw thousands of creatures flooding about the mystic-purple fountain. Lucian tied the door handle to a railing before going up the weakened stairs, avoiding the trap they had set right there. It bought them a few more seconds of upward travel.

The door soon crashed down. With Bruce and Valeria at the rear, they kept spears at the ready. The first fenrhor leaped up, landing to landing, catching up to them in moments. Valeria landed a stab through the shoulder, bracing her footing to pull the spear back out. The internal pressure rose, utilizing the spider-limb joint as a barb trying to pull back on Valeria. Bruce jabbed the beast's head three times before Valeria lost her spear. Before dropping the weapon, however, she lowered herself, generating leverage to thrust the creature up and forward, toppling it. It bought them a few moments at best.

The rumble of stone against stone reverberated down the stairs. Below them, amidst the sounds of broken glass, creature stomping, and various clicking, some of the bottom steps collapsed. Griffith first reached the new opening, confused and rushing with adrenaline.

"Tunnel!" he called, ripping open four strength gels and consuming one. Valeria grabbed the two spears laid against the side and continued up to grab the gel from Griffith, who descended half a flight to meet them.

Sharp metal-against-stone tapping filled their ears as a spider sprinted through the tunnel barely above them. Full speed upstairs and ahead of the others, Lucian used a cable as a rope dart to make the spider hesitate before he swung it around, trying to wrap a few legs in a tangle. Bruce made it up next and used the longer alpha-spider's leg to shallowly stab the smaller one's body. It swung almost all its limbs up and to the side, slamming the spear to the ceiling. Crouching down, it leaped forward as fast and as powerful as it could within the instant, meeting Griffith's powerful jab before catching up to the retreating Bruce.

"Keep going!" Griffith said as he purposefully dropped a collection of vials Lucian dedicated to noxious gas down the stairs. He did not fully understand how it interacted with the skin and internal mechanisms of the creatures, but he trusted Lucian enough not to doubt. Hopefully, with the gas there, the bottom of the stairs would continue to decay until only the best climbers could make their way up. A pile of bodies would be the next step, blocking all the travel up until bored through. By then, they would surely have sealed the stairs.

Lucian could not shake the feeling that he had forgotten something important in the basement. *Too late to even think about that now.* It felt as though he were restarting all the progress they had made on the planet, regardless of the knowledge, training, and experiences they now carried with them. Finally, they made it up to Tanho and Victoria.

"There's more," Victoria told them.

Tanho continued, "They seem to be moving to the side we came from. If we went back towards the ship, we would just run into them when they go back out of the bunker. If we need to leave here, we'd have to make a break for an opening on the opposite side. We'd only have what we remember from the sim."

They caught their breaths as Victoria and Tanho had their strength gels. Everyone except for Victoria took a full stamina gel. She took half of a vision gel they hadn't experimented with much and half of stamina. Victoria felt like she could run for miles; it probably would not be an issue.

"They've definitely got our scent, and that tunnel opened, so we're definitely being flushed out into the open," Griffith confirmed in a considering manner, thinking with an upward glance.

Victoria responded, "Then we need a play, the Hail Mary. I remember some rock structures away from where the monsters entered. If we go now, we may have a lead on them. Besides, we need some time to get across the water." Her signal phrase was received.

They had mostly forgotten about the water creatures already. Step after step, Tanho and Griffith paced the room, contemplating war strategies and the condition of their survival so they could live for the most time possible. Taking a gamble with lives on the line in a short time was always the most challenging, burdensome step, but with a cocktail of information, insight, instinct, and integrity, the battle of wits could be won. A cool, calm, and collected approach was ineffable. The war was on– steps and forced behaviors had to be strategically avoided and played into; strong hands and bluffs must be played through the insight of and about an opponent, especially with six lives, their lives, on the all-in. *Deception.*

With as many gels as they could carry, they climbed the final steps out of the bunker that had provided their momentous survival much longer than they thought possible outside. The gleaming metallic walls shined a dull red. Lucian tapped a few signals into the transmitter as everyone began their way up and over the wall. He awaited a response as the second, third, and fourth went to the outside world. *Creatures today, and no signal once again.* He lingered until Valeria called him over.

"It'll be alright; we have all that we need already. Come on," she told him calmly.

He left his equipment behind, glancing back every few seconds to where the light should have been emitted if contact had been made. As he took the final step over the barbed wire, he imagined seeing the light flicker, even for a moment, although deep down, it could not be true. Now, in his eyes, they were radically isolated.

With the cameras' small size and practically invisible nature, along the vast networks of artificiality, there was no telling how many cameras there could be and where. They used sticks to disturb the water towards the monsters' access point, hopefully attracting anything that swam through the opaque liquids below. After throwing a rock toward the opposite shore, seeing the bubbles of octomorphs, and moving to the other side of the island, they all stood on the singular raft. Paddling slowly to not disturb the water, make noise, or create even the smallest of whirlpools, they felt the serene environment with cold shivers, the wake of their shelter's invasion and collapse renewing their human vulnerability.

Lucian stepped off first with one of the backpacks and a knife, making his way to a grassy field, surely sheltering malevolence.

They watched as it spread everywhere, from the grass to the trees, signaling their time to move. Lucian lit another region on fire to create as much smoke as possible. With highly flammable liquid, only a few drops and a well-placed spark could provide them a smokescreen, eliminate heat-detection, and camouflage their direction as long as possible. They went forward a few hundred yards before circling back, bringing fire towards and away from them. They'd have to keep moving, keeping them out of any open plain. The creatures, too, were shrouded by the smoke, some likely passing in the fire or hopefully after being drawn out. It quickly eliminated oxygen, reducing what the creatures could absorb and breathe. The six of them finally felt an advantage.

Speed would be key, the light breeze helping accelerate the fire's spread. Each of them noted their breathing, inhaling, then exhaling, slowly and deeply, timed for pockets of increased visibility for less carbon dioxide and other potentially poisonous fumes. Victoria chose their direction to favor the wind, still carrying their scent towards the creatures if they could even interpret it, but shoving and spreading the flame in their direction of travel. If their first fires went out early, their direction of travel would be given away– they sprinted and avoided any creature they thought capable of sending signals.

Reaching a dead end between two fields of dense, interlocked grass, they could either go around or wait for the fire to burn through. Griffith looked up and to both sides, estimating the time they'd have before they were exposed from above or before breathing would be hindering. They lit another fire to the left and crept slowly, allowing the fire to rise. An explosion rumbled the ground roughly every thirty seconds, sending flame and chunks of wooden debris far into the air. The light crackle of fire and the air waving the smoke blocked the sounds of wood falling back down, avoiding them entirely. The heat built as they ran, leading them to shed an outer layer and carry them.

They arced around the tunnel and continued back towards the crash site, retracing their steps over the rivers and streams with fervor. The liquid in some sections was slightly flammable, helping them justify the fire making the crossing.

"In the willow forest! There's a pygmy dragon!" Victoria told them after looking through a sliver of visibility through smoke.

"... and behind us there's a toxilizard! And they're a lot bigger!" Valeria alerted.

They turned around to see how far it was, and another two appeared, following their trail before the fire could mask it. They crawled fast, determined to kill; at the speed they chased, the toxilizards were sure to catch up.

The weight of the chemical packs warranted using them whenever needed, especially without the safety of a shelter or a true destination. They went slightly right, moving alongside the edge of the increasingly warm inferno. Victoria spiked a vial behind them, sending a fireball into the air, blocking the lizards' vision and forcing them to walk through or wait until it burned away. Victoria gave the crew enough time to change courses and mask their scent with a neutralizer, baking soda. It was a temporary fix, but hopefully, it was enough to give them another, farther lead. Unsure of the true intelligence of the toxilizards, they resolved to evade by zigzagging, backtracking, and providing a dead end. It only took an extra half-minute but increased their chance of making it to a defendable location– their first rocky shelter would not cut it this time. They had seen firsthand how so many layers of defenses could not hold for even a few minutes. The creatures had even taken the bunker by storm, utilizing wicked tactics alongside some omnipotent controller they sought to expose and destroy, somehow, someday.

"I think we're far enough to move past it," Griffith stated, the fire beginning to move too slowly for them. With their lead, the goal was to either hide or prepare a region to fight their last stand. Without a doubt, they would be fighting more today. It was about noon and quite a pleasant day. The mostly unfamiliar fresh air amplified their enhancing drugs. It had been around an hour since they left the shelter, and luckily, the creatures had just about all been drawn to the base. If they found some valley or tunnel through a mountain, they could direct all their weaponry one way.

Birds began scanning from above, free of the smoke; tree cover was now more essential than ever before. Victoria imagined the birds as military helicopters, searching and scanning the dense brush for survivors– or criminals. Hopefully, these helicopters and drones were not equipped with infrared.

A mystic blue forest was their destination, the canopy so dense the plants below glowed opal and sapphire blues. Fungi-like flora lined the cracked bark of the wise trees, seemingly an indicator of toxins– they would not be the first to test. The ground was covered in a soft moss that cushioned every step. They could not be sure if that emitted toxins either. Somewhere in the middle of the woodland, they rubbed baking soda through their hair and clothing, spitting on their hands to remove it from the skin more easily. Eventually, they would have to wash it out of their hair, but being hidden was essential.

In a particularly dense region, they placed their two bags each on a different tree roughly fifty feet apart. They walked to and from the bags to learn as much as possible about the environment; in their previous training, they had practiced combat in new environments where almost all of the learning happened during a fight. Utilizing the scene was their key to potent combat.

No water was running through the region they chose; it could have helped them hide themselves even better, and they could have used its acidic properties to divide up some of the creatures. Not having running water was helpful, too, however, as each sound could be localized with more precision. Their rather enclosed space created an echo in every direction except upwards– loud and sharp noises would pierce but also could disorient the creature who produced it.

With an emphasis on the first word, Griffith said, "*When* things go bad, and we need to split up, we meet back at the caves or at our first shelter. If you can't leave your position, use smoke or another signal at dawn. We'll come for you eventually."

Victoria told them, "We probably won't get another chance for this, so I'll say it's been an honor to serve with you all. May each and every one of us make it back to a life of tranquility."

Taking a half step forward and meeting everyone's eyes, Lucian furthered, "As cliche and impossible as it may be, I'd still say we can make it out of this one. The odds never favored us, but we were never ones for the odds anyway."

Chapter 19

TORRENTIAL CRESCENDO

Light growls and an echo of rumbling footsteps permeated the forest all around them.

"I guess they're here," Valeria said, initiating a round of hugs and comforting hands on shoulders.

"Farewell, friends," Tanho chuckled glumly.

"Farewell, family," Bruce declared, first to walk away and disappear through the dense forest.

Lucian called loudly, "If you have the opportunity to take *them* down, take it." With that, they separated despite their close proximity, weaponry in hand, and gels stowed. It would still be over two hours until they could have additional enhancements, but a gut feeling told them they would be there for a while.

They fully split up and got silent, awaiting the creatures indeed on their trail. The dense and wide trees would slow some of the larger creature's attacks. It *must* be enough. Closed eyes and deep breaths heightened their hearing and calmed their conscience. Through training and learning, they each set a bar for their mastery and excellence goals– in this fight, here and now, that bar would not suffice. A new prospect, perfection, would have to be achieved for even one of them to have a chance to make it home. Now crouched or on a knee, breathing exercises harnessed adrenaline and kept a slow heartbeat pulsing blood through their veins.

With the wind-rustled leaves shielding aerial sounds, the exact moment of their approach was impossible to anticipate. When they arrived, however, the force of their charge rumbled throughout the entire forest, the mycelial tendrils standing on edge in a pulse.

Griffith first experienced the coordinated power of arachnoids and toxilizards, the leading creatures who rapidly flung themselves toward him. The first two who appeared were arachnoids, staring at him with large eyes and more than fourteen legs; they jumped horizontally from tree to tree, leaving an indent where they landed and leaped from, able to instantaneously spring themselves in his direction with impeccable aim. Instead of being able to land an attack to bring him some momentum, he was forced to lightly retreat around the tree for another angle.

As Griffith rounded his tree, Victoria met her first challengers: arachnoids, charging full force, imbued with an eerie determination. They were quiet, mostly uncommunicative; Victoria thought the dense woods caused confusion. She prodded the ground to test its hardness and response as the arachnoids closed in around her. Only three had found their way into her clearing so far, but they quickly formed a triangle, spreading out in front and to both sides of her. If she were to attack any one of them, the rest were sure to attack from the opposite side– it was a relatively predictable type of attack, something great to further warm up with.

She tested their reaction times with a lunge to the right and a pivot to the left. Leaping into the air towards a tree, wasted adrenaline metabolized as she watched the spider back up. She counted on it, though, kicking off the tree to land straight below and advancing in the other direction with a backhand swing of the spearpoint. The blue phosphorescence absorbed the falling blood and the sound of the collapsed beast. On a glance to ensure it was dead, she saw its sharp eyes, now yellow and reflective– seemingly a night hunter.

A group of orange-purple pygmy dragons approached Bruce slowly, stalking through the forest. *I thought they were rare, hunted alone, and were pygmy– things have changed.* He watched the spikes that adorned their armor, likely all armed with venom. Their tails swayed opposite their turning, balancing their mass over and around tree roots and trunks.

Approaching him head-on, they had no weak spots. So many options– he was sure to be incapacitated. Prey caught in the open, despite a forest surrounding, held their interest and fueled the urge to kill. Saliva dripped from their leader's mouth, burning away the blue below. Moments later, without a chance to advance further, liquid shot from the canopy above. Dissolving ensued with sharp hissing and a run through the forest. Bruce was confused but relieved.

Valeria crouched between a larger group of trees, hearing the rumble nearby. Following her mental map, she appeared as Tanho speared a reptile through the head and into the ground. With six more toxilizards moving forward, he could not finish the kill. The demonic creature followed its brethren.

They saw Valeria and largely ignored her, focusing on Tanho in a unified attack– hunting as a pack was effective. Tanho's vial broke against the toxilizard's rough hide, glass and acid falling to the glow. High-pressure darts of liquid shot into and around the toxilizard, paralyzing three of them. Everyone and everything momentarily paused.

Lucian held vials in both hands, relaxed but focused. His eyes observed the leaves, his skin searching for breeze in the humid-brisk blue hue. A lone arachnoid descended from the canopy. He could not be sure if it had fallen; he had to consider their flank. It met his gaze and advanced slowly. *Why move so slowly?* He countered by, too, walking forward, angled slightly left to stay near the tree line.

The vial was easily deflected, falling somewhere behind it without even a crack. Lucian put the vials away and two-handed the spear, an obviously deadly instrument. Watching the tip of the spear, the chemical burn on its left side was shocking.

Lucian was pleasantly surprised that it worked, too. He smiled as the target was paralyzed– he now had a better weapon.

Griffith wove between trees and left his fight for a better angle on something else. He hoped the mixing scents of so many species would mask their humanity, limiting the creatures actually attempting to hunt them down. After looking around and trying to sense their directions, he fell back to where he set his axe to be used for close-quarters combat.

Swinging it around lightly, he could maneuver through the denser sections providing less visible area. Each earthy step was cushioned as if clouds stood around them. Petrichor– water invading the dirt and soil and diffusing geosmin through the air. The blue luminescence braved a similar scent, earthy, an extension of their home-field advantage. An arachnoid flash-flooded the corridor he stood in, run-rolling with multiple spears aimed at him. A fake lunge caused it to slow down and center its aim; a wide-edged slash deflected at least eight limbs; the spin and half corkscrew brought the point fully into and then through the immediate carcass– shock and unknown traumas of mass damage dropping it where it was. Griffith remained largely unscathed.

Weaving through the trees, she wrapped back around her target, sound dampened. Victoria felt along the back of the spear until she felt the coarse ridge where they had previously separated it from its host. When she felt the cold air settle around her, she rocked forward, allowing the stomp of her right foot to begin the tendon chain that thrust the leg further and further, true in attack.

She stabbed its flailing body over and over through where its eyes were until it completely stopped. In front of her again, another spider monster sprinted forward. She closed her eyes, her ears ringing, reflexively surging the spear upwards as her eyes recalibrated, vaulting the arachnoid behind her. It landed, and she still could not hear over the pangs circumnavigating her head. It came for her again and was met with the end of a spear, impaling itself slightly to get a slash onto her forearm. After finishing the fight, slamming it against a tree, she wrapped her wound and moved away from the spilled blood.

Three pygmy dragons walked around their fallen companion cautiously, Bruce grabbing the cold vials from his right pocket. The leading enemy met Bruce's gaze as the glass clinked together lightly. The vials left his hand faster than he had ever thrown something before, speed and energy flowing through his veins. He felt tingles through his chest and arm watching the scatterbomb of acid break against the ground and an unlucky tail-swing, eliminating the group of them in a fury of bolts.

He looked around and back from where he came, seeing no leftover indentation. The tingles flowing through his body made the spear feel light– it was good, but a weapon of more weight could do more damage to a fleshy creature. Now moving right, he kept a mental map of where everything was and the general regions they would be. *A crowned? How did the frogs get here already?* He had watched the others fight the crowned in simulation but never fought one himself. The vial soared through the air and was swallowed whole by the crowned. He almost laughed, realizing he had wasted his third to last vial. Seeing two large spectres adorned in maleficent yet alluring floral armaments and two large, teethed claws, Bruce left without hesitation.

The pack of toxilizards stood strong together but halted, allowing Valeria to finish Tanho's kill. They backed up slowly, turning to the safety of the trees. Valeria took pursuit with two vials.

"Hey! Where are you going?" Tanho yelled to her.

She was already behind the first layer of trees and knew the sound would not travel for longer. "Communication!" was all she got out before passing behind another layer of trees. A vial flung through the air, followed by her spear, killing the leader and allowing liquid to explode another. Retrieving the spear, she stood stunned by the multi-fanged, appropriately named giant pangolin, who accidentally squashed the last toxilizard. As the blood drained and interacted with the blue mycelium, lasers shot from above and splattered off the giant pangolin's resistance. Alright.

After Tanho understood what was meant by Valeria's word, he began to follow but was interrupted by a spider behind him. *Behind me? From Griffith and Lucian?* He shrouded a vial he held in his pocket and began moving towards the arachnoid.

It watched him intently, reading his heat, stress, and movement patterns. Tanho kept approaching, tilting his head ever so slightly to his left. The swing came spontaneously, his heat patterns relatively unchanging and the tenseness of his body still unfamiliar. It was unlike anything it had ever seen– its eyes squinted slightly, jumping and offering two limbs to test the force of the blow– strong. The chemicals from the strange creature's skin were enticing, a sweet blend of salt and unstressed proteins.

In a decisive maneuver, it darted left. Tanho, being the experienced huntsman he was, rotated the other way, following his own swing to dodge.

Now it was lower, bending its back legs to lunge forward and extending the front to jab at the thinnest portion of the leg– his ankle. Tanho redirected the spear as a blocker and pushed down, repelling him. The spider's spear-clash reverberated into Tanho's hands as they slid to the end, accompanied by light pain. Three of its eyes caught the moment the jab was met with some resistance– it quickly hit a round and dense structure. Its arm tensed to conserve the torque, afflicting maximum damage, but the protrusion of his lateral malleolus deflected it. Eight eyes caught the motion of a shiny object flying towards it, quickly perceiving its distance. In a brisk darting, it moved back and further left, distancing from the bipedal creature and allowing the object to pass between its legs faultlessly. The shattering of glass attracted both of their gazes, safe from each other momentarily. The wheels and interconnections of whole-body widespread neurons spun with the arachnoid's association, almost instantaneously deriving insights destined to be artfully deployed.

Lucian wove through his section of the trees and met a crowd of toxilizards, which he let chase him shortly to group them together before letting streams of hellfire rain from above. A crowned leaped through the trees, appearing beside the stream of corpses. Lucian observed from the side of a tree as the crowned made its way to the toxilizard bodies and ate two before audibly tasting the air and looking around. As two arachnoids entered the scene, the frog fell over, immediately entering a state of stiff rigor mortis– a different reaction to those that had been shot.

The arachnoids became the next target. The spiders engaged him immediately, counter-circling each other to prevent a read and induce confusion. Lucian let his spear fall backward, drawing some attention as he half-stepped back with it, filling both his hands with three chemical vials and immediately throwing one from each in a high lob. With the assistance of the added strength, he flung one vial from each hand at once, slowly but directly at them. The momentum of his swing continued to the next in a half-awkward windmill that, accompanied by twist and follow-through, accelerated the remaining throw from right hand to left arachnoid. His right arm was more accurate anyway, allowing the panicked deflection and dodge to result in a kill and a hesitation from the right arachnoid in watching its family die from liquid spikes both there and behind it. Despite its quick reaction time, the hesitation was all Lucian needed to kick the spear and throw the remaining vial, just as calculated. As the spider blinked rapidly and delegated legs to block the force of the horizontal spear, the vial passed below. It broke, burning tissue before the molten bolts ultimately reduced its suffering.

Thunderstruck, Tanho nervously matched the inquisitive gaze of the dark arachnoid, darker than the others he had seen. *Older, perhaps? Unimportant right now.* It tucked its legs in and rolled, an unavoidable attack if it were not for the remaining vials he had with him. The arachnoid had somehow seen the wrist flick, *maybe a glint off the vial,* as it sprung up and to the side too fast to be caught in the air. His spear was relatively useless now, the flurry of legs shielding any jab or slash.

He could win, just as Griffith had that time he refrains from talking about. There would only be a few chances, the enemy learning so quickly, an electric pace where underhanded tricks could only be performed once before futility. Tanho tensed his left arm, watching the veins rise. Unsheathing his knife in a reverse grip in his left hand, he rotated his wrist to rid any stiffness. He held the spear just two feet from the spearhead in his right hand, keeping his eyes locked onto the torrent foe ahead.

In an instant, the two gladiators collided in an upward swing, Tanho's left arm braving the points of several legs to get close enough to jab parallel to the spider's right side. In the arachnoid's kick-off, blood flowed down both Tanho's left and right side from the arm and mid-torso. Without a second thought, Tanho bolted from the tempestuous storm's path, retreating into the confines of the unfamiliar forest, a noxious purple trailing behind him.

The force of his swing decapitated the slightly deformed toxilizard, unable to fend off attacks from the right side, just as the next round of creatures arrived. *How do they know where we are? We couldn't have left that obvious of a trail.* A mandibles approached; Griffith observed the hide and exoskeleton of the two-segmented ant-beetle-dragonfly-like creature, which had strangely not been on their all-encompassing simulation. This one also seemed larger than they had seen before, albeit only from security cameras– it looked to be seven feet long. As enclosed as they were, its wings could only be used as a deterrent. The mandibles was fast on its many three-inch-wide legs, but anything could be killed.

He tossed the axe end over end, two revolutions before impact. The weight of the crystal drove through the insufficient blocking attempt, embedding itself a few inches into the right of its outermost eye. Griffith had created a blindspot and weak point for his spear, allowing a simple counterclockwise approach to help retrieve his beloved weapon.

A shadow caught his peripheral vision. *Another spider, great.* He spun quickly, driving the end of the spear into the undefendable back of the mandibles, ripping insides in the direction of his axe. The spider watched. *Thanks.* Griffith sidestepped and lunged at the mandibles' head, dodging the giant pincers, horn, legs, and mace of a tail. The strength and accuracy of the jab tore open its wound considerably, knocking the axe to the ground and creating a borehole from a quartering-away angle.

Nutrient flow to the eyes decreased, concussing it so the next jab finished the job. Griffith noticed he was sweating more and more– the onsets of dehydration. He turned to face the spider, angling his body so his stronger right arm was forward. The arachnoid, which had not moved for the remaining duration of the mandibles' fight, squinted and ambled forward. Griffith counter-arced left to meet it, closing distance quickly within their mostly enclosed, blue space.

The variance between the arachnoids had always been subtle, only a few inches from individual to individual, discounting the apparent changes since their first encounters some one month ago. *Something is different with this one, though, but I can't figure it out.* He padded the gels in his pocket with the axe, enabling him to take more risk with another layer of safety– half a packet... for at least another few hours.

He backed up to watch it a bit longer, calming his heart as he had trained. With a bead of sweat approaching his eye, he swiped his left arm over his face. The spider did not change his approach or even pause. Comfort was the name of the game; Griffith tossed his axe into the ground in front of him and lunged, wide-slashing the spearpoint to its maximum range, bringing it closer to conserve angular momentum and spin faster. The second slash, which certainly would've made leg contact, he faked, stopping his momentum entirely and slinging the spear almost side-armed.

He stood up slowly while picking up his insignificantly dulled axe. He did not expect the spider to offer negative defense, allowing the spear to pass the whole way through and close distance. Before he could react, Griffith's left arm had been impaled three times and was being pulled. His right arm swung with the strength of a guaranteed hit, snapping two limbs at the joint before knocking the arachnoid back just a few inches, enough to recoil his arm with the lubricant of blood spilling out.

He remained quiet through gritted teeth as he jumped backward with the axe, attempting to catch as much blood as possible and escape the danger. The arachnoid also backed up, conscious of the liquid darts, allowing Griffith to retreat between the trees.

"Victoria!" she heard from behind her amidst the light echo. She turned to face Tanho, who was also bleeding.

"I think we've got a problem. One of the spiders is learning. It's different." He caught his breath, wiped sweat, and took half of the recovery gel while trying to tend the wounds that ached more and more by the minute.

"We should group up and warn the others," she said, looking at her own wound and Tanho stuffing some of his remaining cloth strips into his wounds while looking up and tensing his jaw.

"Cleavers!" Tanho announced, lowering his gaze and beginning to jog. Two heavy-tailed serpents wove river-bends through the lush, blue landscape they were rather unfamiliar with. He recalled one of their first encounters with the old cleavers, paralyzing their target and cutting off their limbs to eat. *There's no way their digestive systems are optimized for human consumption– why can't they just let us be?*

Victoria waited for Tanho to pass her, jabbing twice at the surprisingly fast snakes before weaving around the trees. Her heart beat faster, causing her breathing to accelerate, which she denied with a mental runner's high.

"Are you okay?" Griffith said with a partially furrowed brow, seeing that all three of them had sustained relatively serious injuries.

"Alright," Victoria responded quickly.

"Yeah, we should reconvene and get out of here; one of the spiders has learned how to fight us," Tanho replied.

"I must've fought that one," Griffith told them, gesturing to his arm as he moved back to their starting center. He temporarily blocked the bleeding as he moved, eyes mostly looking up to avoid and evade any surprise attacks.

Bruce and Valeria drew weapons, startled by their swift approach.

"Injured?" Griffith asked, cutting to the point to optimize time.

"We're good. We're good," Valeria replied, staring at their bloodied arms and hands.

Victoria suggested, "You should take your recovery now while you can."

Tanho looked at the tree canopy and added, "There's a spider who can fight. Where's Lucian?"

On the move to Lucian's section, Valeria chuckled as her mouth raised and lightly quivered, saying, "We need to get out of here." They did not even bother calling out for Lucian– nothing traveled through the sullen flood of blue. As they approached the carcass of a spider deductively killed by Lucian, another spider entered the space. Immediately, a single vial was thrown, and three spears pinned the beast to the tree backstop.

Several jabs from Bruce's spear finished the kill, and Griffith, Victoria, and Tanho retrieved their weapons. As they tried to follow the trail of insufficient carnage, the clouds of bioluminescence below their feet began to darken and rise fractionally more by the second.

"We can't split up, and we can't stay here for too long," Tanho forecast, insinuating the bad omens.

"We can't," Griffith stated, moving faster.

Victoria corrected, "We shouldn't, but we can." The five of them ran and saw the carcass of a crowned and a few toxilizards.

"Wonder how he did that," Griffith said in passing.

"Lucian!" Valeria shouted.

With his deeper voice, Bruce yelled, "Lucian!" effecting a boom. They were undoubtedly drawing attention, but they waited a few seconds for a reply.

"Alright, we'll catch up with him later," Tanho announced, looking over to Griffith.

A few seconds later, with no visible red blood on the ground or the forest becoming more tempestuous by the second, Griffith said, "Yeah. Yeah."

They continued straight as best as they could until the blue returned to brown and orange, dense and rough compared to the flora, but provided more traction on their somewhat worn shoes. They stood but fifty feet from the blue before turning back around, not moving but observing.

Hoping Lucian had followed the light depressions they must have left, they lingered enough to watch the forest build and swell to a flash flood of liquid lasers. Valeria looked away, and they followed.

Victoria drew an arrow into the ground, dulling the tip of her spear. After catching up, they picked up the pace while trying to enjoy the peace of nothing around them but wilderness, occasionally drawing another arrow.

Chapter 20

Noxious Maelstroms

"We've still got a few good hours left before nightfall," Victoria announced, watching the sky give them a glimpse of the prismed sunset they wished to see once more.

"A few good hours for Lucian to make moves. I wish you luck, brother," Griffith said to the boundless ceiling.

Roars and rumbles trembled the air, vibrating the blood still slowly dripping and drying. They were powerful, doubtlessly, somehow heading their way. With the fear already understood, inevitability of the situation denied, and stimulants empowering their hand, they knew to continue with whatever they had.

"We're not dying today," Bruce told them plainly. The warning rumbles increased in frequency until purple flames breached a neighboring ridgeline. They stood in the open, barely considering seeking shelter or hiding.

Without words of acknowledgment, they noticed a goliath to the right. They split up and began moving forward so the fights would not interfere with each other, just in time for a sea of vex to crest between the beasts.

"Make fire!" Valeria yelled, watching the dauntless and goliath invade. They all emptied their pockets of vials and some gels, realizing none of the chemicals were labeled and Lucian would be the only one with a real idea of how to accomplish their immediate task.

"Throw everything when they get close enough," Griffith said with the rising buzz of wings flapping and hitting each other. The dense wave of vex prepared to crash, aiming needles and some kind of talons.

Vials flung and broke, causing varied layers of vex to burn and fall depending on the breaking angle. As four of them slung vials, Valeria opened their extra gels, collecting them in cloth or opened wrappers. Before they were out of their few vials, she launched both gel bombs. They soared through the air slower and in more of an arc than the vials but spread out just the same, if not more. As the gel dripped down and fell to the few corpses below, the blaze erupted and exploded.

They fell to the ground to shield themselves from the heat, rising again quickly and frowning at the plume, dauntless, and goliath coming at them. Again splitting up, Griffith and Bruce took on the fire-breathing dauntless, Victoria and Valeria engaged the goliath, and Tanho kept watch to coordinate.

They each did not notice their sigh of preparation amidst locking onto the targets. Griffith tore the top of a gel packet, keeping it higher in his pocket. Fighting dauntless in the simulations was surely easier than in the field, but the silver-plated mouth and jaw would still inflict the same damage. He was not entirely sure what he would do with the gel. Still, if it exploded with similar ferocity as just earlier, especially if he could close its jaw, Griffith could effectively drop a live grenade, decapitating it in a single attack.

Bruce intended to reduce its eyesight with a throw as soon as possible, hopefully giving him and Griffith enough time to kill it and face whatever was next before it approached. He was never one to gamble, considering the possibility of being defenseless a calculated risk– it was the endurance of the team he was procuring. Its monstrous size did not scale well compared to the team– it would be impossible to climb up or get anywhere close to its head, and they had no means to cut it down limb by limb, especially without dying in the process.

The distance was closed, and they immediately had to focus on evading. In an instant, they were feet from being crushed. Griffith dove to the right, propping the butt of the spear onto the ground and locking it in with the curve of the axe and handle, flipping himself to see the dauntless swing and miss his legs and femoral arteries as he tucked them up. Bruce held the spear as a javelin, envisioning the dauntless for its actual size without scale, and held for the swing of its slender neck. The strength infused in his muscles led a familiar finger-hand-wrist-forearm-tendon-elbow-bicep-shoulder contortion as an applied weakness to two large and keen eyes. Its menacing eye-slit dilated as the corner of its eye was pierced, the straight, true, sharp javelin passing through almost the way to the other eye, almost entirely embedding the spear. It barely reacted, although its vision was most definitely shakey.

Victoria slowed her pace, waiting and watching for swing indicators. She immediately gauged its dominant foot, and they began provoking sweeps, enough to jab a few times into its supporting leg if they timed it well enough. With only the spears, they would have to jab several hundred times to do anything substantial. It quickly caught on and planted both feet to swing its makeshift club, making distance the only dodge. Crumbs of Chaos flung over them, masking the light tremble of more approaching beasts.

They fought with less effort now that they had set the pattern, keeping it engaged and breaking it down slowly until another opportunity would make it easier. That opportunity formed in the junction of gluttony, too large to leap but incomprehensibly strong. They seemed natural enemies on the one night the group had watched them. Valeria waved the goliath as an angry bull chasing red heat, connecting the heat of injury and rage of the fight to a charge directly at the giant frog.

They felt their injuries and aches enhance through the blaze of their withdrawal. Calf tightness and Chaos' eruption, trembling and tremoring the arrival of the three creatures. A beastly spectre crested the hill opposite the pack-alpha fenrhor; they both were adorned in silvery daggers and spikes. They observed the battlefield, making their way to the flank of the goliath's clash for a piece of the prize.

A stark green dolus appeared last, the bulb on its maneuverable tail brightly flashing white periodically. The group had never seen the deceptive creature in the day, not even in simulation, and never green. The beasts' congregation impassioned Chaos into a picturesque bonfire of chemical composites. The biggest and strongest warriors of their world altogether, dispelling the alien threat disrupting their natural order, temporarily aligned interests rooted in their most profound influences of behavior; it was almost as if human scent secreted neurotoxins that induced annihilation.

Tanho eyed down the fenrhor, looking back to his team in battle, and transitioned from walk to jog to almost sprint in moments, bearing the cold, pointed staff under the sun's berating and ever-unyielding bloodred rays. He approached until the fenrhor watched him only. Its wretched but omnipotent howl reigned the air. Tanho was certain its army was about to emerge, looking side to side to see if anything could kill. With Victoria and Valeria's idea the only viable option, time departing, and strength and recovery propelling him forward, he engaged the wolf creature several times his weight and size.

Simultaneously, Bruce peeled off to hold off the spectre, perhaps the most ruthless killer they'd yet encountered. It was fast, relatively thin but durable, distracting, and ate its prey alive after immobilizing it. With the spear to counter its very long range, he could only hope to land multiple forceful jabs to its joints as they had effectively done before. The sigh was habitual.

Griffith called, "Get ready to pit them against each other! It's our only chance!"

Tanho continued, hoping the beast would face him directly so he could shove the spear down the length of its body and reduce its mobility. Once it held one shoulder forward to demonstrate its hunting mastery, Tanho pulled back and waited for the call. Victoria and Valeria had fully disengaged, but the goliath and gluttony did not stay interested in each other for too long. Bruce waved the spear forward and made sure not to overextend. Griffith made the call and beelined away from the dauntless, prompting the chase to ensue.

At once, they ran for each other, using their size as an advantage; the spectre did not see it the same way, slowing down as the colossal and dangerous monsters bounded closer. The other four beasts bathed in confidence and tunnel vision as they were brought within range. Once the giant's swing hit the dauntless, the battle of Titans commenced, giving room for them to dodge and dance their way out.

They met Bruce with the spectre and engaged, Bruce throwing his axe from the far right and shallowly embedding it in its lower abdomen. Through the roars behind them involving the four beasts, they set up a feign. Victoria swung around behind them, jumping up and slightly forward off Bruce's back. Tanho swung the other way behind all the pointed spears and launched his spear through the side of the spectre's head. It lodged halfway through and provided quite a weak spot. Sensing the vulnerability, it backed up and brought its raptorial forelegs to the sides of its head, ripping the spear out the front of its head through its mouth.

The crunch of keratin breaking and hitting the ground was stunning but respected. It surely would not be able to eat anything until it healed; *hopefully, we're saved from that one demise,* Bruce thought.

Half of its head was already cut through, weakening the strength and security of its perception of the world. With that obvious of a target, it held its arms slightly higher. Its lower body was never really a target, with so many legs and insufficient blood.

Tanho, without a weapon, had a chance to turn around, keying into the sounds of battle. The gluttony shot its tongue at the left shoulder of the fenrhor, which scratched in retaliation as the goliath swung at the dauntless, catching the club in its teeth and crushing it. He turned back and began a half-flank on the spectre without drawing too close– just enough to warrant some attention. *Not gonna question where the other creatures are.* Tanho caught its eye in a fake kicking motion and took a half-step back.

How do we finish this? Victoria thought. She held her spear, one hand in the middle and the other at the back, stepping forward with a jab and quickly backing into formation again. Griffith and Bruce stood on either end and arced around, pushing it backward. It quickly became apparent that it was not interested in fighting the group like this.

"Let's back off," Valeria said, reading the same behaviors.

They agreed and disengaged. The spectre came closer but did not engage again or lunge with an attack. *It definitely has a goal. Luring? Time-wasting? Waiting for a slip-up? Not sure,* Bruce analyzed.

They saw the dolus to the right of the cooling battle, so they went left. The beasts again determined they would not be able to kill one without leaving themselves vulnerable in the process, leading to a standstill and the dauntless shrugging off and turning away. They felt the breeze slightly pick up from behind them– their scent would be carried through the giant beasts and in the direction of the horde.

"What do we do now? Valeria questioned, shrinking.

"Rest while we can," Griffith said, recovering his and Tanho's weapon that had been dropped to the floor. "Enjoy!" he said, returning the bloodied spear to Tanho.

"Thanks." They both went to a crouch and just observed. The spectre remained behind them, possibly trying to cut off an escape route, but they paid little attention. They all crouched or sat down to rest their sore and injured limbs.

"We could ignore the rule and take another gel, I think it has been over two hours at this point," Victoria suggested.

Tanho responded, "I think those rules are meant to be broken. If its half-life is four hours, which the directions seem to suggest, we're probably safe from toxicity unless we take like six... maybe five to be safe if we're riding the upper dosage, as long as we only take a quarter gel."

Griffith spoke up quickly, "Makes sense to me. I think I'm the most injured; I can test."

"What? No, let me. You're more needed on the field," Victoria said, gesturing to her dominant forearm in bloodied wraps.

"I disagree," he said calmly with a light smile, unwrapping a strength and swallowing a quarter of it before she could react more.

Tanho observed the lightly injured dauntless and admired its strength and boldness, even as it turned towards them and began walking. "Our dauntless friend is incoming."

With the unspoken and temporary pact of the giant beasts, only the dauntless approached, the spectre still observing from behind them. It took its time, likely also recovering oxygen through its skin or some other unknown way. As it drew closer, they saw liquid bleeding from the entry wound at its eye– the stretching, movement, and jaw power must have moved the spear around internally and opened space for blood to flow.

"If it keeps moving its head around, it shouldn't ever stop bleeding, right?" Valeria asked.

Griffith looked at it and envisioned the spear inside. "Yeah, as long as any healing doesn't push it out like our healing would do to splinters."

Tanho agreed, "These guys definitely have some mechanism to remove foreign substances."

Victoria slightly countered, "Well, with the rate of death here, we can't be too sure."

By now, the dauntless had closed in, and they had no spare spears, leaving them back where the giants had fought. If they threw their spears, there was still a strong chance they would be unable to kill it, or it would just leave much faster than they could chase it.

It began breathing fire, warming itself up again for the fight they both knew would ensue. The spectre took its chance to team up with the dauntless. They, too, observed the dolus approach on the right.

"I'm thinking the third gel is safe; I'm feeling it the same way as before."

"I'm waiting longer," Tanho said, Valeria agreeing. Victoria and Bruce took strength as Tanho. Valeria and Griffith defended them. Griffith kept watch on the dauntless as the others turned to the spectre, disliking the idea of a dangerous adversary on their rear and being surrounded.

They engaged quickly, arcing right to make an escape route and a solid backstop. Thrusting two spearheads down and one middle mass raised its head in a backstep. Tanho jabbed up to force it back down and jabbed again to lower it further. Valeria threw her spear, and Victoria feigned another, forcing weight to shift to one side for Bruce to flick his wrist imbued with strength, launching his javelin into the spectre's head. Amidst some confusion and Tanho flanking, Victoria got a powerful hit onto the end of the partially embedded spear, applying a strong impulse into multiplicative torque that broke through all of its feverish eyes.

Griffith backed up with the opened space, just watching the dauntless so it would not attack in the safety of surprise. Once the spectre had been basically decapitated, it was no longer a real issue, although it seemed able to move around and attack, only blindly– all the sense organs on its head dysfunctional or gone altogether.

The dauntless clearly did not trust the spectre to aid it in battle, watching and patiently waiting its turn. With the dolus still approaching but around a hundred yards away, Victoria and Griffith went right while the others went left. It immediately blundered, shooting fire toward the group of three and arcing forward through the gap. It left a clean opening for Victoria, brimming with renewed adrenaline, to lead the spear through its left eye. The angle was not clean, only getting through one eye before barely piercing through the hide towards the bridge of its nose. With each step, gravity flung the spear back and forth, opening both wounds and completely disabling its left eye, if it was still partially operative just before.

In order to evade the imperial flames, Valeria, Bruce, and Tanho cut their arc farther left and away, giving more time as the fire traveled and was blocked by the air between them. The warmth was somewhat appealing, momentarily.

The dauntless passed fully through the gap, scratching the spear free and aiming everyone through its right eye. The dauntless was one of the only creatures they had seen with two eyes; it was rather remarkable that it was still selected for.

With their connection bridge built and the dolus closing in, they grouped up, having to get closer to the other giants in the process. Putting everything to one side by backing up, they took the moment to rest and regain composure. Victoria hopped up and down in nervous anticipation and attempted to preserve adrenaline, now without a weapon.

Chapter 21

SACRIFICE

Through clandestine conflicts, the unceasing cut to courage on chaos lay demonic wraiths incarnate to rest. A calm, unobscured sky and adjacent kin procured all hope, containing their connotative home.

The hellish hunters of this unearthly birthplace held the highest of strengths– hypermutation selecting for harmful behaviors hindering only the heaviest links in the chain. Heroes challenged such a natural order through relentless hardship, deathly hurdles, and hindrances, hearing out their hopelessness.

An abstract planet harboring arcane arcanum remained amply unexplored, but foul play was readily apparent within the atomic fraction. Humanity may have already arrived some time ago.

Organizing and optimizing, assistance was an obvious out from the ominous onset of death. Time was seldom an opponent but offered no more options for going home.

A last stand, surmounting themselves or subduing chaos, set survival on the line. Susceptible as they always were, subsisting was the sensible solution despite that scant chance of success.

"Watch out!" they heard from back and to the side. They all spun to Lucian's voice, the charge of an arachnoid immediately drawing their eyes. Victoria and Bruce went forward to it, allowing Griffith, Valeria, and Tanho to keep an eye on the dauntless and dolus. The dauntless seemed more uninterested, facing more away than it had before. Within a few seconds, it moved farther away and seemed to try and clean its wounds, trying to remove the lodged spear from its eye socket. This green dolus was much larger up close, sporting a twenty-foot-long, meaty but armored tail, six legs below the large body, and a terrifying head. They had never really inspected it as they now could, building an anxiety which they let flow and then fade from the several-foot wide jaw and hundreds of fangs, reversed, signaling compression power and surely excruciating chewing.

Lucian was far behind the arachnoid, catching up; they would have to fight the spider before regrouping. It moved just as the others had, but Tanho immediately identified it.

"That's the one!" he exclaimed moments after turning towards it. Griffith and Tanho tagged in, having fought it before and wearing a slight grin of vengeance and retribution.

"Victoria, help us here," Griffith requested, nodding to Bruce and Valeria, trusting them to battle the fearsome dolus. Both sub-teams moved forward and gave themselves space, the arachnoid closing that distance the fastest.

Its confidence was frightening but warranted– it had clearly bested three of them in battle. Drawing on their experience fighting arachnoids since the first week, they thought through Lucian's dissection and the venom they had dipped some of their first spears into.

Out loud, Griffith examined, "We just have to cause enough damage to shock its systems, and it might shut down." The arachnoid clicked the air as it prepared for a first strike, but they did not flinch at all.

It observed their eyes lightly squint and the corners of their mouths raise. Slightly confused, it pondered for a second before engaging Bruce on the left side.

Victoria, stepping forward to match Bruce's half-step back, told them, "The pause is good; it's still wary of us. It's worried for itself, too." She lowered her spear along with her center of mass, allowing the arachnoid, if it wanted, to impale itself at an angle that it could not impale further and hit her. They still had a substantial range advantage.

Tanho took out a recovery gel and, as Griffith with the axe and Victoria with his spear fought, told them, "I'm gonna let it get to me. Kill it when it's stuck on my spear." They disapproved but did not voice it, the arachnoid still successfully parrying and avoiding their tricks, and danger increasing as time went on. Lucian got closer but was unarmed, blood down his shirt, pants, and shoes.

Tanho charged around and, with Victoria's lunge, forced it to make a play; it put all of its arms into deflecting and parrying, knowing Griffith would not throw his only weapon on a whim. Through the opening now created when it landed, it backed off and prepared to re-engage.

"There's more on the way!" Lucian said, moving behind them quickly.

Valeria and Bruce had only managed to keep it from killing them thus far, unable to get close due to the tail and unwilling to throw the spears as their only weapons. With the edge of a yellowish forest in view to their right, their move was simple: drop it off inside.

"Stick together, no matter what," Bruce said.

"We go on three." She counted down slowly, "Three, two, one, go!" She ran into the forest, waving the spear up in the air. It followed, interested in the human scent and easy meal– worth whatever energy it had to expend if it could just catch the larger target.

As he ran, he thought of finding somewhere to trap the dolus and how splitting up with the group, after all this, sucked. *Let's make this quick.*

As Bruce and Valeria crossed into the treeline, pursued by a several-ton creature, a band of six arachnoids caught up. Without a weapon, Lucian could not fight, leaving them outnumbered by over two to one, the single strong adversary already challenging the three of them.

"I lost half my arm; all you, best of luck," Lucian lightly scoffed, ending in a chuckle. He could not run away to the woods either– he was much slower than them. It was a miracle that he got away and found them, too, although he followed the spider to do so. Lucian looked to the sky with a wishful eye, nodding and lingering his gaze amidst the soon-to-be setting sun.

"Maybe don't go for that trick anymore. I'll take a few normals out if you're up for the big guy," Griffith told them. He swung his axe around and tossed it in the air once, adjusting his grip and squeezing tightly to secure it. He held it cross-body and held his other hand up but loose, primarily to block any attacks he needed to and stabilize his body, conserving momentum– anything helps.

Without another word in some subconscious attempt to hold onto energy and oxygen, Tanho and Victoria, in front of Lucian, stepped up to the darkened spider, likely a burn survivor, to re-engage. It was, as with many other fights, but most certainly here, during this fight, that their training and endurance were to be tried and tested. A field-tested team of trained astro-explorers, rediscovering what it means to be human and rediscovering what it means to survive.

Tanho timed his breaths with his steps, feeling the blood rush through his veins warming his fingertips and toes, chaos below his tired feet, rustling of wind through his now longer hair, and light sunburn on the back of his neck reconnecting mind and body. Victoria, too, took a deep breath but instead focused on the spear as an extension of her arm that she could flex, bend, and expose. The spear was a bit front-heavy, ideal for throwing and increasing the torque of a hit, but not much for maneuverability– she would have to hold it a little forward, decreasing her range, but only sometimes. She flexed each individual finger around the spear, assisted by her forearm, before working the biceps and shoulders and back, with a solid and light-footed base joined by a slight bend in the knees– springy and flexible.

On that awfully barren and roughed-up field, odds had no place. As the light gust died down, the fight commenced. The swing of Victoria's spear, testing waters, sliced the air with a loud slash. Holding the spear point down, Tanho tried a new technique, feigning a jab with the back-end before kicking out the bottom and accelerating through his reverse-grip stab. As the arachnoid reinforcements finally joined the battle, Tanho's hit landed, leaving a puncture wound at the mouth. It moved its mouth back and forth subtly and stepped back for two companions to proceed.

Griffith had hoped for three but was instead fighting four at once. Moving far enough away from the others to not impact their battle, he was quickly surrounded on all four sides. They took little time to engage, multiple at once, with respect to a seemingly worthy opponent they were confident would lose. The spider to his left launched itself from ten feet away; with that much time to react, he ducked right in a half-spin, grabbing the lead leg by its end as he swung the spike end as hard as he could in the momentum in chase. He was nicked several times on the chest and on both arms, but the one was sure to bleed out.

From directly behind and right, he was quickly put off-balance. Using the broadside of the axe, he deflected one attack to half-step and crouch back just out of range of the other. The bleeding arachnoid joined with another to coordinate high and low attacks. The sounds of clicking from their apparent leader, fighting Victoria and Tanho, were inaudible.

A spear stuck the injured arachnoid to the ground, where Victoria ran in and ripped it out, flinging the heavy spider several yards back. Griffith had dodged the airborne enemy as Tanho reconnected. They were now surrounded by six many-legged, intelligent monstrosities. Victoria set up the same feign and kick that Tanho had done before, performing it on the lead spider, taking up space as Tanho and Griffith backed up and turned to defend against as many as possible. The torque of the kick lightly bent the spear shaft, initiating an entry angle that straightened out post-puncture, locking it farther toward the end of the spear instead of passing all the way through.

On Griffith's side, an arachnoid aimed at Victoria's undefended legs. Griffith got in the way with an underhand swing that clashed against legs and dissuaded it as Tanho similarly planted the spear between one and Victoria. Griffith kept forward and ended Victoria's kill. On the recovery and step forward, his left-center calf was hit. He gave out a light scream and grit, now likely unable to walk on it.

Before Victoria or Griffith could swing their weapons back over, he was stabbed again just inches below the previous. He did not make a sound, but it was apparent pain, complete with red spilling down to the ground. Griffith finally swung and chopped off eight legs at once. Victoria quickly finished the job with an immediate, undefendable follow-up to his hit.

Bruce and Valeria had made it far into the relatively empty forest, surprised they were still being chased. *It's definitely not getting enough energy if it catches us to make up for this chase.*

"Can we even run it out of breath? It seems to be doing well," Valeria asked between slow breaths.

Not wanting to expend too much breath to compensate for his weight, he simply said, "We're built for distance; it's not."

Valeria spotted and pointed, "Over here, some trees are close together." Passing the one to three-foot diameter trunked trees with little to nothing but short grasses on the ground, it was peaceful. *This place would be a nice camping spot on Earth... without a ten-ton monster chasing me though, preferably.*

They led it to the trees and passed through at a slight angle to hopefully wedge it further. Making a wide arc, they were careful not to get hit by the crazy tail. It successfully lodged, but the dolus immediately began swinging its tail, clawing, and biting its way out.

"Let's get back there!" Valeria exclaimed.

They made the return trip in an almost sprint, arriving to the battle out of breath as Tanho and Griffith lay on the ground. Victoria was fighting four, including the different arachnoid who had stood back, almost supervising. Victoria focused most of her protecting attention on Griffith with the worst wounds and shorter weapon, but it did not look good for them all.

Valeria and Bruce entered the battle from the side and helped redirect the creatures to Tanho's side, away from Lucian, who held Griffith's axe in his remaining hand. Three on three was okay, but with the addition of two more humans, the leader rejoined the battle– that itself felt like three or even more normal arachnoids, although as they fought, the subordinates were picking up the patterns and strategy.

"We need to move and get away from the big guys. Lucian, try and move them," Valeria suggested. Lucian gave Griffith his axe and pulled him up, anchoring his left, weakened side against him. Tanho got himself up, but his ankle and dominant right arm were mostly shot– he could still get himself around, though. Where they had sat lay pooling and dried blood, chaos thirsty for blood, as it always was and would be; nature reclaiming what was rightfully hers, an eye for an eye in the mystic land of fruitful and fruitless bravado, lay stability and long-term hopes to waste.

The largest, darkest, scariest, and most dangerous arachnoid spun from one attack to another, defending against both Bruce and Valeria, successfully. They all backed up, glad that the arachnoids shared a sense of camaraderie and did not want to injure each other. The leader seemed not to care, but the others stayed out of the way. It meant they had superb synergy, but the home team shared that advantage.

The flurry of spear jabs and under-extended parrying helped them continue backing up, nothing but expended energy resultant.

"What's our play?" Victoria thundered, angered and progressively more exhausted– a dangerous combination.

"We can charge the one." Bruce asserted.

"Or feed it gels."

"Won't work. Cover me," Victoria said confidently. She took out her last gels, three strength and one recovery, the one for vision falling to the ground. Tearing the wrappers off faster than ever, she consumed all four and reached for the vision on the floor.

"What are you doing! You're killing yourself!" Valeria yelled while an arachnoid shot at her legs, forcing her backward again. From her left, Bruce was pushed in the same direction by another one doing the same thing.

Bruce focused on the fight, partially entrusting the also silent Victoria to make her play. She unwrapped the vision and slid it into the somewhat hollow back end of the spear. Holding it closed with her sore and injured right hand, she made shallow jabs to the spiders on Valeria's side, allowing Valeria to help keep watch on the biggest spider.

The minute passed fast, her body craving the sugars after expending so much energy. When she felt her heart beating through her chest, and each muscle seemed to bulge and expand with power, she knew it was time, and the arachnoids had no idea what was coming. She cut between Valeria and Bruce to the worst and most wicked beast Chaos had to offer, the malignant cancer to their survival.

In the fluid strength of her swing, she closed distance while knocking the heavy, metallic legs farther away, allowing the spear to twirl and, with the lunge of her left foot, implant the back end of the spear first one, then two and three and four inches into the malfeasant. She drove it further and further in until she was hit three times in the right leg and three more times just above the hip before Valeria could dispel them temporarily. Through profuse bleeding, she managed to shake the spear back and forth, allowing acidic blood to take up the gel and begin dispersing before it knew the difference. She took one additional stab from the beast itself as she held it in place as long as possible, stepping once to match its initial backpedal. It must have stayed in place longer to stab again and again and leave her side open for the others, but it led to strange feelings.

Twenty or thirty-some seconds later, the beast, partially imbued with gels and energy, stopped and backed up off the spear, shaking some, just as Victoria began exhibiting, and allowed well-placed jab after well-placed jab to induce bleeding. Valeria, with the help of Lucian, successfully held off the three remaining arachnoids from Bruce, Tanho, Victoria, and Griffith long enough for arachnoid hemorrhaging.

After the most intelligent thing on chaos backed up and retreated to heal, so did the other arachnoids. Bruce fell to the ground and helped Victoria induce vomiting. Picking her up, he realized she had a hole through her collarbone and could bleed out from three separate places. He got their shirts and cloth once more and pressed on and in her side and collar against her whimpered wishes. The punctures were deep and likely filled with chaos– hopefully, through all the harm it had caused, it would assist clotting; that's all that mattered now.

The goliath approached quickly, despite just walking, joined by the forbidding roar of the dolus they had just escaped.

"We got to go," Griffith managed, blood loss the most similar thing among them. Bruce carried Victoria, now partially unconscious, in the direction opposite the two beasts ready and eager to re-engage. The arachnoids retreated to the forest, likely camping out the rest of the day– hopefully at least.

Lucian said, "There's gotta be a river up here; maybe we can find a way across." They hobbled and hopped as quickly as possible while Valeria scouted ahead as much as possible.

"Left fifteen degrees!" she called from over a hill, lining them up to pass a valley. As she jogged, she saw a crowd of creatures, indistinguishable in the quarter-second she looked before yelling, "Nope! Go right!"

Going up the hill was the hardest thus far into the short trek, primarily for Griffith and the blood soaking through the cloth stuffed into his wounds, rubbing and moving around a bit with each hop. His right leg was also injured, but it was not noticeable in comparison.

They made it over the hill and sped up on the way down, meeting Valeria, who directed them to the right of a correctly deduced river. Their only sanctuary could lie in a forest– the nearest one in that direction being several hundred yards.

"We're not making it there–"

"We're trying," Lucian told Griffith sternly without stopping.

"Without me."

"Without me, too."

"We're making it."

The warmth of the sun shining through their thin, dark hair; the chaotic breeze whistling by, zephyrs of tranquility; a crimson matching their delightful sun flowing smoothly with the wash of aquamarine a bit to the left; left quite some mystery unraveled, tangling again in the blinding haze of blood, sweat, and tears.

"Keep moving! Don't stop," Valeria encouraged as best she could, watching the goliath get closer and closer with every step. It clearly calculated its vengeance for Victoria and Valeria's earlier attacks and how their speed would not let them reach the forest before he caught up.

She stopped and let them pass her, holding two spears, one of which hers and the other Victoria's, which had been Griffith's previous.

"No!" Tanho yelled, relinquishing himself from Lucian's aid. Griffith followed suit and just stood with his axe. He used his left hand to bend his leg back and stand his ground. Lucian gestured for a spear, and Valeria gave one over.

"Farewell, family," Griffith led, catching each of their eyes for less than half a second each, wanting to watch the goliath in his final moments and reduce any burden they may self-impose.

"With love," Tanho softly spoke through a tear. Valeria ran back to the others and sheltered tears.

"Goodbye," Bruce said, focusing on his mission.

"Memento mori, my brothers," Lucian ended.

Unheard by the four others, Griffith and Tanho whispered, "Memento mori." At that moment, time stood still and refused to pass faster. An angry giant stood there; beaten-up club in his right hand, *how peculiar, it is not left handed; a blue-green something was mid-charge, I wonder why it hasn't given up; a swarm of things that should be fighting were not, haha, I always thought those crocodiles were cool.*

Griffith looked up to the darkening sky filling with purples and greens and warms and cools. Stars and northern lights blipped and swirled together galaxies harboring cool and warm and gaseous planets. Wormholes, mysterious and fascinating, time and space manipulated; they were probably trillions of light years away. He watched the galactic swirls intently, centered by stars and black holes; he was always fascinated by the latter. Griffith had accomplished his dream, going up into those places and marveling at its up-close beauty, and he had made family too, although he knew that would happen.

His eyes squinted, and he fought them from closing. He had fallen to the ground on his back some time ago but did not realize it. *No pain, that's good.*

The wind felt nice and peaceful. He heard low thumping and high-pitched thumping, the world becoming brighter and darker and brighter again. *Am I dead? Is Valhalla real?*

Valeria struggled to drag Griffith the twenty yards, getting Lucian's one-armed help for the second half amidst thunderous and incessant communication-blocking soundwaves. No thoughts ran through her head as she watched the goliath fall to the ground as she held Griffith by his hurt arms. The dolus scampered off, deterred, declaring them now obsolete. The army crowd remained incoming at something shy of full speed; once the dolus had been discouraged, attention turned to the horde. Bruce set Victoria down and helped Tanho up the ramp.

"Get in, now!" a voice boomed as hundreds of strange and genetically chaotic creatures leaped over each other in slow motion. Tanho's quick glance shrouded pain sent to his brain with layers and layers of movement.

Bruce pulled Tanho up the final few feet and helped with Griffith as they raised up into the air, a deinodile and pygmy dragon jumping up off other creatures to try and catch on. Once the crew was out of range, he could not help but stare as chaos ensued, enemy rediscovering enemy– *it was a facade all along.* Through the steady stream of creatures, epicenter now at their liftoff point, thousands must have been massacred. Natural selection could only favor those intelligent enough not to fight, those not equipped with human interest; *maybe we'll come back. No. No way. Memento mori.*

Valeria and Bruce finally sat down after the doors at last began to close. Wide-eyed and still in shock, they managed to smile, similarly despite the cumulative amount of blood lost.

"Is there first aid here?" Valeria shouted to the front of the ship. The ship they were now in had the same exterior as theirs but was smaller. The inside was also more broken up, affording more rooms instead of carrying so many people.

The signal, it worked! Lucian thought. As soon as he smelled something strange, his eyes widened and his pupils dilated more than when they were being rescued.

"Hold your breath! Gas!" he yelled. Lucian felt the onset of nausea and drowsiness as Valeria tried to get up but fell back down. Victoria and Griffith were already knocked out.

Bruce was taller, giving him that much longer to react, stand up, and get a good breath in. He was also heavier, requiring more of the gas. *We're already trapped; it's now or never.* He fell down as convincingly as he conceived possible, using his hand to try and support himself before allowing it to fail. He held his jaw as loose as possible to simulate his unconsciousness and slowly relaxed his muscles with his unfocused and slightly opened eyes, allowing him to close them whenever he saw anything or could not keep them open longer.

He waited a full minute with partly irritated eyes before it went dark around them. With the optimal speed of their ship, factoring in a size difference, he estimated they should have reached space, but he had not felt nearly enough turbulence or G-forces pulling him into the floor– *we're still on Chaos.*

A door opened, and a set of footsteps and gas-masked breathing entered. In the darkness, there was no method to any madness, but with little time left, he made a break for where his mental map placed the open door.

It had to be another airlock, or light would come through from somewhere up front. Their ship had something similar– it should be laid out the same, or at least he hoped. Bruce only made it three steps before he was tased and fell over, breathing in enough of whatever knockout gas filled the air.

Chapter 22

FINAL STRANDS OF HOPE

"Is anyone awake? Victoria! Victoria!" Valeria called as she shook her. Victoria slowly opened her eyes and pushed herself up through aches and full-body soreness. *Where am I? I think I was bleeding out earlier,* she reflected, a bright and warm light forcing her to almost fully close her eyes.

"Hi," Victoria groaned, "What happened?"

Valeria was stunned, "You're alive! We were about to die and then we were rescued by someone. They knocked us out and now we're here. Help me wake them up."

Victoria opened her eyes more and saw four other bodies, everyone laid out in a circle around a few backpacks. As the memories of Chaos rushed back, she threw up her arms and checked her injuries, only scarring remaining. She stumbled over to Lucian, who now had both arms and hands.

"Lucian, get up!" she half-yelled, her voice struggling to adjust. As she reached to grab his arm, she checked his facial hair; based on the last time he cleaned himself up, it must've been a week that she had lost.

Valeria tried to wake up Griffith by lightly shaking his shoulders, but it did not work.

"Hey how do you feel?" Victoria asked, deciding not to do much without more people awake.

"A little out of it, and stiff."

"Yeah, same. At least we're alive, I was sure I was a goner."

"Yeah, Bruce carried you for a few hundred yards after that fight, it's a miracle you're right here– a miracle that we're all right here."

"Well, it seems we'll have some more survival-time together," she said, taking a deep breath and looking around at the stranger of an environment they were surrounded by. Red-trunked trees forked hundreds of times to make an intricate web holding thousands of red-orange leaves, too far to discern shape, although they seemed to resemble sunflowers, also clearly facing the sun. The star they now orbited was blue, creating an illusory hologram glow. They sat trying to process everything until Lucian and Tanho finally got up at similar times.

"Hey hey, good morning! Get up!" Valeria told them while looking towards Tanho.

Lucian and then Tanho sat up, Tanho squinting his eyes farther open before saying "Where are we this time?"

Lucian looked at the backpacks and the red tree-trunks, "Oh gosh." He laid back down and took a deep breath.

"No no, get up," Victoria softly asserted, pulling him back up. "Look, you've got your arm back."

"Oh, that's nice."

Victoria laughed and looked at Valeria, "Yeah, he's still very drugged."

Bruce and Griffith took the longest to awaken– likely receiving a higher dose fading slower with a relatively low metabolism. Waiting for them,

Tanho, Victoria, Valeria, and Lucian tried to piece events and memories together.

Lucian added, "And the sun is blue! That means this sun is much hotter than Earth's, like at least four times as hot. And I can't believe my arm is back!"

"Yeah, can we talk about how that's even possible– it was fully gone," Tanho said. "And so were you, Victoria, I'm sure you were close."

Victoria inspected her arms again, "Well I seem all here, so that's all that matters now. If it came down to it, I'd do the same thing again."

Valeria told her, "I'm glad you're here," chuckling.

Lucian thought about his arm, "They must have grown my arm back on something else and aged it. That's what they're doing on Earth at least, although the aging to match the rest of my body is pretty finicky." He inspected the light scarring from where it must have been surgically reattached.

"Why are they helping us now?" Bruce asked, reattaining his thoughts.

"Helping, I'm not so sure. Using, maybe," Victoria addressed the group, answering him.

"We just need to figure out what they get from us being here," Lucian posited. He moved to the backpacks and slowly began opening them, cautious in case anything dangerous was inside. After opening all the pockets of every black, military-style backpack and peeking in, they began taking each item out for an inventory.

Griffith scooched forward to the items and said, "Only a few backpacks of items? If they're trying to help us they could've at least given some more stuff. Anyways, Lucian, what do you think the situation is?"

"I'm thinking whoever drugged us wants us alive but doesn't fully care. I think that they lose something if we all die, and they gave us these items to make this time around easier."

Valeria looked up and asked, "So was our crash because of them? Why kill so many of the crew?"

"We probably would've all survived if not for landing in the water. Maybe it was a miscalculation."

Bruce spoke up after recollecting, "After you announced the gas Lucian, I held my breath and waited for them to come in. I'm pretty sure they're human; I heard boots and gas masks but the lights were off, so night-vis too." They were all listening intently as he continued, "There were at least six, one for each of us, but they seemed to go towards Victoria first. I tried to get to an airlock but got tased, so they have tasers too."

"Suspiciously Earthy, but since when did home have quick access to a red star and a blue star, and with habitable planets, and by Lucian's hair, be able to travel between them in about a week," Victoria questioned rhetorically.

"Okay, with all of that, we must either be in a simulation, or in some– quote– parallel reality, or both!"

Griffith confusedly looked at Lucian and said, "Explain."

He spoke quickly and with assertion, "Humanoids with human technology but seemingly more advanced space travel than we had. We would know about cutting-edge tech, and our closest red star was four to five light years away while the type-B, blue stars, were about eighty. In any type of space travel like that, we would've had to have been frozen, but I'm not feeling any different. So, because we couldn't see this blue star in detail, and I assume we weren't tidally locked with it– only showing one side to each other, these humanoids must have more advanced cryotech, where we were only unfrozen for roughly a week, and in that time, my arm was fully regrown and Victoria is all good and everyone else's injuries seem healed. Thus, this isn't near the milky way and we traveled somewhere in the universe where these humanoids live, and we're being played with to some regard, in a simulation or otherwise. Of course, I'm also open to the possibility that this is all a simulation, but Earth, at least the one I knew, did not have enough energy to sustain something so complicated. But of course, on the Kardashev scale, a type two or three civilization could produce lots and lots of energy which, with the right resource access, could make these planets or sustain such a simulation." He gasped for air once as he finished speaking, everyone around him subtly aghast with the explanation that seemed all too true.

"Okay, I get that, now what do we do to get back to home, if home is home, which I want to assume it is?" Valeria asked.

Griffith scanned their inventory, "I say we make our immediate plans to survive while we can and with this daylight, and work through getting home as we learn and can come up with things. I mean, we've gotta be bugged and being watched this time surely– although there's a chance they don't understand english."

They agreed, acknowledging their completely new situation as Victoria went through their gear, "We've got four backpacks, four metal water bottles, new sets of clothes, thirty gels including a new one for intelligence– gosh that must be fun but we've got six of each. Anyway, there's our knives, sword, two shields, Griffith's axe– they must've gone back for that, a slingshot, hammer, that atlatl thing, some of those crystals, and this unlabeled bottle of pills."

"Wow what a mind game," Bruce chuckled, "Will it kill us or help us?" He wondered if their captors would give them all of these things just to kill one or more of them with this bottle of pills. It was plausible that they were being tortured, in a sense, being placed on Chaos and wherever they were now.

Psychological deduction through profiling is possible when you can get a sense of one's decision-making and nature through questions and answers as well as prompts and responses, physical and not. In the case of complete mystery and potential brain development changes, however unlikely, making a deduction so risky could be impossible. The group had experience making life-and-death decisions founded on what was known at the time, but sometimes what you know may not be enough, and deceptive strategies may be utilized to gain that edge once more. They were powerless, though, sheltered unsheltered on this planet with no access and no real answers– deductions can only go so far.

Their captors were smart, too, turning off the lights to shroud their identity, as the night sky's emptiness had done to the Chaotic creatures they had fought what felt like yesterday. They used the same style ship, in identical colors, which could only be achieved by a preconceived scan or some unappreciated surveillance. *Life is complicated... but I guess– isn't it always?*

"Alright, I guess we shouldn't waste more daylight," Tanho initiated. "Two groups of three, meet back here or a mile towards the sun if this place is compromised. If it's nighttime, stay hunkered down– we should move when we can see. Don't make unnecessary noise et cetera et cetera."

"Sounds good to me," Victoria told them.

"Yeah same," Griffith said. They concurred and started walking, Valeria, Griffith, and Bruce heading hypothetical north and Victoria, Tanho, and Lucian due hypothetical south, following the setting sun as setting west.

Through trembling trees traveling east, three distant mountaintops enclosed them. Red-rooted, regal flowers raised high over the ground leafery, leering at them as if the coarse dirt they disregarded in light of radiant mushrooms were more remarkable. Instinct insighted peril, inciting their ignoring in intuition of the illusory ravines to their right, which upon investigation yielded stygian despair. Artificial architecture was absent– the landscape was absolute in its arbitrary maturation. Layered leaf litter piled in low contours, leading rainfall and clouds to be torrential along lots of lightfall– the land dry.

They kept going on their makeshift path, keeping the sun to the right and distance between anything where a creature could attack from. Valeria held onto a knife, Griffith his axe, and Bruce carried the hammer.

Bruce told them, "This place seems pretty peaceful, maybe we could build an actual house somewhere."

Shutting him down kindly, Valeria responded, "Oh come on, you know there are going to be plenty of deadly things here." She thought about it for a second, *what if they just want us to live out our lives? That's crazy, no way! But there's some chance.*

Griffith led them to a taller stick pile, pulling some of the longer and straighter ones out to be used for spears or staffs or defenses. They made sure not to get too close, and watched for creature movement, but nothing jumped out at them.

"We still need cordage of some kind, it would've been nice of them to send some with us." Griffith paused, "Oh wait, these shoes we have on have shoelaces, I guess they did give some to us, just not a lot."

Leaving the dried sticks on their path, besides one ruby-red walking stick each, they knew they had to find at least a contender for a defensible shelter. After walking and jogging for roughly fifteen minutes, absorbing the scenery of multicolored megaflora and hundreds of uniquely-shaped trees, they summited a hill and came across a cliffside.

"There's an indent over there, and the cliff isn't that high. We could make something here and be blocked off by a few sides, as long as the rock and dirt doesn't fall on us," Griffith analyzed while turning slightly left to get closer.

Bruce stepped forward, saying, "Here, let's try this." He threw the hammer roughly twenty feet up the cliffside, making a loud smack before hitting the ground, leaving no indent either time.

"Seems good to me," Valeria told them, "Now let's hope they found a decent way to get water." Griffith, Valeria, and Bruce walked back with the spear poles they collected, listening and looking for signs of any type of life. Just as Chaos was that first, confusing time, there was practically nothing. The planet was either devoid of animals or everything was consumed whole. *Qui vivra verra.*

Earthen elements exchanged with the exotic ecosphere, experimenting and exploiting their preconceived notions. Red roamed freely, renovating flowery prowess through reflective highlights and entrancing Fibonacci rhythm. Regions of remote, royal rivers, remarkably broad, ran far and wide within the miry depressions to their right. Orderly, orchid-like, floral vines organized themselves on only some tree outgrowths, an outbreak looming. Reigning mountain ridge ranges rose to recover the horizon and its favorable vantage.

Victoria led with the sword and shield, approaching some small hills to observe the surrounding landscape, all approaching the wall of mountains. Tanho and Lucian took the back flanks, with the atlatl and slingshot, respectively. Tanho had five shots, and Lucian had ten– he began collecting rocks to preserve the metal ammo for later needed accuracy or other potential uses. Between the searching for life and the survival necessities, Lucian thought of their predicament– it was likely and probable that, with the advanced technology present, their brain activity and thoughts and vitals were being monitored intently, and they had no way of knowing. Implanted devices could even be swallowed and invisible to almost all detection. If they really were in some alternate or parallel universe, they could only hope the technology and way their captors' intellects, thoughts, and even vitals worked was different enough for the tech to be obsolete.

"The water's just up ahead. Let's fill up the two bottles and rendezvous, there's nothing else here but trees and those mountains," Victoria logically proposed. Descending the mountain, they experienced deja vu of their previous first day's exploration. Life, at least in plants so far, was flourishing, but they had much to learn with the high likelihood, by association, that the planet would grow chaotic come nighttime.

The water was slightly transparent but with a deep, permanganate purple look that increased with the depth. Tanho estimated the visibility to be around a foot, which gave no clue as to the river's actual depth. The section they arrived at was the thinnest for a significant distance at around thirty feet. Before collecting any water, they watched for any surface disturbances beyond the typical rushing current and wave.

Lucian took one bottle and submerged it bottom first until only the top was above the surface, angling it so he kept his hands out of the water while filling as much as possible. Upon pulling it out and screwing the cap back on, they waited a minute to be certain the liquid was not corrosive or destructive like gallium. It did not smell at all either; once he acknowledged that, he thought, *this planet must have a very similar atmosphere to Chaos–*

I don't seem to be having any trouble acclimating. They filled their other bottle and sighed looking around and listening to the empty breeze.

The way back was lustrous, that blue glow showing off the adjacent sides of some of the flowers, trees, and random sparkles dangerously far in the distance, not worth exploring yet. They returned first.

"Hey, what did you find?" Victoria asked them after waving.

After they got closer, Griffith said "Found a cliff face for potential shelter and Bruce tested the wall's durability with the hammer– seems good. Then lots of big plants and mushrooms and trees. Pretty peaceful, although it seems we're blocked in by mountains that way."

"What about you guys?" Valeria asked.

Tanho told them, "Yeah we got mountains that way too, but some large rivers and a marshy area and then trees and such. We've probably got to head through the forests to find something more sustainable. The cliff face seems enough for tonight, probably safer than going out on a limb and having a second first night."

"Yeah, let's not do that again," Lucian said. "So we head to make our shelter and I'll get to work on trying to sterilize the water– the metal water bottles are going to be amazing, and we get to drink purple water!" They went back quickly, realizing that if there were mountains through the trees, they would have much less daylight.

Approaching the spot, Tanho said, "Yeah, this seems pretty nice, better than nothing I suppose. As long as nothing can bore through and get to us, we could probably defend it for the night."

"We've got this," Griffith affirmed with confidence as he slung the backpack back off his shoulder and lay it against the wall. After making an initial structure, lying larger and easily accessible sticks upwards, leaving plenty of gaps, Tanho began working on a contraption.

"Just wait, this'll be cool, useful, and worth the time," he said.

Griffith began sharpening the sticks and poles and preparing some to be used with the crystal spear points. Within an hour, their camp was very sophisticated, each person utilizing their strengths without managing-co-ordination– they knew each other a bit better this time around, and the fire was burning wood quickly.

Another hour marked the initial dulling of the sky and then soon after, the ground. Tanho had finally completed his gadget, packing many long and pointed poles point outward from their structure, back-end into the ground. Using his understanding of wood-joints and a lot of tedious, manual sanding, he made an activated wooden-spike fence that would impale anything that ran into it. In his demonstration, he walked through how the angle could be adjusted to account for the strength and target. He sectioned them off in three groups, each controlled by their own stick in the shelter, where once pulled down with strength and locked into place with another stick-joint, they stayed up.

Their angled walls had holes for light to escape or the slingshot to be fired, with respective plugs just in case. They were extremely cautious when choosing their sticks and opted only for specific types of leaves that Lucian tested for at least some safety. As a result, their bedding was thin and their structure needed more smaller sticks over the top to hold in the heat and light and prevent the rain that would fall on the front end of their shelter, luckily drawing away from them from the erosion patterns.

Once their shoelaces had lashed spears and more stakes were driven into the ground, they sat by the fire, finally feeling prepared and a bit safer through their obvious, pure smiles. They were right about the mountains that way too, not much time passing from the initial set to darkness.

Through the safety of their firelight, they stood outside and listened beyond the crackling and the wind's rushing over the cliff above them. The darker it got, the more red the sky became, not in a literal sense, but in a blending of colors and lights and hopes. vibrant blues and spiritual greens of the setting blue sun made purple with the reddish atmosphere.

"I've never seen anything like it," Bruce said in awe.

"It reminds me of those bioluminescent beaches," Lucian connected, observing the air density and upper-atmospheric wind-patterns making waves of purple through the sky, drawing out the multicolored stars that sparkled in harmony. The symphony of color, wind, and illumination set their little world to shame, creating colored-in constellations greater than they could comprehend.

"I'm drawing this scene when we get back home."

"Wish we could take a picture. I know I'm partial to the night sky, but this place might beat Chaos," Bruce decided, still looking up.

Tanho told him, "Don't be too hasty, we need to learn some more before making crazy conclusions like that one. I think tomorrow, we ought to climb up one of those mountains and see what's really out there."

"This place, although very red, really is something. The flowers are just spectacular," Victoria said calmly. She put her hands up to her face and felt its warmth, exhaling, before initiating a group hug.

Griffith told them from the outside of the hug, "We can conquer this place too."

In taking rest while they could, Victoria and Griffith being the most tired, likely from the healing they had done while asleep before, they laid down and tried to sleep. She slid her hand over and met Griffith's, who lightly squeezed it once before settling again with an exhale, still holding her hand. Their warmth shared and equalized in comfort.

"You're incredible, you know? A luminary."

"I know."

Tanho, Valeria, Bruce, and Lucian took the first watch, the spectacle of the sky and rush of thoughts, given their relaxation, keeping them up.

Tanho held onto the slingshot, just in case, while he surveyed the darkness. Despite the stars, the forest was just light-insulant enough to block everything out, reminding them of Chaos more and more.

If it were not for the darkness, their new residence would be peaceful and tranquil; the temperature had dropped only a bit, reminding of Earth nights in the summer but without the pesky bugs.

Bruce admitted, "You know, the more I'm out here with you all, the less I miss my old life. Maybe it has something to do with our chances of getting off of here, but hey, we got off of Chaos."

Valeria said with Lucian nodding along, "Well, we're close enough to be family now. There's no getting rid of us. We're here for each other until we're gone."

Tanho followed, saying, "We'll make our own fun and persevere through whatever they throw our way. We don't have anything to toast with, trying to save our water, but I'd say: to friends, to family, to survival; we live to fight and fight to live– live with each other, our memories, our growth, our revival."

"I'd cheers to that," Lucian supported.

After a few more minutes of increasing darkness, the bending of light around the mountain lessening and fading with the lost sun, Valeria went inside to try and rest. She smiled seeing Griffith and Victoria.

Tanho, Lucian, and Bruce remained outside, now in silence, appreciating and observing. Once the sun fully disappeared over the obscured horizon, the wind began to pick up and whistle passing over the cliff.

"Glad we didn't make a lean-to or something out there," Lucian said. He knew the wind carried the cold and would probably make quick work of the smaller sticks they used for extra insulation.

"Yeah, definitely; and I think I ought to go get some rest," Bruce said ending in a yawn and shoulder-shrug stretch.

"Wait."

"Tanho, what is it?" Lucian asked, clueing into his sudden increase in attention and pupil dilation.

"Shh." Tanho looked around, closing his eyes in some orientations to focus on what he was hearing. Lucian and Bruce searched for it too.

Moments later, a mass appeared from the darkness, somewhat blurred and confusing. They looked at each other, silent, with equally confused and unknowing eyes. They stood still, keeping their eyes as closed as possible while still being able to see to reduce the movement their eyelids would take to blink.

There was life on their planet after all; blood flowed faster throughout their bodies, resisting their attempts to control their heart rate. Oxygen influxed to muscle cells in the legs to engage their flight-response if it was needed. They did not dare to move or ring the alarms, observing for as long as possible, the creature now stood not but fifty feet from them.

Tanho watched it more intently than Lucian and Bruce did, being the only one searching for weak spots and realizing that the creatures here likely did not have the same anatomy as on Chaos. Its body was rather compact and it was tall, but still blurred. *A little too blurred. Maybe it's distorting light somehow.*

Then he realized. Through its sway, the creature had long grass-like blades that it raised and re-placed along its support-structure. The blades all moved together, limbless, and the light was not being distorted– the light was hitting it, but the creature, primarily hugging the trees, was mirroring its background.

A few seconds after Tanho's realization, Lucian and Bruce caught on. They slowly turned and looked at each other, hair standing on ends, a familiar shock and adrenal rush keeping them on their toes and aware of the position of each individual limb, finger, and toe. The jolts through their empty stomachs felt as though they had too much caffeine, a discomfort and persistent anger, almost betrayal. Lucian mouthed, *that's Victoria's design!*

Acknowledgements

This was one of the most challenging and rewarding things I have ever attempted. That being said, the supports and inspirations of my family and good friends were cornerstones in this novel's production. From the exchange of ideas to deep, late-night conversations, I am forever grateful for those I have the pleasure of being friends with.

I would firstly like to thank my dad for those hours of conversation indulging my interests in survival and the wilderness. Those years becoming an Eagle Scout, fostered by him, gave me material and a profound curiosity for we do not engage with on a day-to-day basis.

Thanks to my mom, who taught me the empathy I use to build personality. I believe that she built my interest in social psychology and profiling, now a major part of how I see the world around me, especially in trying to articulate it.

Starting with not even the slightest idea of where to begin such a massive project, my parents facilitated my stake in learning and trying new things– especially challenging ones. Without their encouragement, this never could have happened (they even let me write instead of work the summer before college, where I made hundreds of hours of progress).

I am inexpressibly grateful to Edward, whose character and good nature remains an inspiration. Through offering suggestions and consistently offering an ear, even hanging out or calling in the early early morning, he was invaluable to my sanity.

I know many of them may justly think I'm a bit crazy for the way I utilized time during this, but I'd like to give thanks for the support, inspiration, and constructive criticisms to some friends: Abigail, Agustin, Andrew, Anthony, Anushka, Ashton, Ben, Brian, Charlie, Cole, Daphne, Edward, Evelyn, Gustavo, Inaya, Jake for his medical knowledge those brisk mornings, Jorge, Josh, Joyce, Kaustubh, Keya, Lillian, Lucy, Marley for her proofreading, Mattia, Mohit, Nick, Nidhi for her knowledge as an author, Pranab, Ryan, Sabine, Shahmeer, Sydney, Timothy, Vaishali, Vikram, Xander, and all my other friends who watched and will watch me grow as a person. I recently talked to my college roommate Gustavo (listed above), and I sincerely believe that we are an amalgamation of those we surround ourselves with– thank you all. It really is the friends we made along the way.

Many of my teachers made writing and coming up with ideas notably easier, even with some conversations with friends occurring in their rooms in the morning or at lunch. Thank you Mrs. Sears and Mrs. Walter especially.

As the reader, I'd like to thank you as well. I hope you enjoyed and continue to enjoy *Wraiths: The Night Sky*. Who knows, maybe by the time you read this I'll have come out with the next installment. I wholeheartedly appreciate your interest and I hope you may continue to follow my writing journey.

I imagine I will read this many times again as I grow older, so here's to my future self and future relatives: I want you to acknowledge the difficult times and events you went through and see how that has brought you where you are today. Alan, starting at 16 bored in classes and looking for stimulating challenges, learned that he could get things done if he had a lot he wanted to do– dreaming big and making strides. I'm still on a similar path at 19 so future me, you need to remember the effort and always strive for that excellence, remember the people, and take better care of yourself. Do more things for *you,* you deserve it. o7

ABOUT THE AUTHOR

Alan Rock has always been a creative and thoughtful individual. From an early age, he stood out for his vivid imagination and keen listening skills, allowing him to excel in school and seek out challenges beyond the classroom. His curiosity and drive led him to explore various interests, including basketball, soccer, and Boy Scouts, where he achieved the prestigious rank of Eagle Scout.

Alan's passion for writing blossomed in the second grade when his short stories, brimming with humor and wit, became cherished family favorites that are still fondly quoted to this day. His love for storytelling only intensified, eventually propelling him to write his first novel. This book, a true labor of love, embodies Alan's unwavering dedication to his craft. He meticulously researched and incorporated a wide range of concepts, even conducting interviews to ensure the authenticity of his work.

Made in the USA
Middletown, DE
26 September 2024

61541527R00201